Sea Sirens

A Trot & Cap'n Bill Adventure

by
AMY CHU
and
JANET K. LEE

lettering by
JIMMY GOWNLEY

VIKING

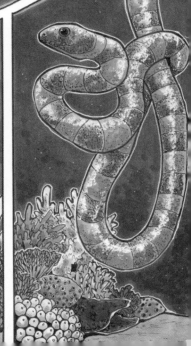

VIKING

An imprint of Penguin Random House LLC, New York

First published in the United States of America by Viking,
an imprint of Penguin Random House LLC, 2019

Copyright © 2019 by Amy Chu and Janet K. Lee

LIBRARY OF CONGRESS CATALOGING-IN-PUBLICATION DATA IS AVAILABLE.
ISBN 9780451480163 (hardcover)
ISBN 9780451480170 {paperback}

Manufactured in China   Book design by Nancy Brennan
1 3 5 7 9 10 8 6 4 2

Contents

To my friend and collaborator Janet Lee who had the initial vision for the book, and L. Frank Baum for the inspiration. Immense gratitude to the incredible force of nature Judy Hansen and the ever patient Sheila Keenan. And much love to my boys Alexander and Adrian for their support, honest feedback and proofreading eyes. —A.C.

For my sister who believed my stories no matter what, for my dad who taught me how to draw, and for my husband who loves me. —J.K.L

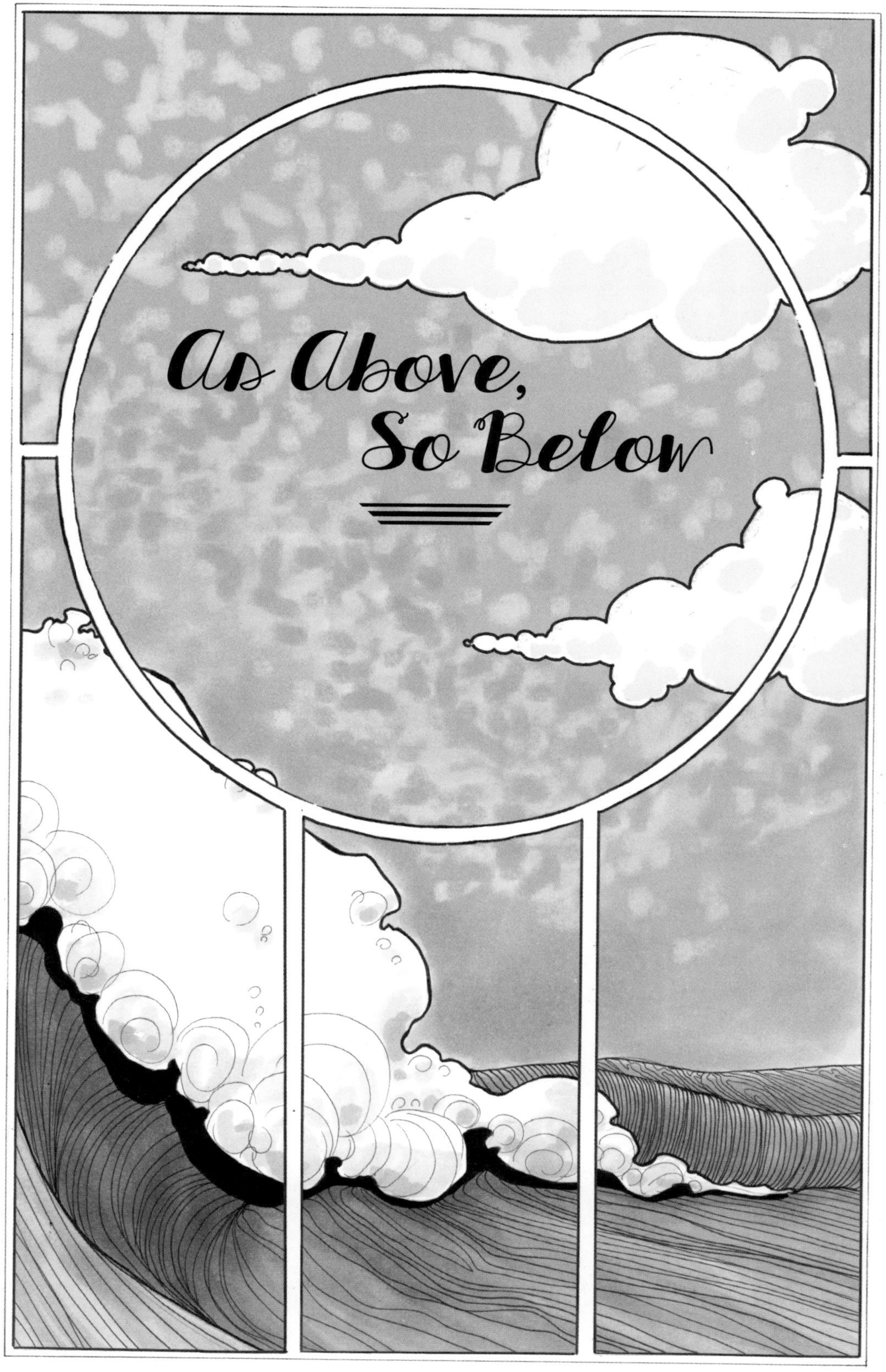
As Above,
So Below

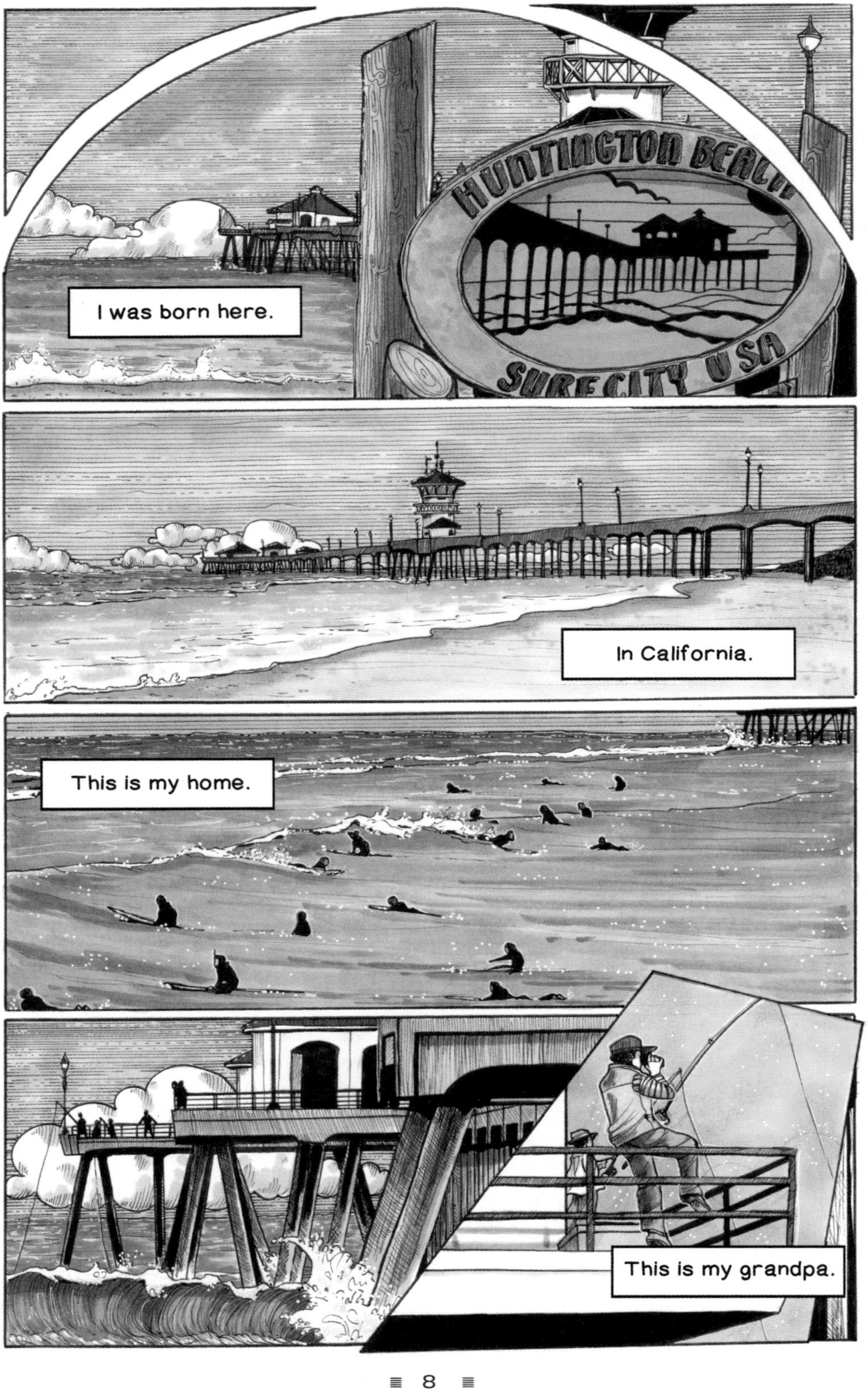
HUNTINGTON BEACH
SURF CITY USA
I was born here.
In California.
This is my home.
This is my grandpa.

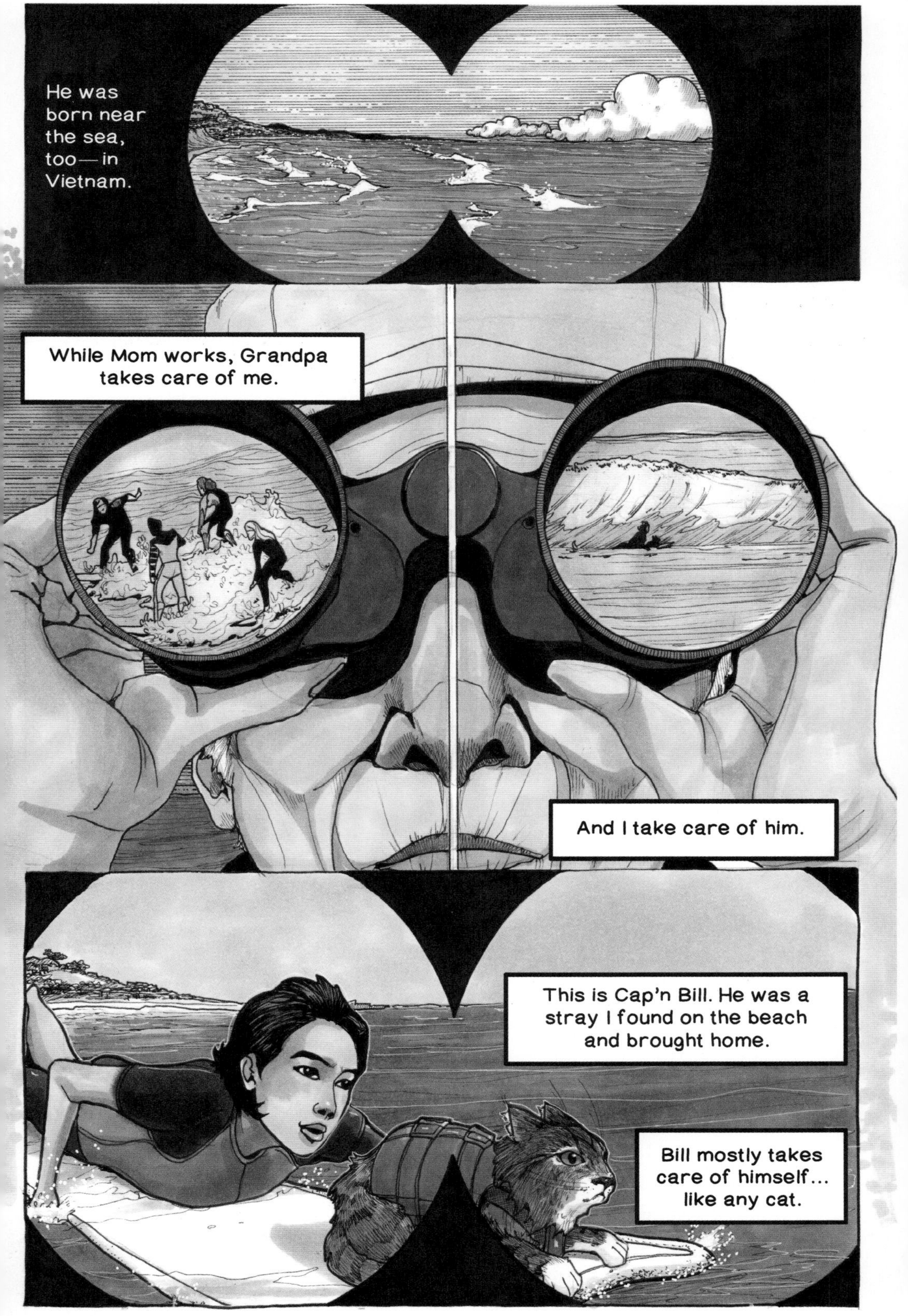
He was born near the sea, too—in Vietnam.
While Mom works, Grandpa takes care of me.
And I take care of him.
This is Cap'n Bill. He was a stray I found on the beach and brought home.
Bill mostly takes care of himself… like any cat.

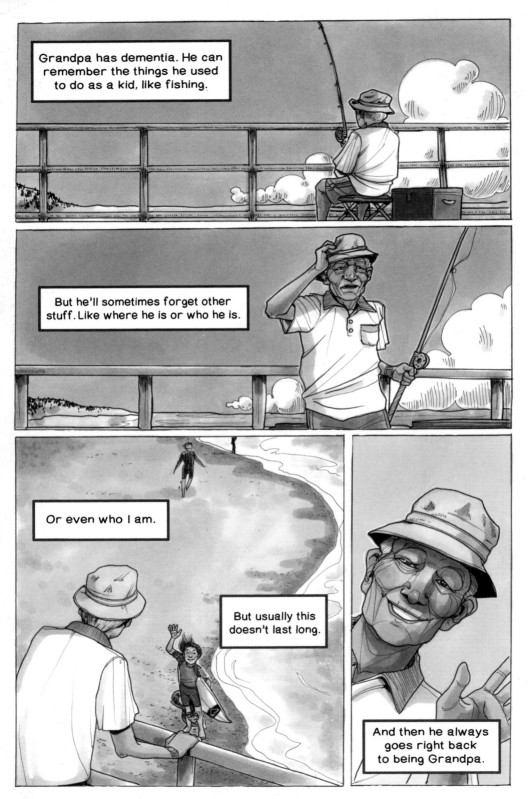

Grandpa has dementia. He can remember the things he used to do as a kid, like fishing.

But he'll sometimes forget other stuff. Like where he is or who he is.

Or even who I am.

But usually this doesn't last long.

And then he always goes right back to being Grandpa.

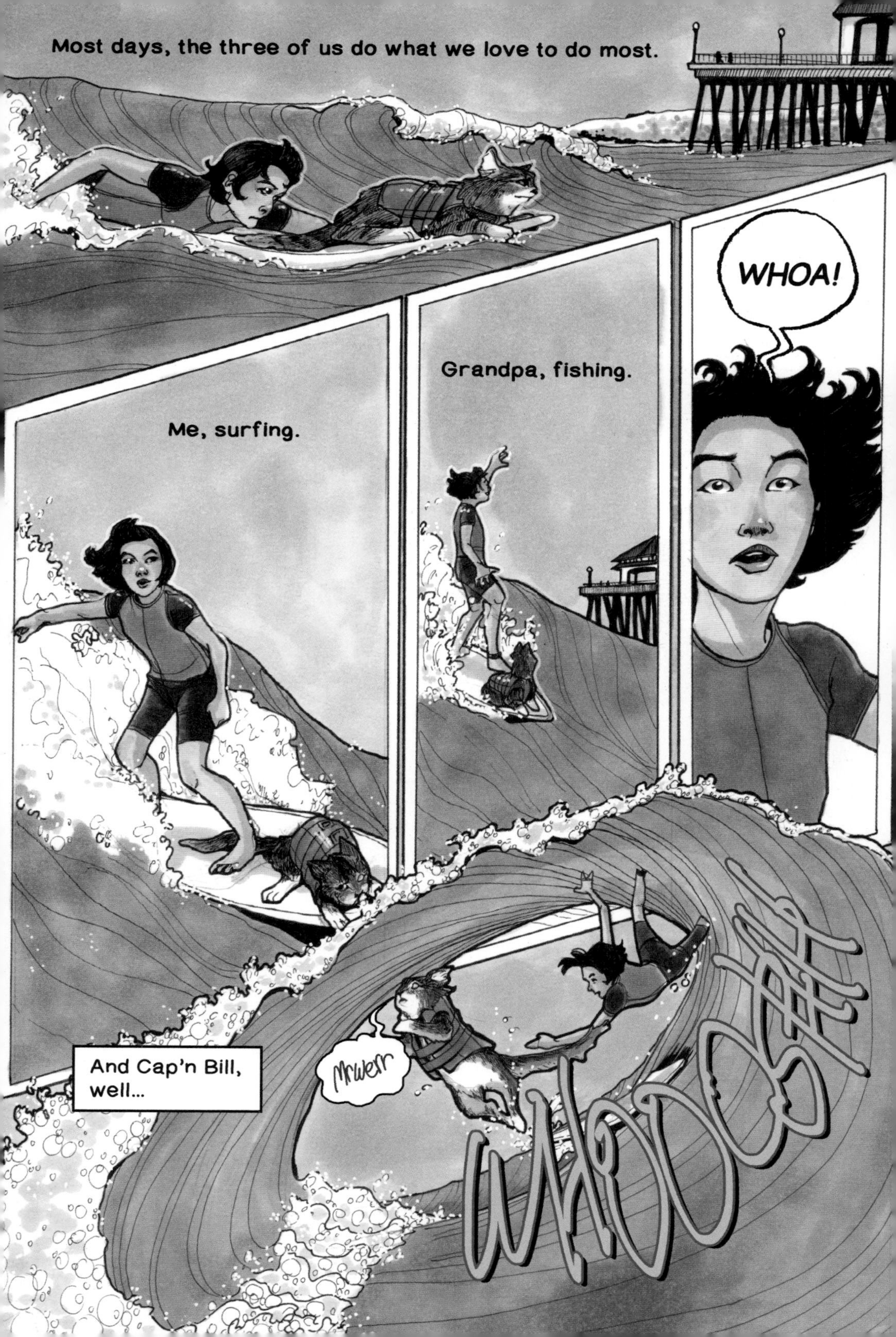
Most days, the three of us do what we love to do most.
Me, surfing.
Grandpa, fishing.
WHOA!
And Cap'n Bill, well...
Mrwerr
WHOOSH

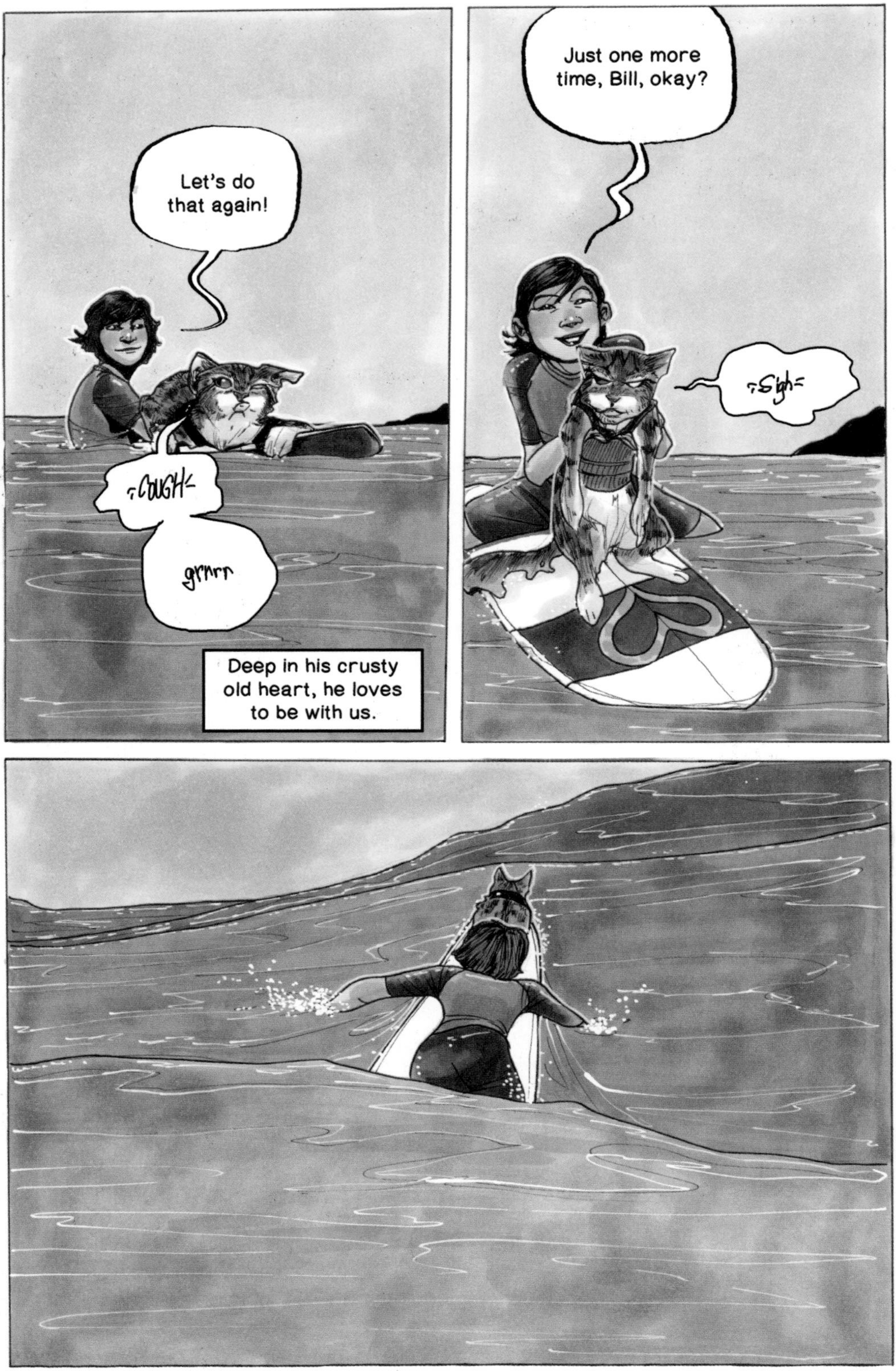
Let's do that again!
~COUGH~
grrrr
Deep in his crusty old heart, he loves to be with us.
Just one more time, Bill, okay?
~Sigh~

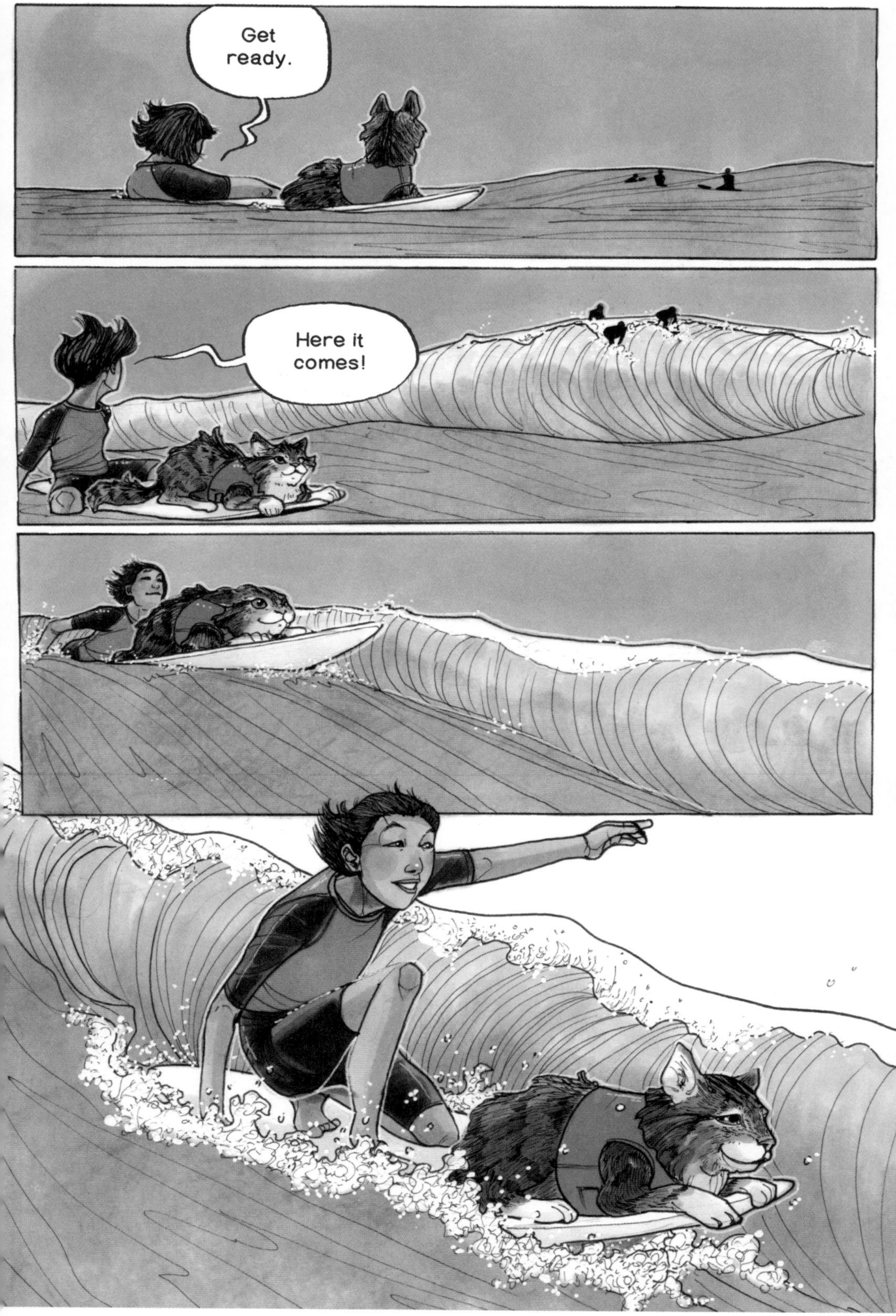
Get ready.
Here it comes!

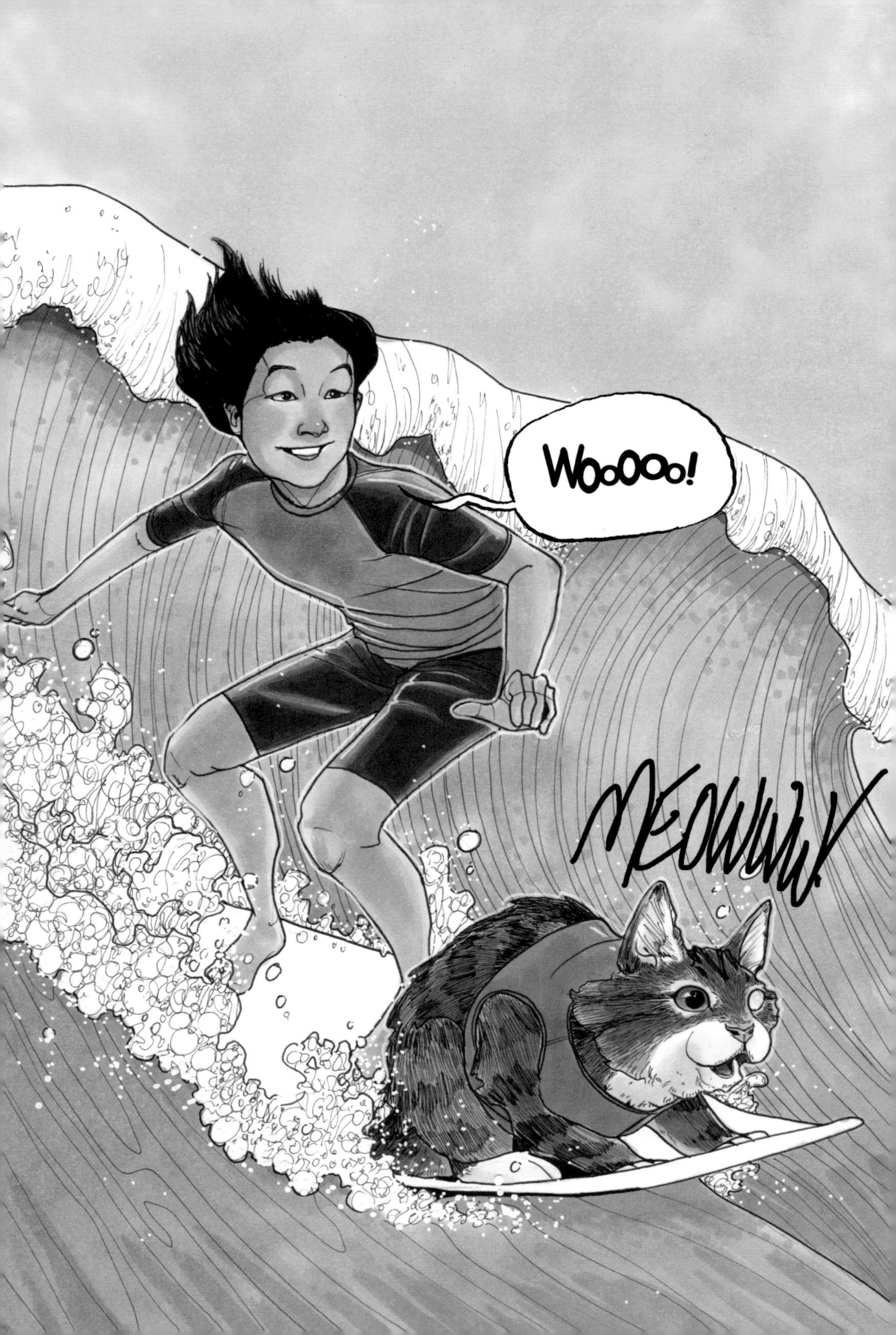
WoooOoo!
MEOWWW!

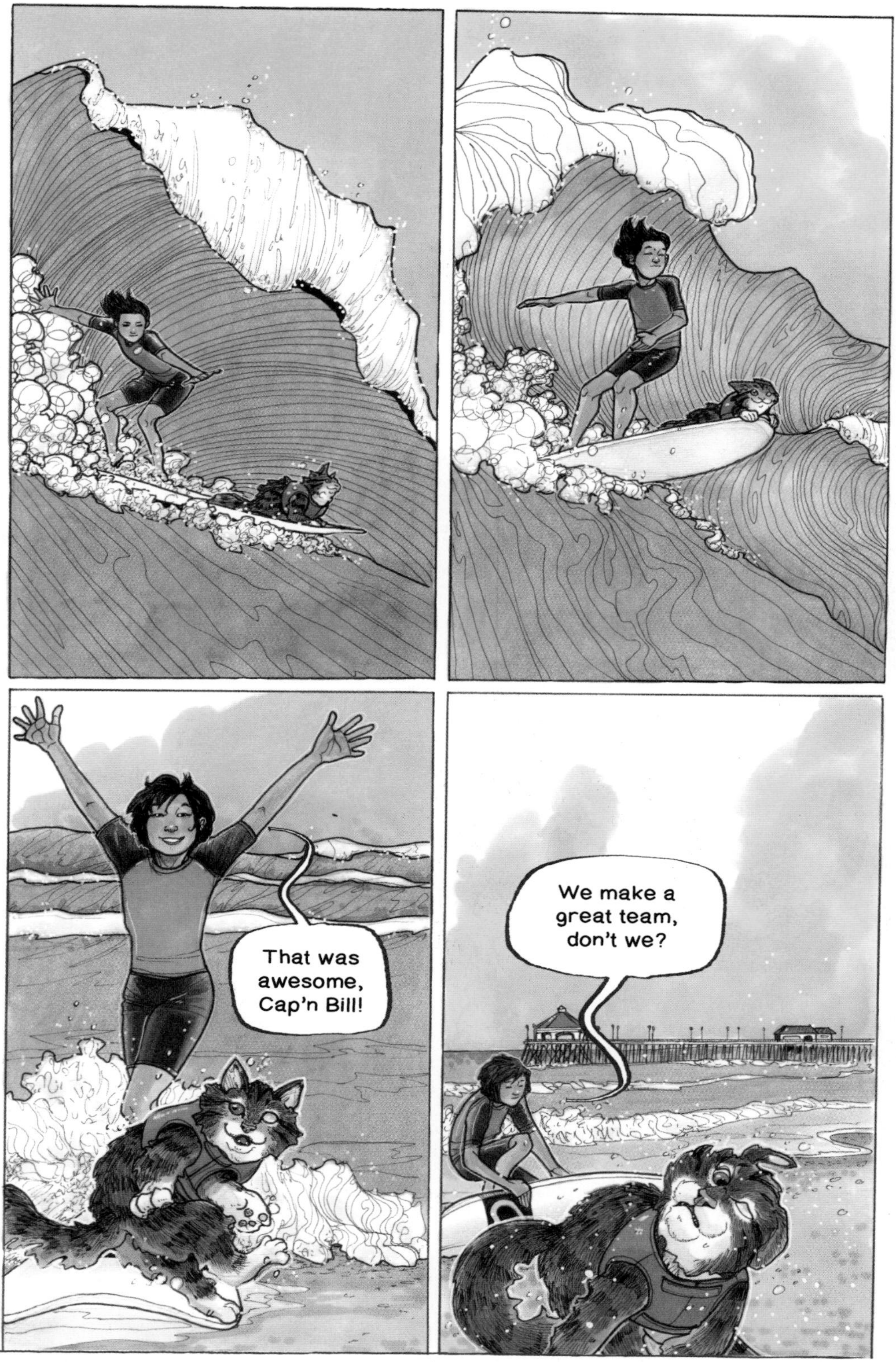
That was awesome, Cap'n Bill!
We make a great team, don't we?

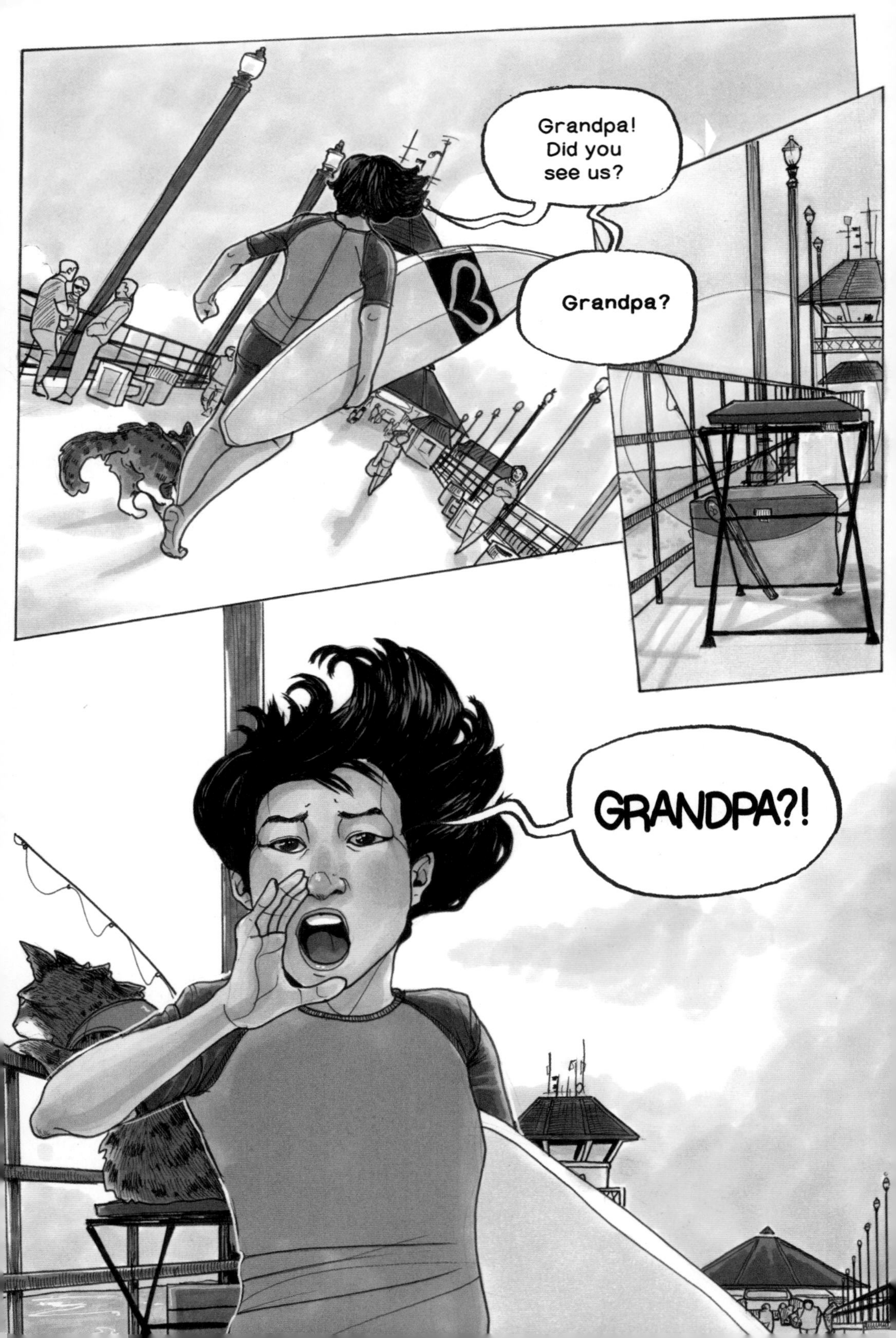
Grandpa!
Did you
see us?
Grandpa?
GRANDPA?!

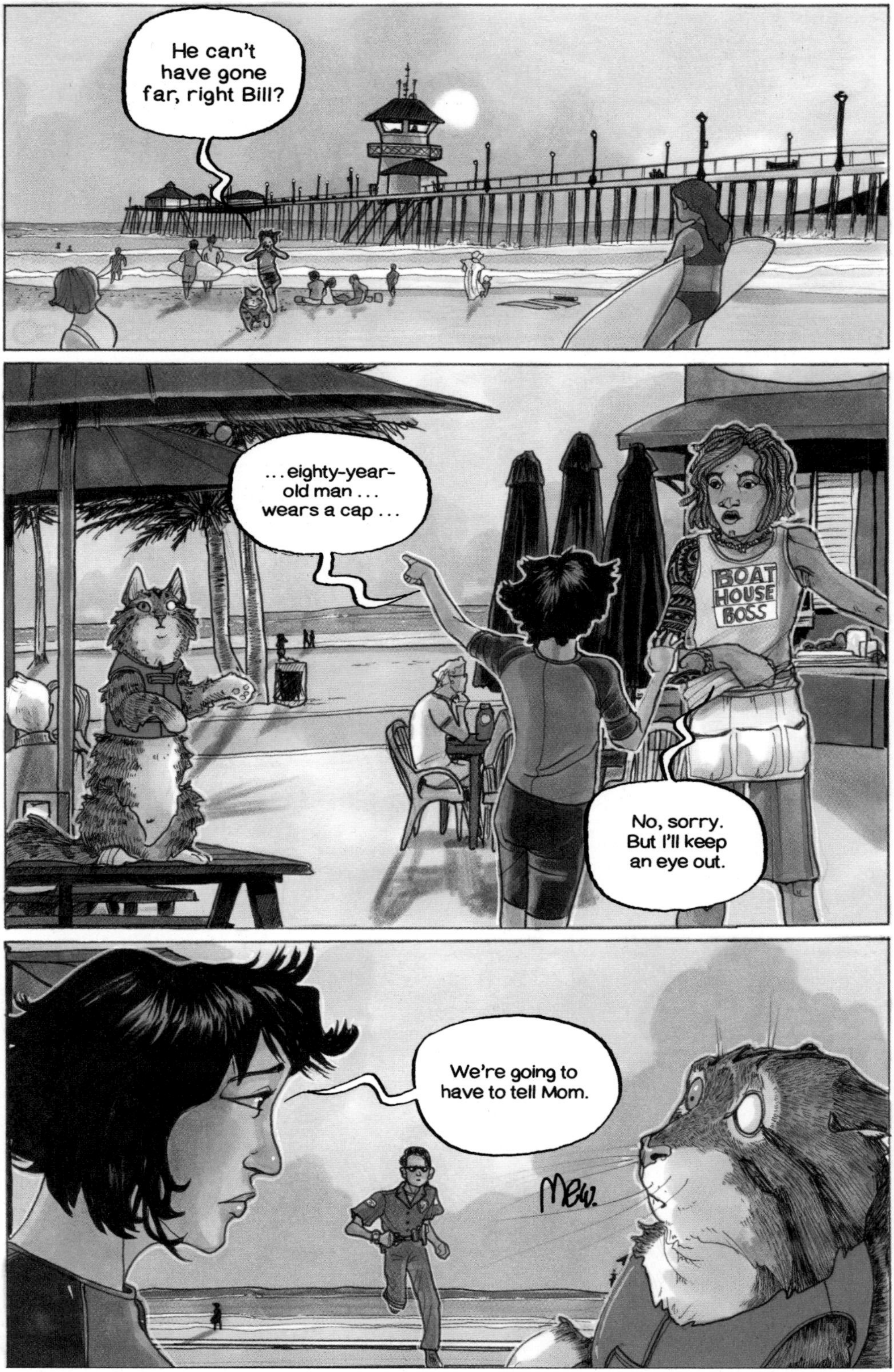
He can't have gone far, right Bill?
...eighty-year-old man... wears a cap...
BOAT HOUSE BOSS
No, sorry. But I'll keep an eye out.
We're going to have to tell Mom.
Mew.

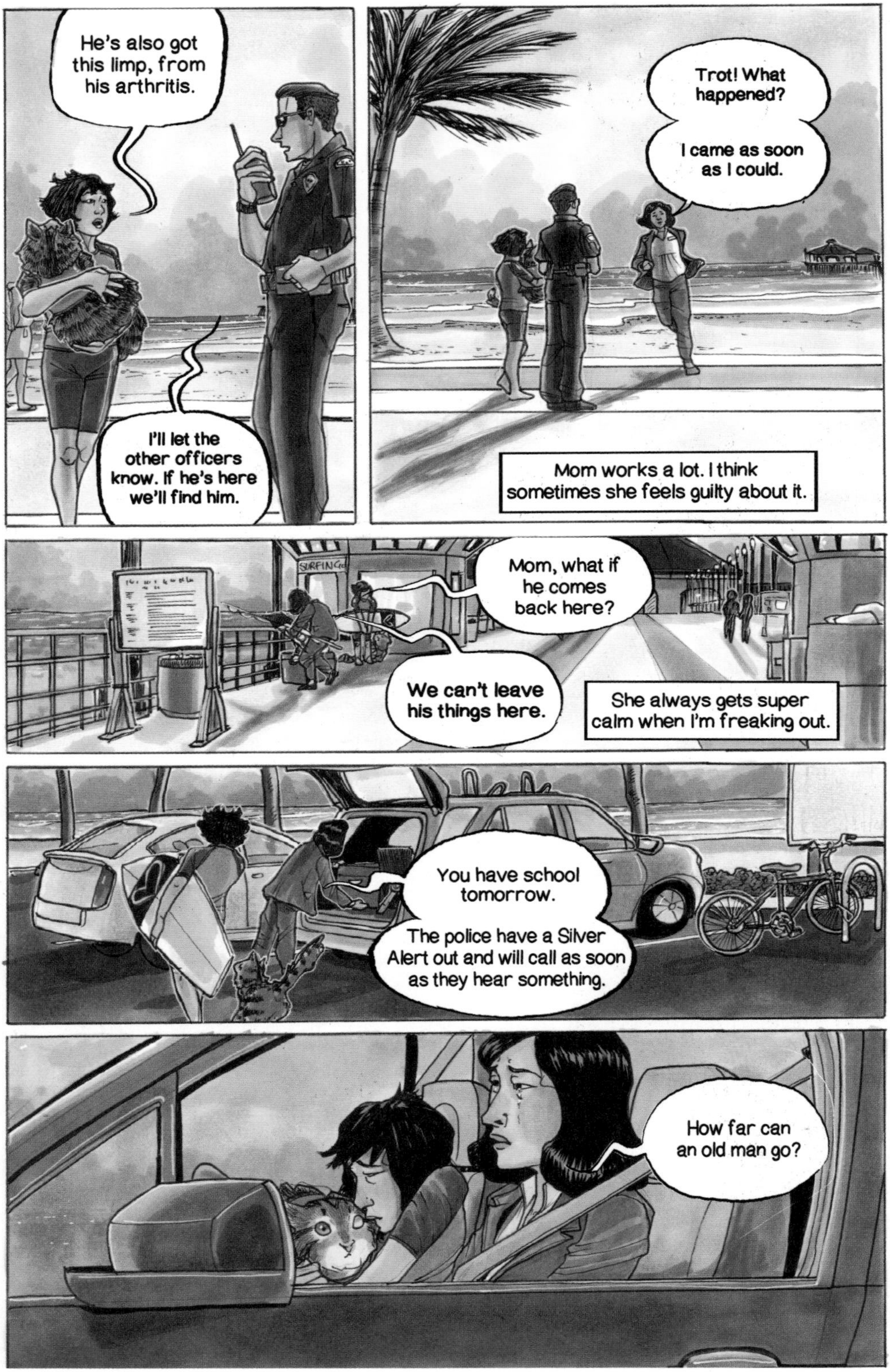
He's also got this limp, from his arthritis.
I'll let the other officers know. If he's here we'll find him.
Trot! What happened?
I came as soon as I could.
Mom works a lot. I think sometimes she feels guilty about it.
SURFING
Mom, what if he comes back here?
We can't leave his things here.
She always gets super calm when I'm freaking out.
You have school tomorrow.
The police have a Silver Alert out and will call as soon as they hear something.
How far can an old man go?

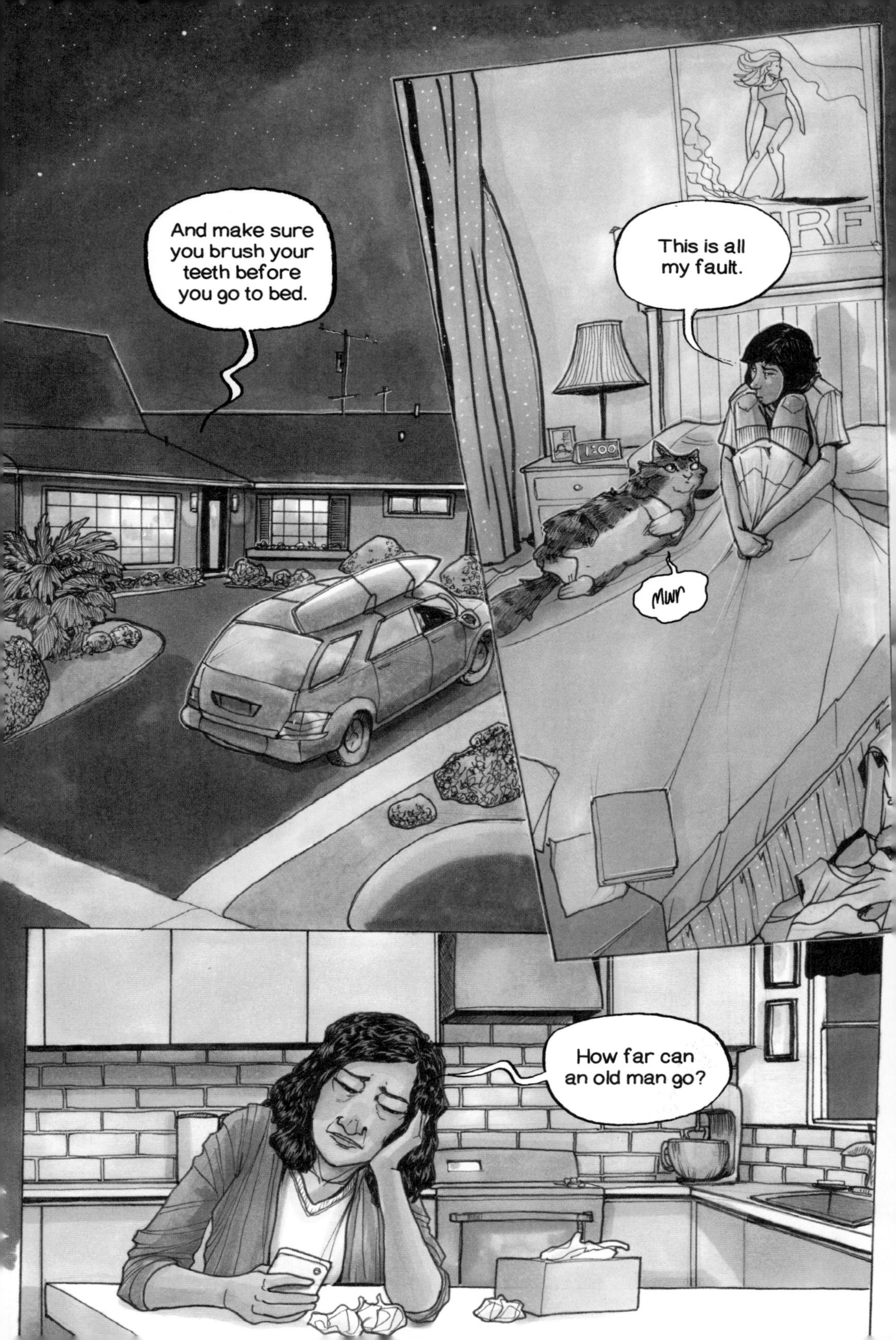
And make sure you brush your teeth before you go to bed.
This is all my fault.
Mwr
How far can an old man go?

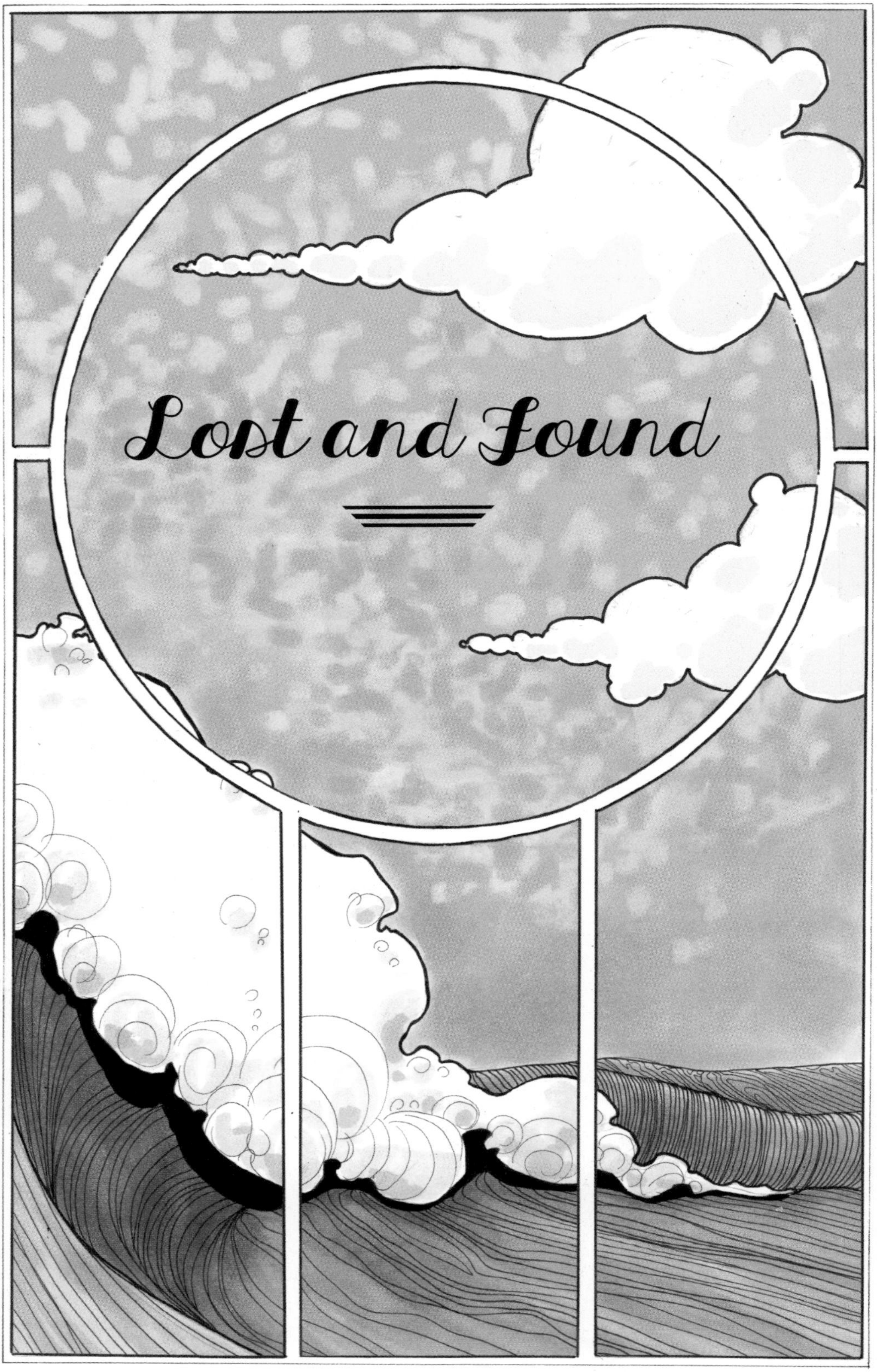
Lost and Found

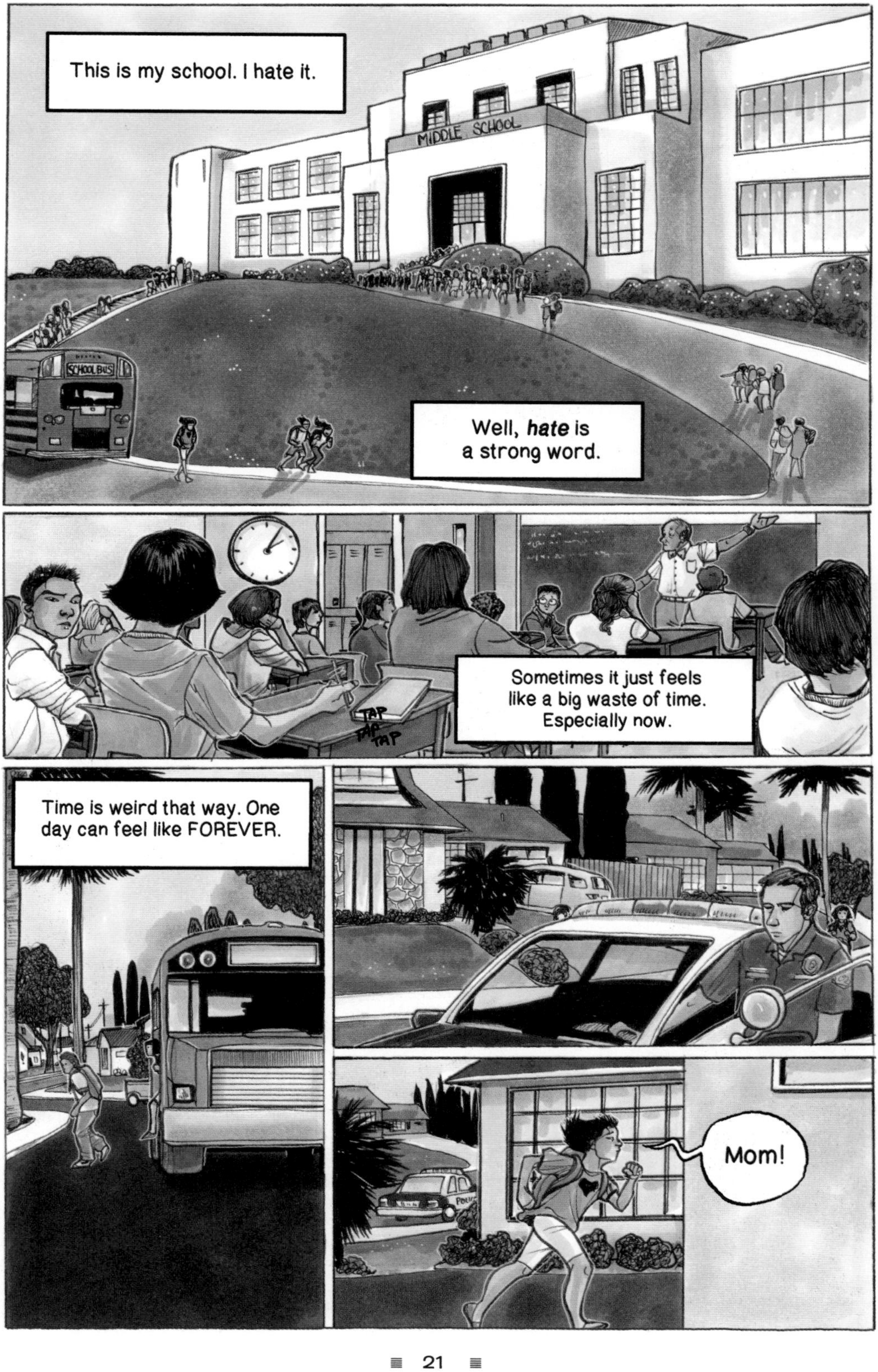
This is my school. I hate it.
MIDDLE SCHOOL
SCHOOL BUS
Well, *hate* is a strong word.
Sometimes it just feels like a big waste of time. Especially now.
TAP TAP TAP
Time is weird that way. One day can feel like FOREVER.
Mom!

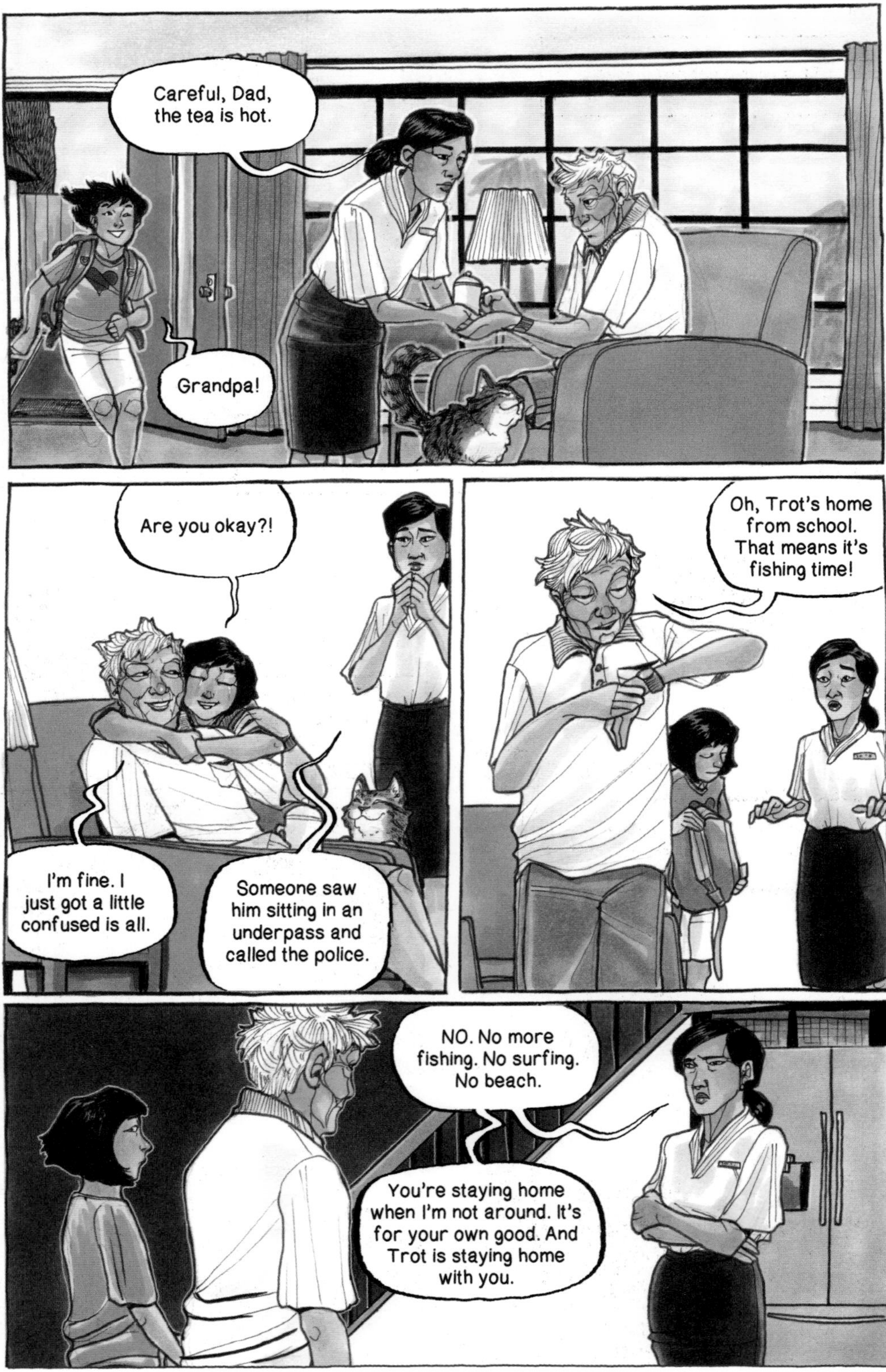
Careful, Dad, the tea is hot.
Grandpa!
Are you okay?!
I'm fine. I just got a little confused is all.
Someone saw him sitting in an underpass and called the police.
Oh, Trot's home from school. That means it's fishing time!
NO. No more fishing. No surfing. No beach.
You're staying home when I'm not around. It's for your own good. And Trot is staying home with you.

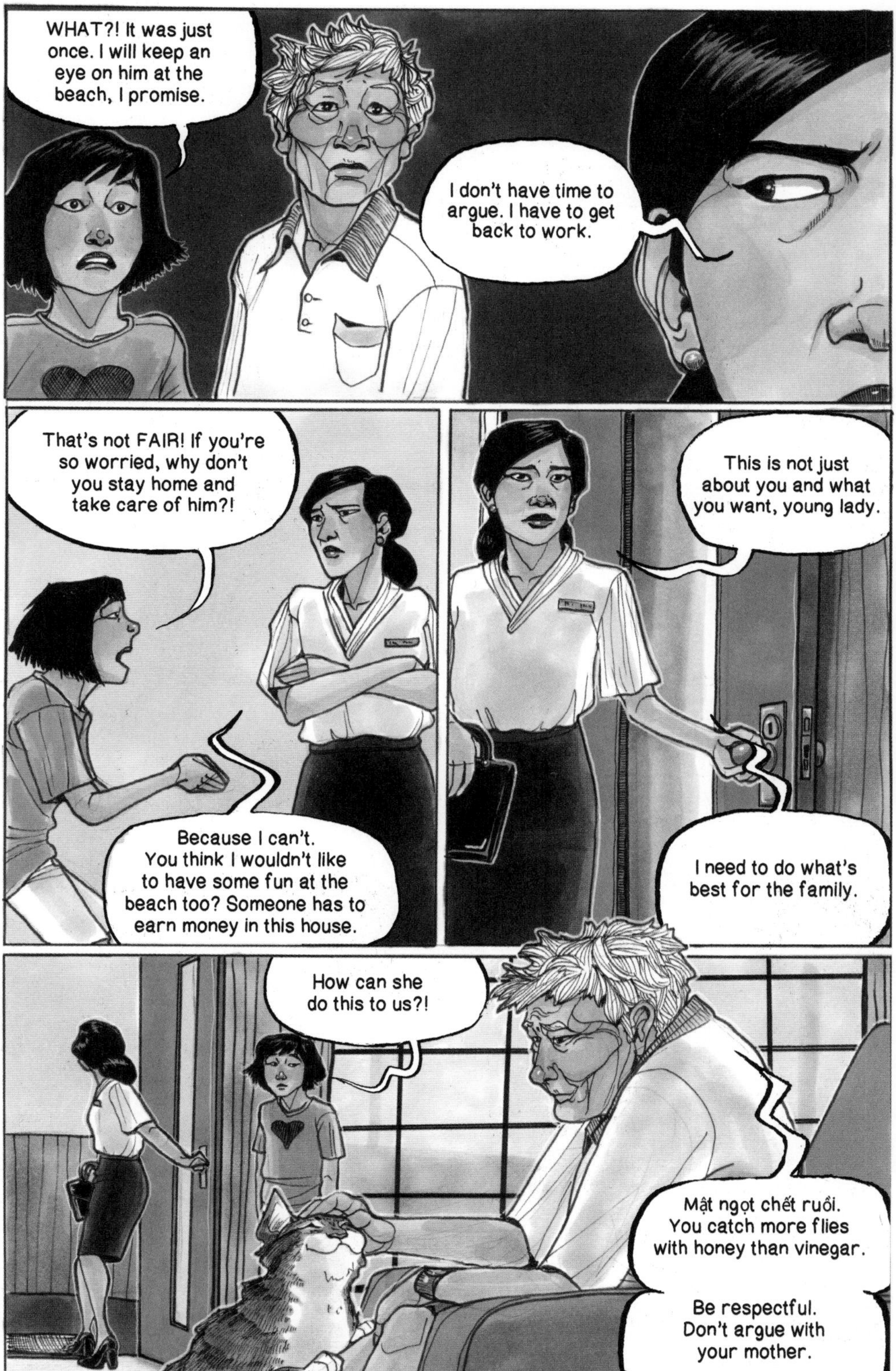
WHAT?! It was just once. I will keep an eye on him at the beach, I promise.
I don't have time to argue. I have to get back to work.
That's not FAIR! If you're so worried, why don't you stay home and take care of him?!
Because I can't. You think I wouldn't like to have some fun at the beach too? Someone has to earn money in this house.
This is not just about you and what you want, young lady.
I need to do what's best for the family.
How can she do this to us?!
Mật ngọt chết ruồi. You catch more flies with honey than vinegar.
Be respectful. Don't argue with your mother.

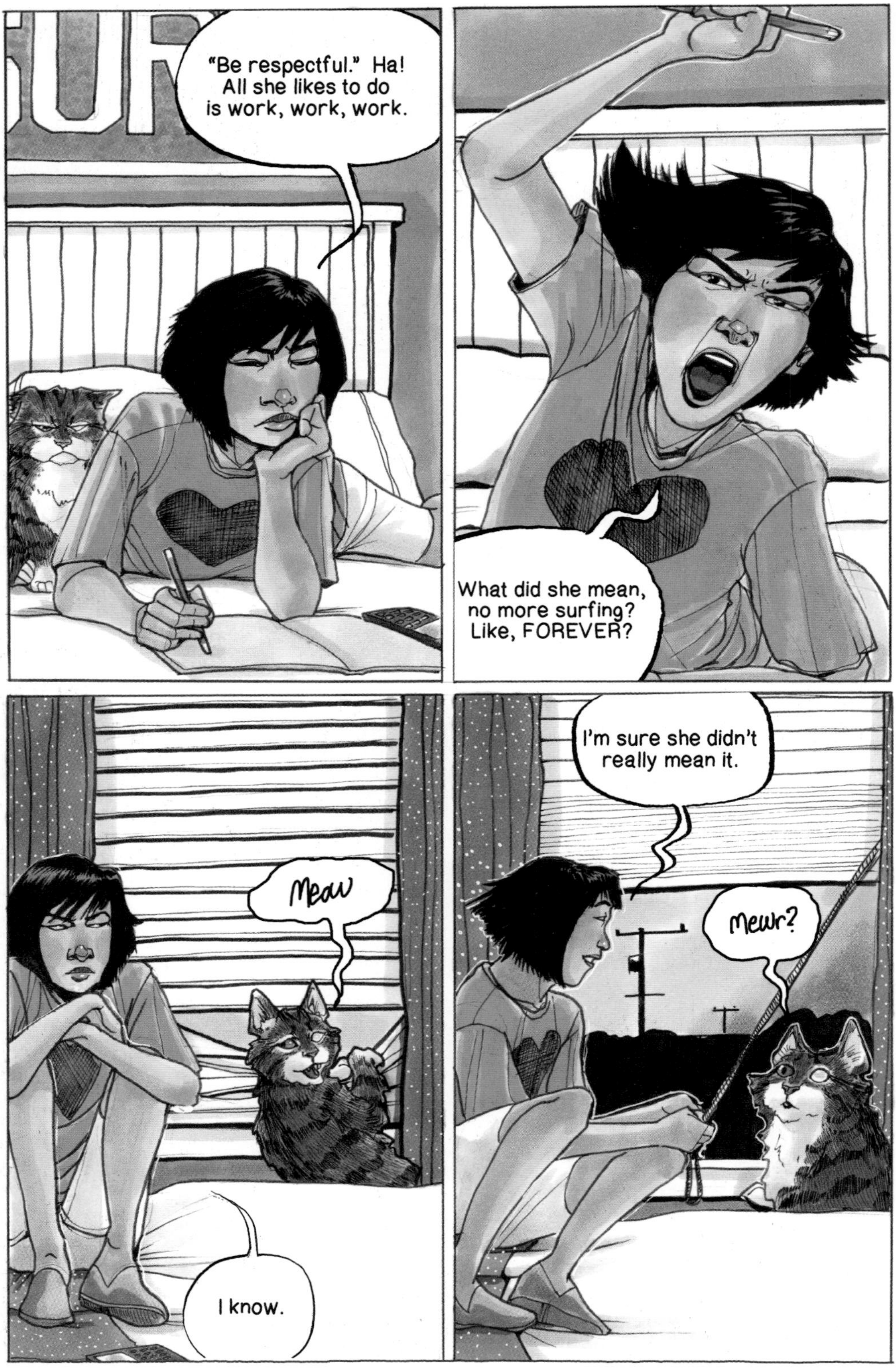
"Be respectful." Ha! All she likes to do is work, work, work.
What did she mean, no more surfing? Like, FOREVER?
Meaw
I know.
I'm sure she didn't really mean it.
Mewr?

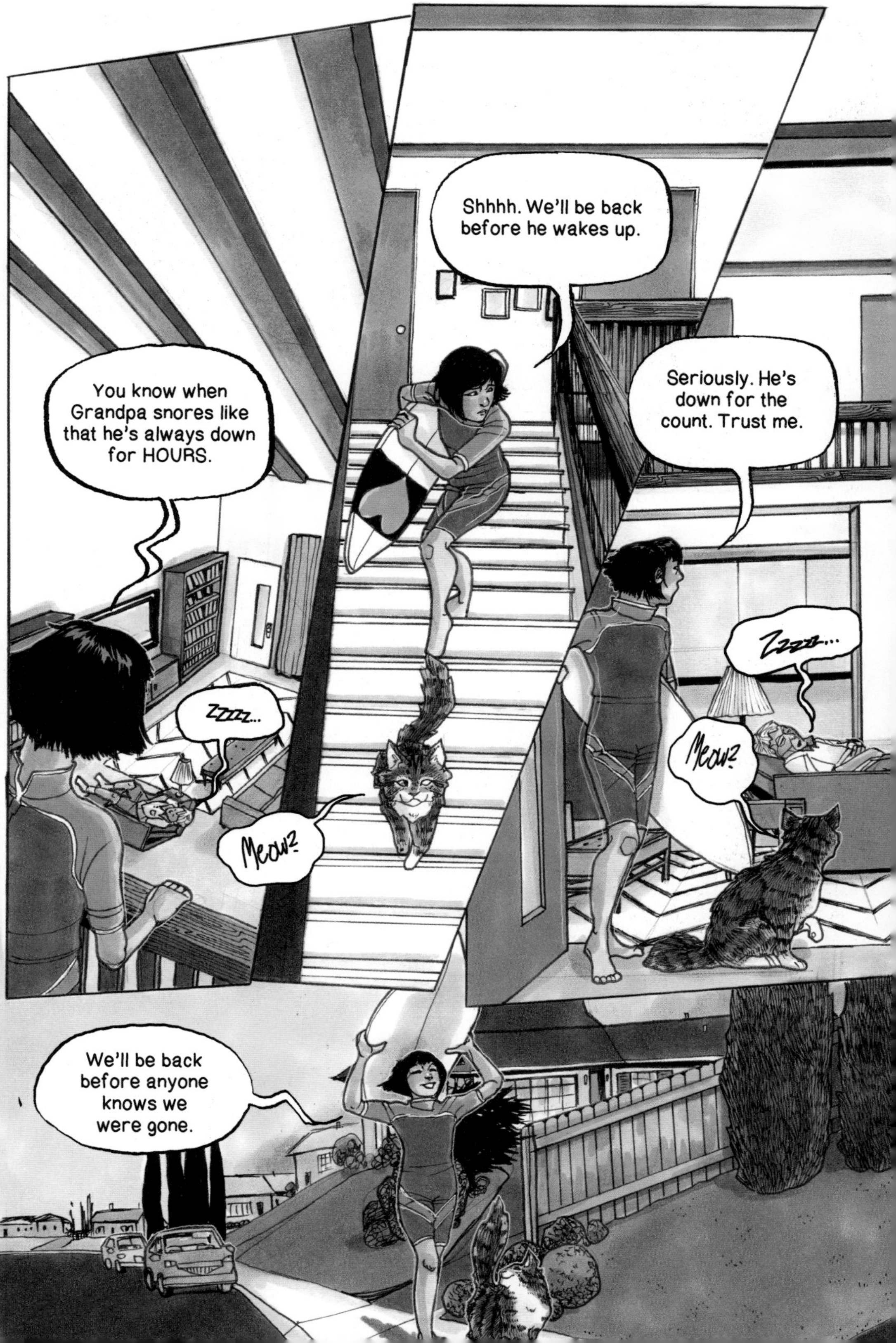
You know when Grandpa snores like that he's always down for HOURS.
Zzzz...
Meow?
Shhhh. We'll be back before he wakes up.
Seriously. He's down for the count. Trust me.
Zzzz...
Meow?
We'll be back before anyone knows we were gone.

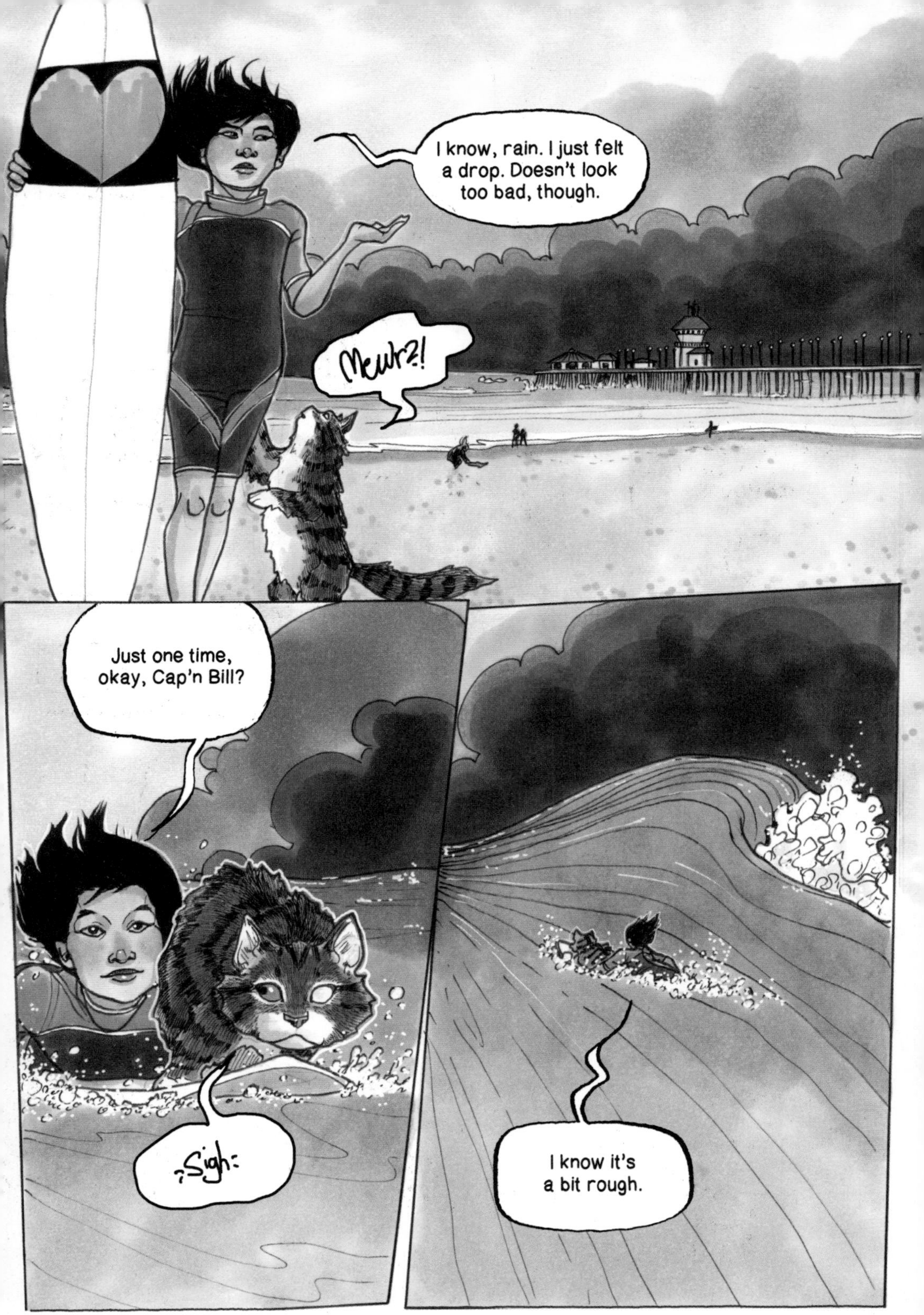
I know, rain. I just felt a drop. Doesn't look too bad, though.
Mewr?!
Just one time, okay, Cap'n Bill?
Sigh
I know it's a bit rough.

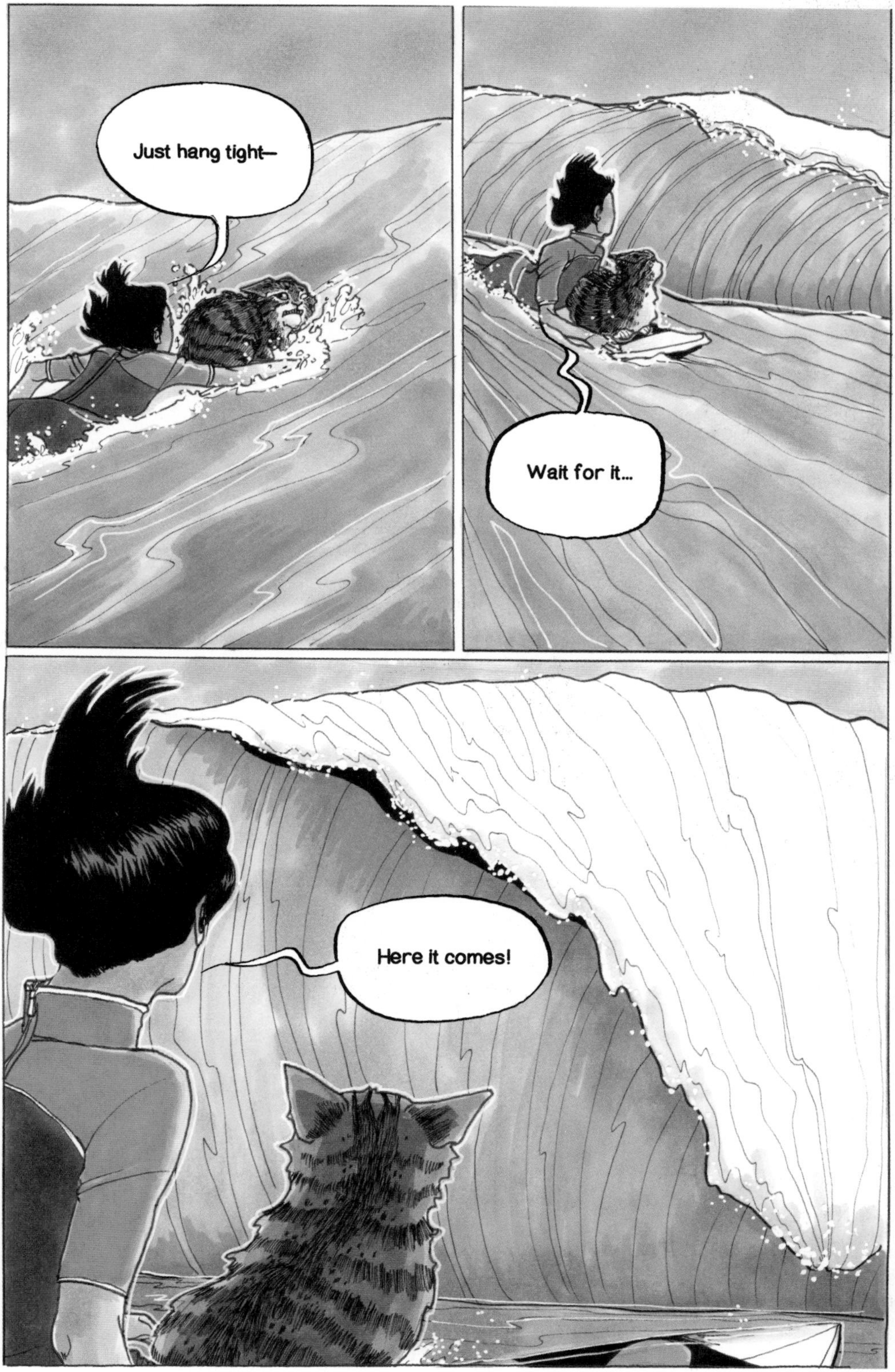
Just hang tight—
Wait for it...
Here it comes!

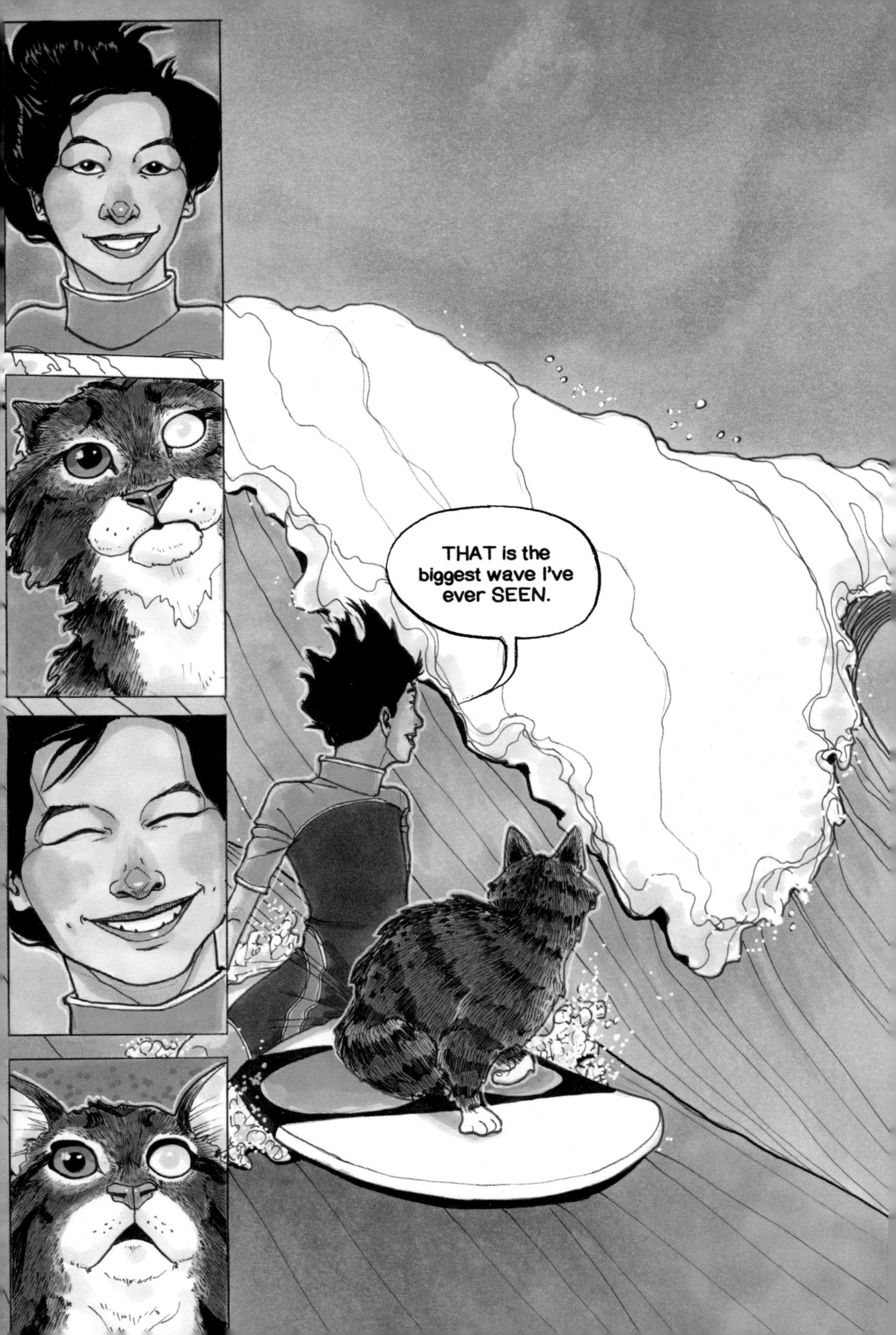
THAT is the biggest wave I've ever SEEN.

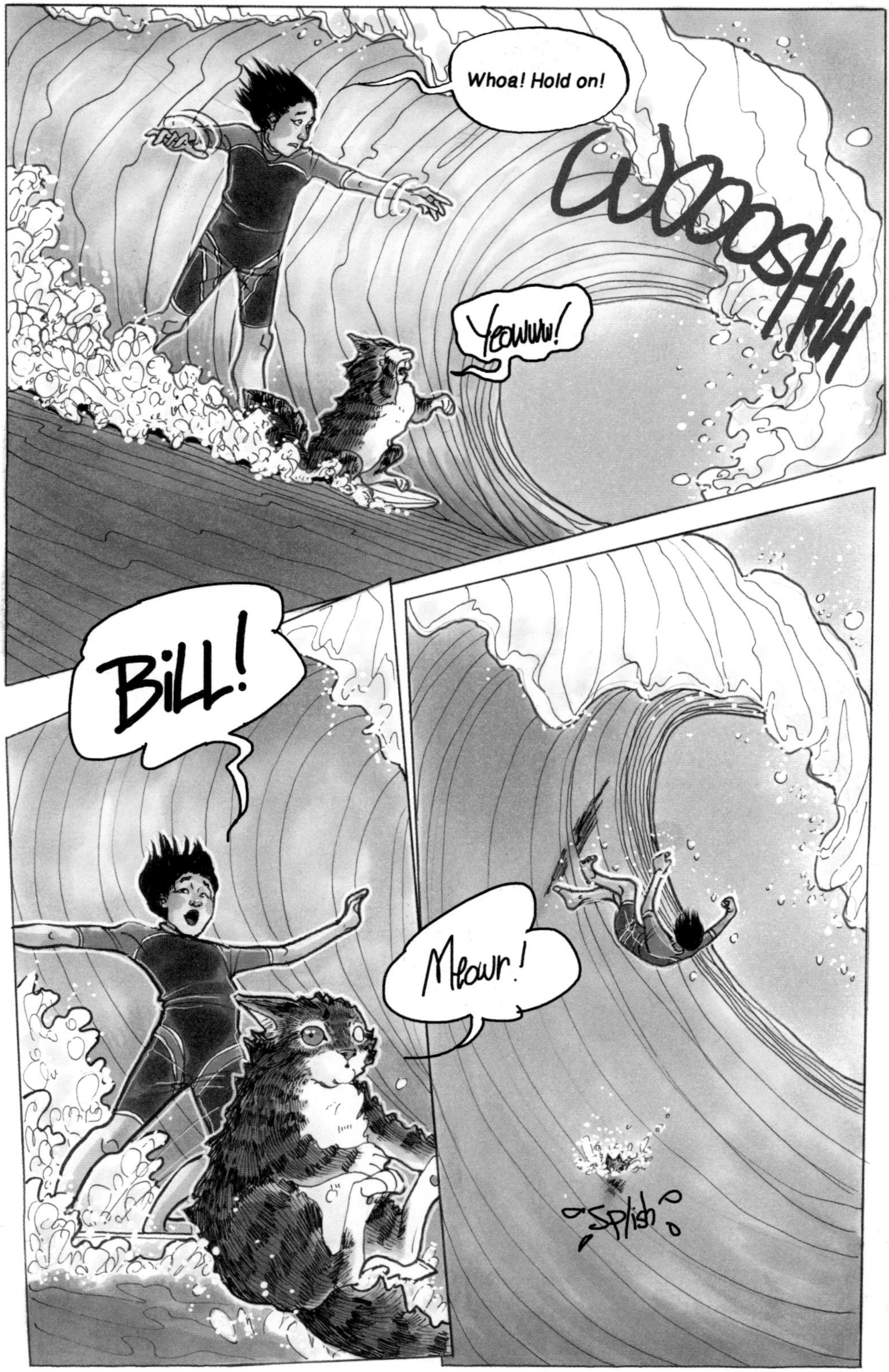
Whoa! Hold on!
WOOOSHHH
Yeowww!
BILL!
Meowr!
Splish

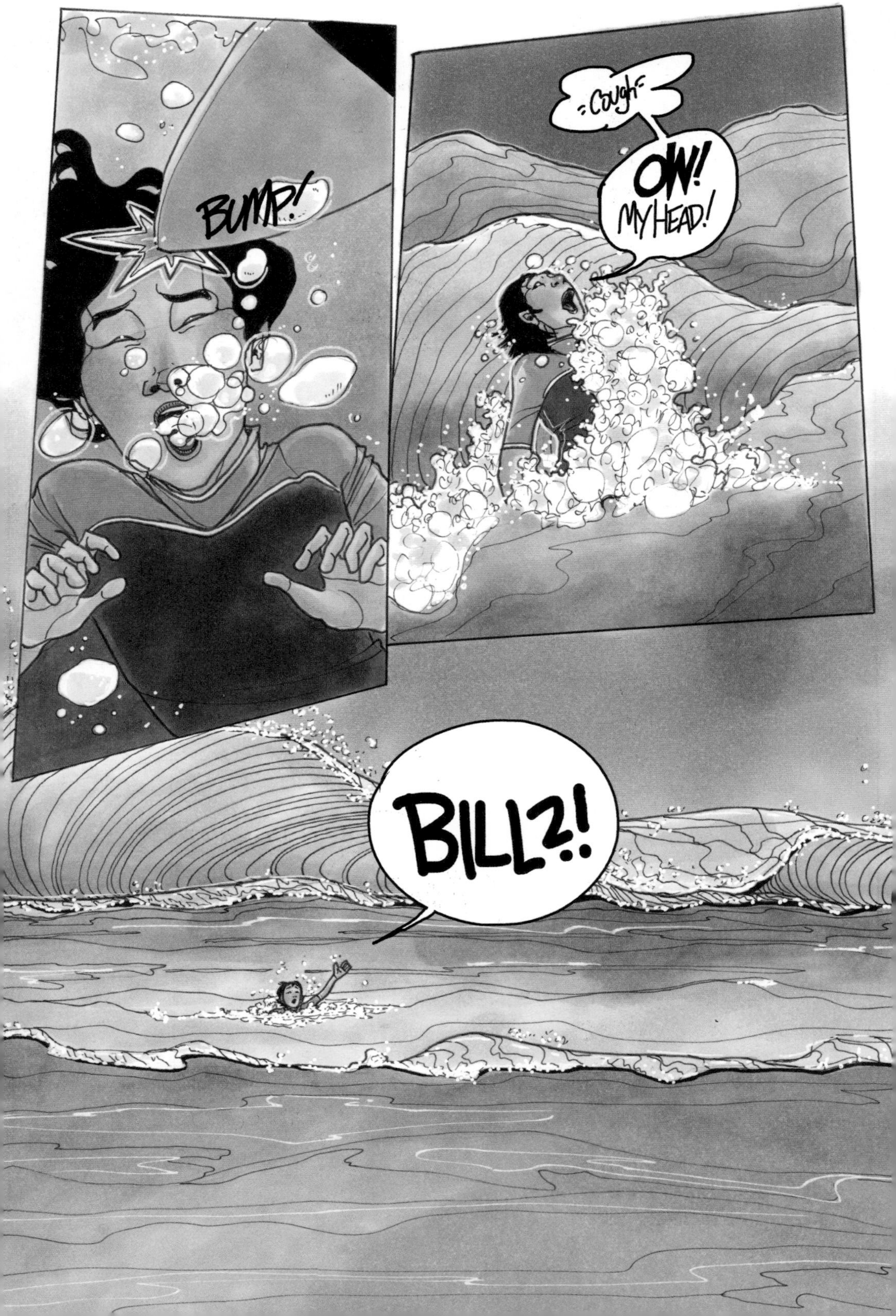
BUMP!
=Cough=
OW! MY HEAD!
BILL?!

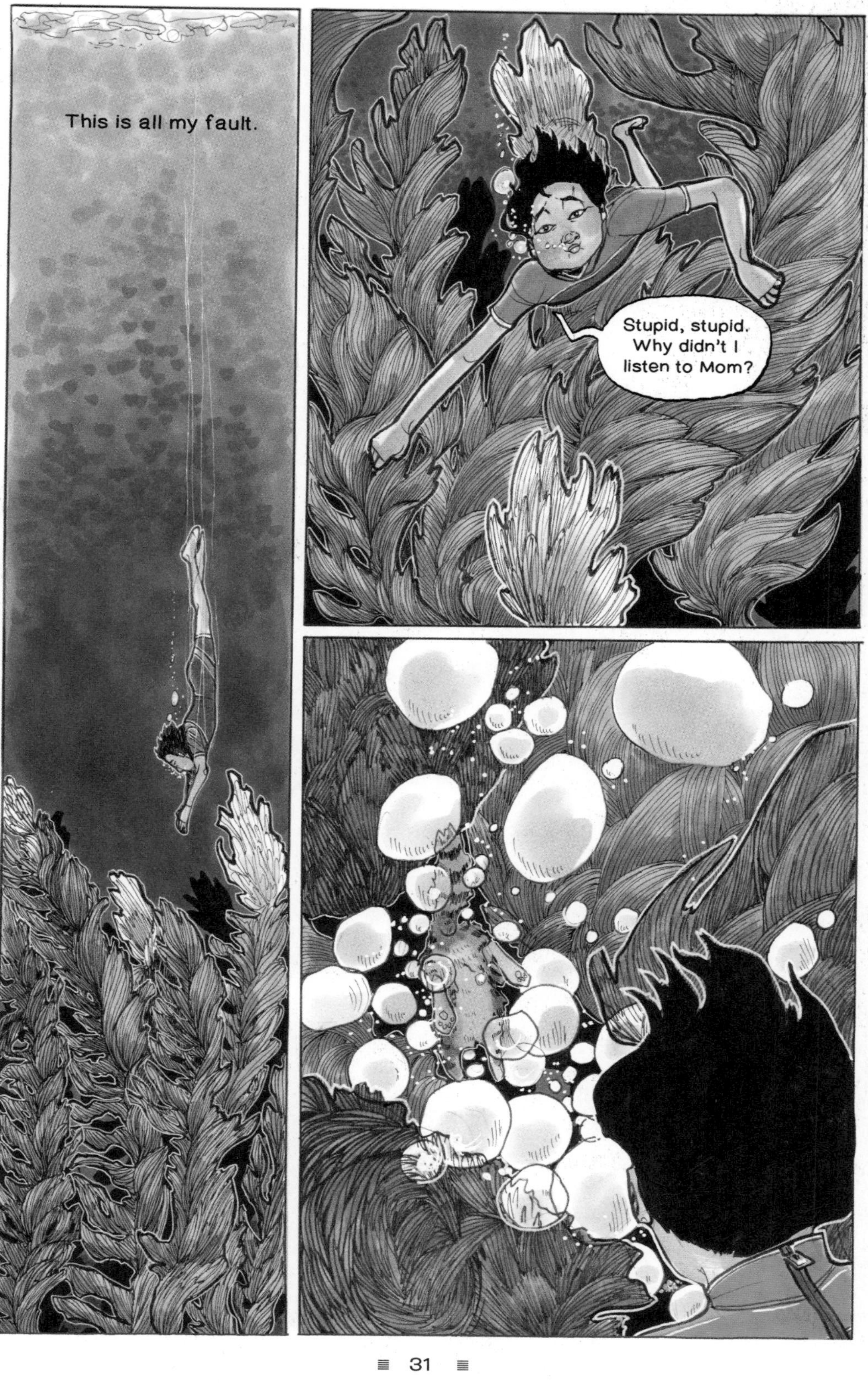
This is all my fault.
Stupid, stupid. Why didn't I listen to Mom?

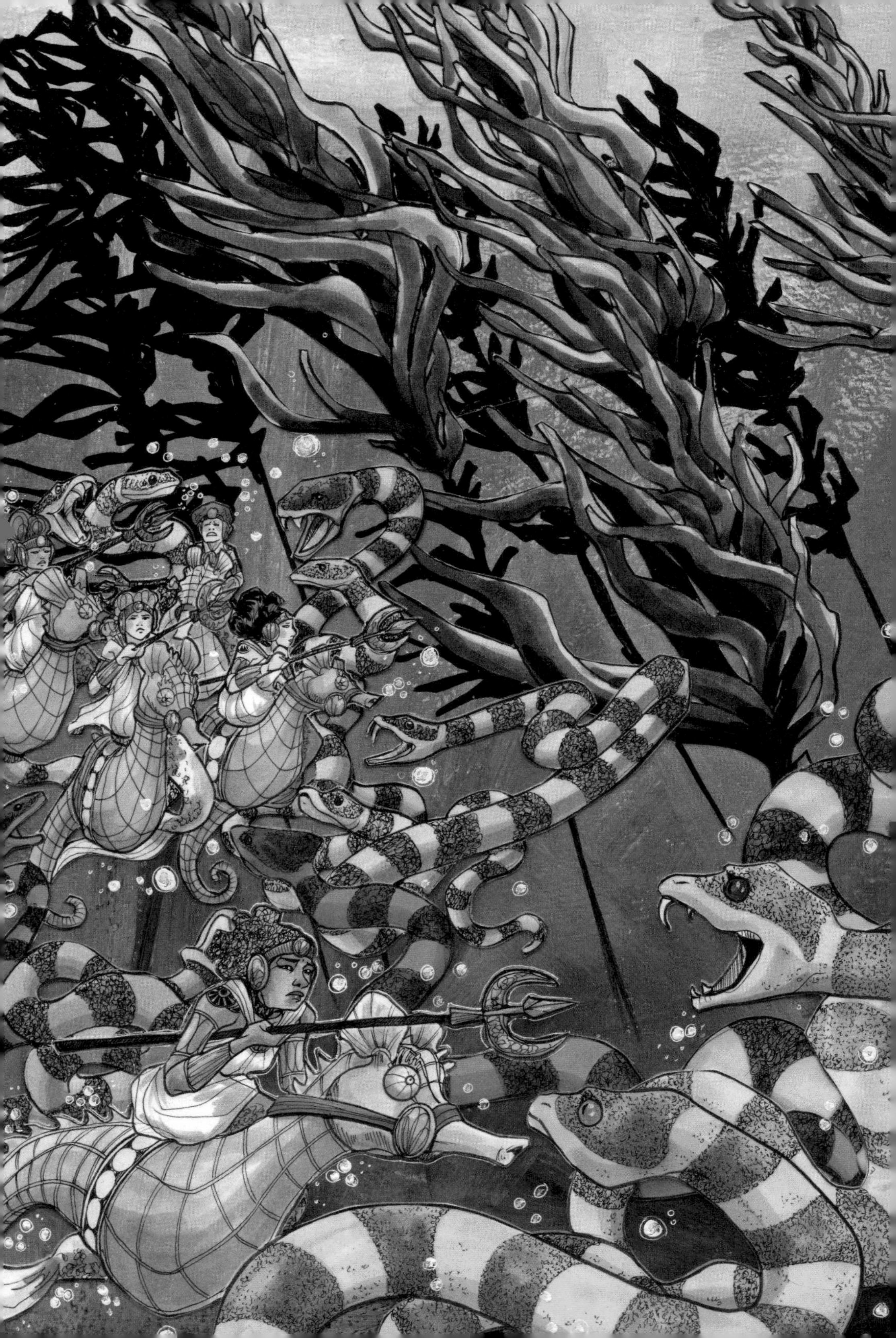

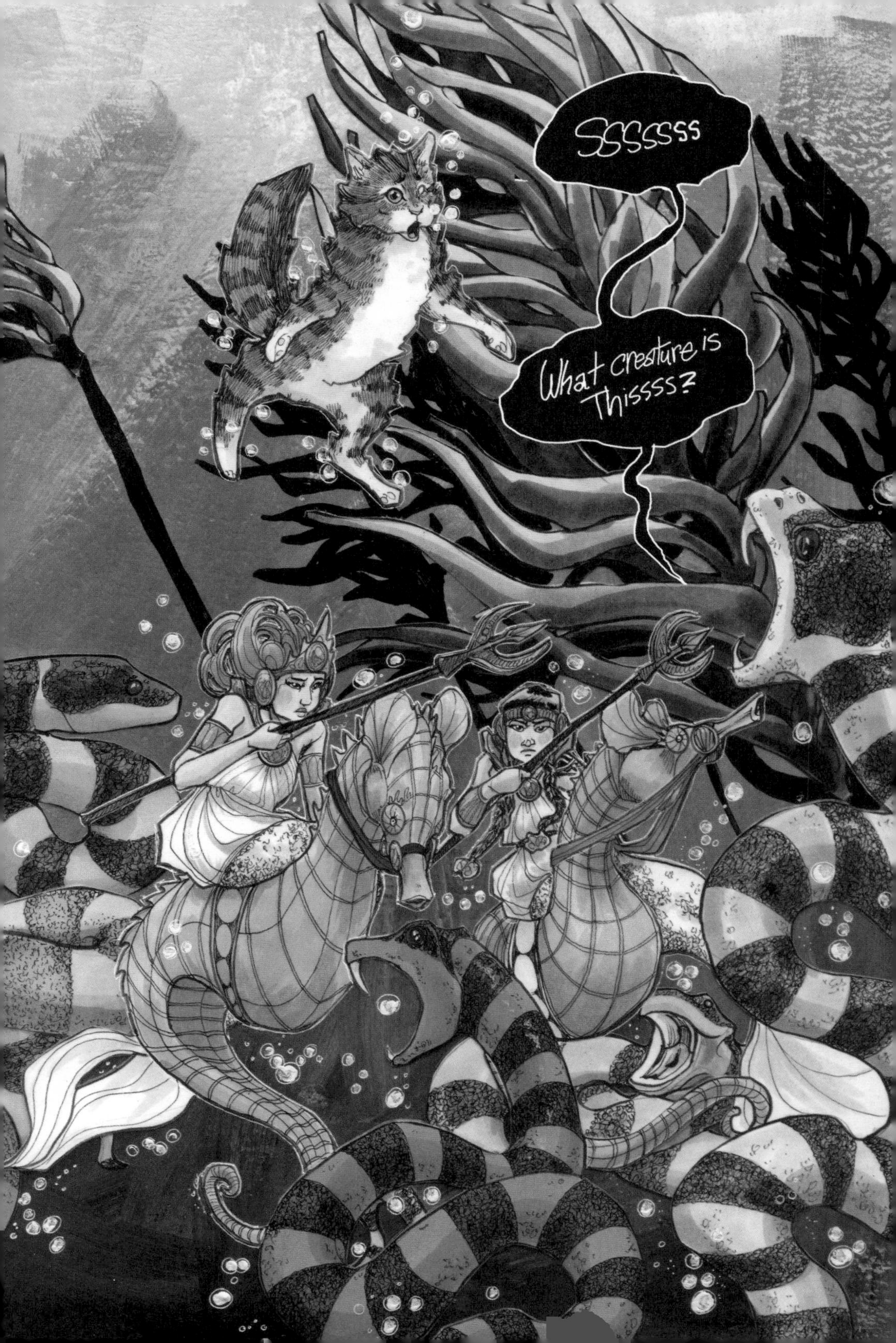
SSSSSSS
What creature is Thissss?

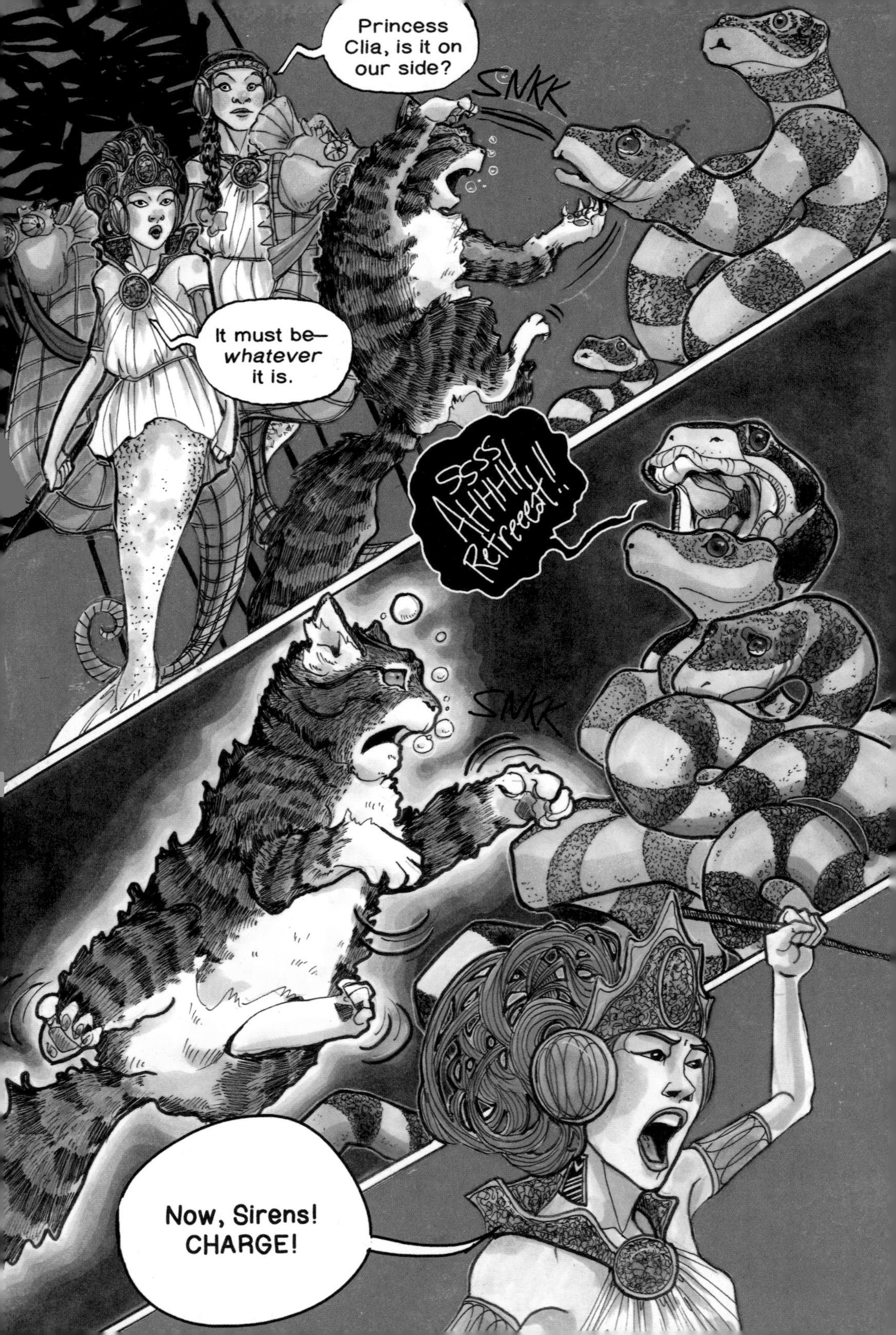
Princess Clia, is it on our side?
SNKK
It must be—*whatever* it is.
SSSS! AHHH!! Retreeeat!!
SNKK
Now, Sirens! CHARGE!

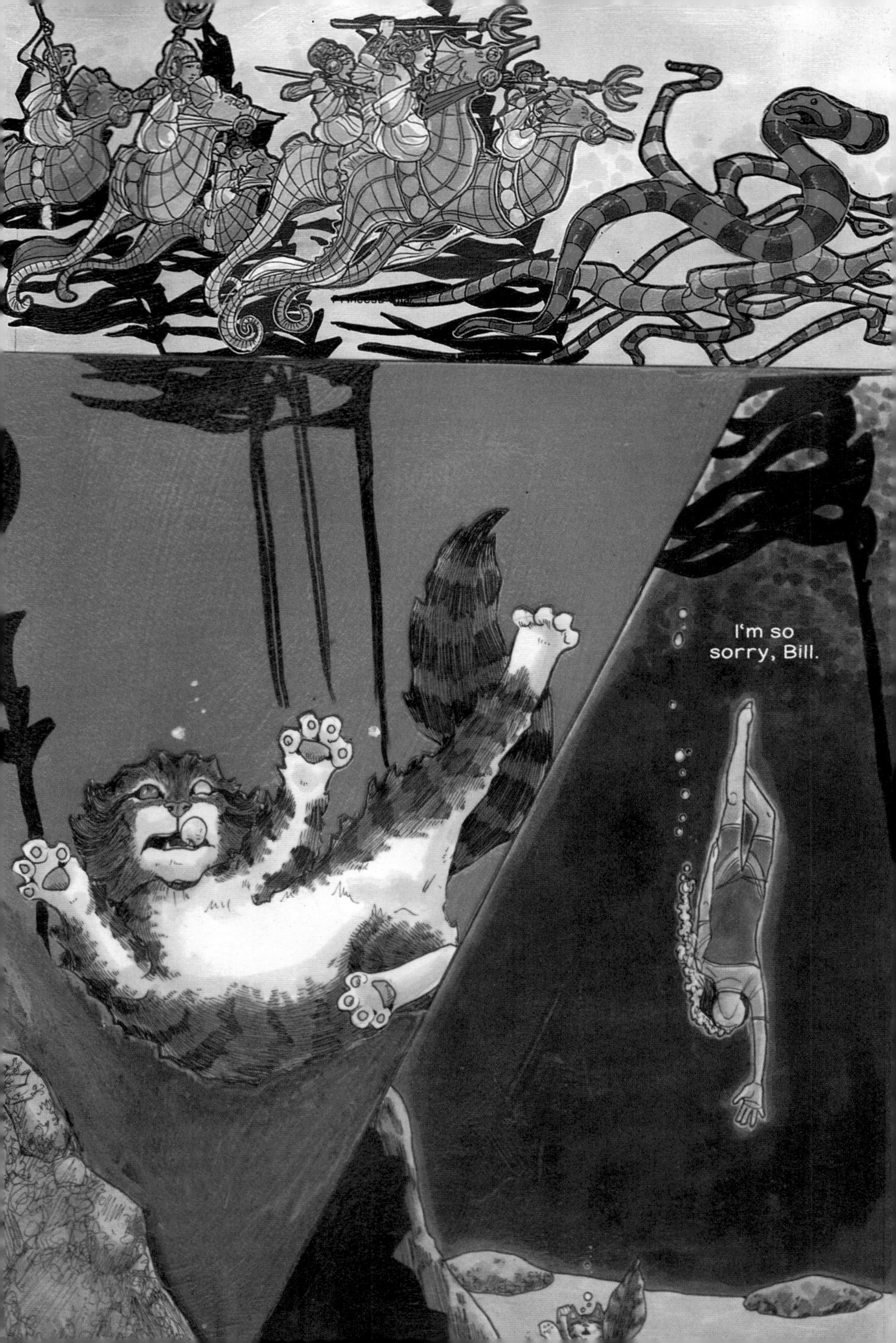
I'm so sorry, Bill.

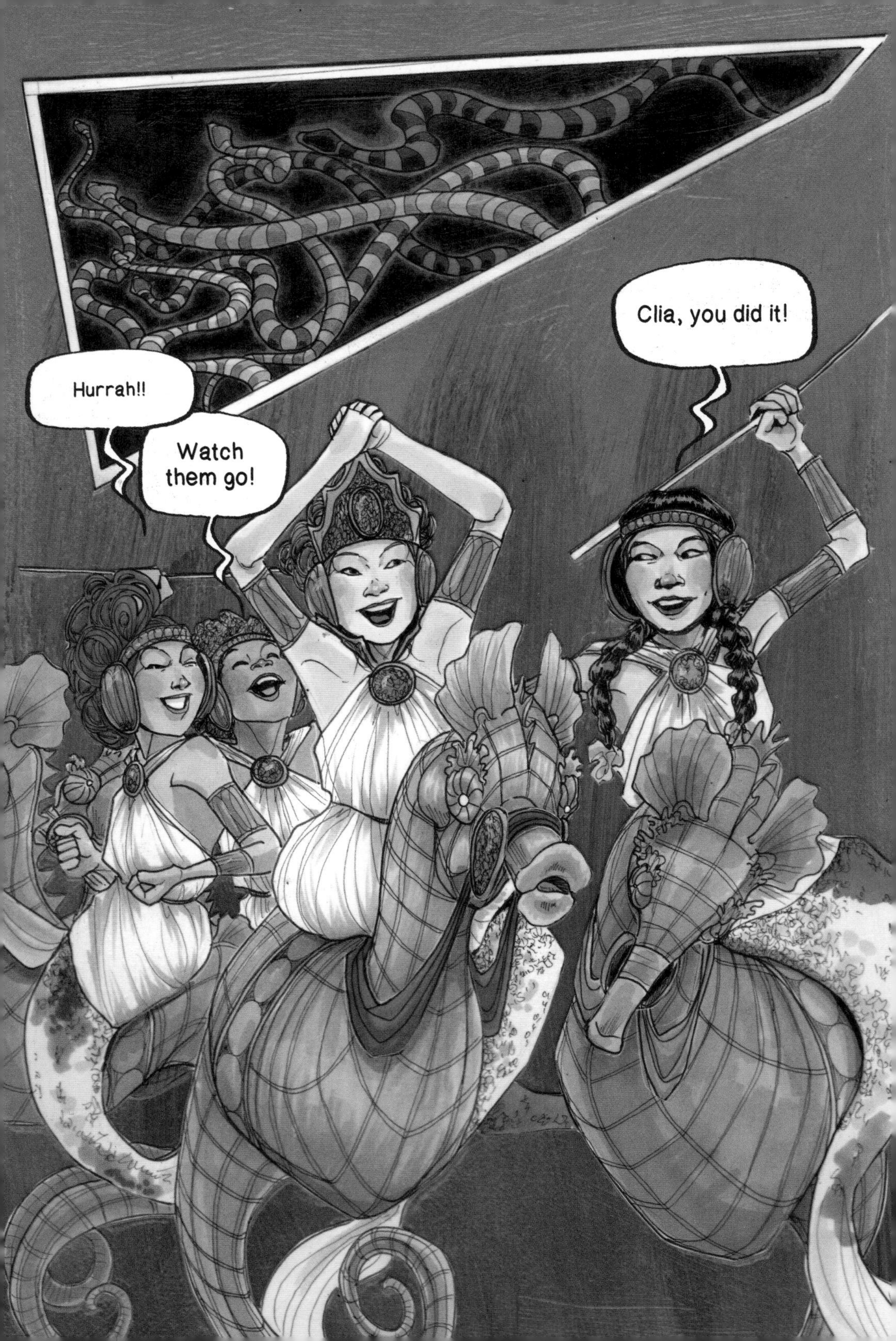
Hurrah!!
Watch them go!
Clia, you did it!

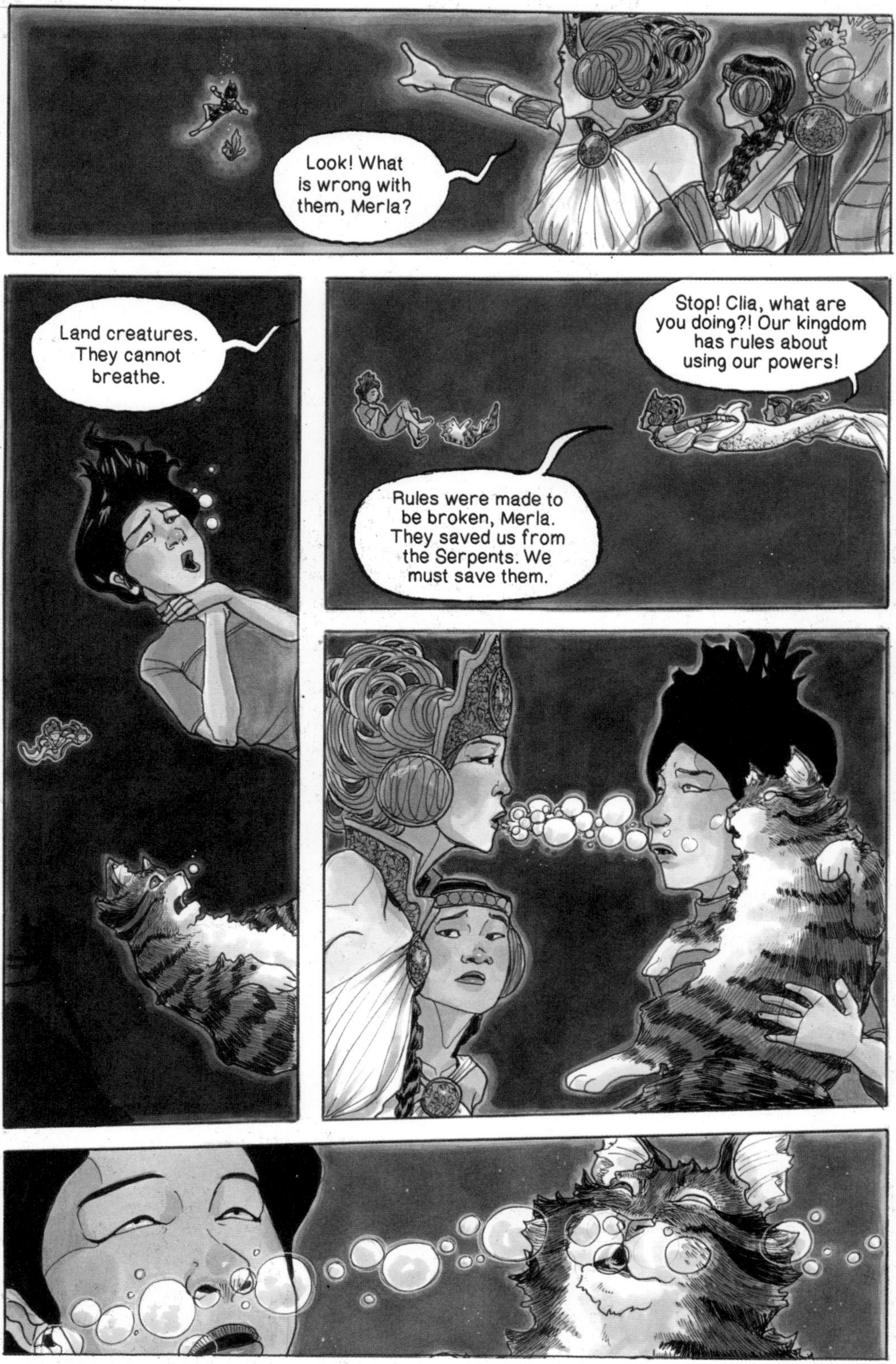
Look! What is wrong with them, Merla?
Land creatures. They cannot breathe.
Stop! Clia, what are you doing?! Our kingdom has rules about using our powers!
Rules were made to be broken, Merla. They saved us from the Serpents. We must save them.

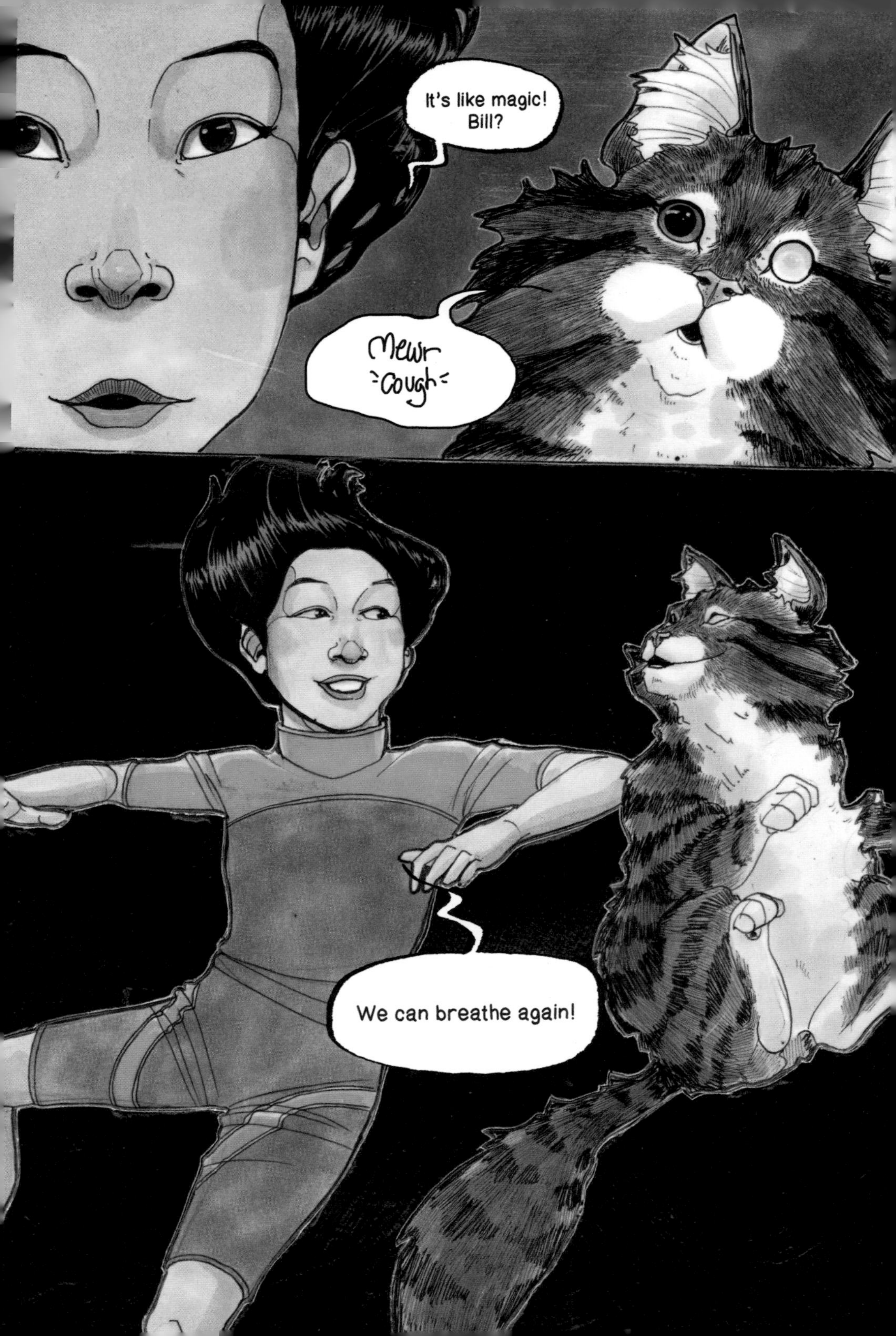
It's like magic! Bill?
Mewr
=Cough=
We can breathe again!

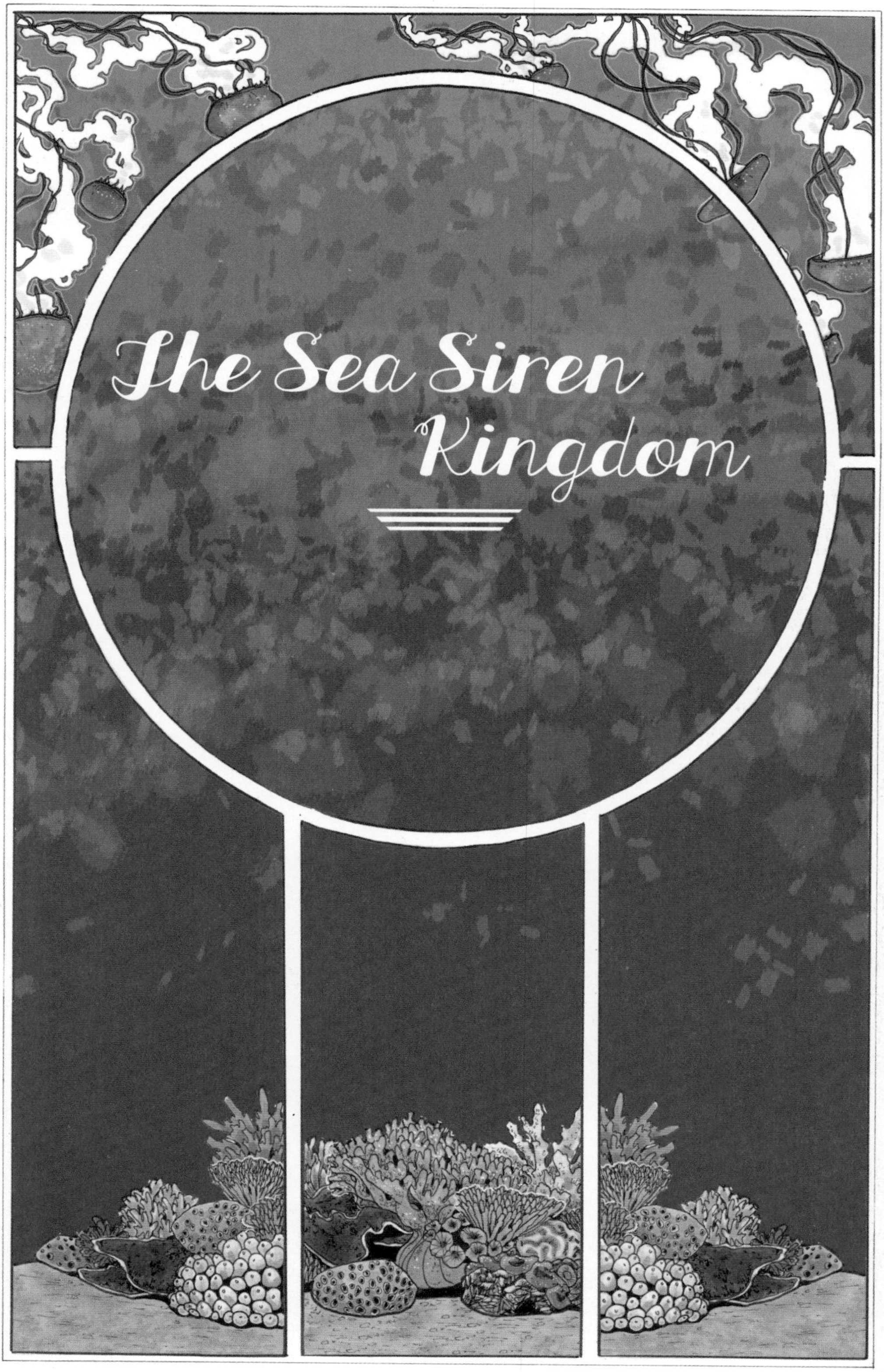
The Sea Siren Kingdom

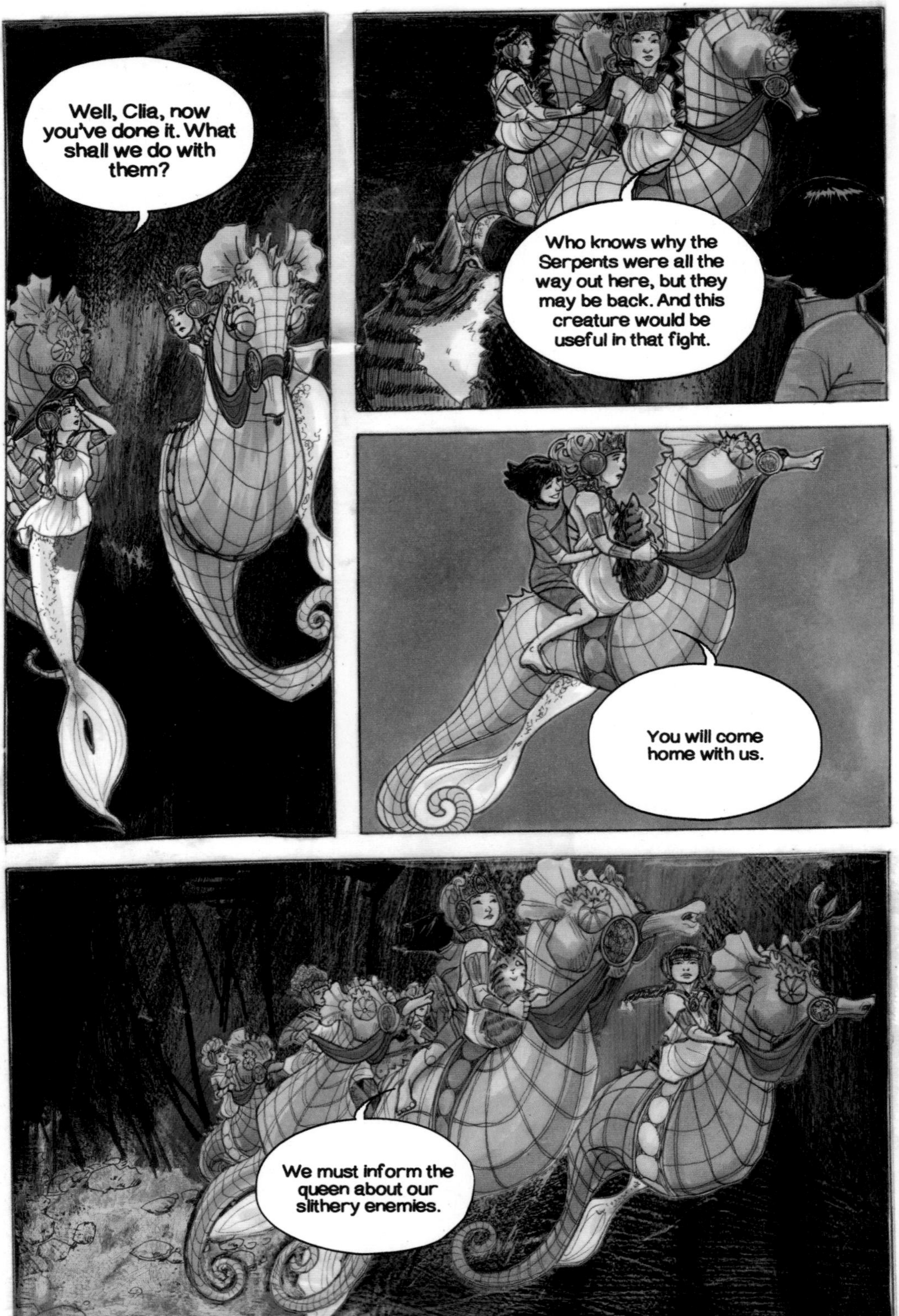
Well, Clia, now you've done it. What shall we do with them?
Who knows why the Serpents were all the way out here, but they may be back. And this creature would be useful in that fight.
You will come home with us.
We must inform the queen about our slithery enemies.

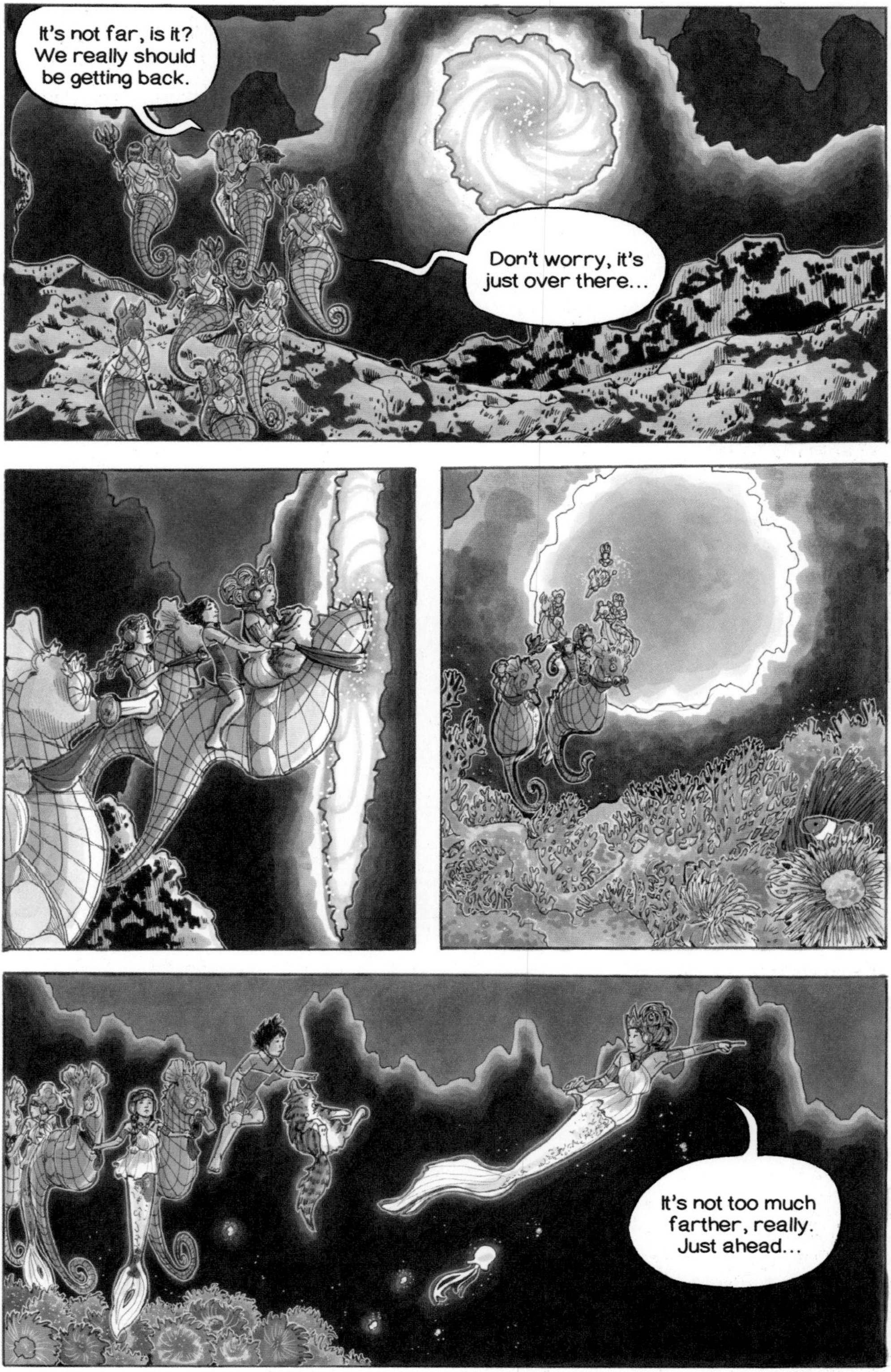
It's not far, is it? We really should be getting back.
Don't worry, it's just over there...
It's not too much farther, really. Just ahead...

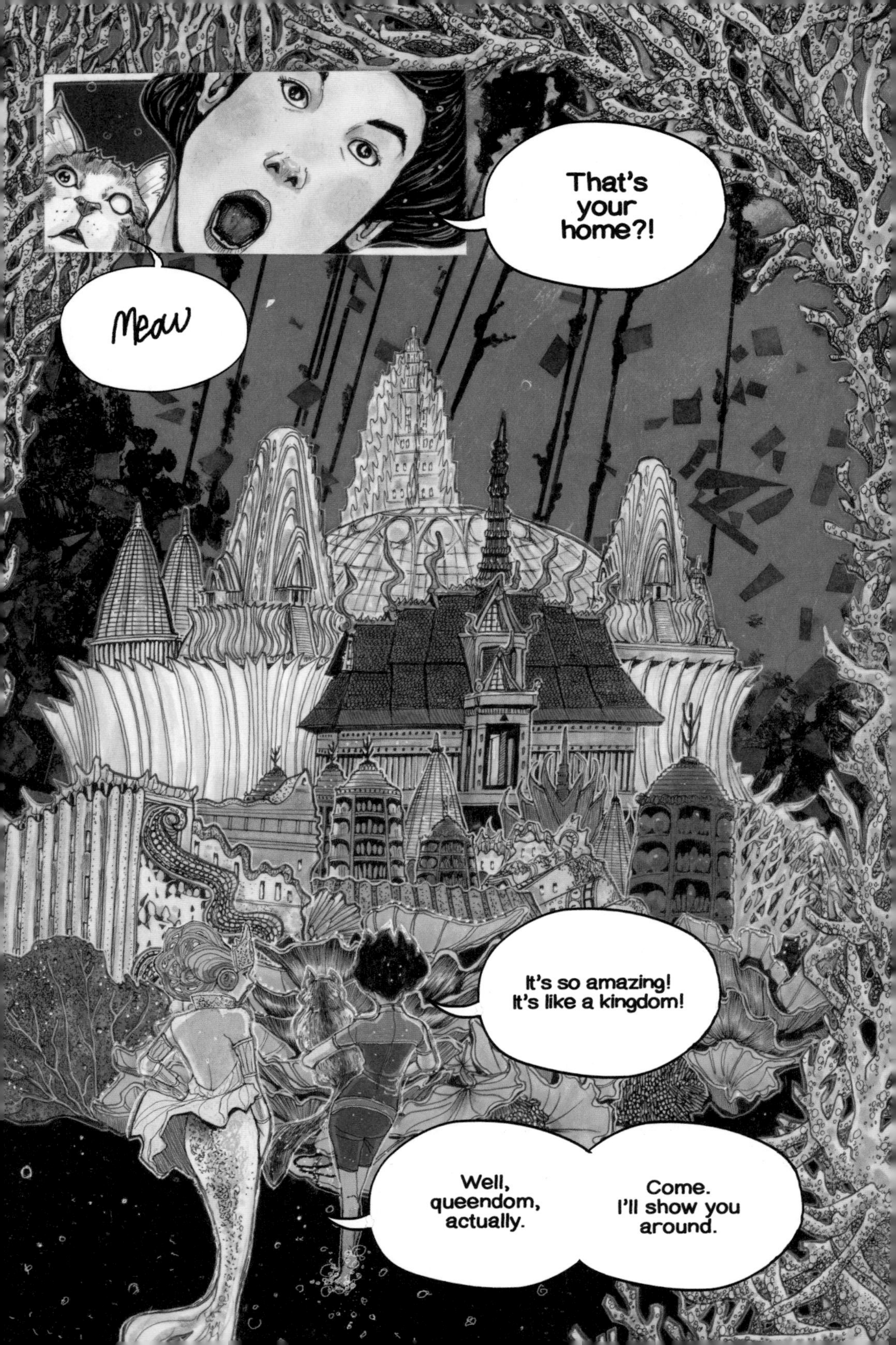
That's your home?!
Meow
It's so amazing! It's like a kingdom!
Well, queendom, actually.
Come. I'll show you around.

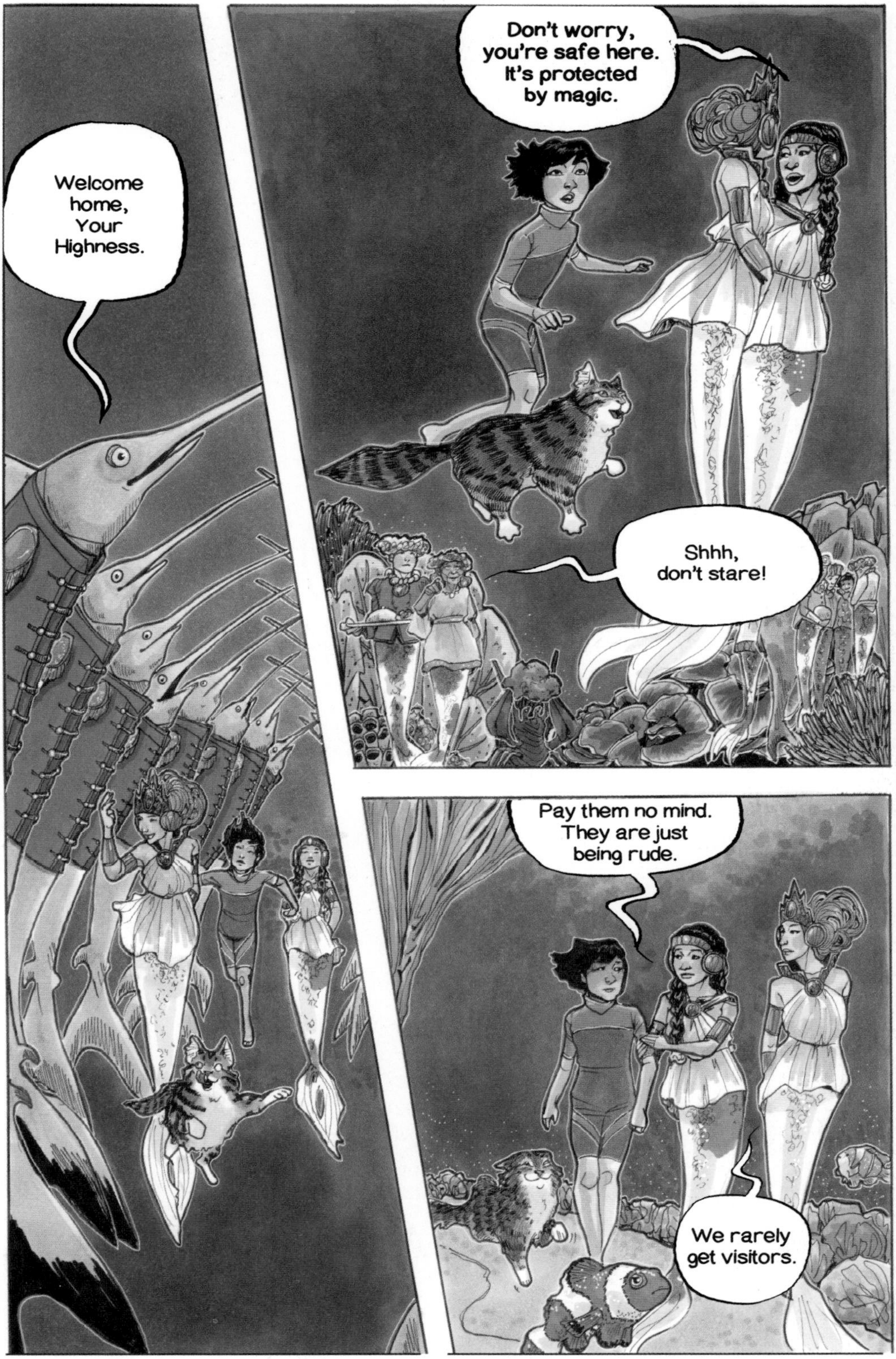
Welcome home, Your Highness.
Don't worry, you're safe here. It's protected by magic.
Shhh, don't stare!
Pay them no mind. They are just being rude.
We rarely get visitors.

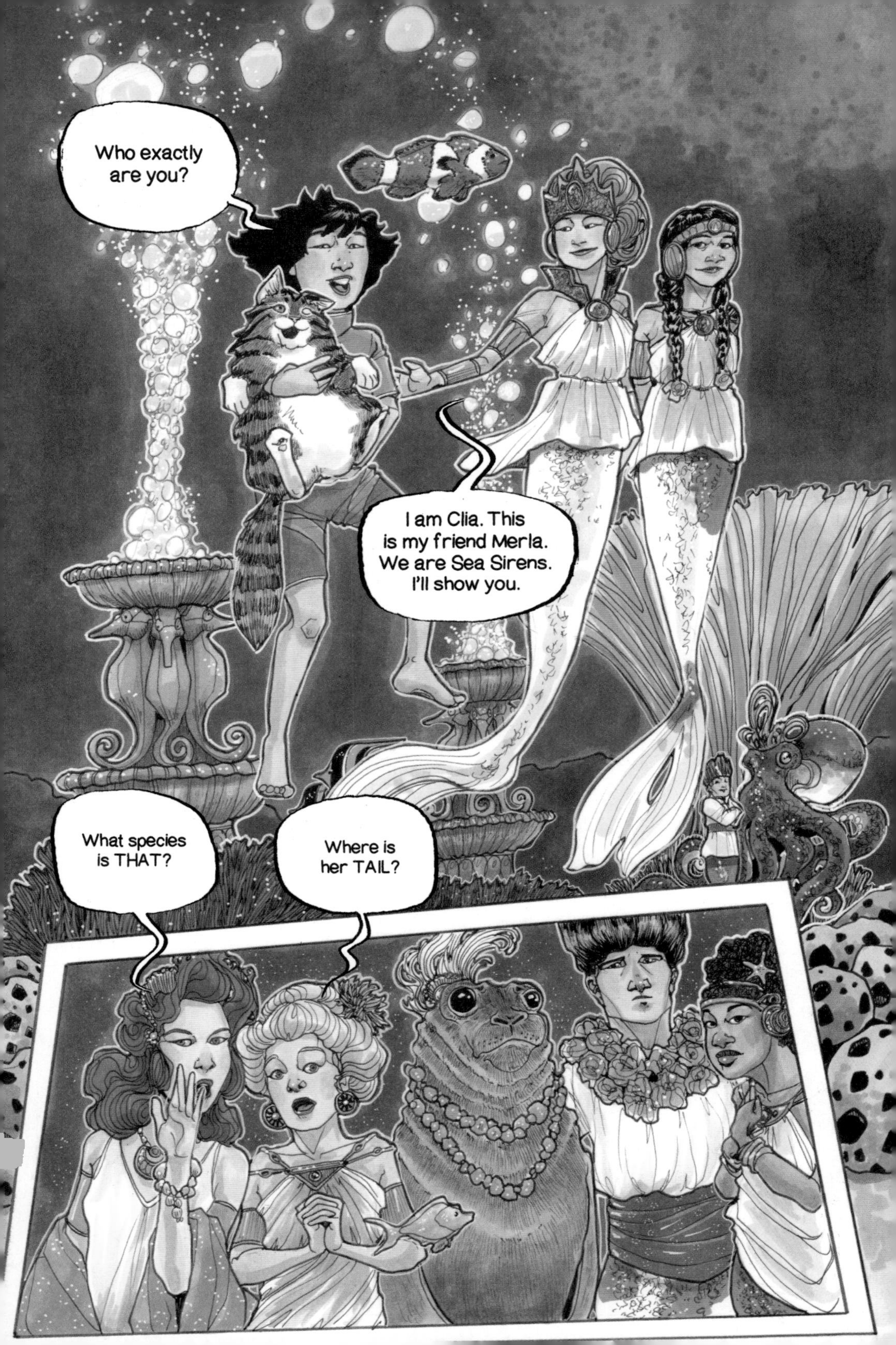
Who exactly are you?
I am Clia. This is my friend Merla. We are Sea Sirens. I'll show you.
What species is THAT?
Where is her TAIL?

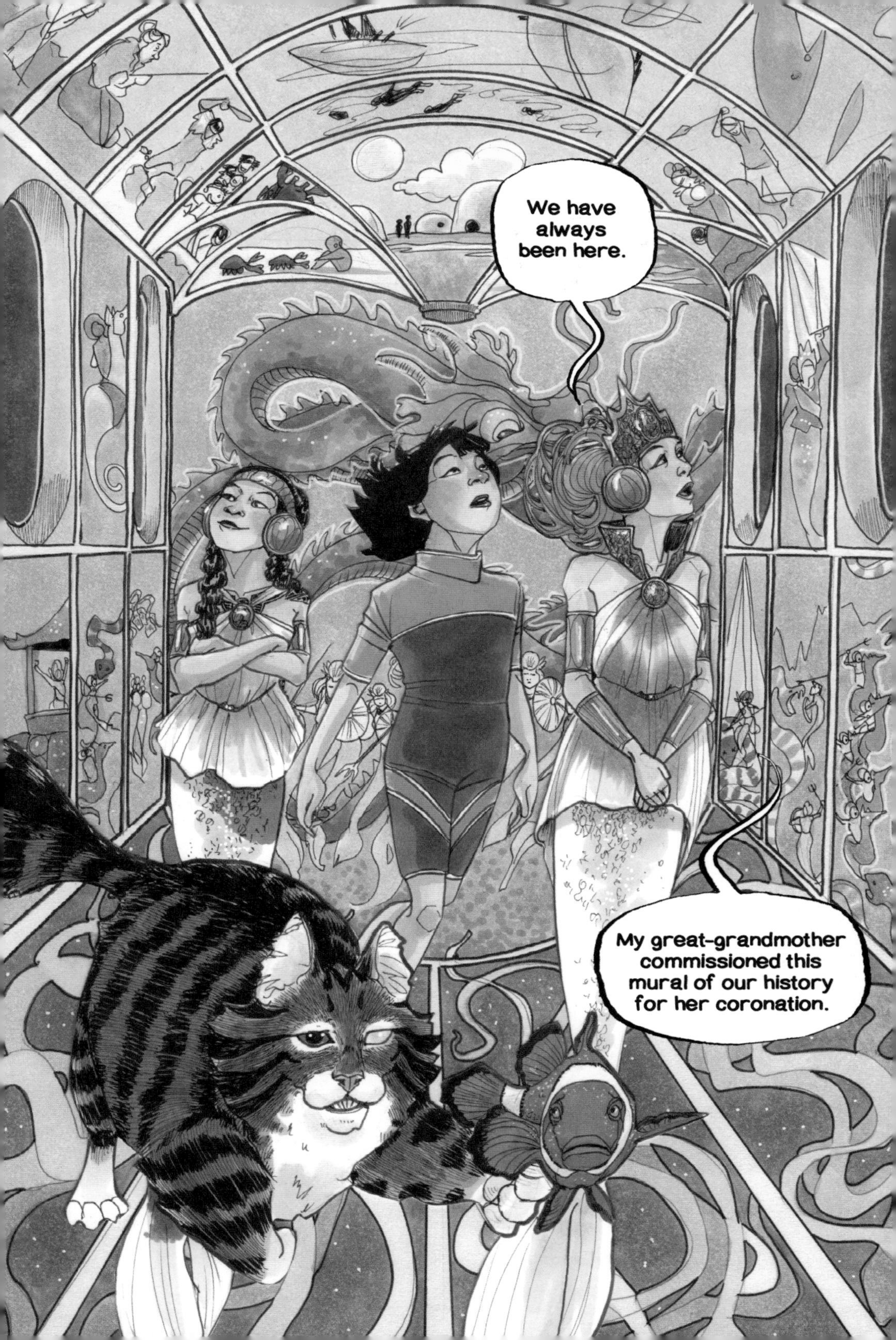
We have always been here.
My great-grandmother commissioned this mural of our history for her coronation.

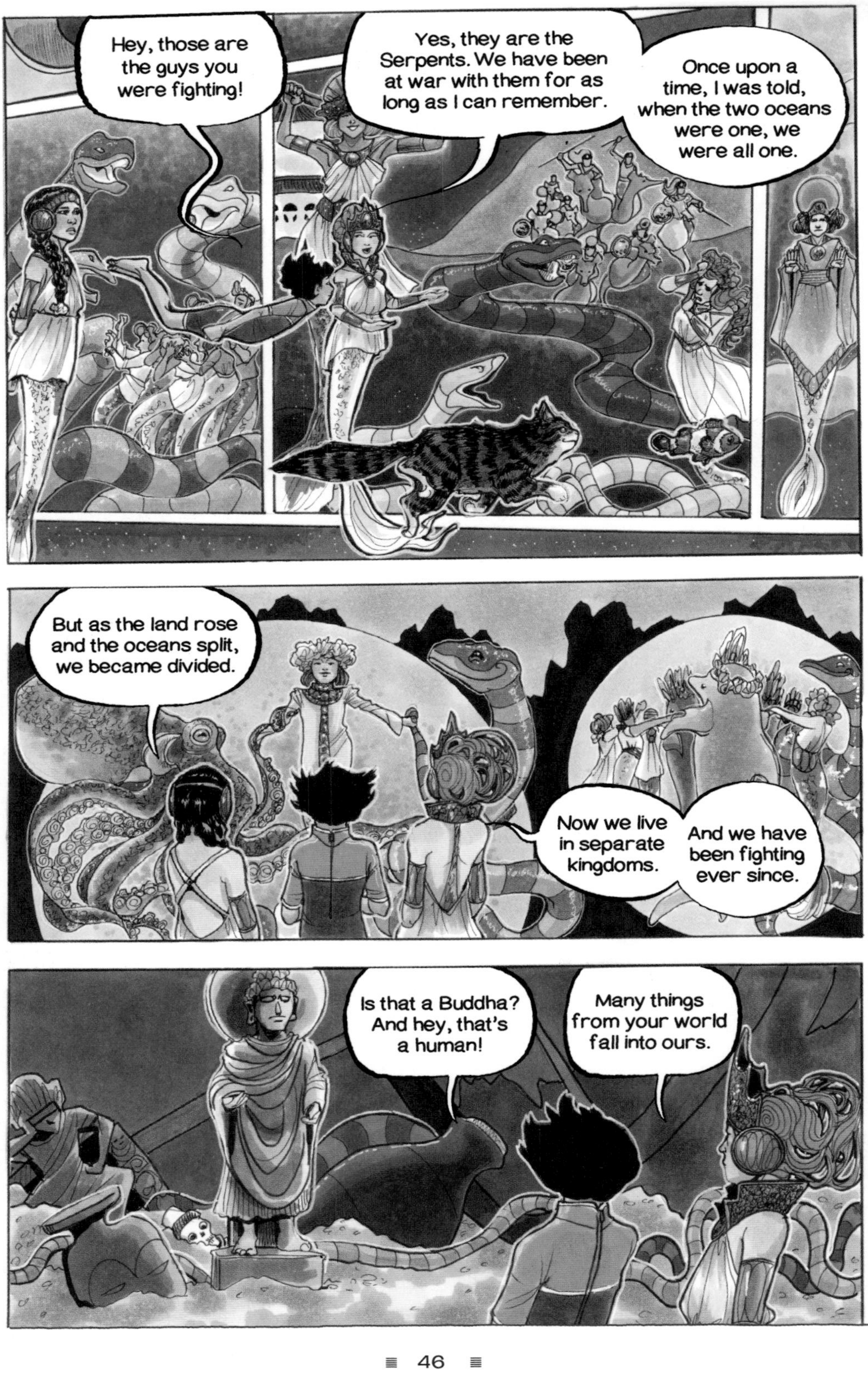
Hey, those are the guys you were fighting!
Yes, they are the Serpents. We have been at war with them for as long as I can remember.
Once upon a time, I was told, when the two oceans were one, we were all one.
But as the land rose and the oceans split, we became divided.
Now we live in separate kingdoms.
And we have been fighting ever since.
Is that a Buddha? And hey, that's a human!
Many things from your world fall into ours.

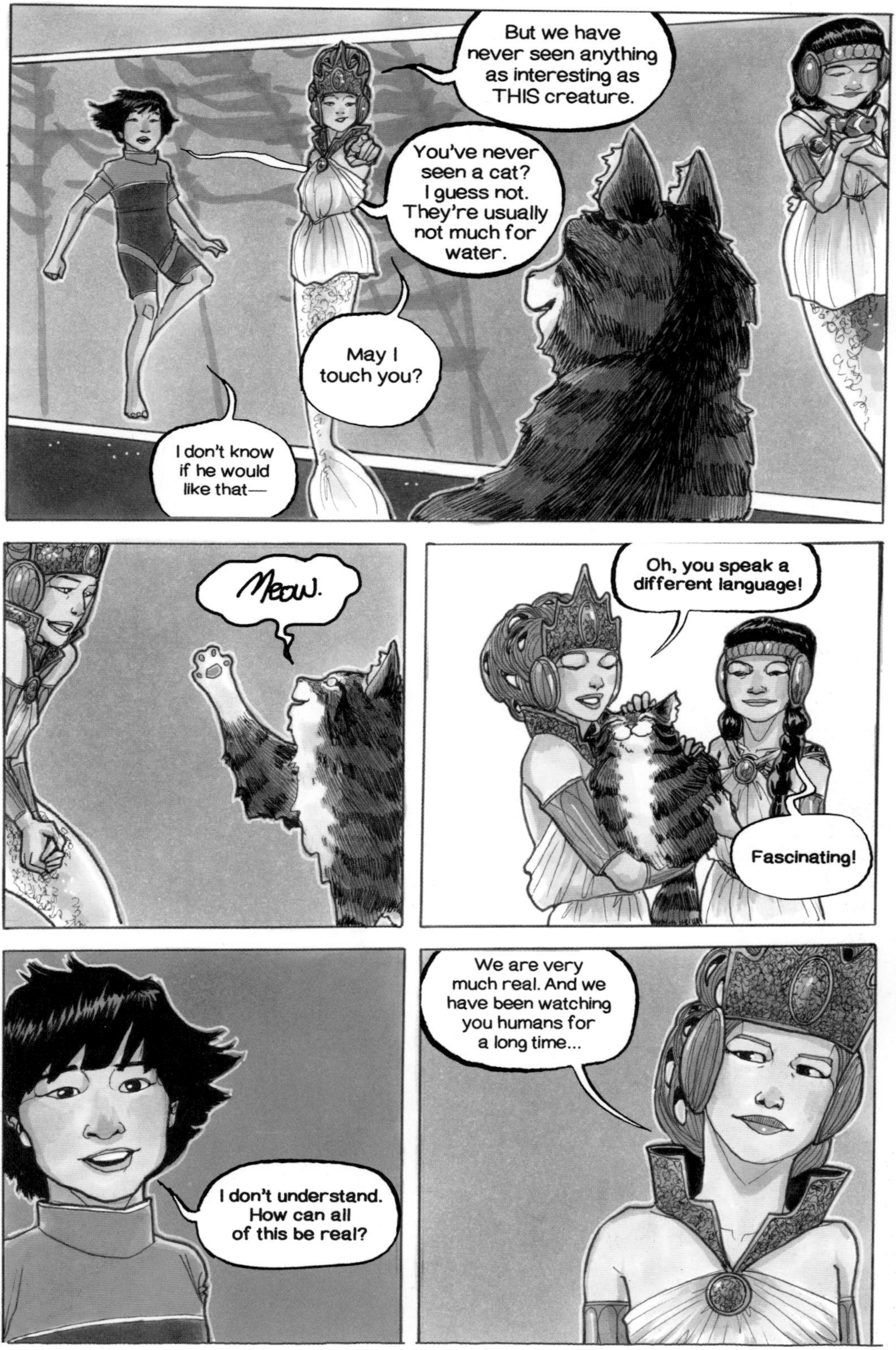
But we have never seen anything as interesting as THIS creature.
You've never seen a cat? I guess not. They're usually not much for water.
May I touch you?
I don't know if he would like that—
Meow.
Oh, you speak a different language!
Fascinating!
I don't understand. How can all of this be real?
We are very much real. And we have been watching you humans for a long time...

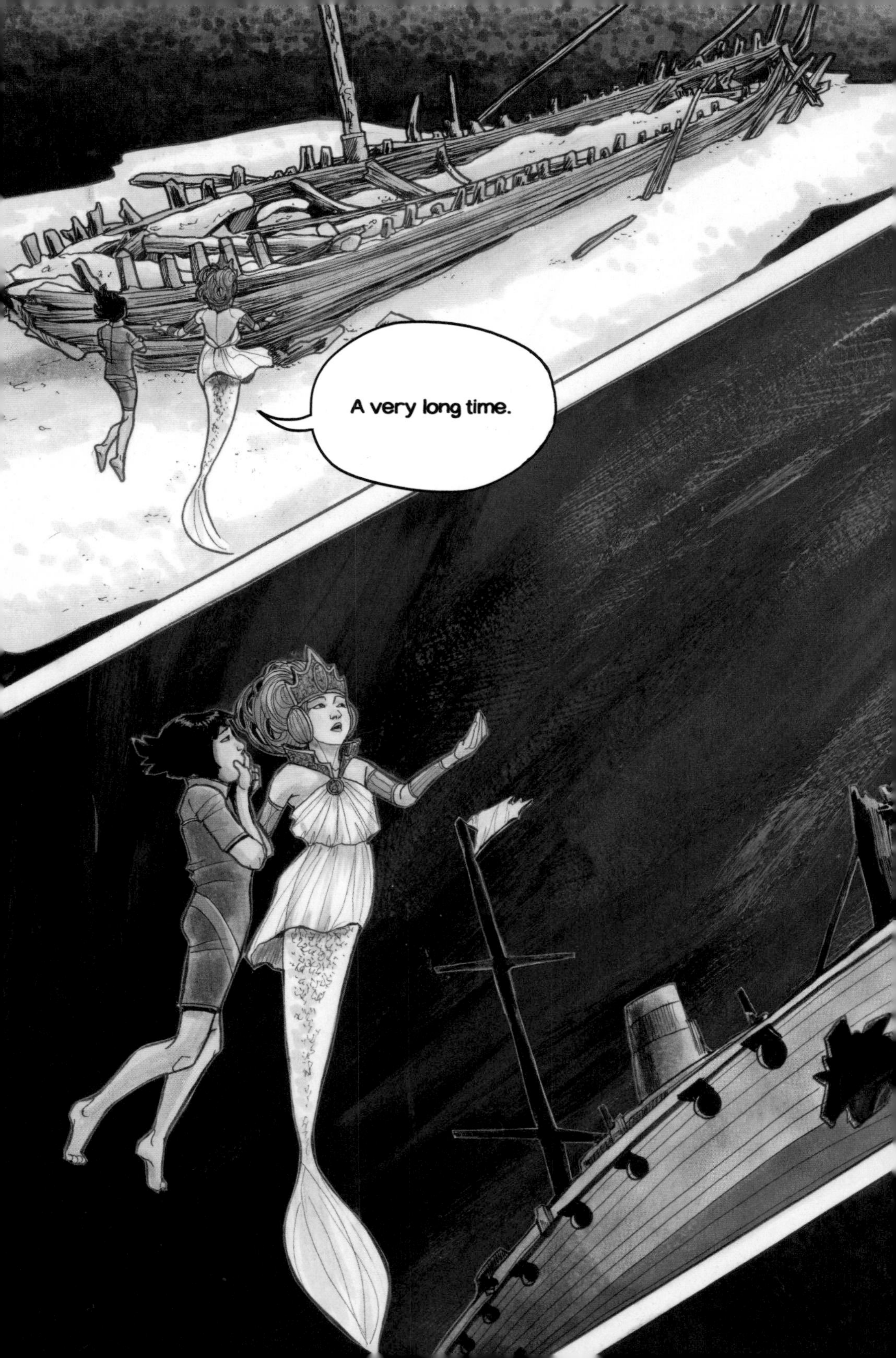
A very long time.

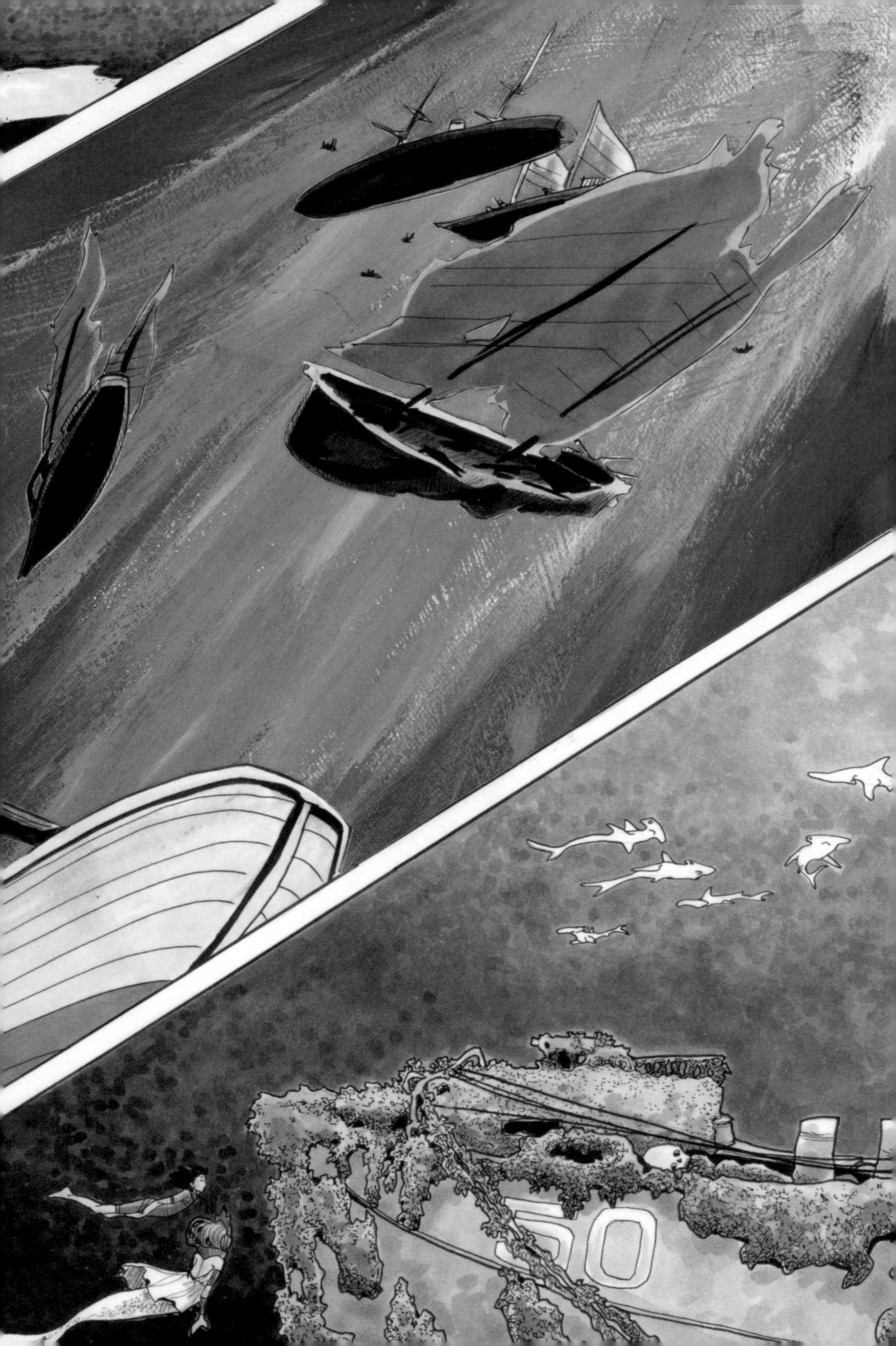
50

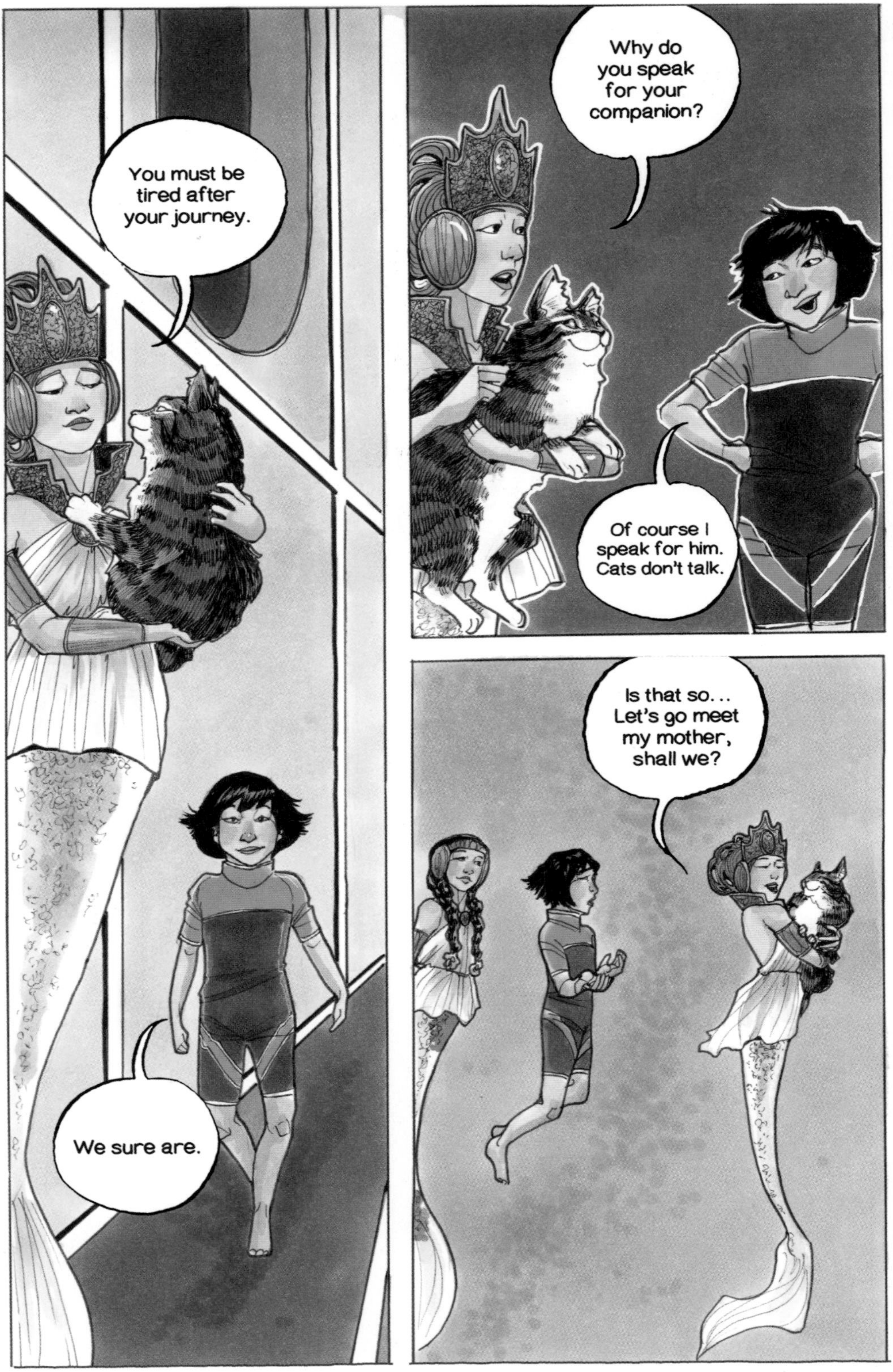
You must be tired after your journey.
We sure are.
Why do you speak for your companion?
Of course I speak for him. Cats don't talk.
Is that so... Let's go meet my mother, shall we?

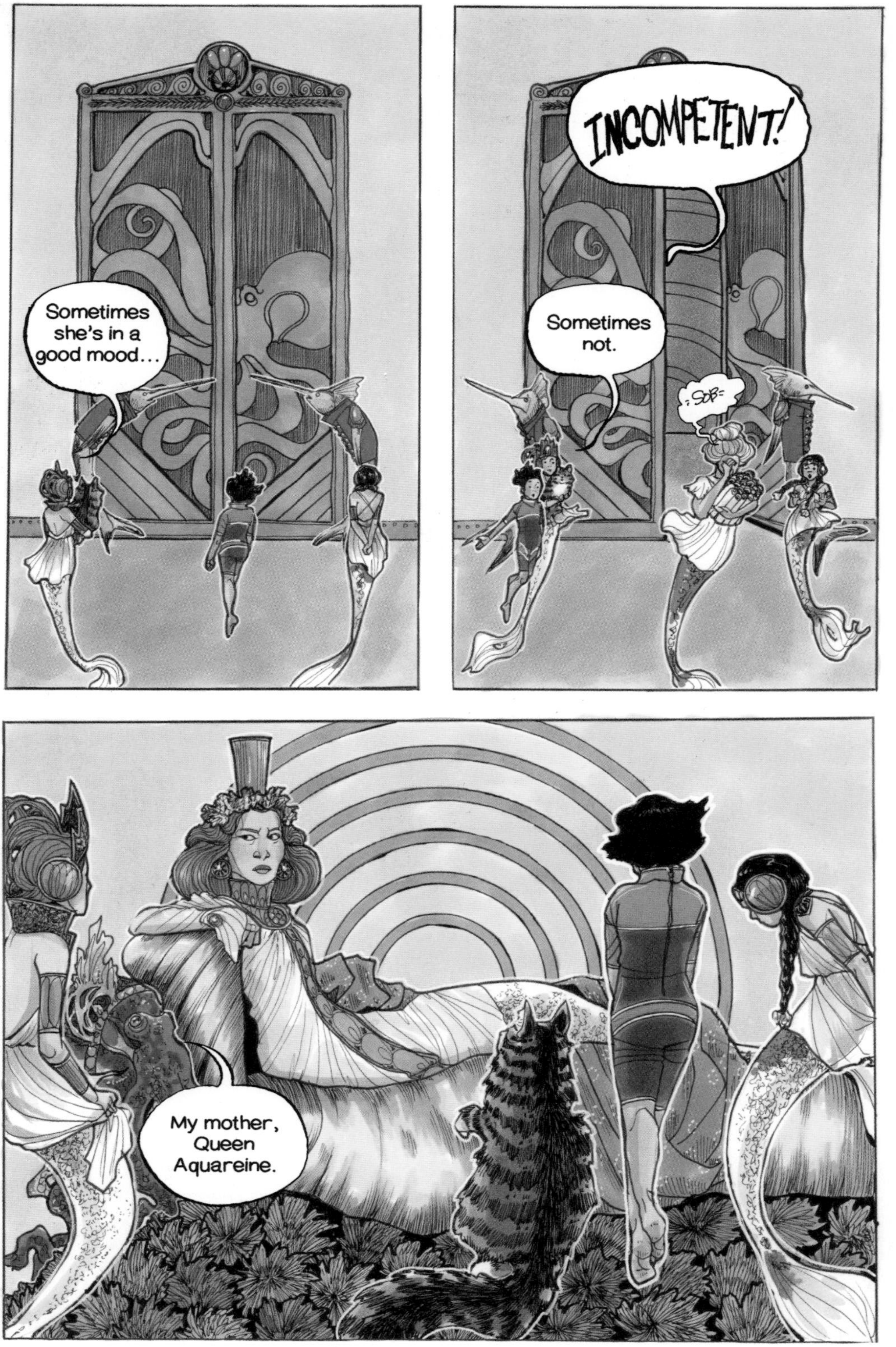
Sometimes she's in a good mood...
INCOMPETENT!
Sometimes not.
SOB
My mother, Queen Aquareine.

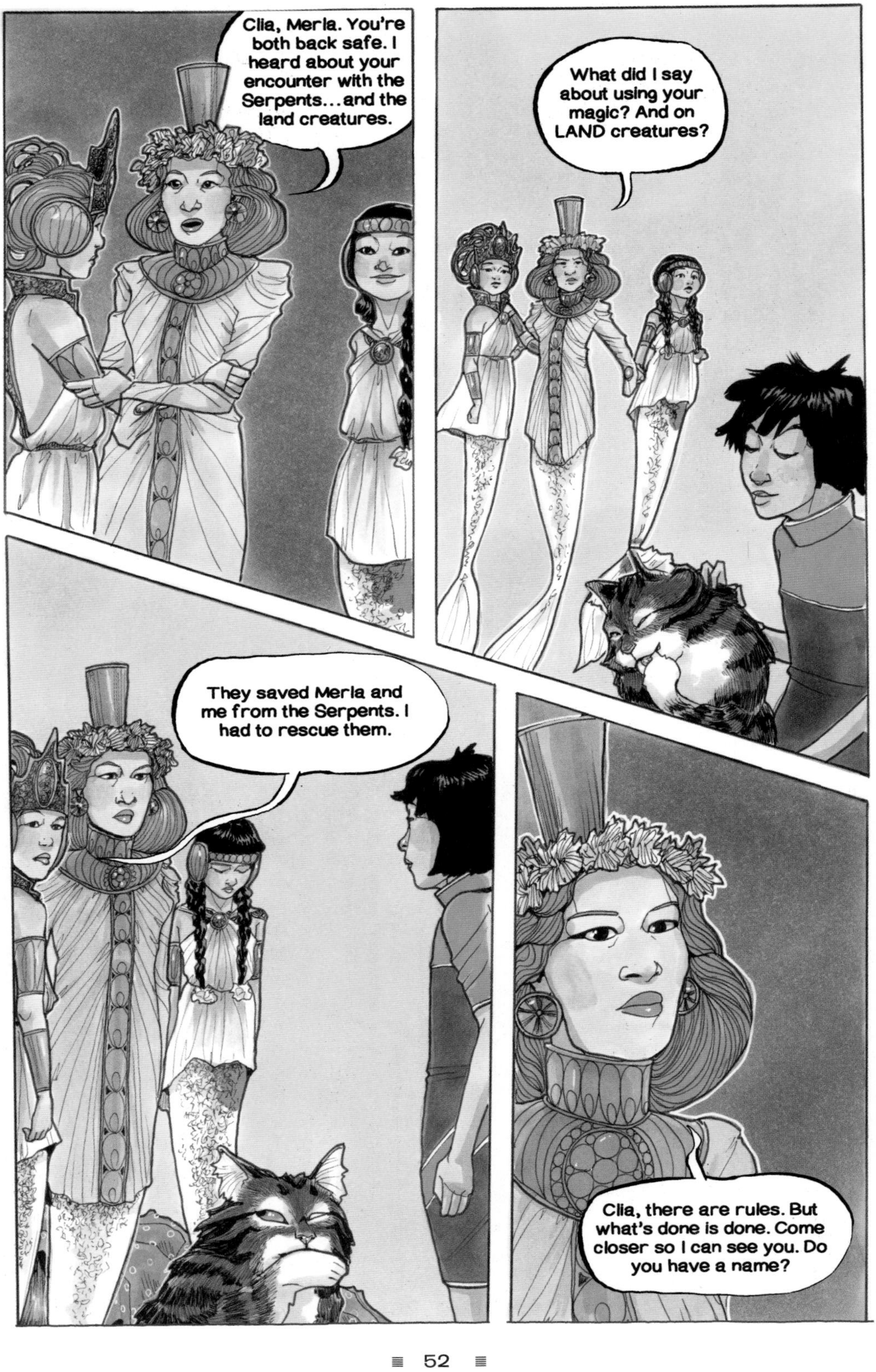
Clia, Merla. You're both back safe. I heard about your encounter with the Serpents...and the land creatures.
What did I say about using your magic? And on LAND creatures?
They saved Merla and me from the Serpents. I had to rescue them.
Clia, there are rules. But what's done is done. Come closer so I can see you. Do you have a name?

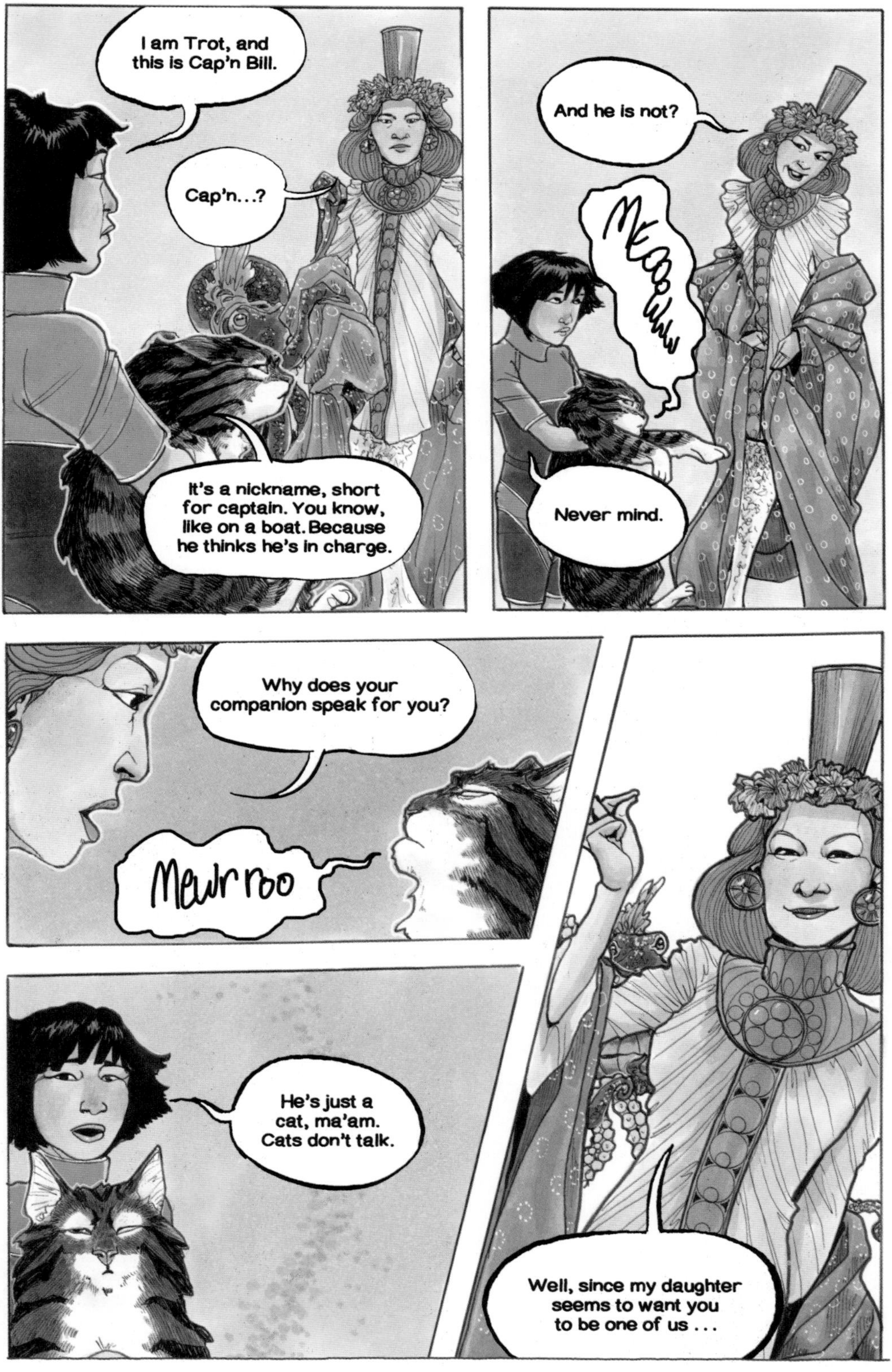
I am Trot, and this is Cap'n Bill.
Cap'n...?
It's a nickname, short for captain. You know, like on a boat. Because he thinks he's in charge.
And he is not?
Never mind.
Why does your companion speak for you?
Mewrroo
He's just a cat, ma'am. Cats don't talk.
Well, since my daughter seems to want you to be one of us . . .

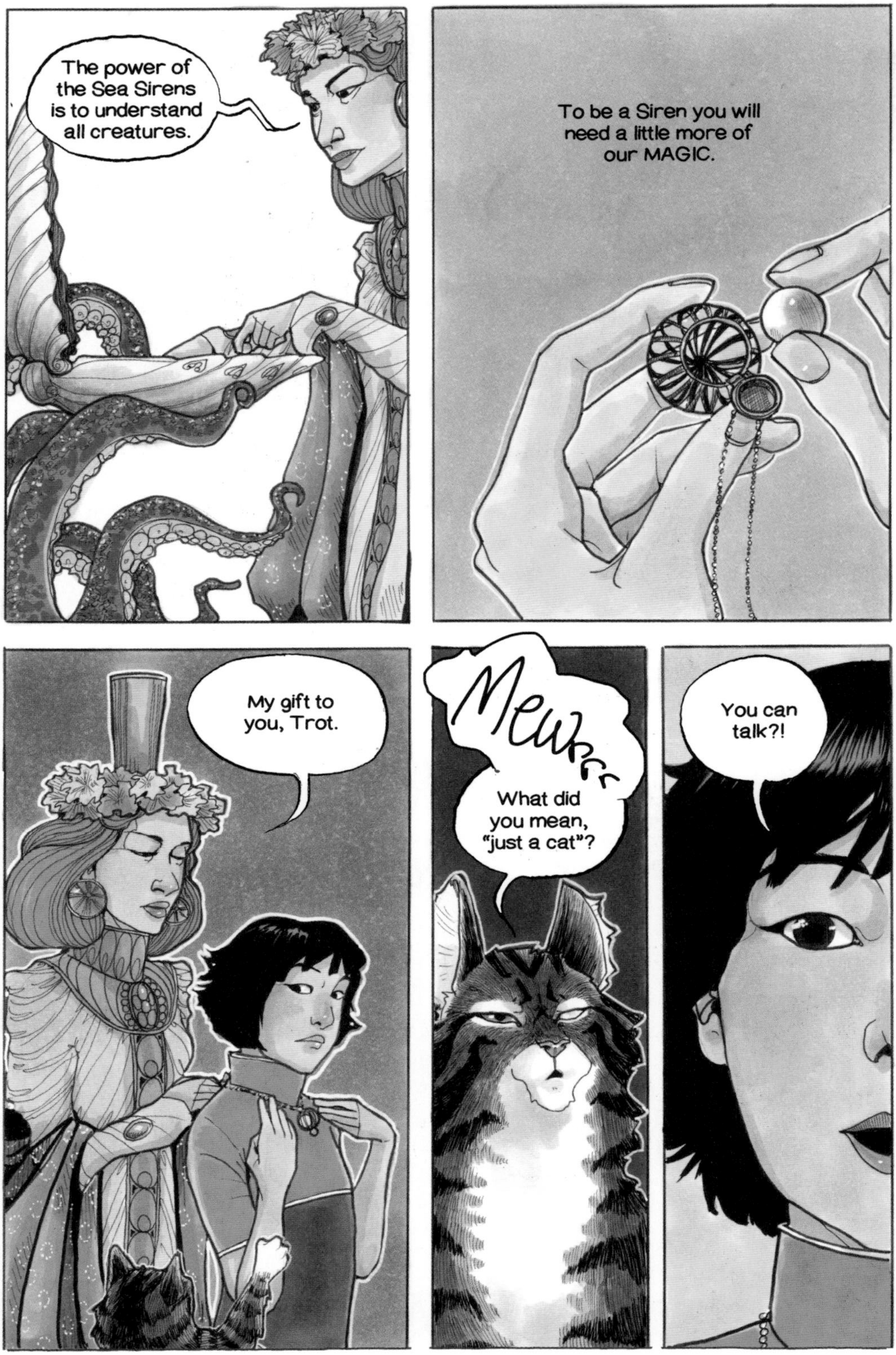
The power of the Sea Sirens is to understand all creatures.
To be a Siren you will need a little more of our MAGIC.
My gift to you, Trot.
Mewrrr
What did you mean, "just a cat"?
You can talk?!

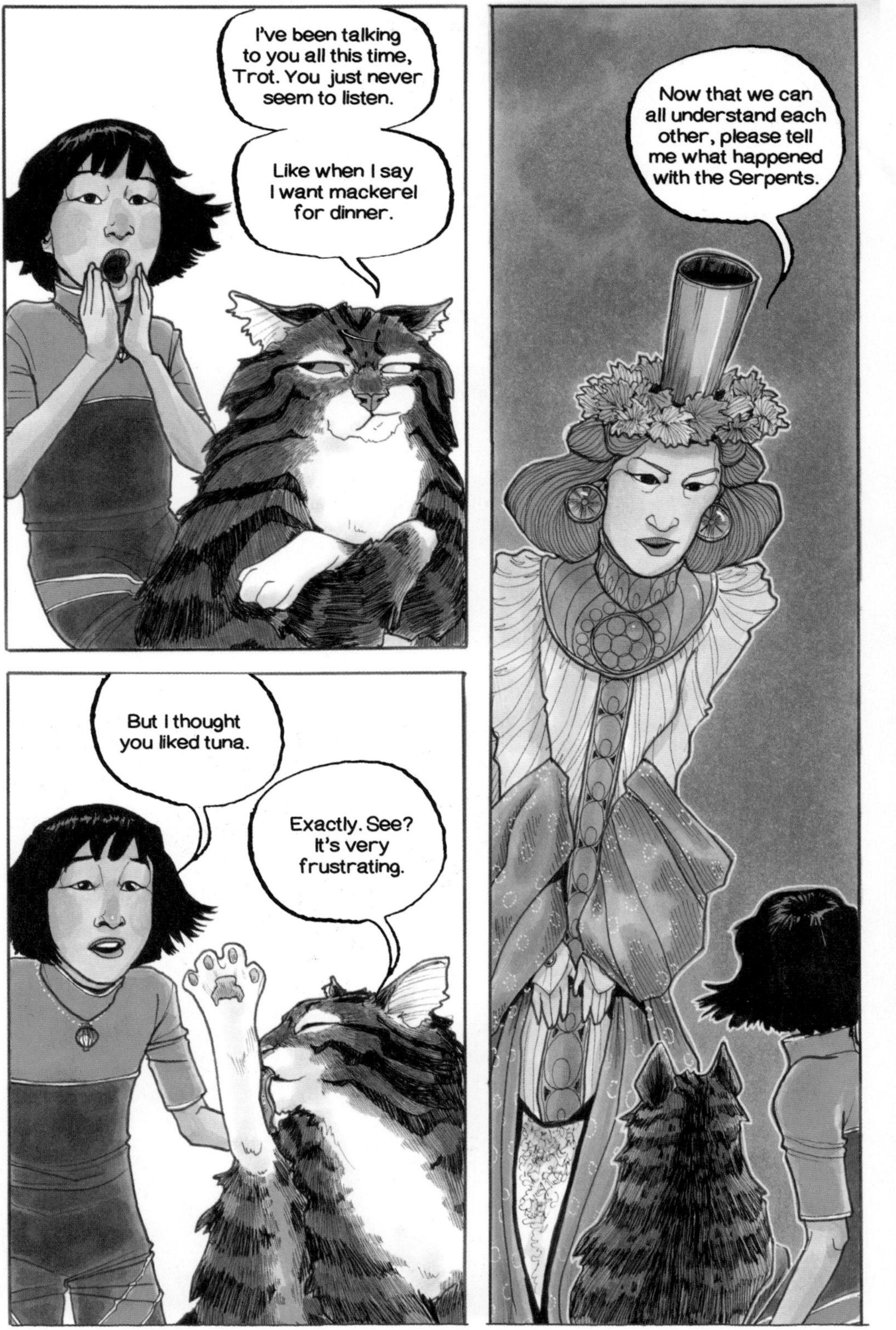
I've been talking to you all this time, Trot. You just never seem to listen.
Like when I say I want mackerel for dinner.
But I thought you liked tuna.
Exactly. See? It's very frustrating.
Now that we can all understand each other, please tell me what happened with the Serpents.

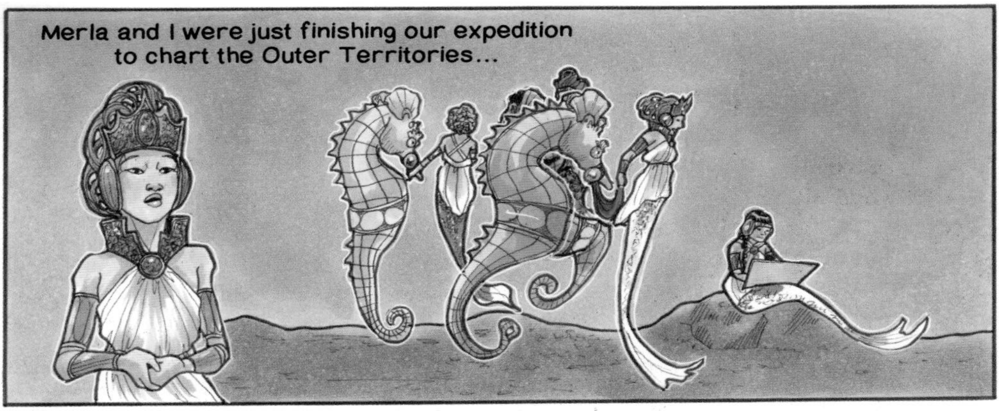
Merla and I were just finishing our expedition to chart the Outer Territories...
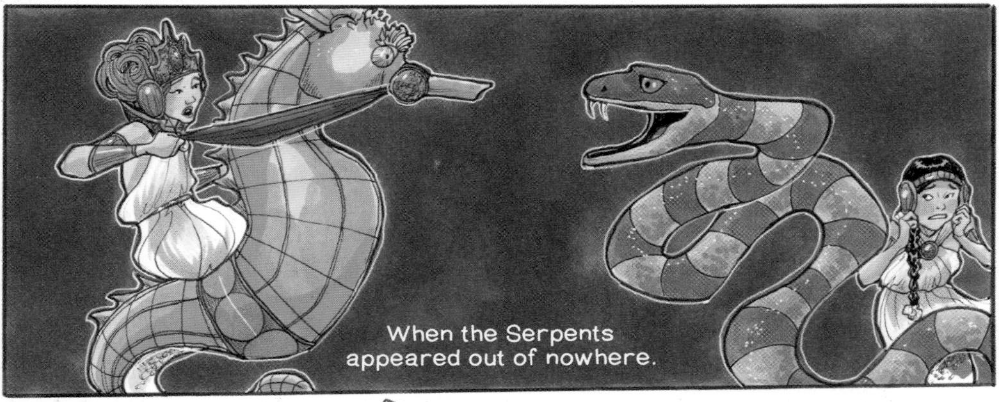
When the Serpents appeared out of nowhere.
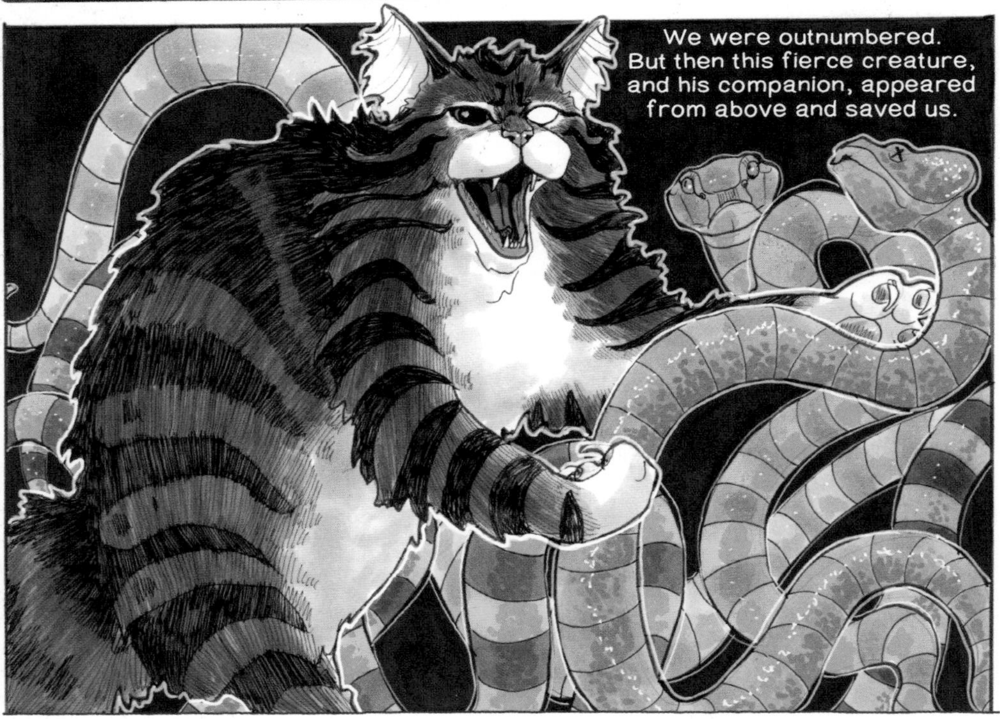
We were outnumbered. But then this fierce creature, and his companion, appeared from above and saved us.

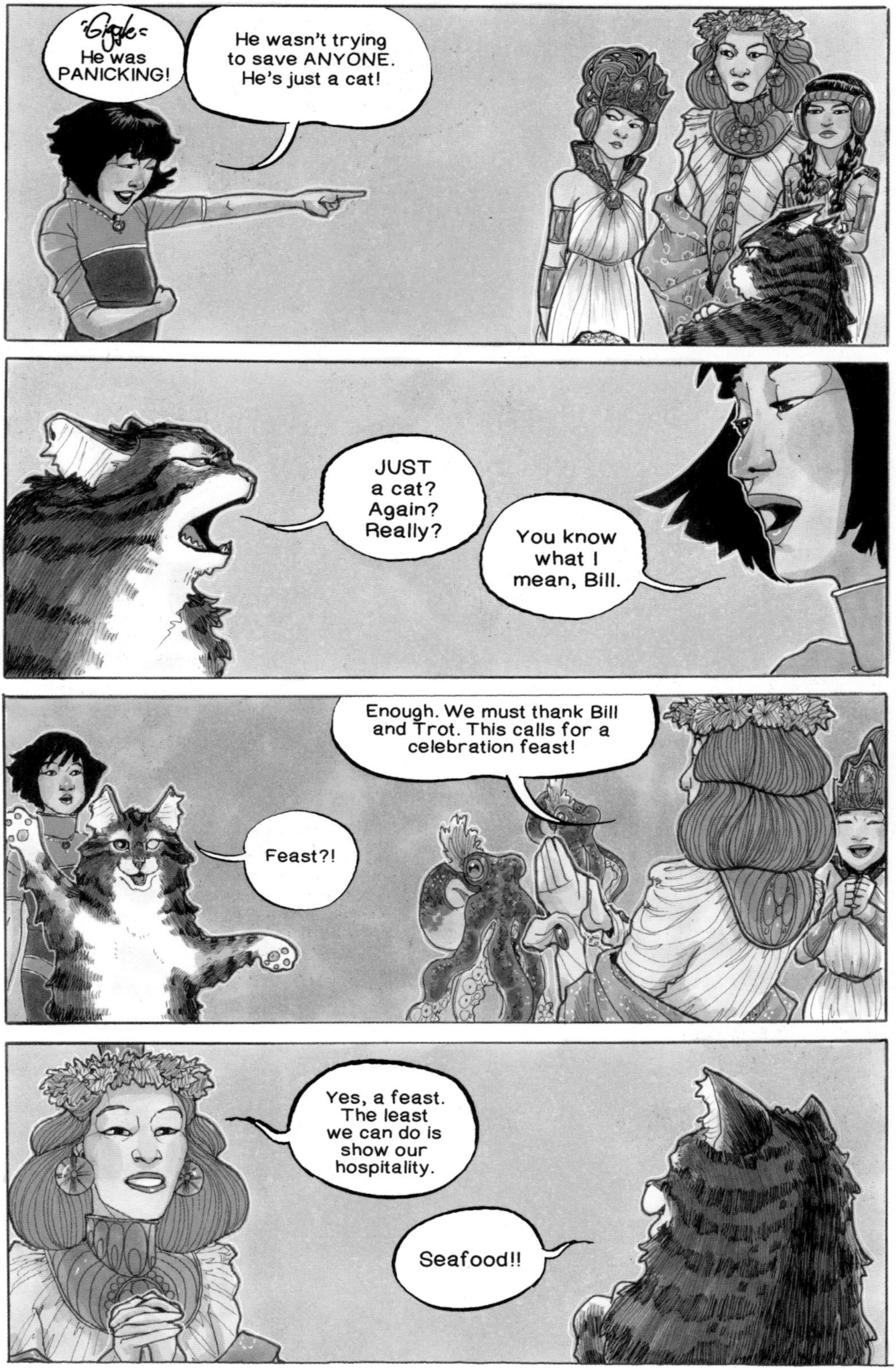
Giggle
He was PANICKING!
He wasn't trying to save ANYONE. He's just a cat!
JUST a cat? Again? Really?
You know what I mean, Bill.
Enough. We must thank Bill and Trot. This calls for a celebration feast!
Feast?!
Yes, a feast. The least we can do is show our hospitality.
Seafood!!

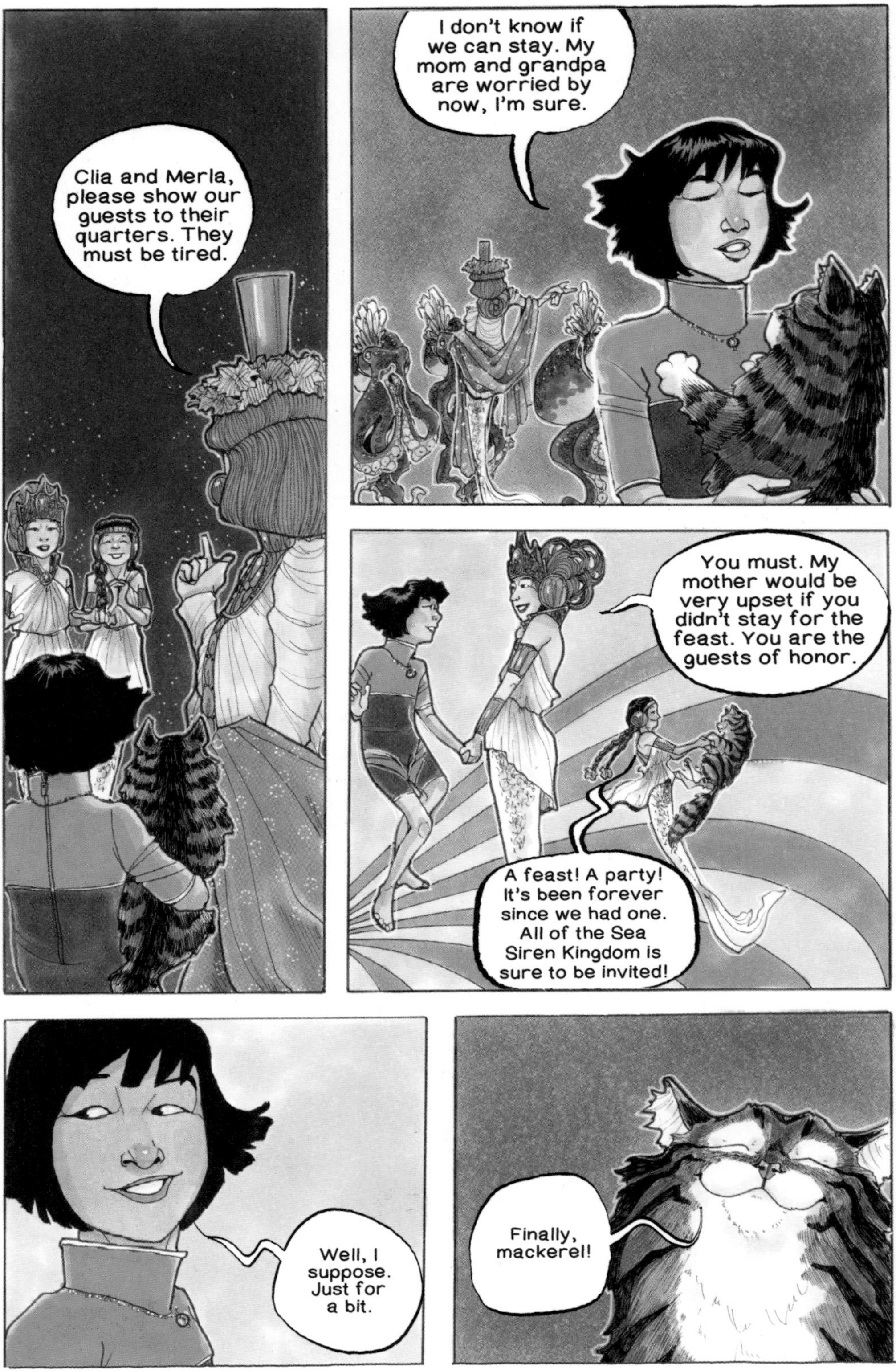
Clia and Merla, please show our guests to their quarters. They must be tired.
I don't know if we can stay. My mom and grandpa are worried by now, I'm sure.
You must. My mother would be very upset if you didn't stay for the feast. You are the guests of honor.
A feast! A party! It's been forever since we had one. All of the Sea Siren Kingdom is sure to be invited!
Well, I suppose. Just for a bit.
Finally, mackerel!

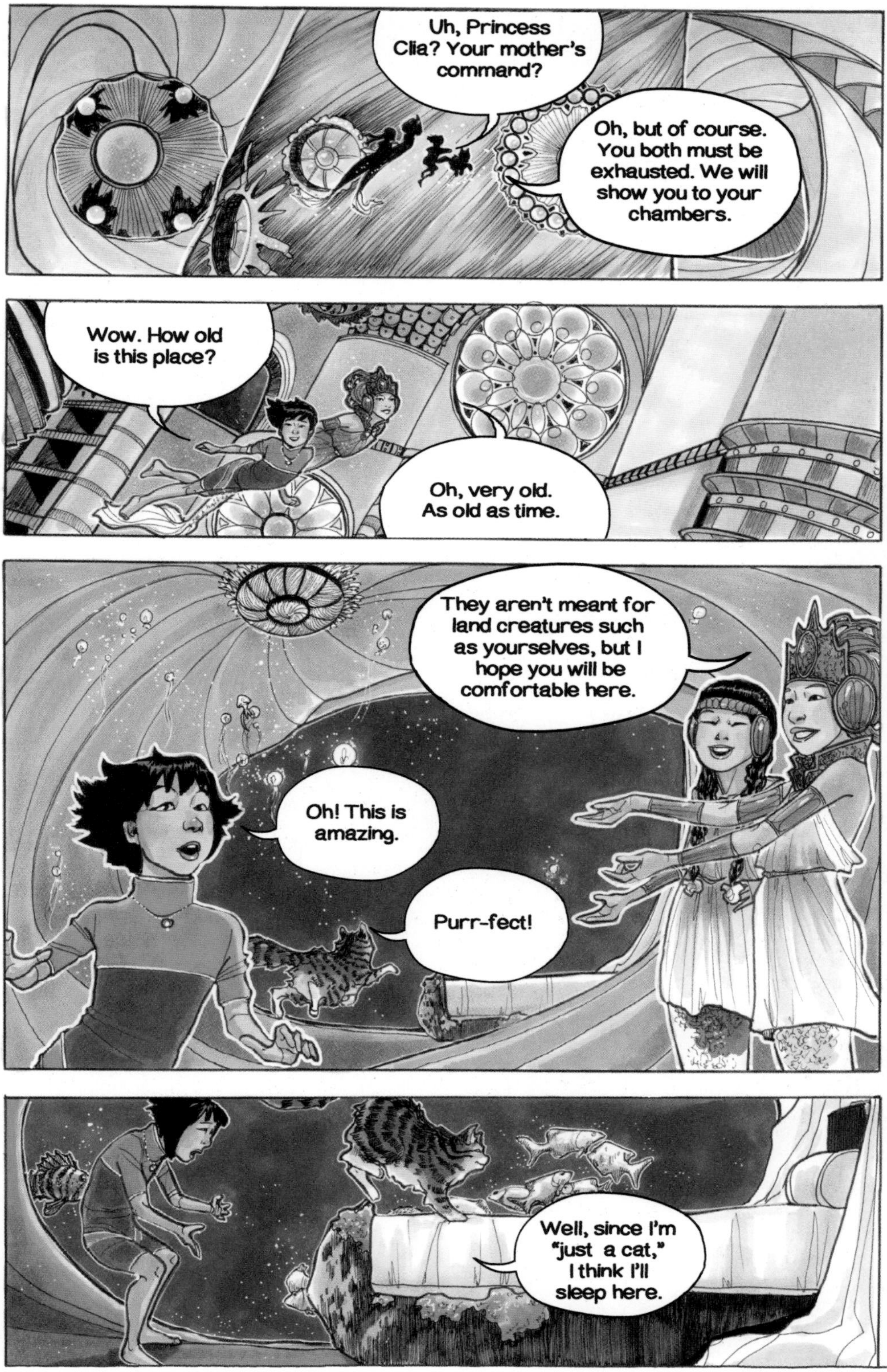
Uh, Princess Clia? Your mother's command?
Oh, but of course. You both must be exhausted. We will show you to your chambers.
Wow. How old is this place?
Oh, very old. As old as time.
They aren't meant for land creatures such as yourselves, but I hope you will be comfortable here.
Oh! This is amazing.
Purr-fect!
Well, since I'm "just a cat," I think I'll sleep here.

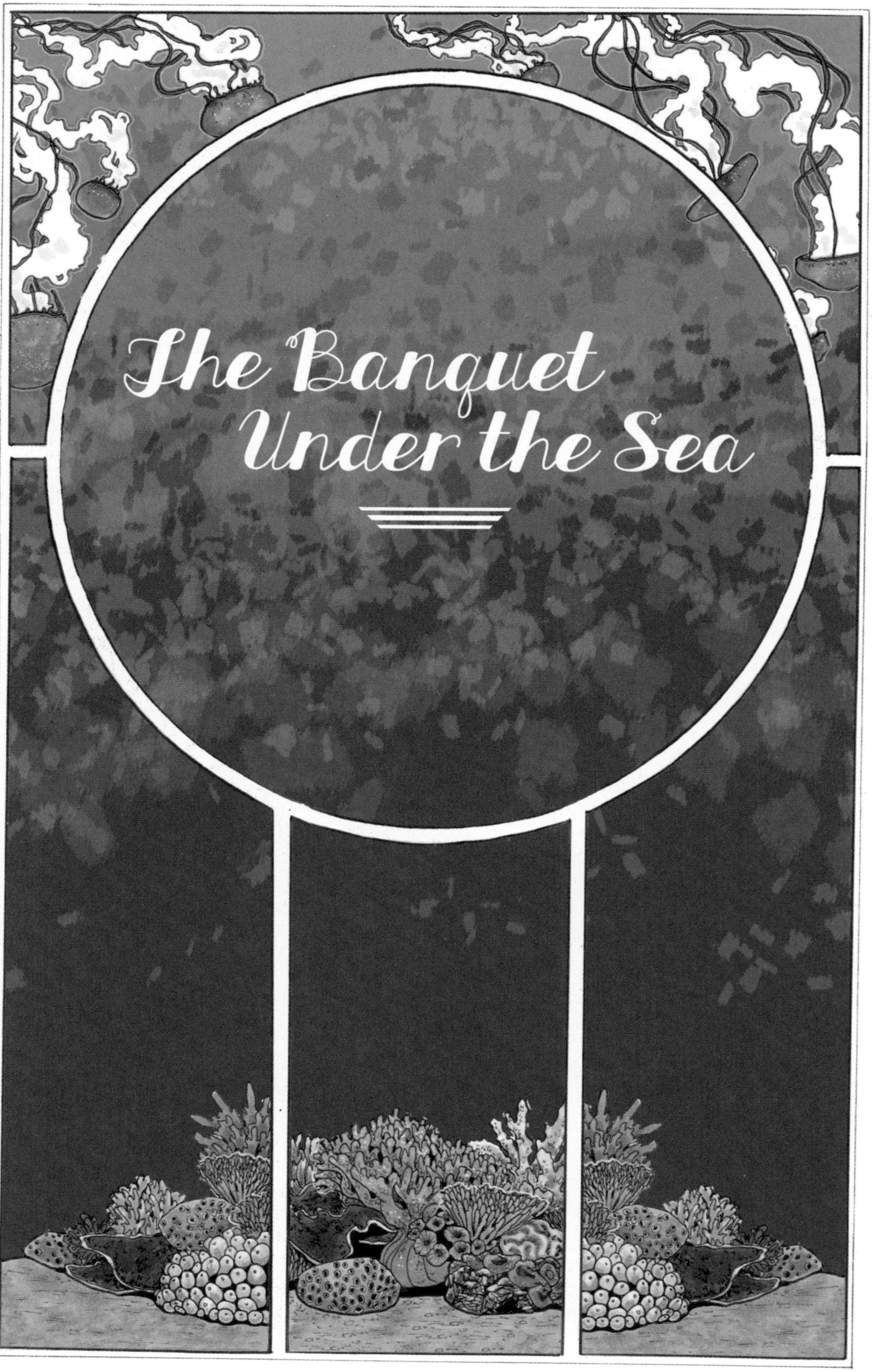
The Banquet
Under the Sea

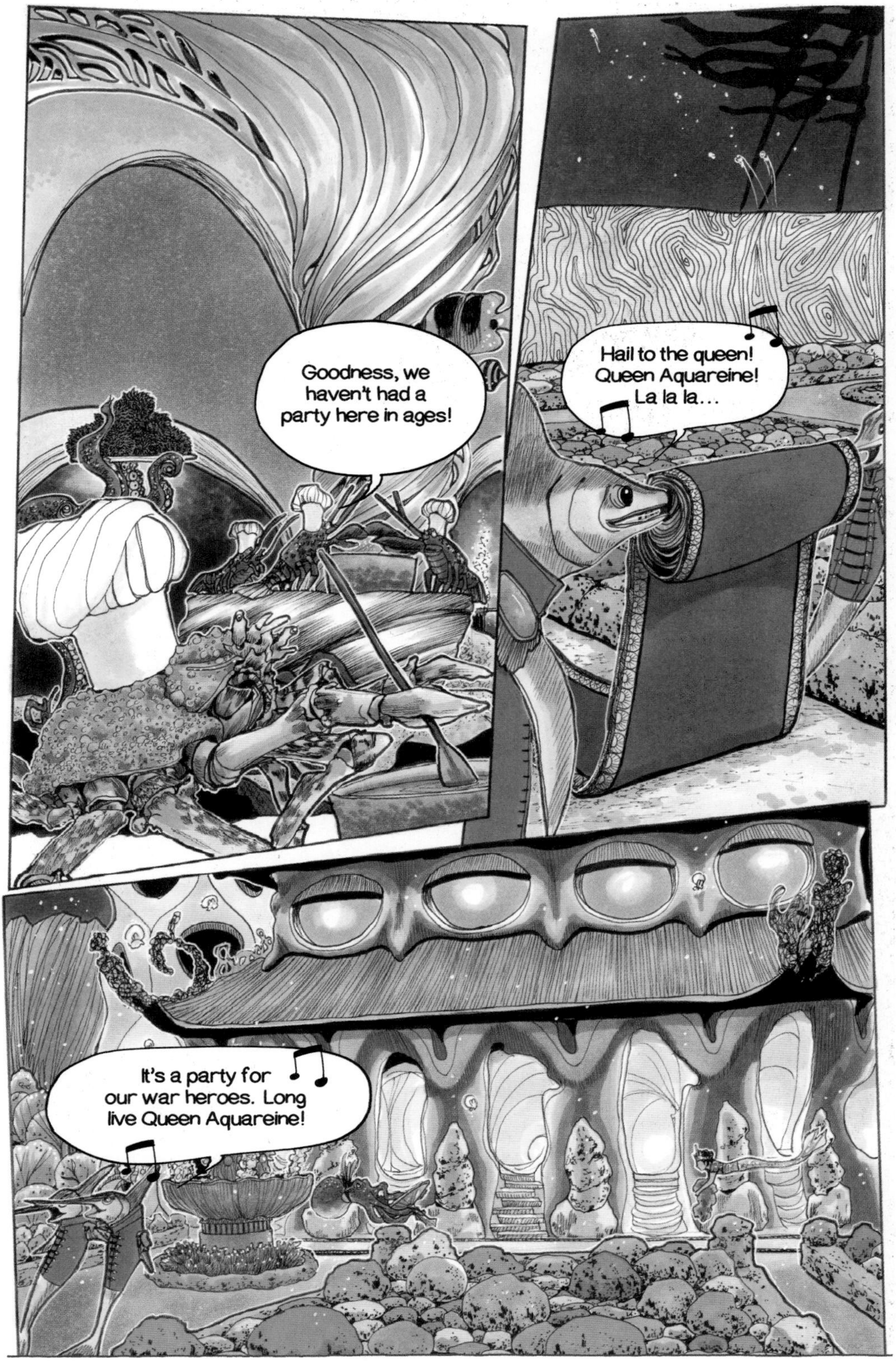
Goodness, we haven't had a party here in ages!
Hail to the queen! Queen Aquareine! La la la...
It's a party for our war heroes. Long live Queen Aquareine!

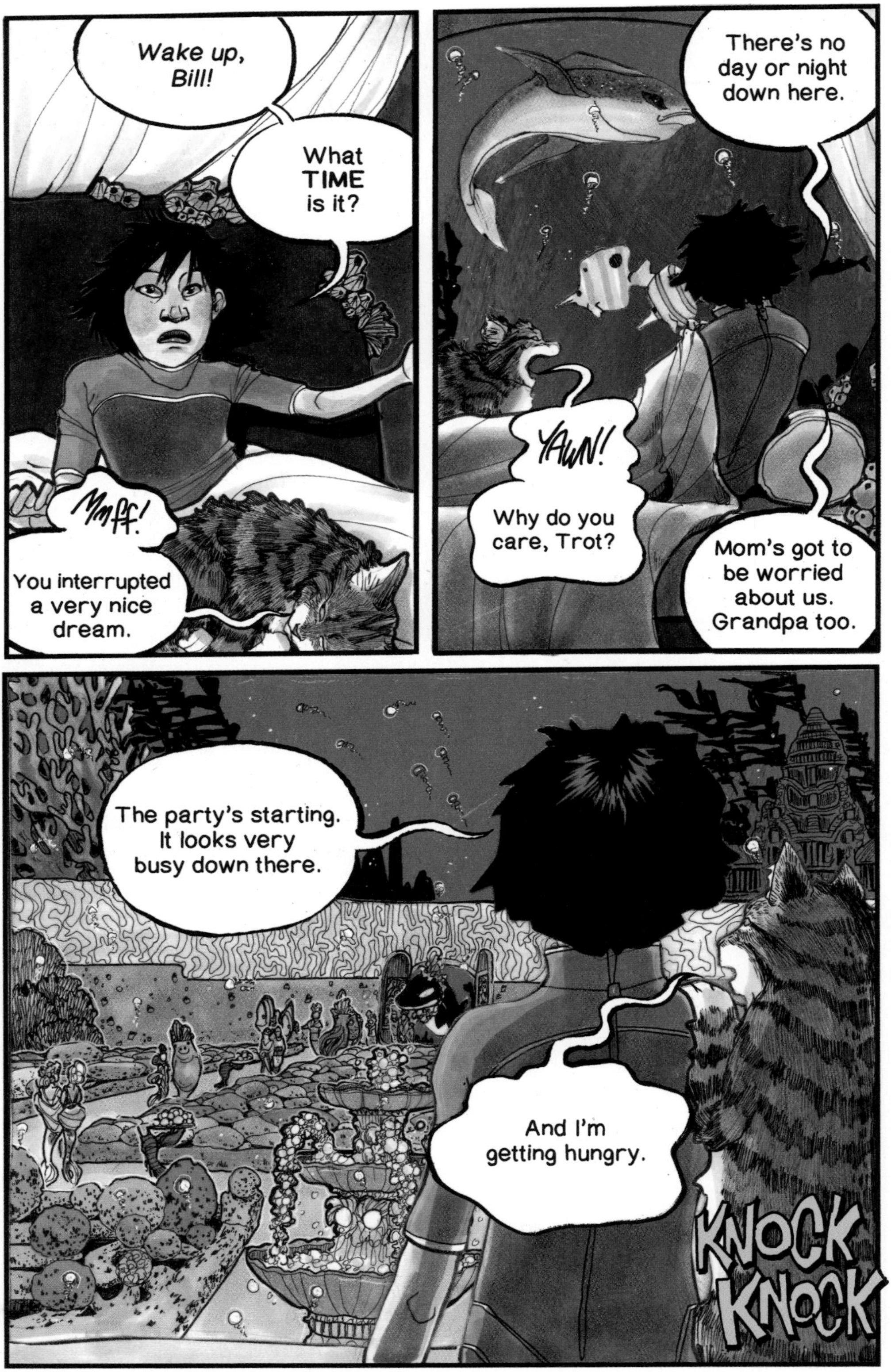
Wake up, Bill!
What TIME is it?
Mnff!
You interrupted a very nice dream.
There's no day or night down here.
YAWN!
Why do you care, Trot?
Mom's got to be worried about us. Grandpa too.
The party's starting. It looks very busy down there.
And I'm getting hungry.
KNOCK KNOCK

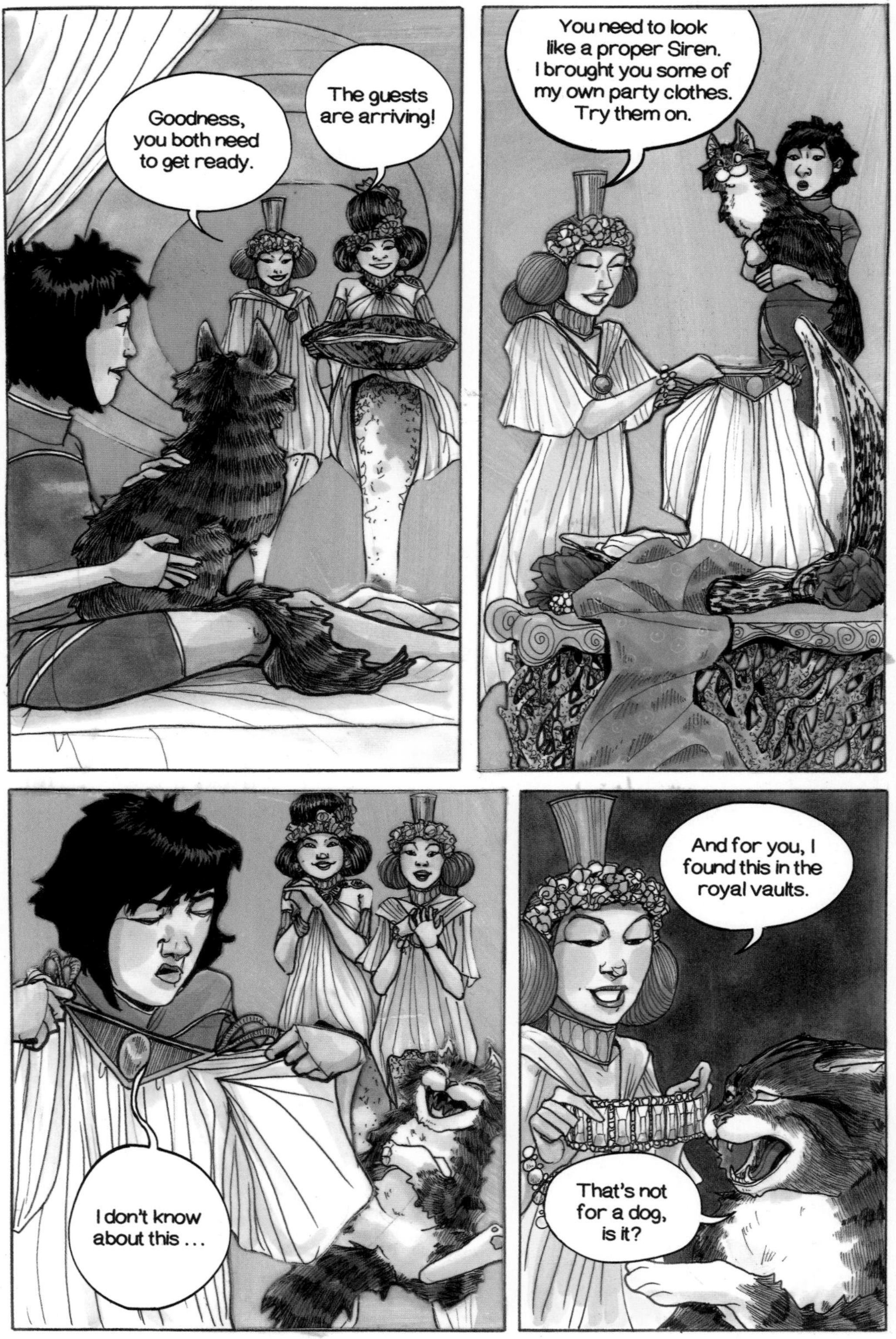
Goodness, you both need to get ready.
The guests are arriving!
You need to look like a proper Siren. I brought you some of my own party clothes. Try them on.
I don't know about this . . .
And for you, I found this in the royal vaults.
That's not for a dog, is it?

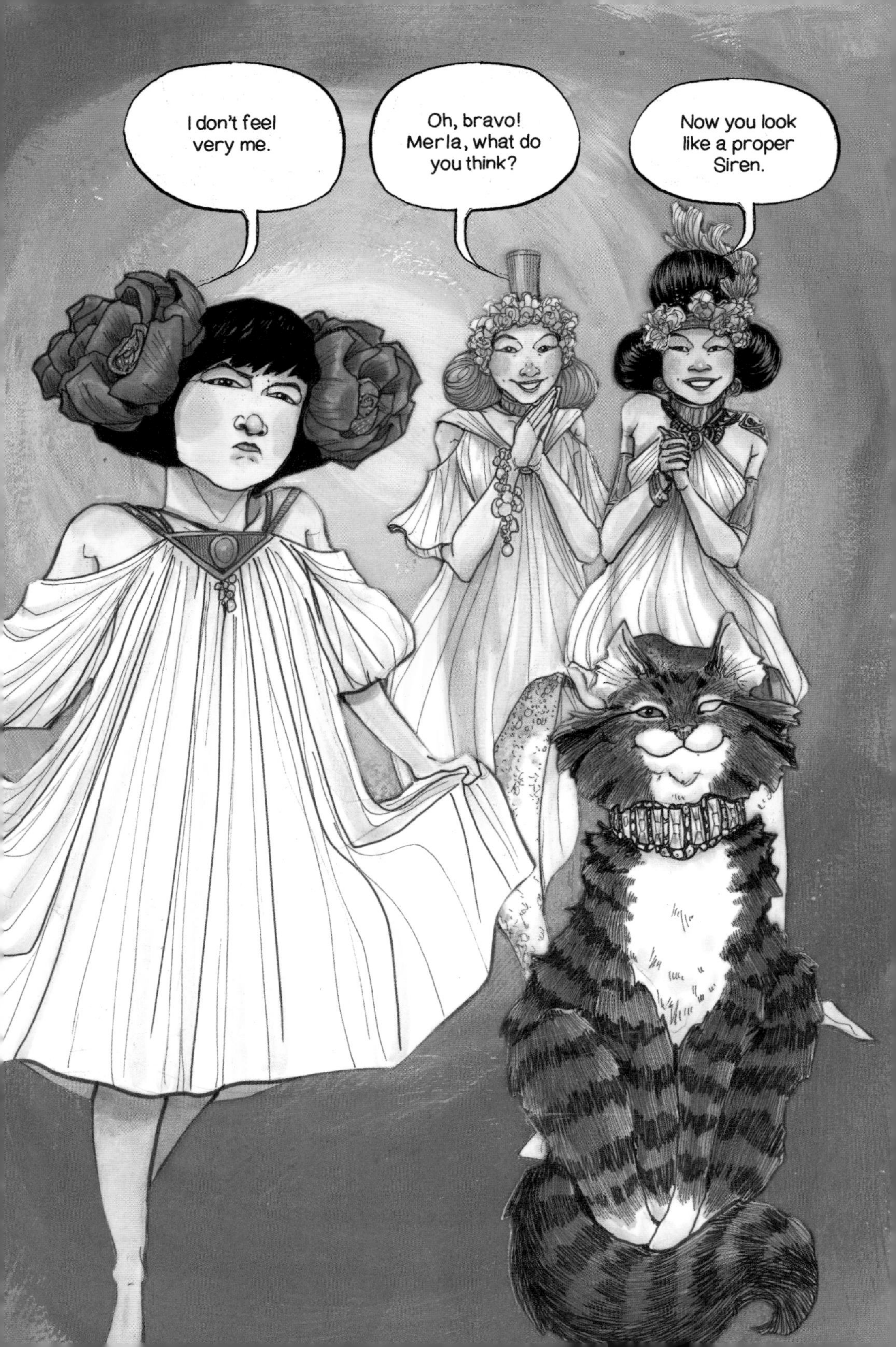
I don't feel very me.
Oh, bravo! Merla, what do you think?
Now you look like a proper Siren.

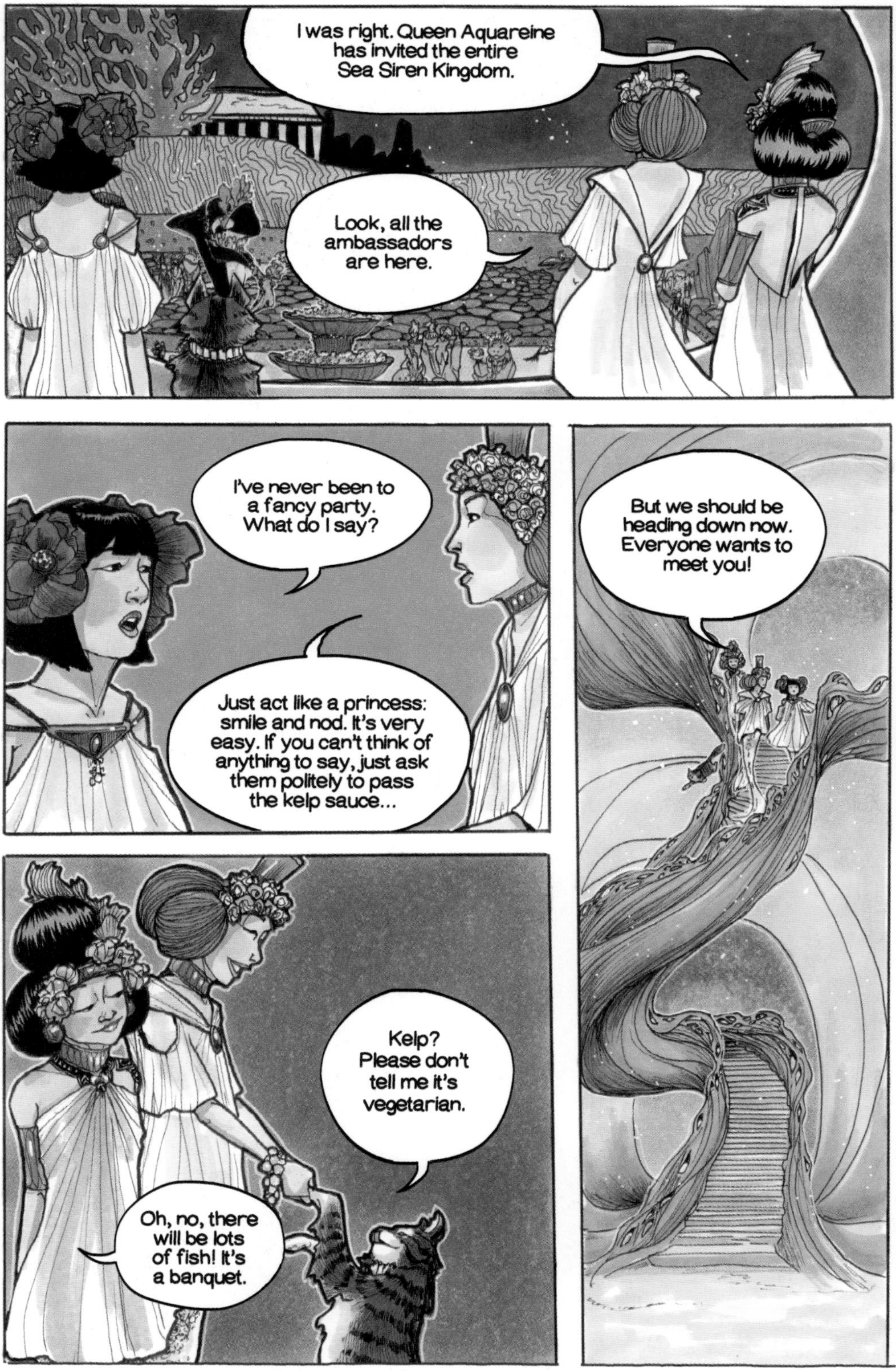
I was right. Queen Aquareine has invited the entire Sea Siren Kingdom.
Look, all the ambassadors are here.
I've never been to a fancy party. What do I say?
Just act like a princess: smile and nod. It's very easy. If you can't think of anything to say, just ask them politely to pass the kelp sauce...
Kelp? Please don't tell me it's vegetarian.
Oh, no, there will be lots of fish! It's a banquet.
But we should be heading down now. Everyone wants to meet you!

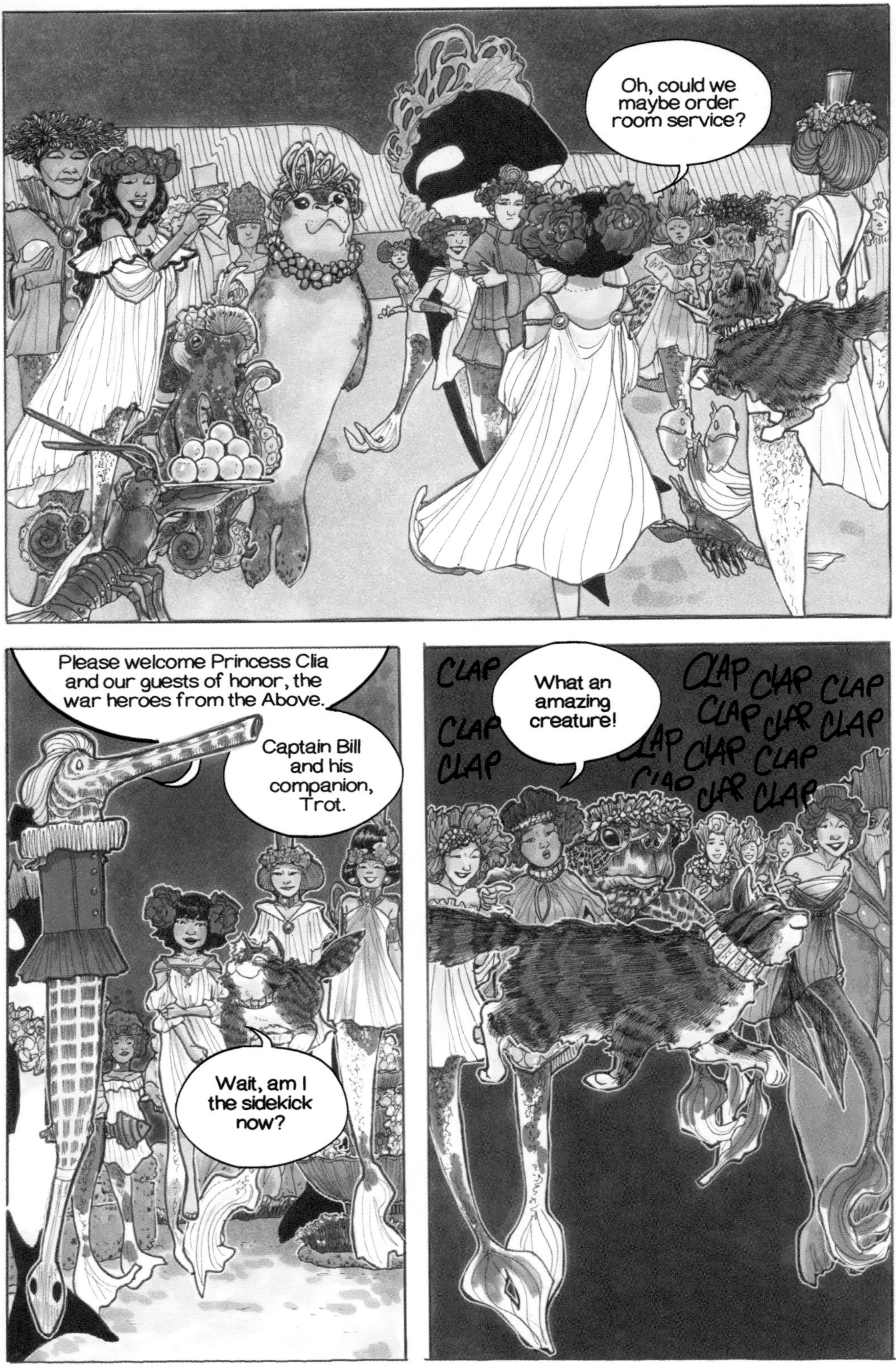
Oh, could we maybe order room service?
Please welcome Princess Clia and our guests of honor, the war heroes from the Above.
Captain Bill and his companion, Trot.
Wait, am I the sidekick now?
CLAP
What an amazing creature!
CLAP CLAP CLAP CLAP CLAP CLAP CLAP CLAP CLAP CLAP CLAP CLAP CLAP CLAP CLAP

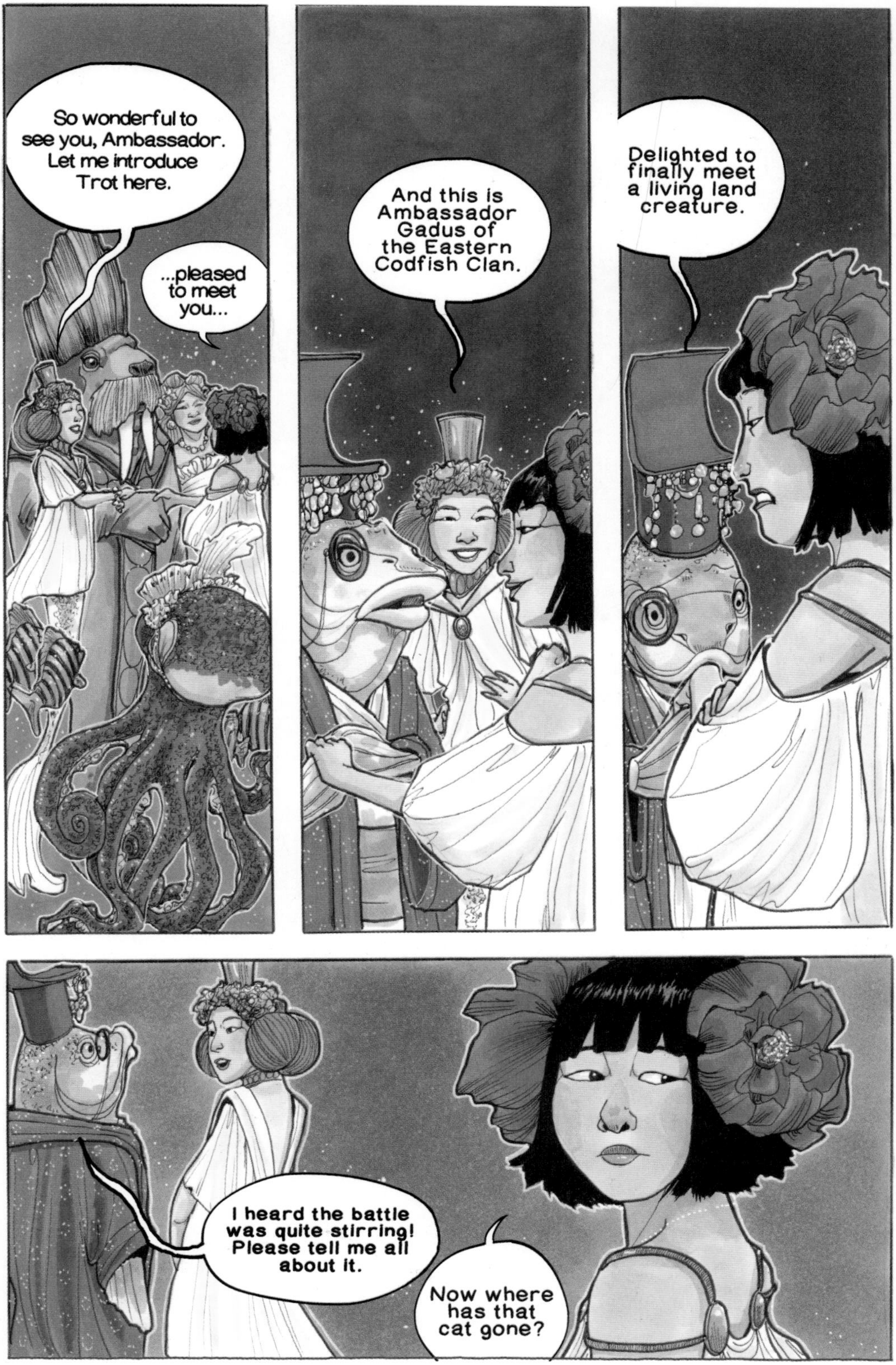
So wonderful to see you, Ambassador. Let me introduce Trot here.
...pleased to meet you...
And this is Ambassador Gadus of the Eastern Codfish Clan.
Delighted to finally meet a living land creature.
I heard the battle was quite stirring! Please tell me all about it.
Now where has that cat gone?

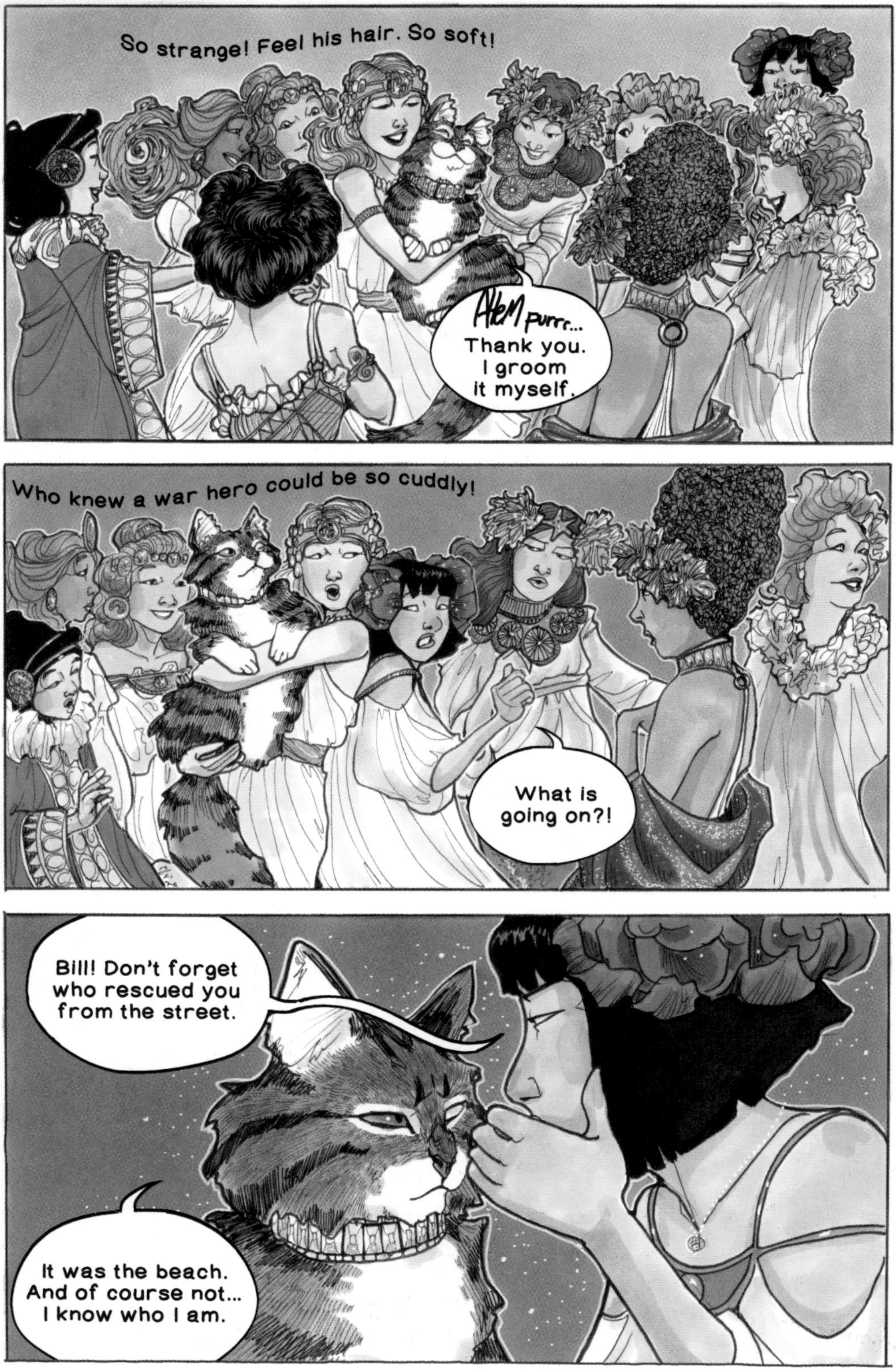
So strange! Feel his hair. So soft!
AHEM purrr... Thank you. I groom it myself.
Who knew a war hero could be so cuddly!
What is going on?!
Bill! Don't forget who rescued you from the street.
It was the beach. And of course not... I know who I am.

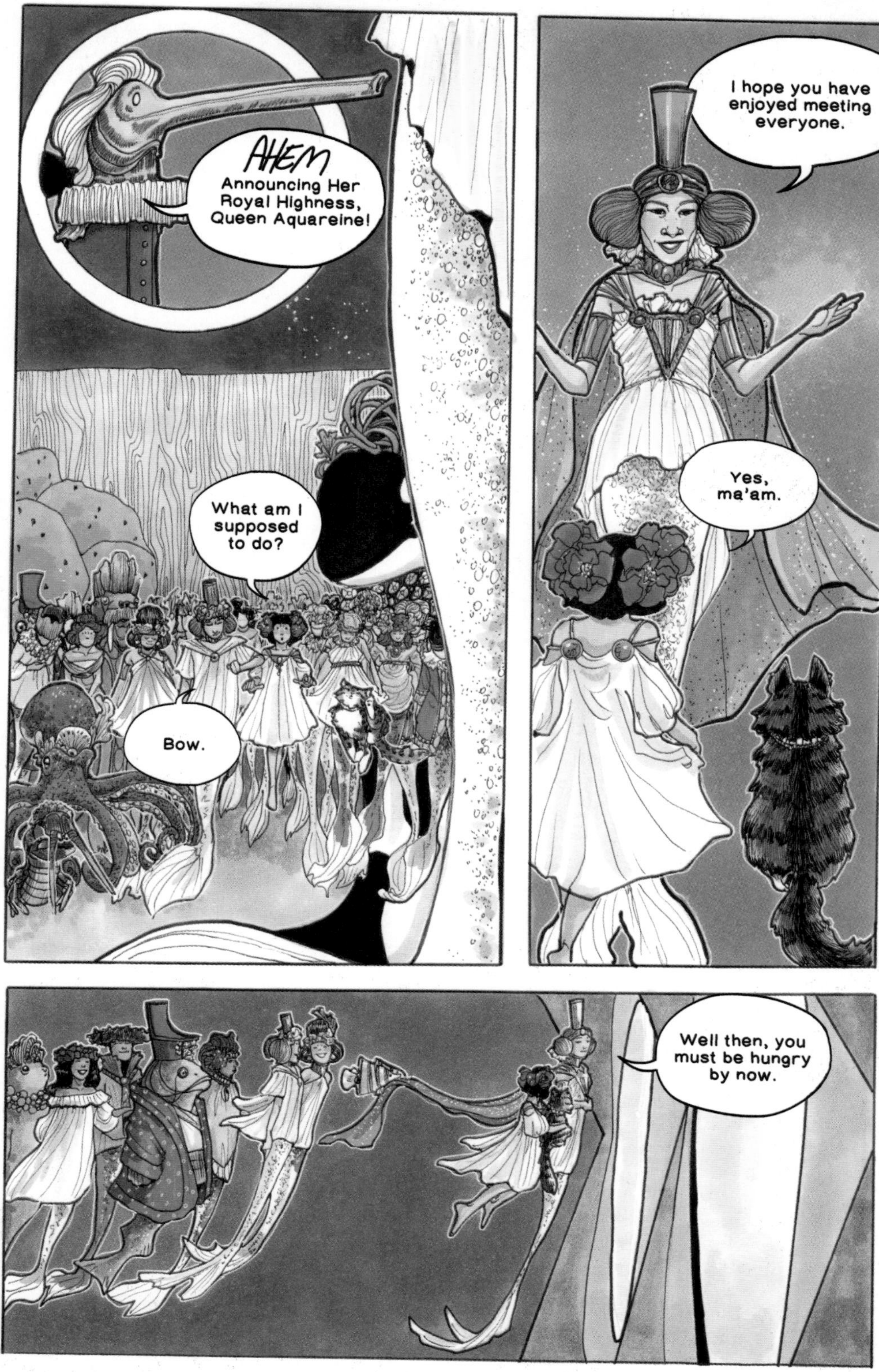
AHEM
Announcing Her Royal Highness, Queen Aquareine!
What am I supposed to do?
Bow.
I hope you have enjoyed meeting everyone.
Yes, ma'am.
Well then, you must be hungry by now.

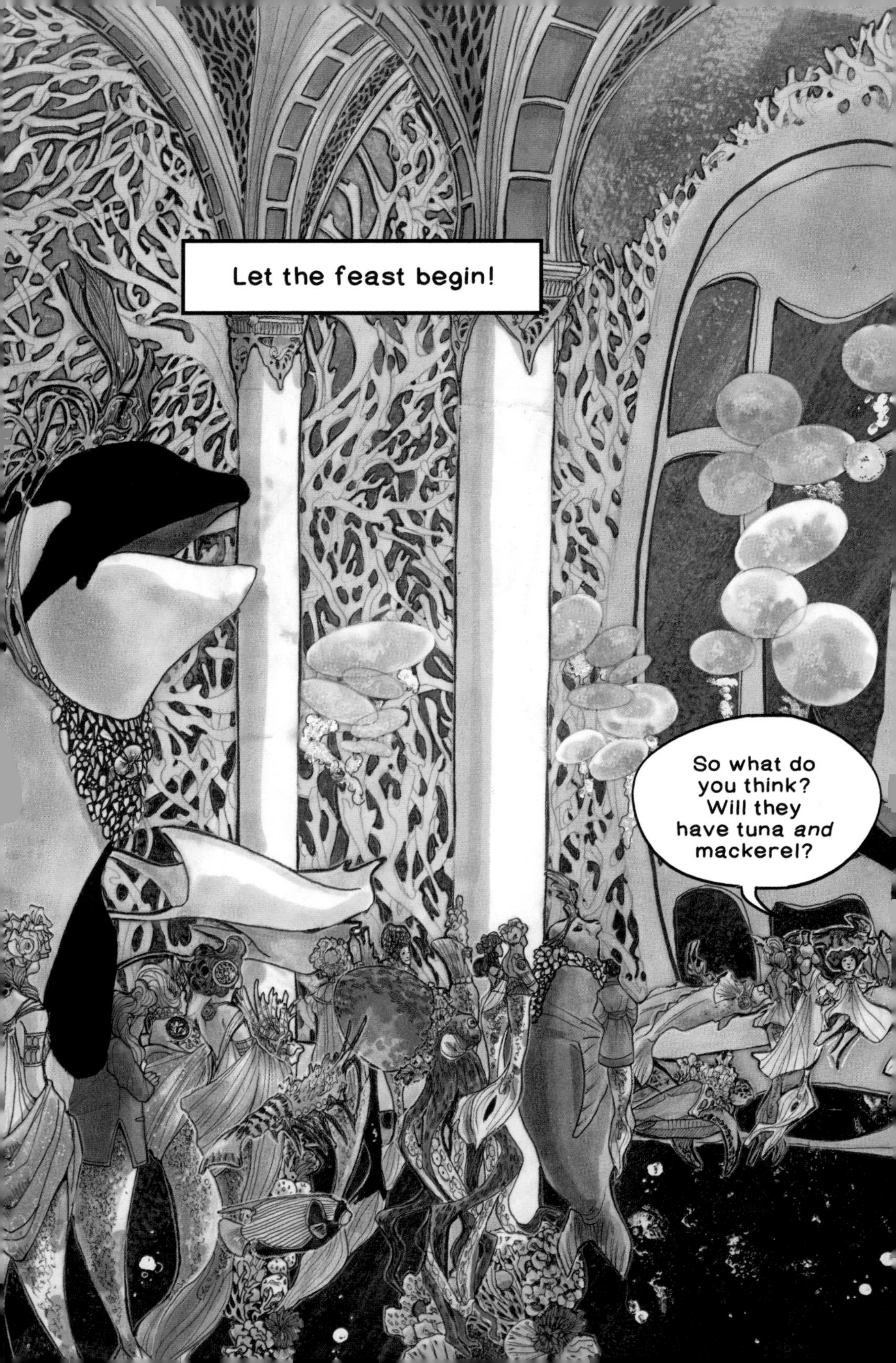
Let the feast begin!
So what do you think? Will they have tuna *and* mackerel?

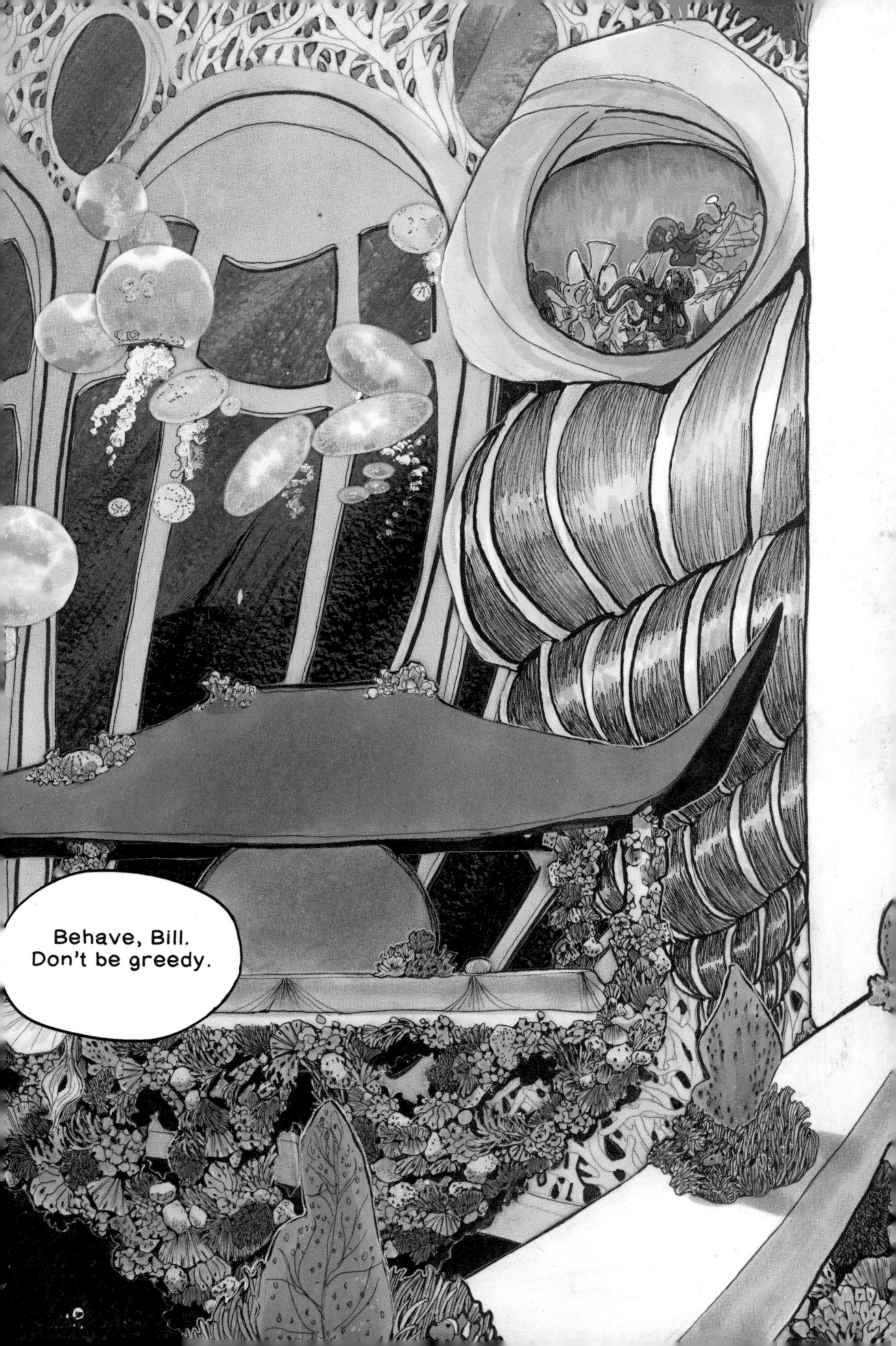
Behave, Bill. Don't be greedy.

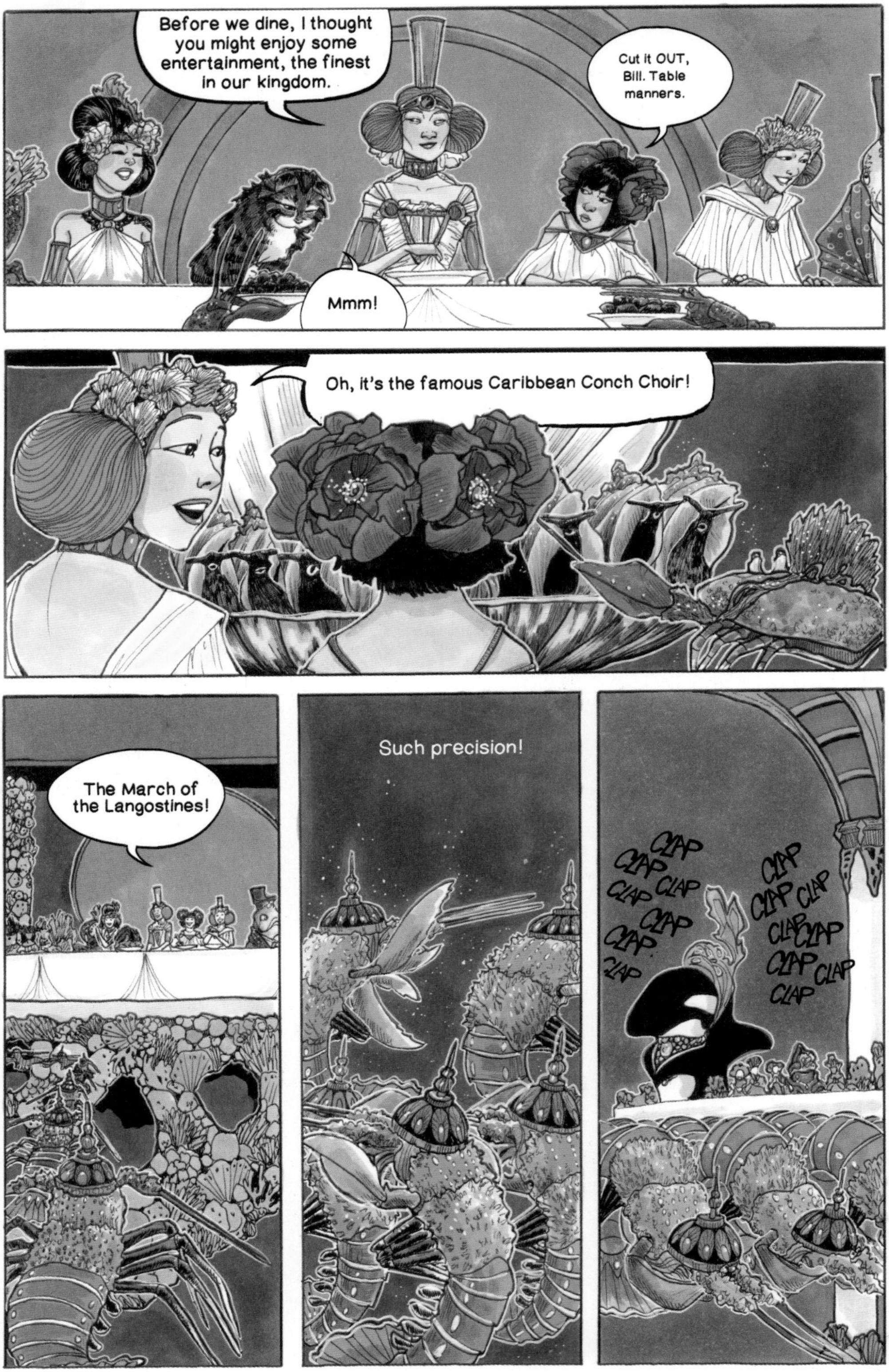
Before we dine, I thought you might enjoy some entertainment, the finest in our kingdom.
Cut it OUT, Bill. Table manners.
Mmm!
Oh, it's the famous Caribbean Conch Choir!
The March of the Langostines!
Such precision!
CLAP CLAP CLAP CLAP CLAP CLAP CLAP
CLAP CLAP CLAP CLAP CLAP CLAP CLAP CLAP

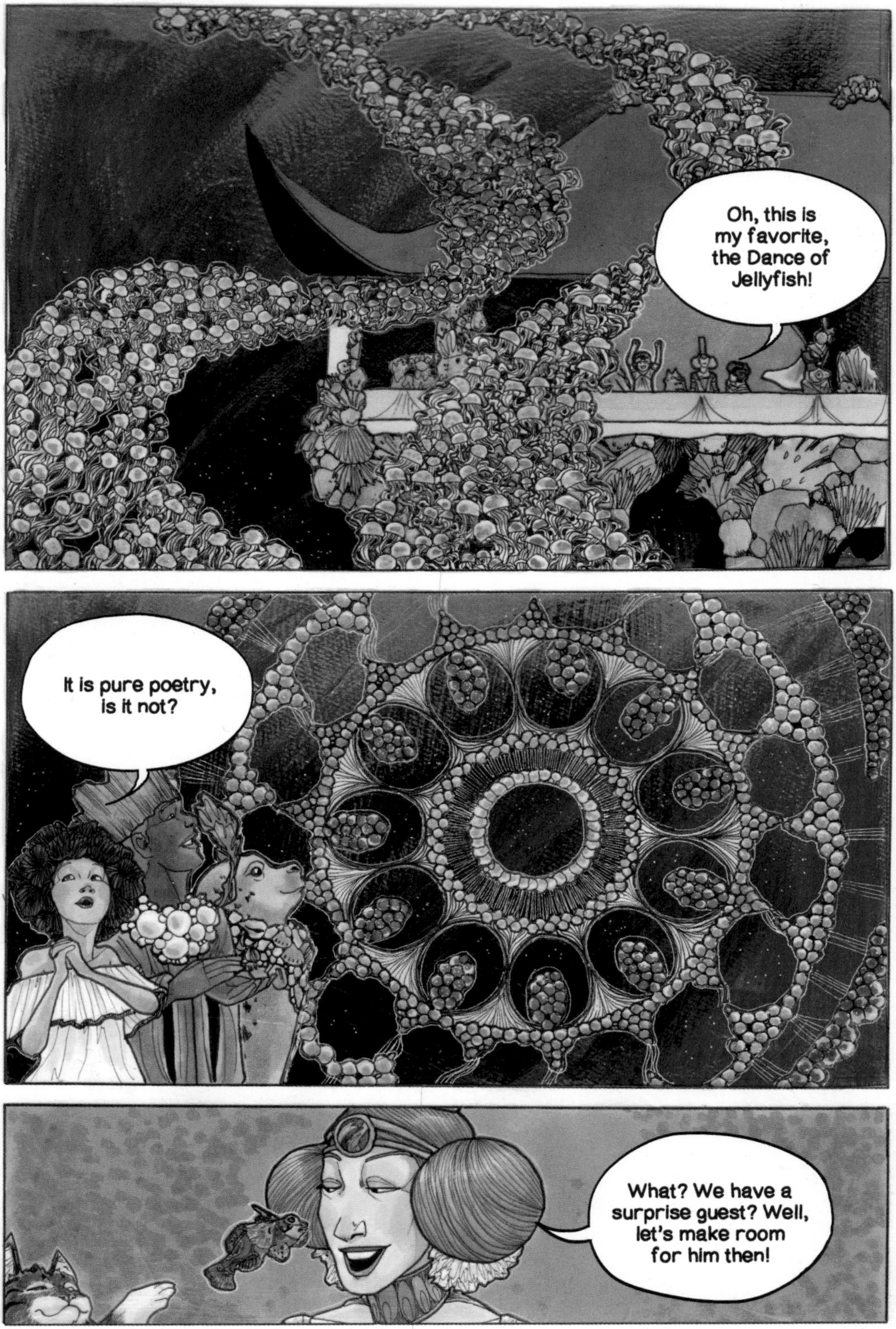
Oh, this is my favorite, the Dance of Jellyfish!
It is pure poetry, is it not?
What? We have a surprise guest? Well, let's make room for him then!

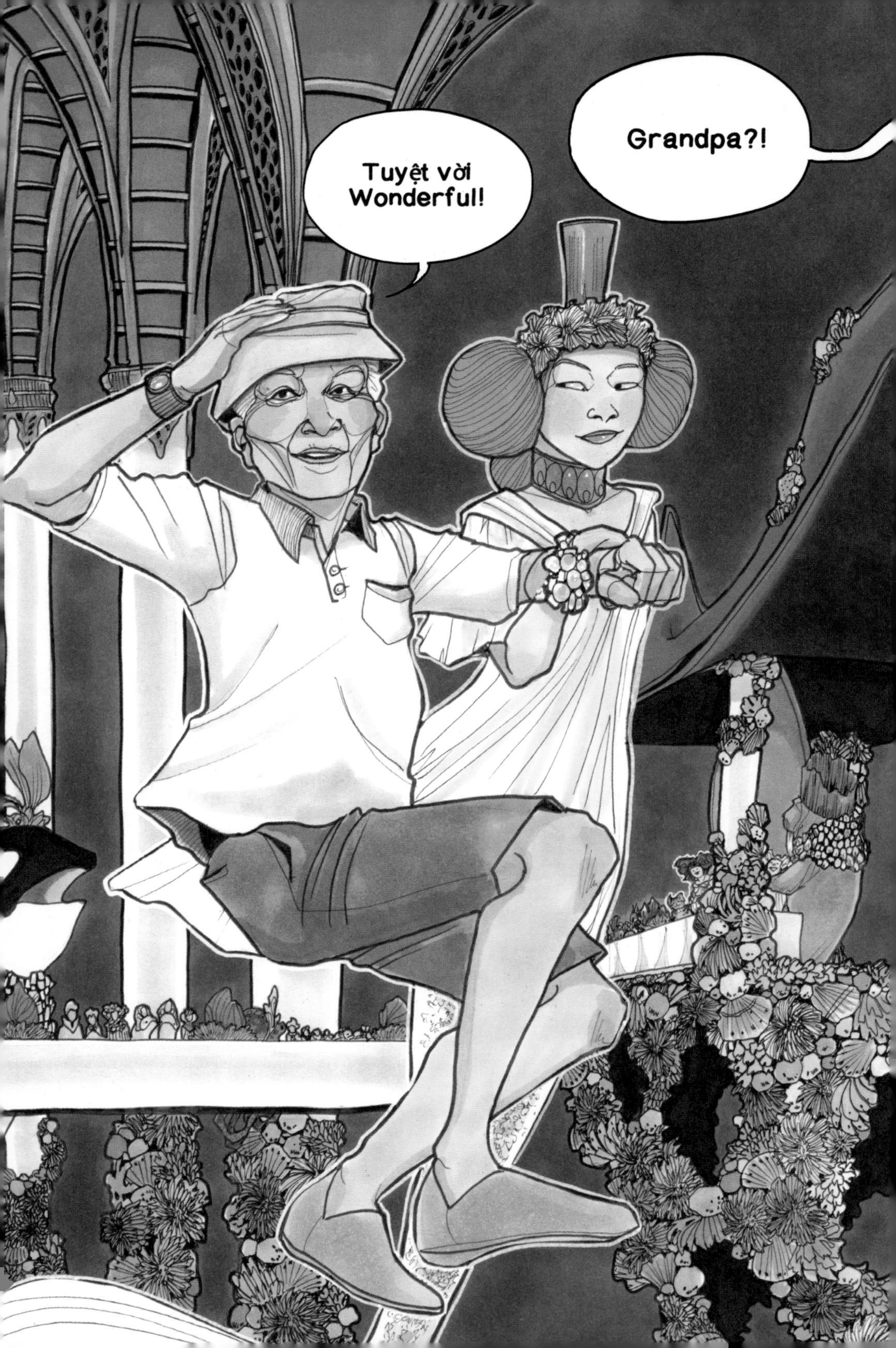
Tuyệt vời
Wonderful!
Grandpa?!

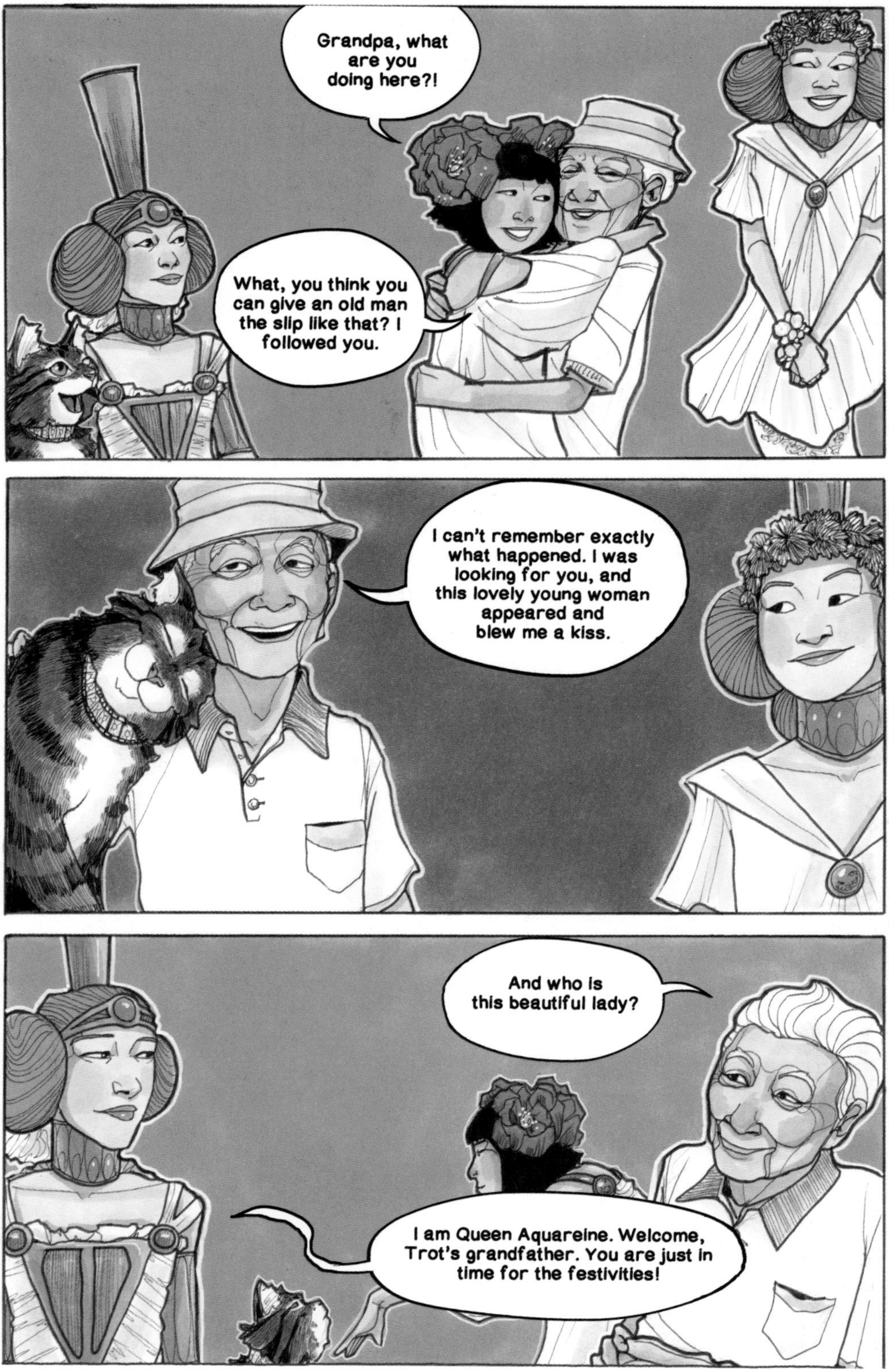
Grandpa, what are you doing here?!
What, you think you can give an old man the slip like that? I followed you.
I can't remember exactly what happened. I was looking for you, and this lovely young woman appeared and blew me a kiss.
And who is this beautiful lady?
I am Queen Aquareine. Welcome, Trot's grandfather. You are just in time for the festivities!

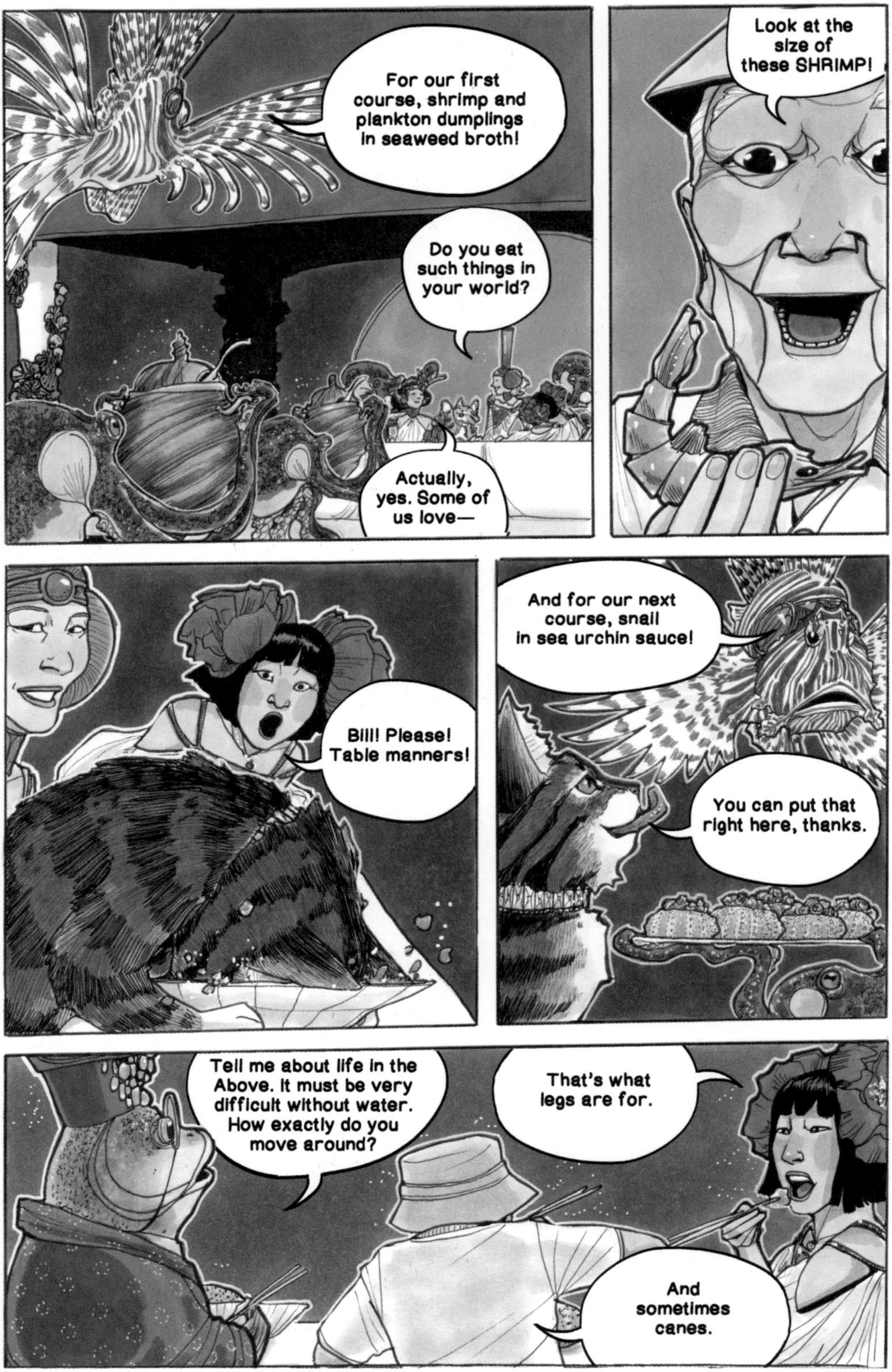
For our first course, shrimp and plankton dumplings in seaweed broth!
Do you eat such things in your world?
Actually, yes. Some of us love—
Look at the size of these SHRIMP!
Bill! Please! Table manners!
And for our next course, snail in sea urchin sauce!
You can put that right here, thanks.
Tell me about life in the Above. It must be very difficult without water. How exactly do you move around?
That's what legs are for.
And sometimes canes.

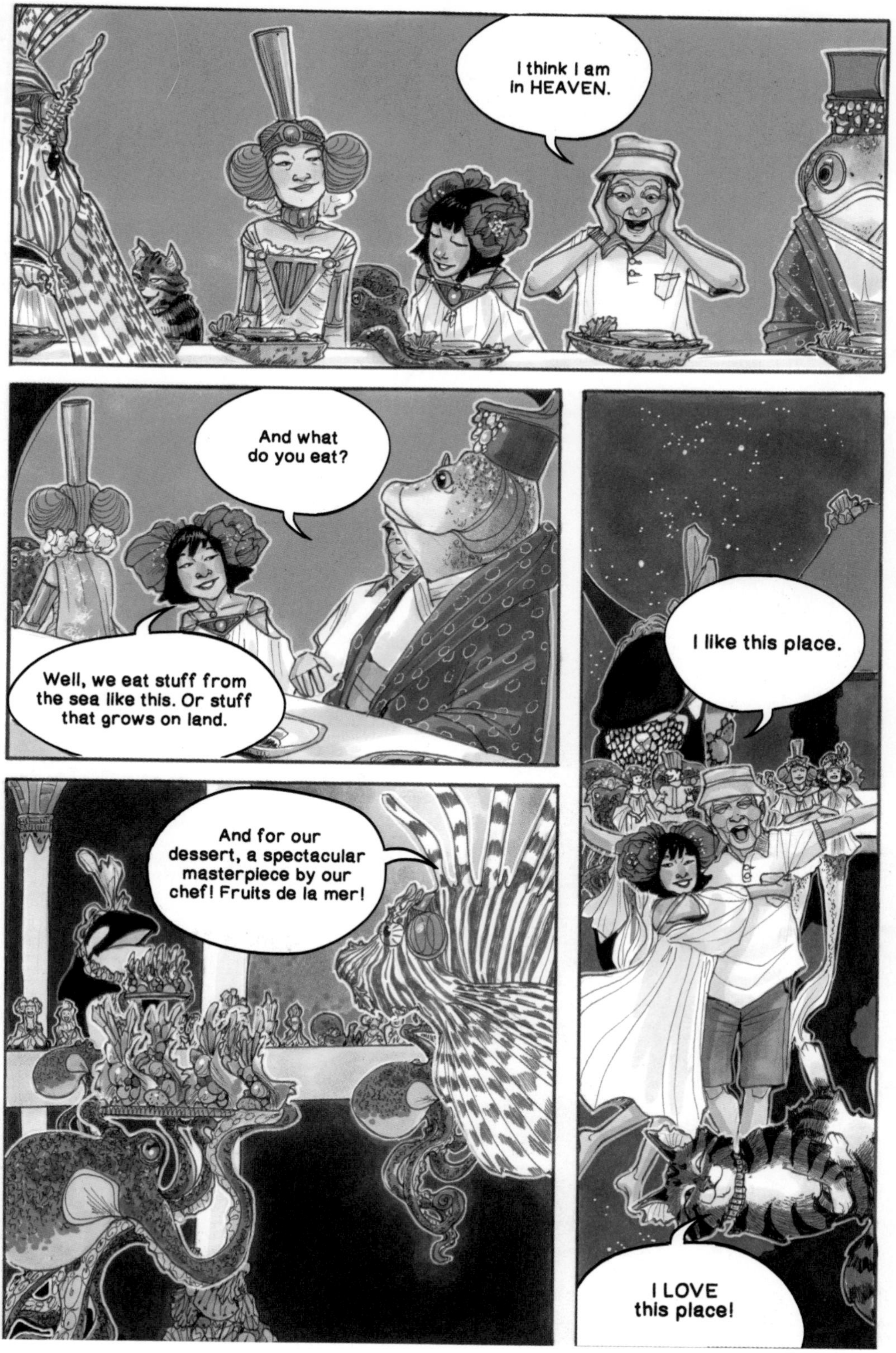
I think I am in HEAVEN.
And what do you eat?
Well, we eat stuff from the sea like this. Or stuff that grows on land.
I like this place.
And for our dessert, a spectacular masterpiece by our chef! Fruits de la mer!
I LOVE this place!

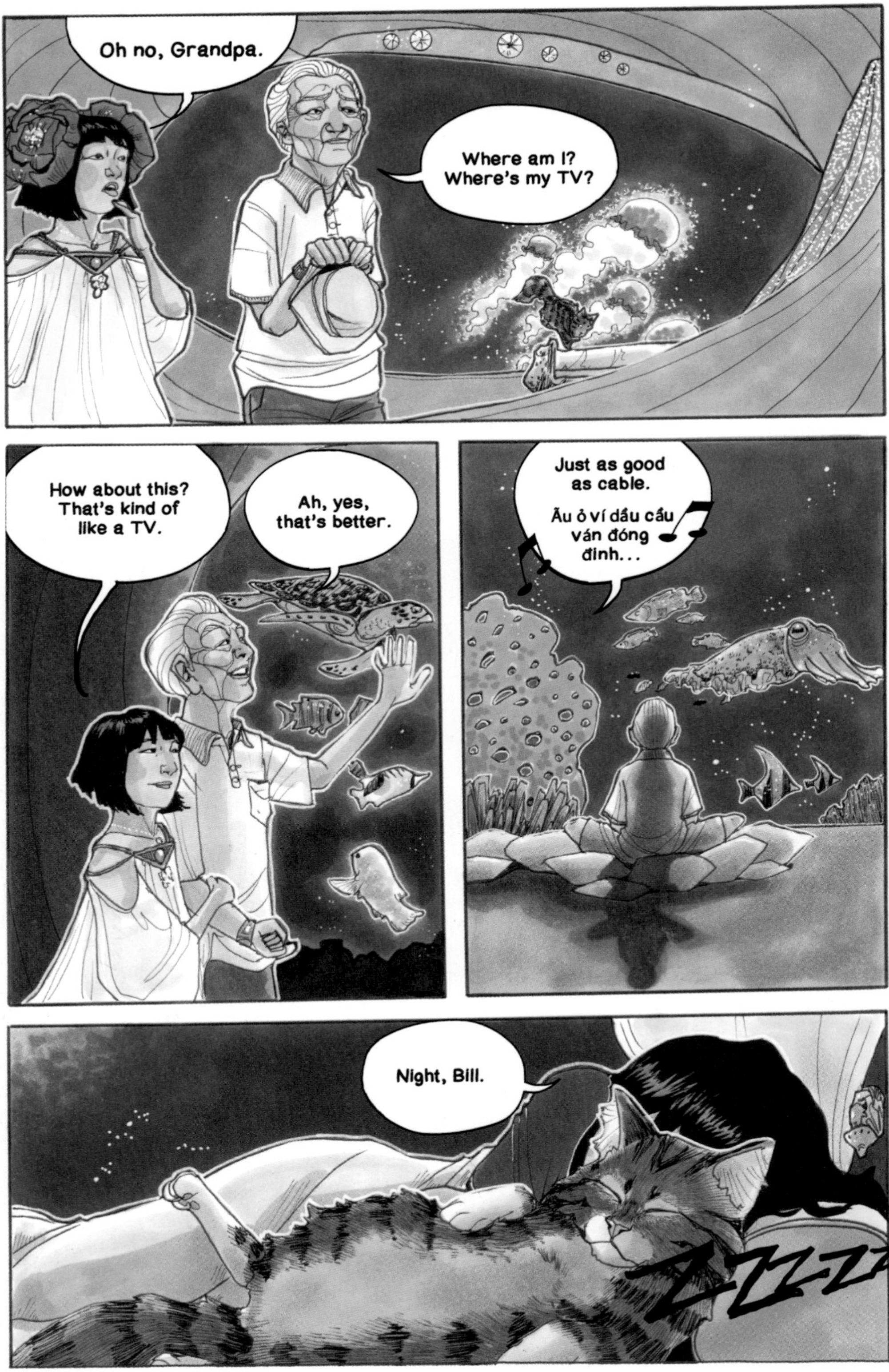
Oh no, Grandpa.
Where am I? Where's my TV?
How about this? That's kind of like a TV.
Ah, yes, that's better.
Just as good as cable.
Ẫu ỏ ví dẩu cẩu ván đóng đinh...
Night, Bill.
ZZZZZ

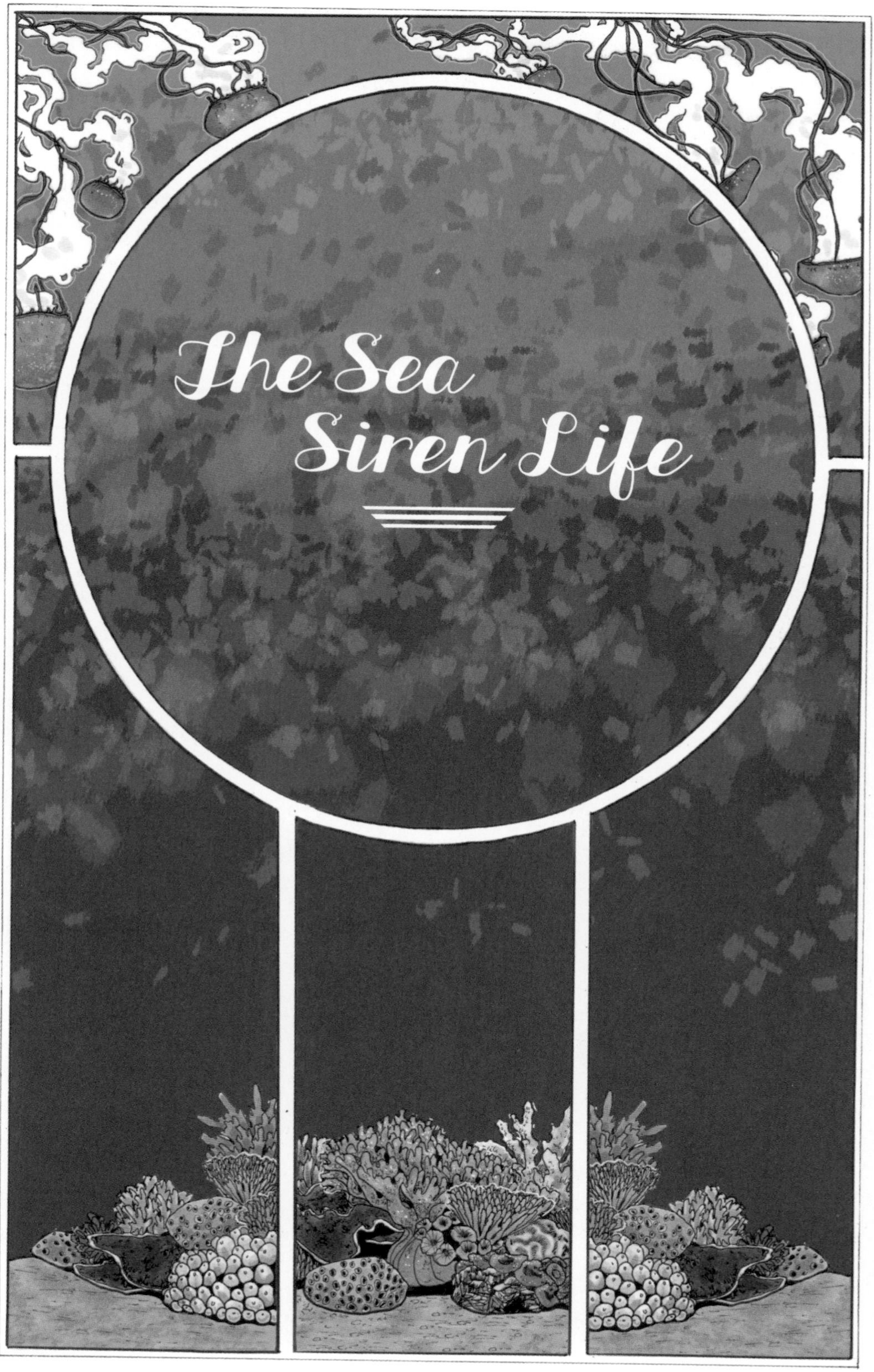
The Sea
Siren Life

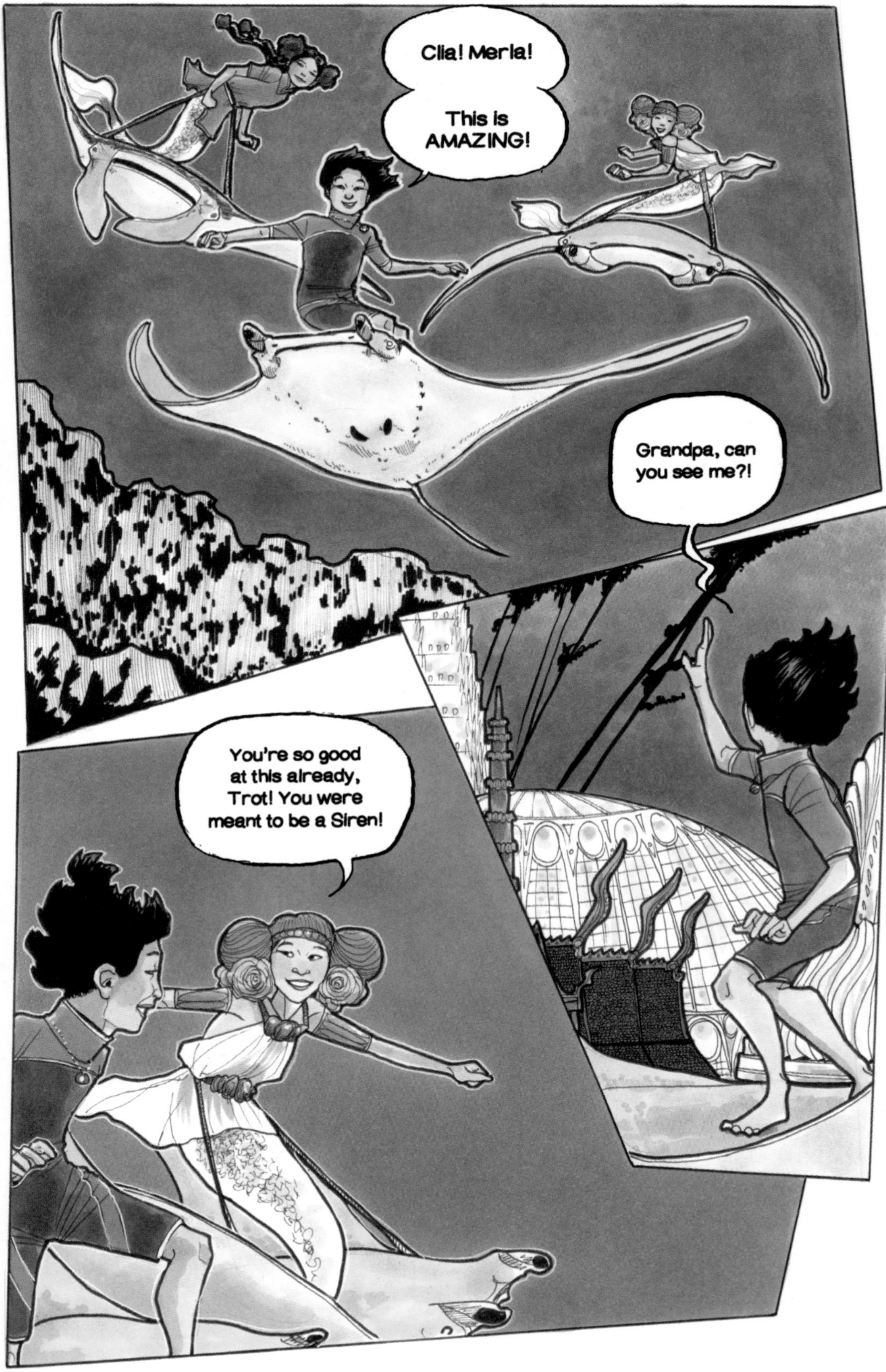
Clia! Merla!
This is AMAZING!
Grandpa, can you see me?!
You're so good at this already, Trot! You were meant to be a Siren!

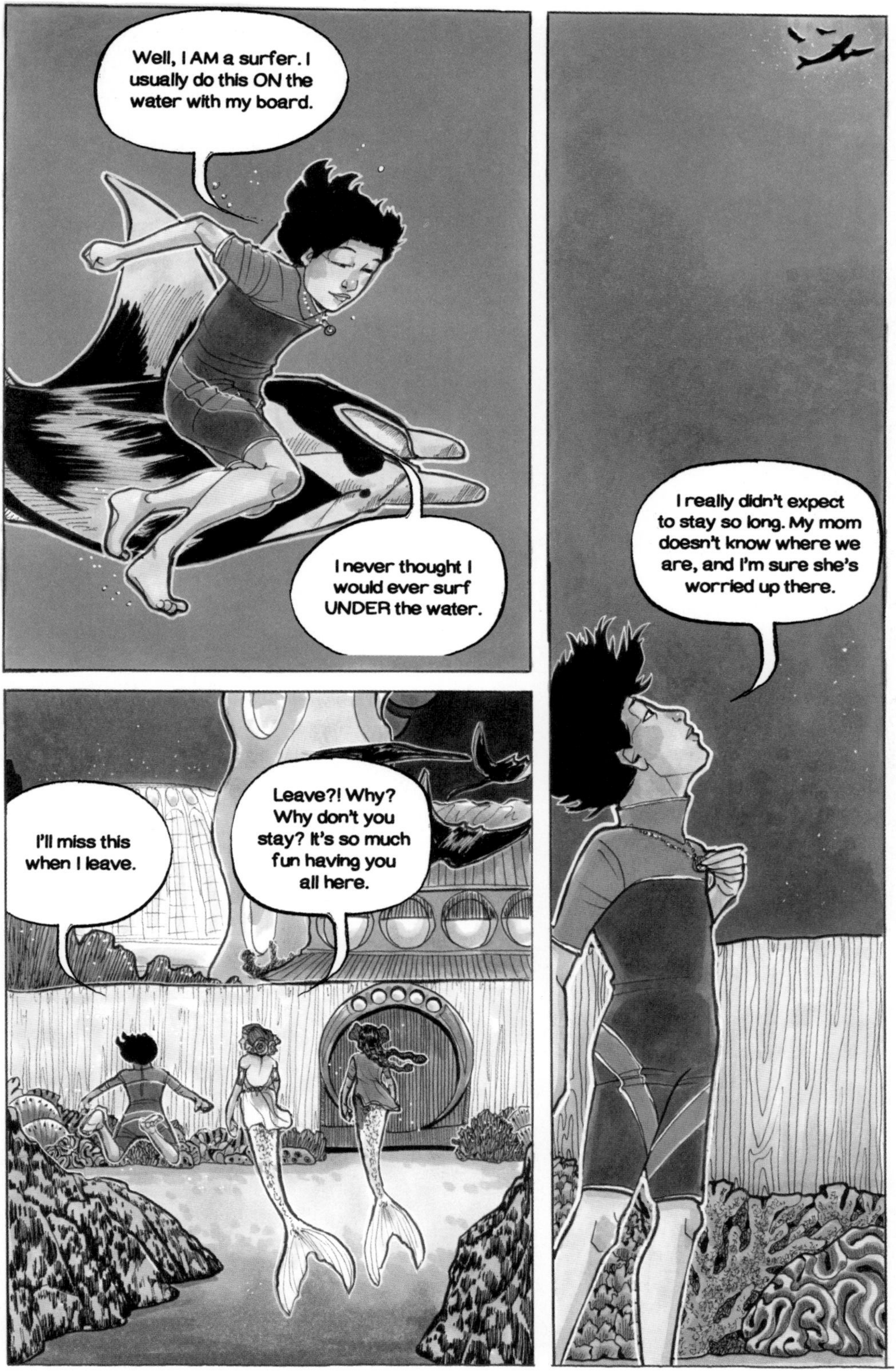
Well, I AM a surfer. I usually do this ON the water with my board.
I never thought I would ever surf UNDER the water.
I'll miss this when I leave.
Leave?! Why? Why don't you stay? It's so much fun having you all here.
I really didn't expect to stay so long. My mom doesn't know where we are, and I'm sure she's worried up there.

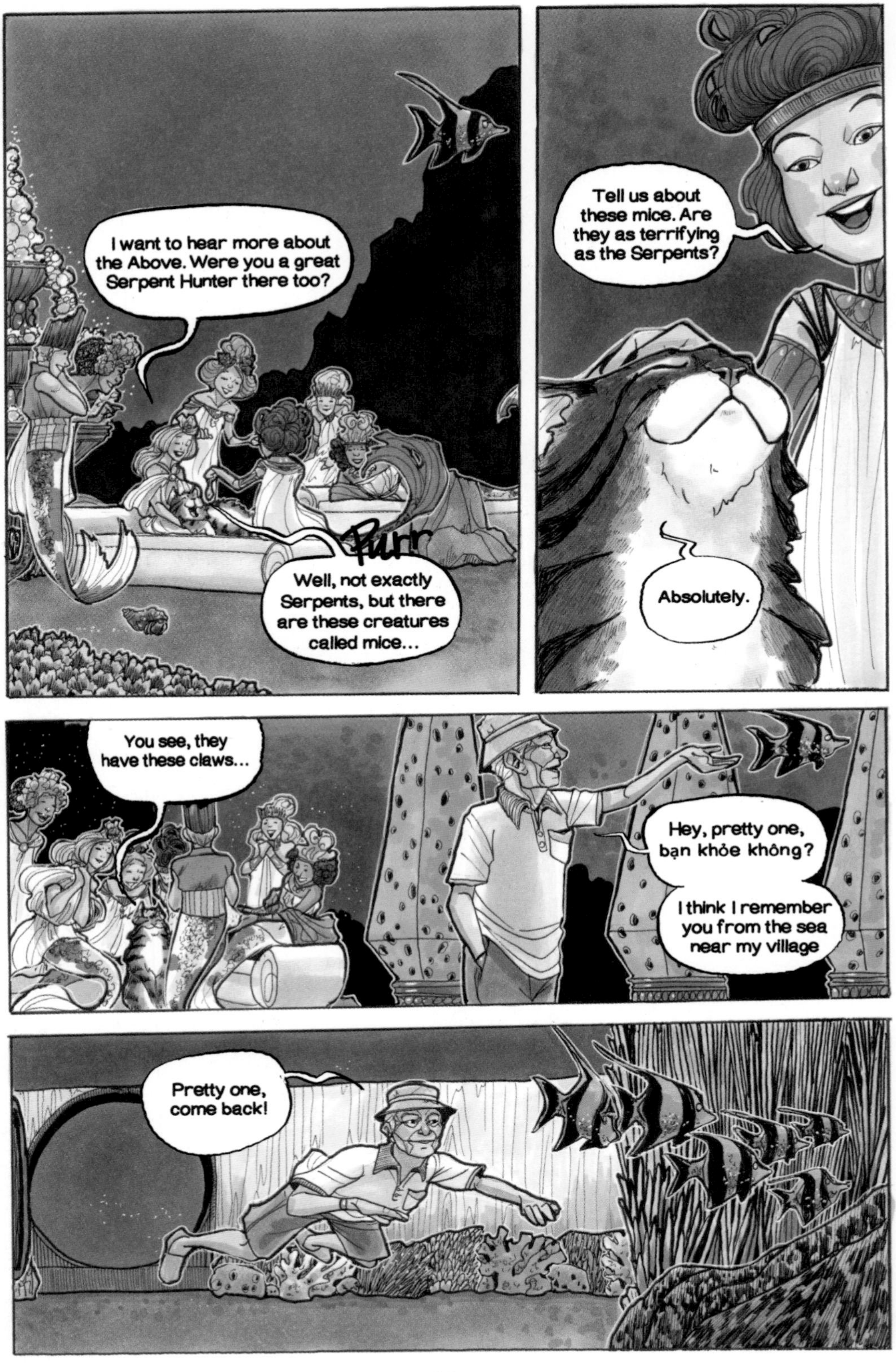
I want to hear more about the Above. Were you a great Serpent Hunter there too?
Purr
Well, not exactly Serpents, but there are these creatures called mice...
Tell us about these mice. Are they as terrifying as the Serpents?
Absolutely.
You see, they have these claws...
Hey, pretty one, bạn khỏe không?
I think I remember you from the sea near my village
Pretty one, come back!

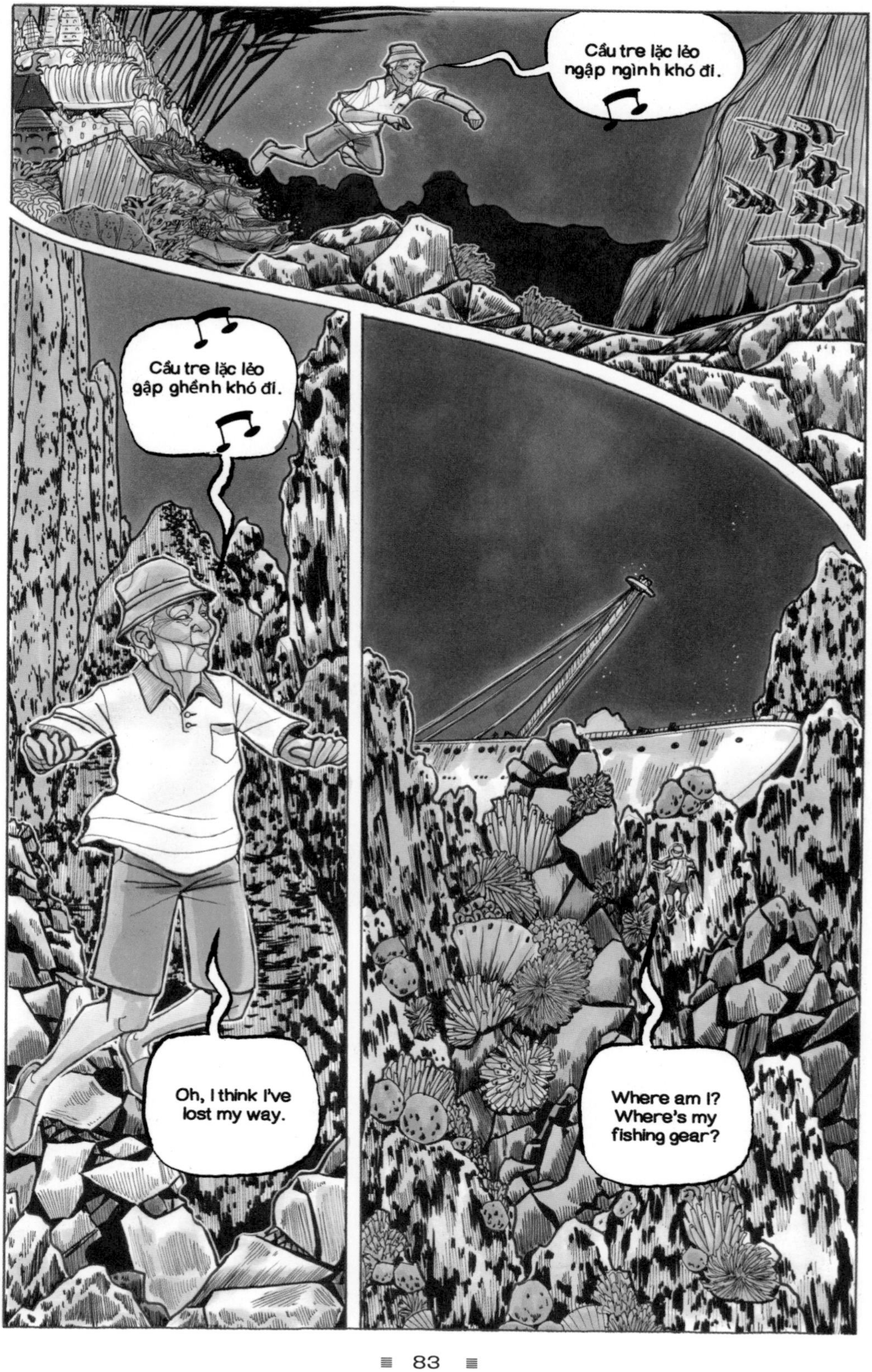
Cầu tre lặc lẻo
ngập ngình khó đi.
Cầu tre lặc lẻo
gập ghềnh khó đi.
Oh, I think I've
lost my way.
Where am I?
Where's my
fishing gear?

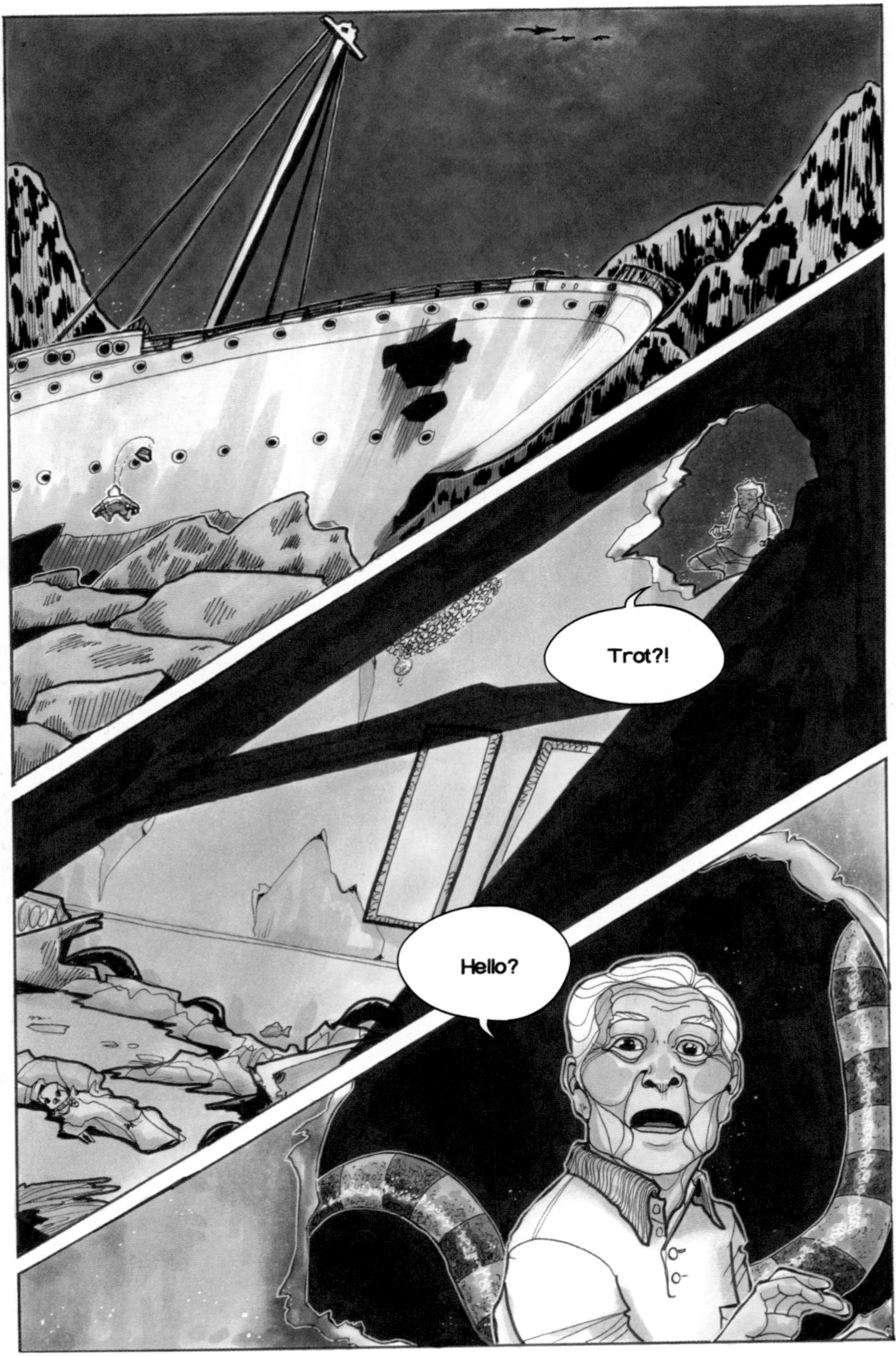
Trot?!
Hello?

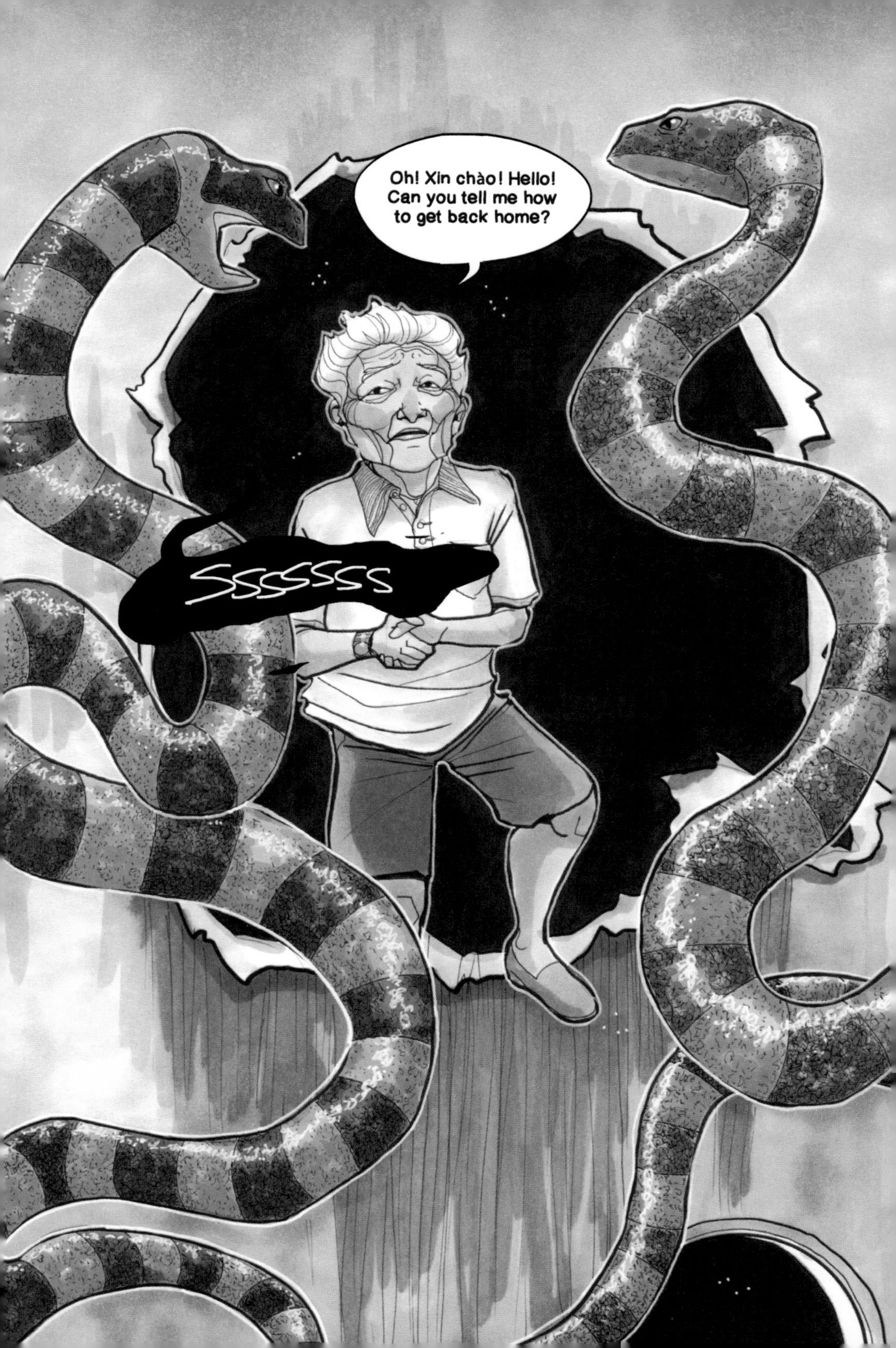
Oh! Xin chào! Hello! Can you tell me how to get back home?
SSSSSSS

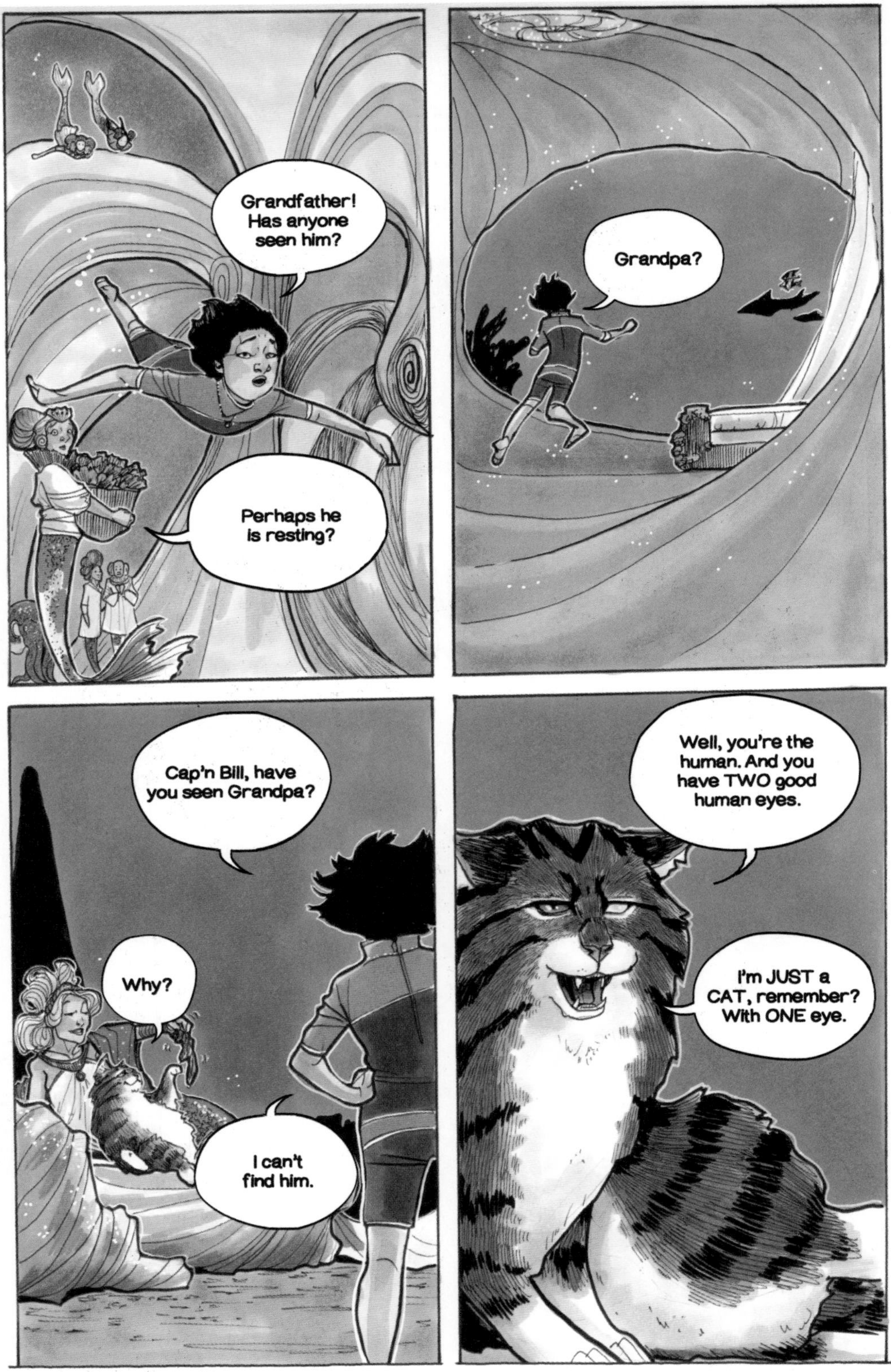
Grandfather! Has anyone seen him?
Perhaps he is resting?
Grandpa?
Cap'n Bill, have you seen Grandpa?
Why?
I can't find him.
Well, you're the human. And you have TWO good human eyes.
I'm JUST a CAT, remember? With ONE eye.

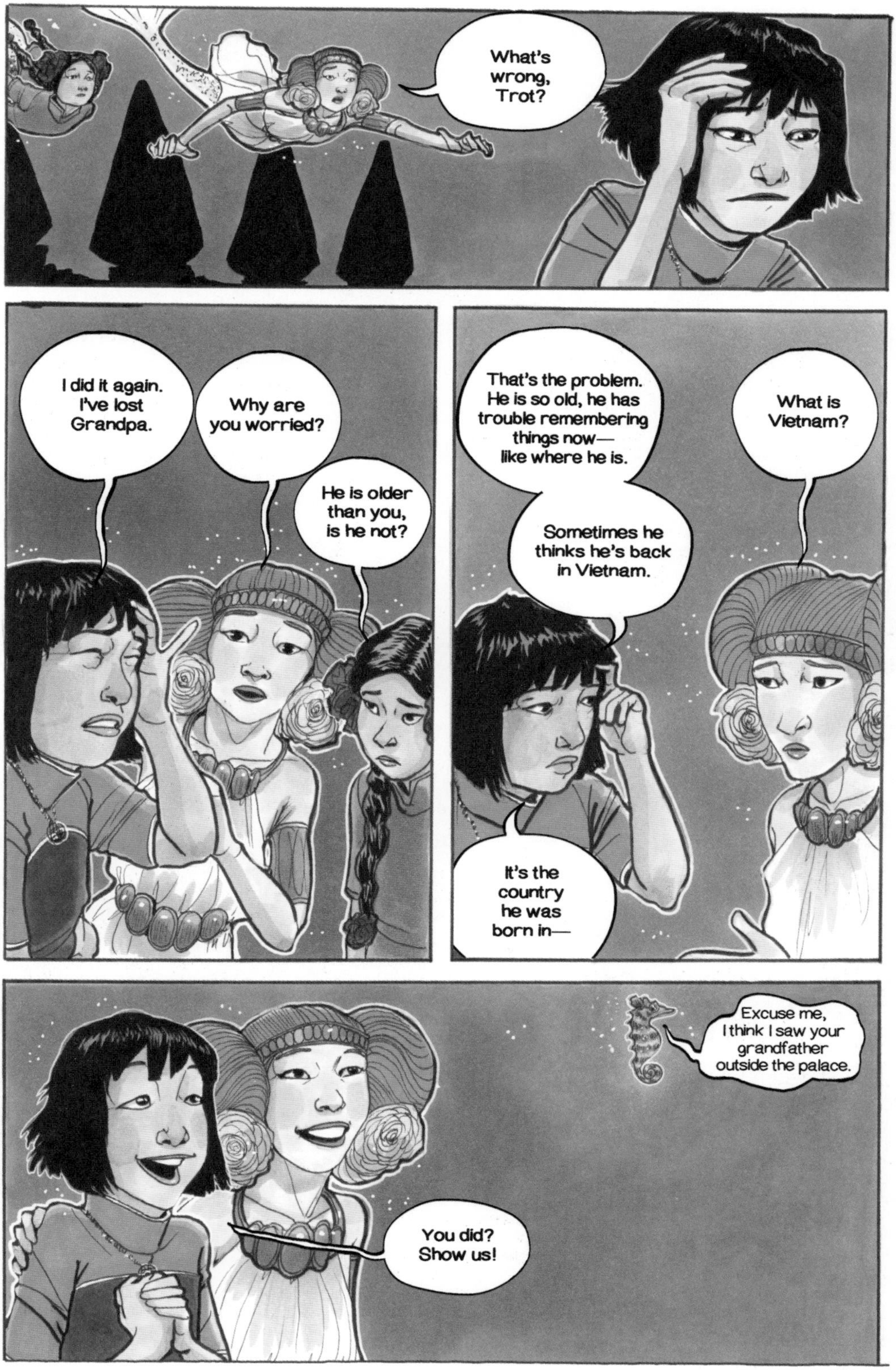
What's wrong, Trot?
I did it again. I've lost Grandpa.
Why are you worried?
He is older than you, is he not?
That's the problem. He is so old, he has trouble remembering things now— like where he is.
Sometimes he thinks he's back in Vietnam.
What is Vietnam?
It's the country he was born in—
Excuse me, I think I saw your grandfather outside the palace.
You did? Show us!

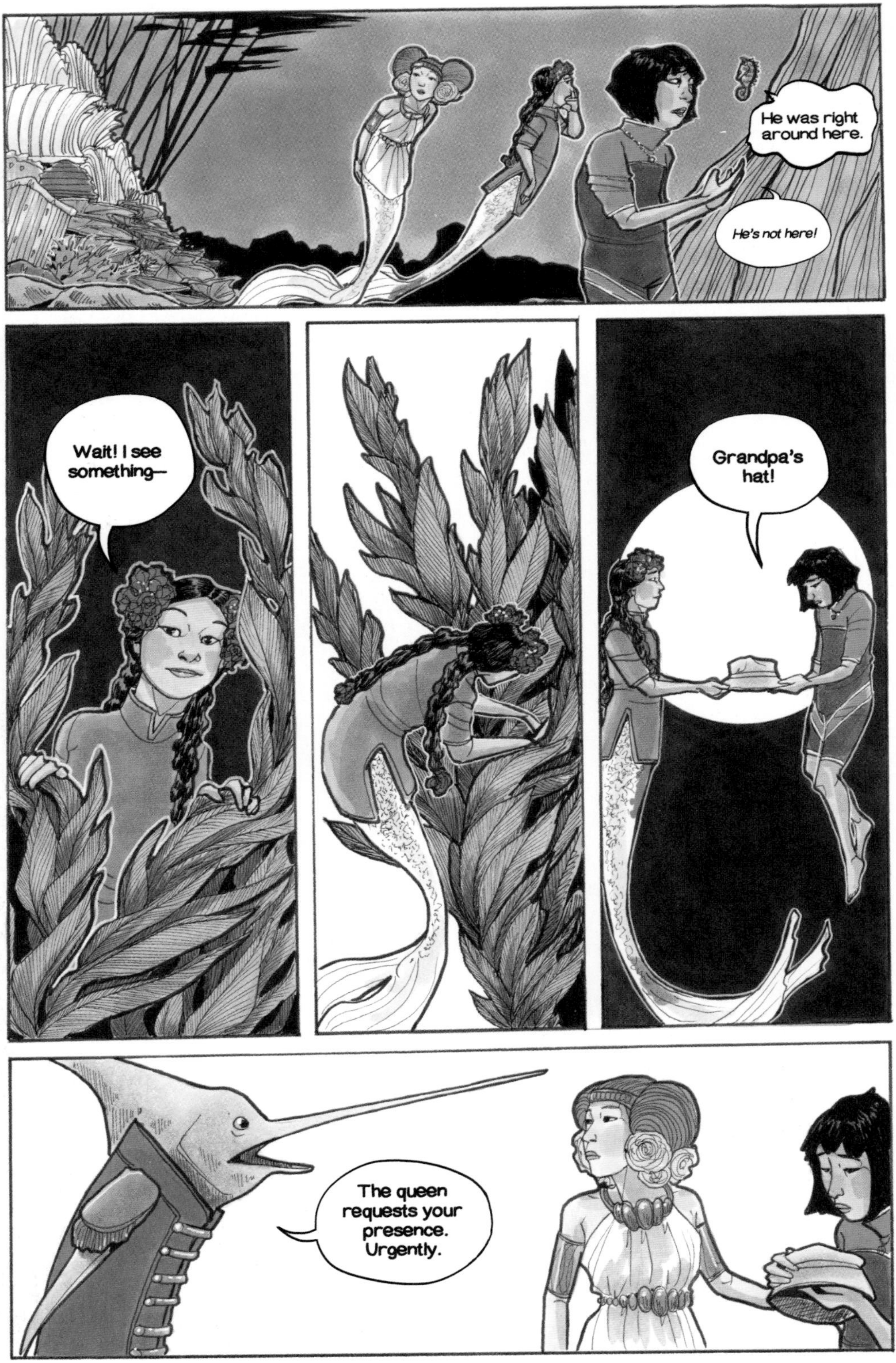
He was right around here.
He's not here!
Wait! I see something—
Grandpa's hat!
The queen requests your presence. Urgently.

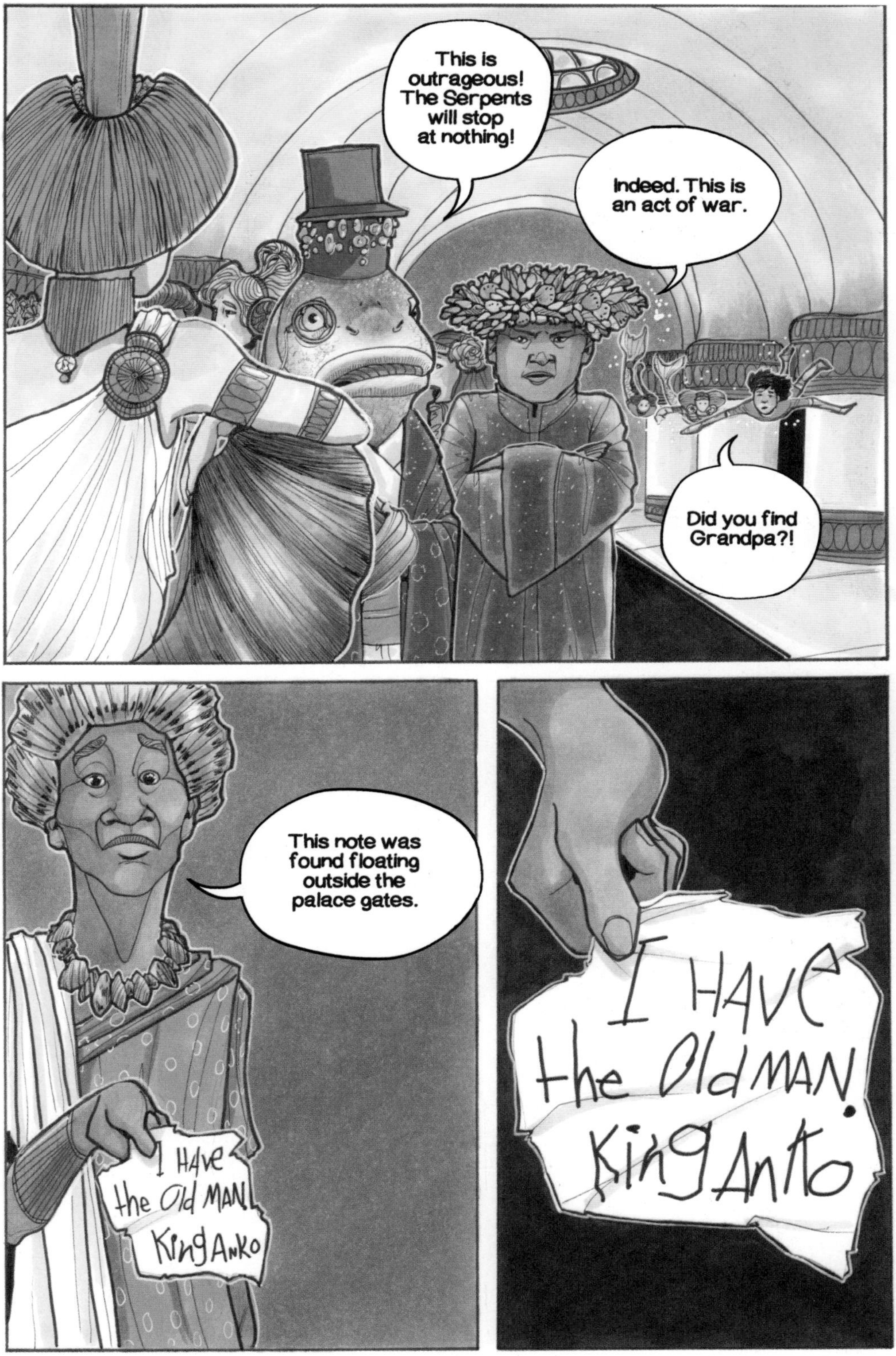
This is outrageous! The Serpents will stop at nothing!
Indeed. This is an act of war.
Did you find Grandpa?!
This note was found floating outside the palace gates.
I HAVE the Old MAN King Anko
I HAVE the Old MAN King Anko

Who is King Anko? What does this mean?

Anko is the King of the Serpents. He and his Serpent army have been terrorizing Sirens for as long as I can remember.

Then we need to rescue Grandpa!

I cannot risk any Sirens in this matter.

Anko is crafty, and dangerous. No one has actually ever met him face to face.

I am not interested in another confrontation with this brutish species. I am sorry, Trot.

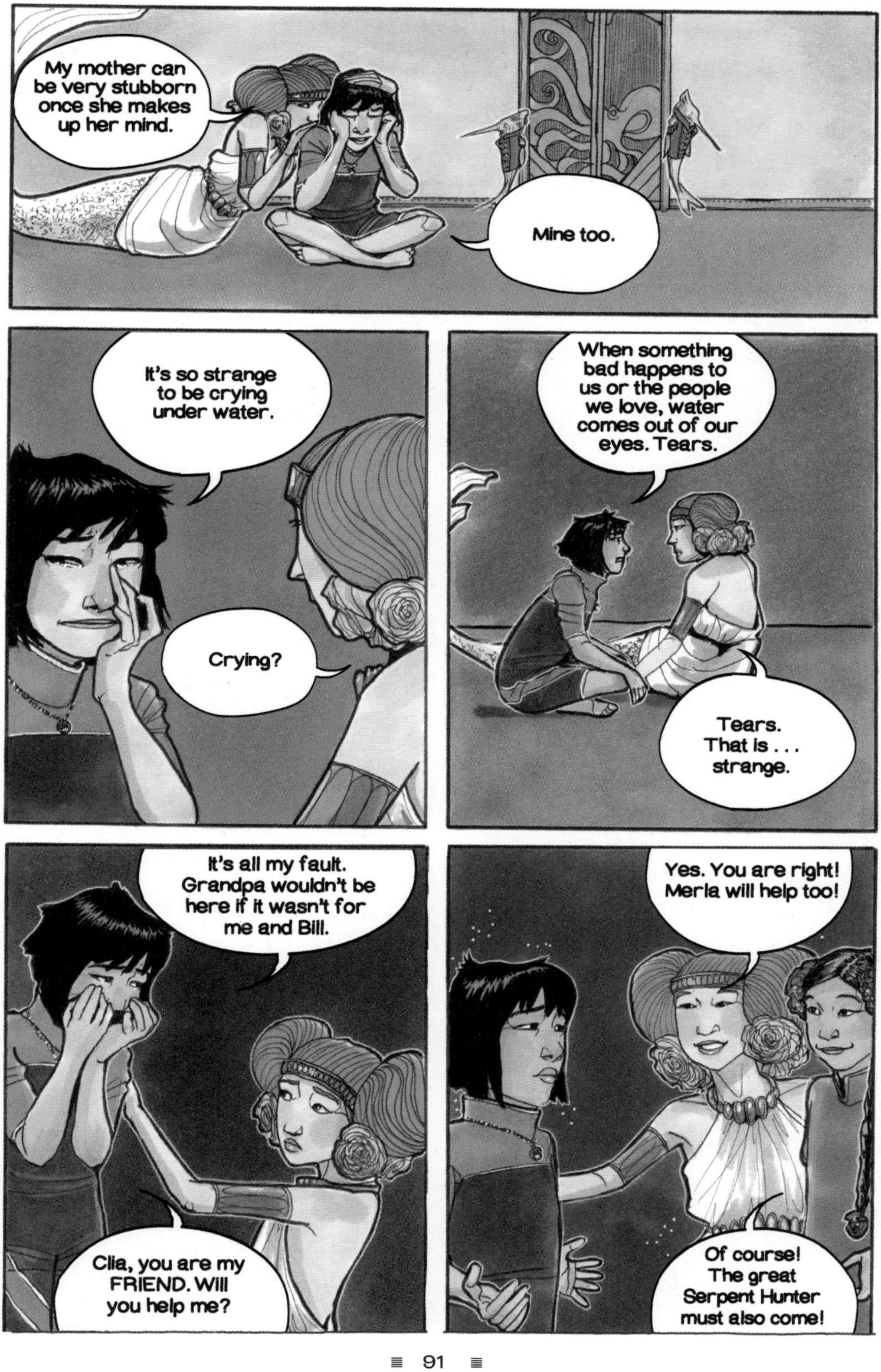
My mother can be very stubborn once she makes up her mind.
Mine too.
It's so strange to be crying under water.
Crying?
When something bad happens to us or the people we love, water comes out of our eyes. Tears.
Tears. That is . . . strange.
It's all my fault. Grandpa wouldn't be here if it wasn't for me and Bill.
Clia, you are my FRIEND. Will you help me?
Yes. You are right! Merla will help too!
Of course! The great Serpent Hunter must also come!

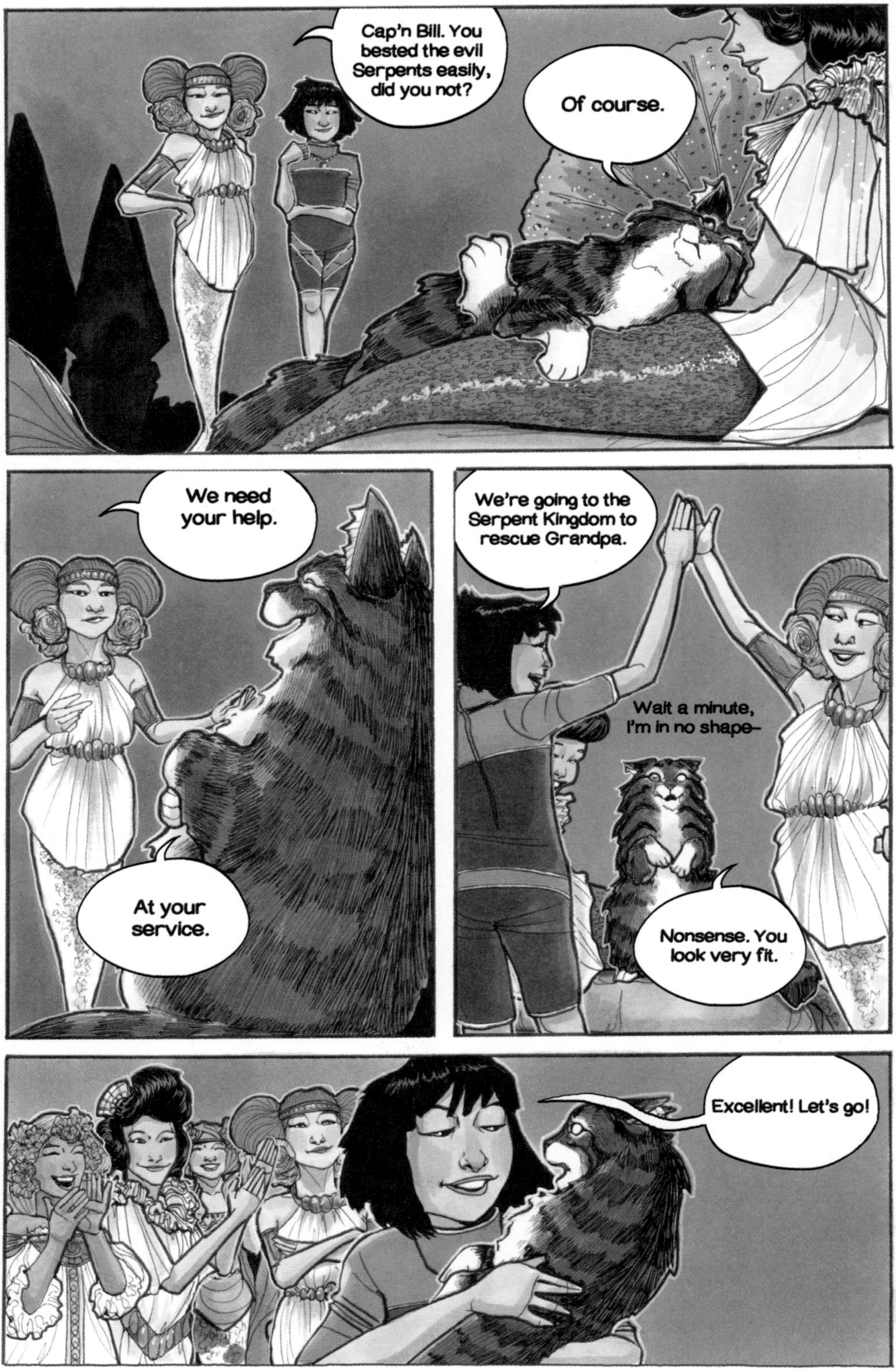
Cap'n Bill. You bested the evil Serpents easily, did you not?
Of course.
We need your help.
At your service.
We're going to the Serpent Kingdom to rescue Grandpa.
Wait a minute, I'm in no shape–
Nonsense. You look very fit.
Excellent! Let's go!

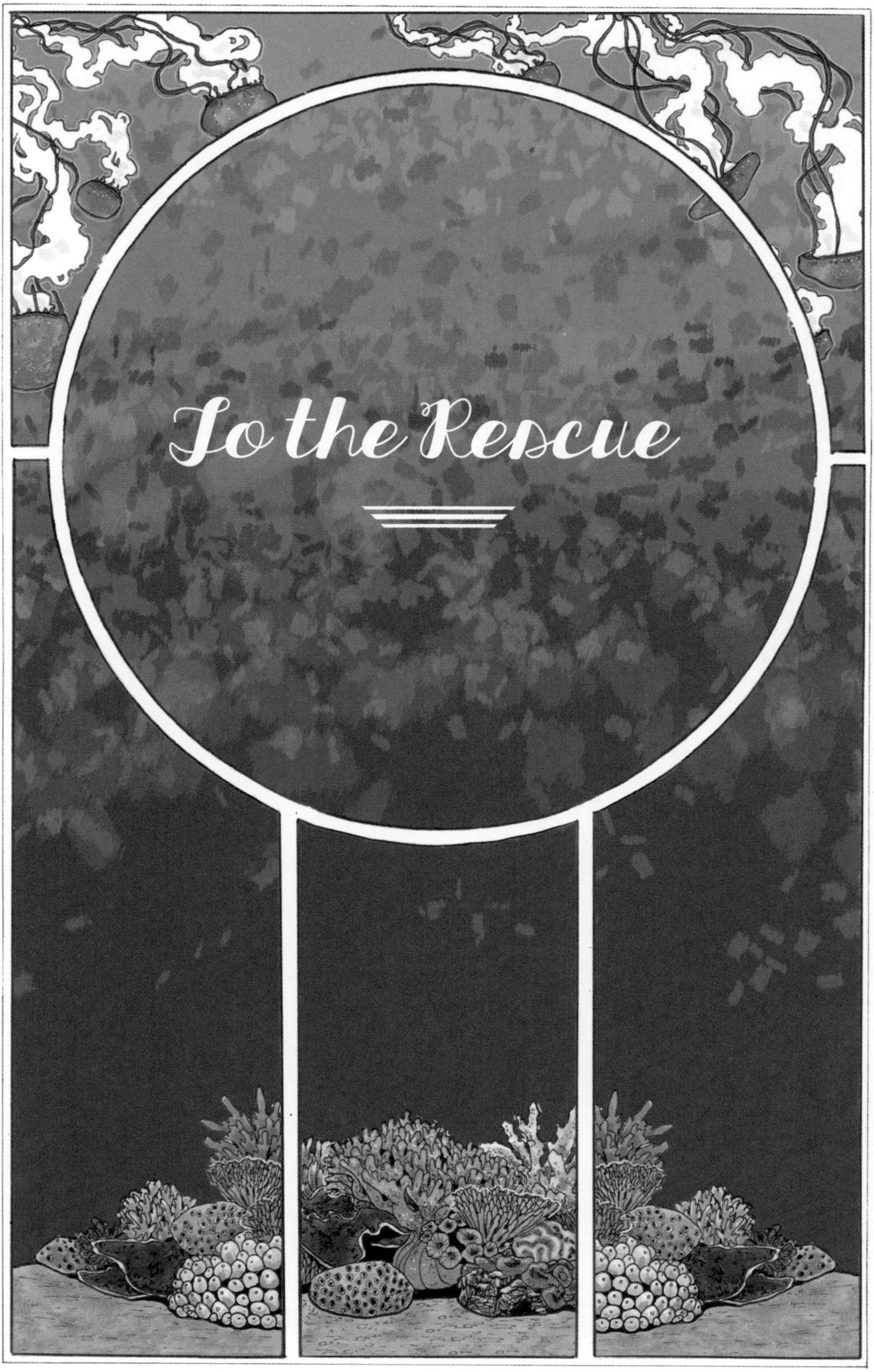
To the Rescue

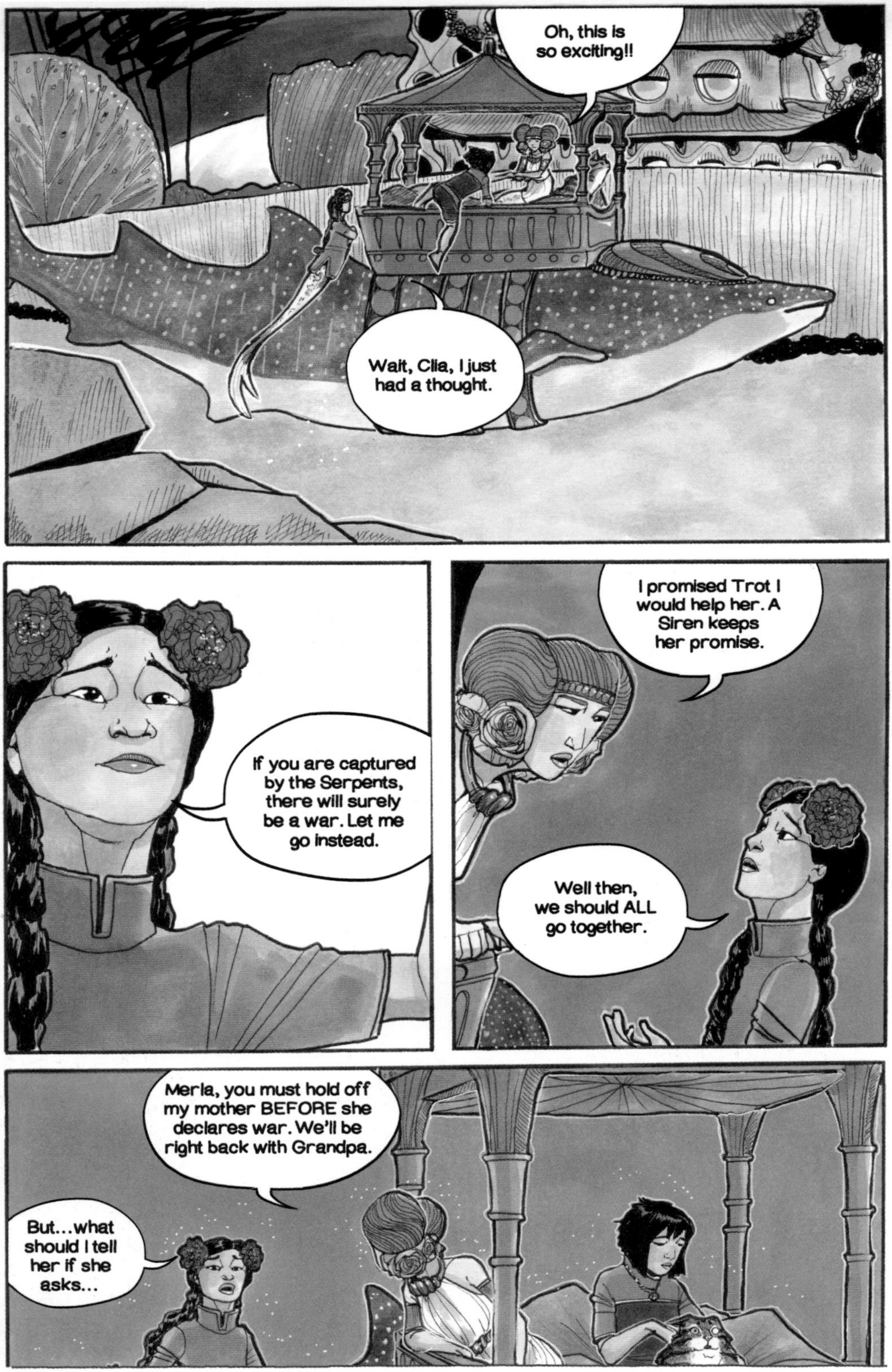
Oh, this is so exciting!!
Wait, Clia, I just had a thought.
If you are captured by the Serpents, there will surely be a war. Let me go instead.
I promised Trot I would help her. A Siren keeps her promise.
Well then, we should ALL go together.
Merla, you must hold off my mother BEFORE she declares war. We'll be right back with Grandpa.
But...what should I tell her if she asks...

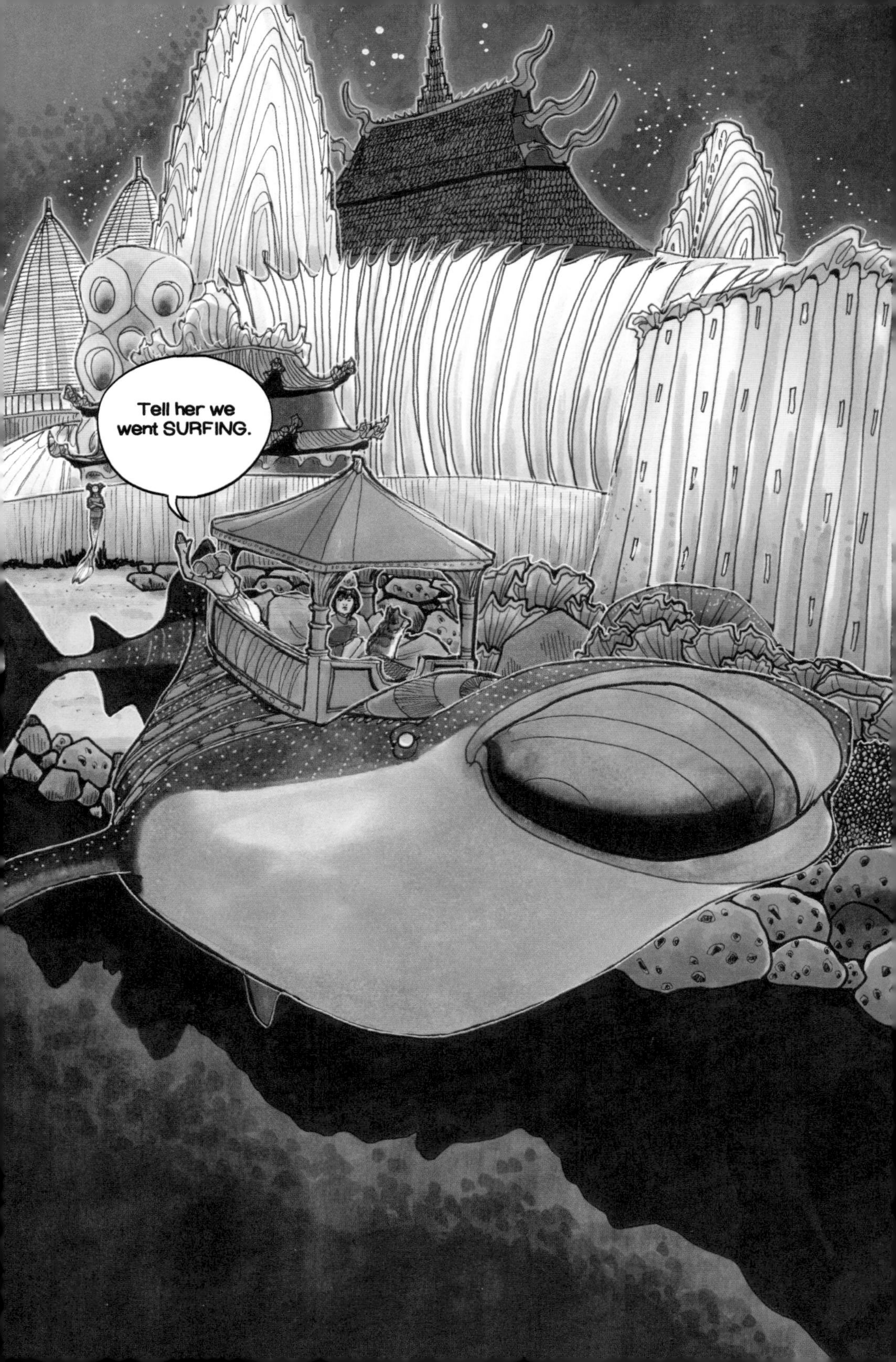
Tell her we went SURFING.

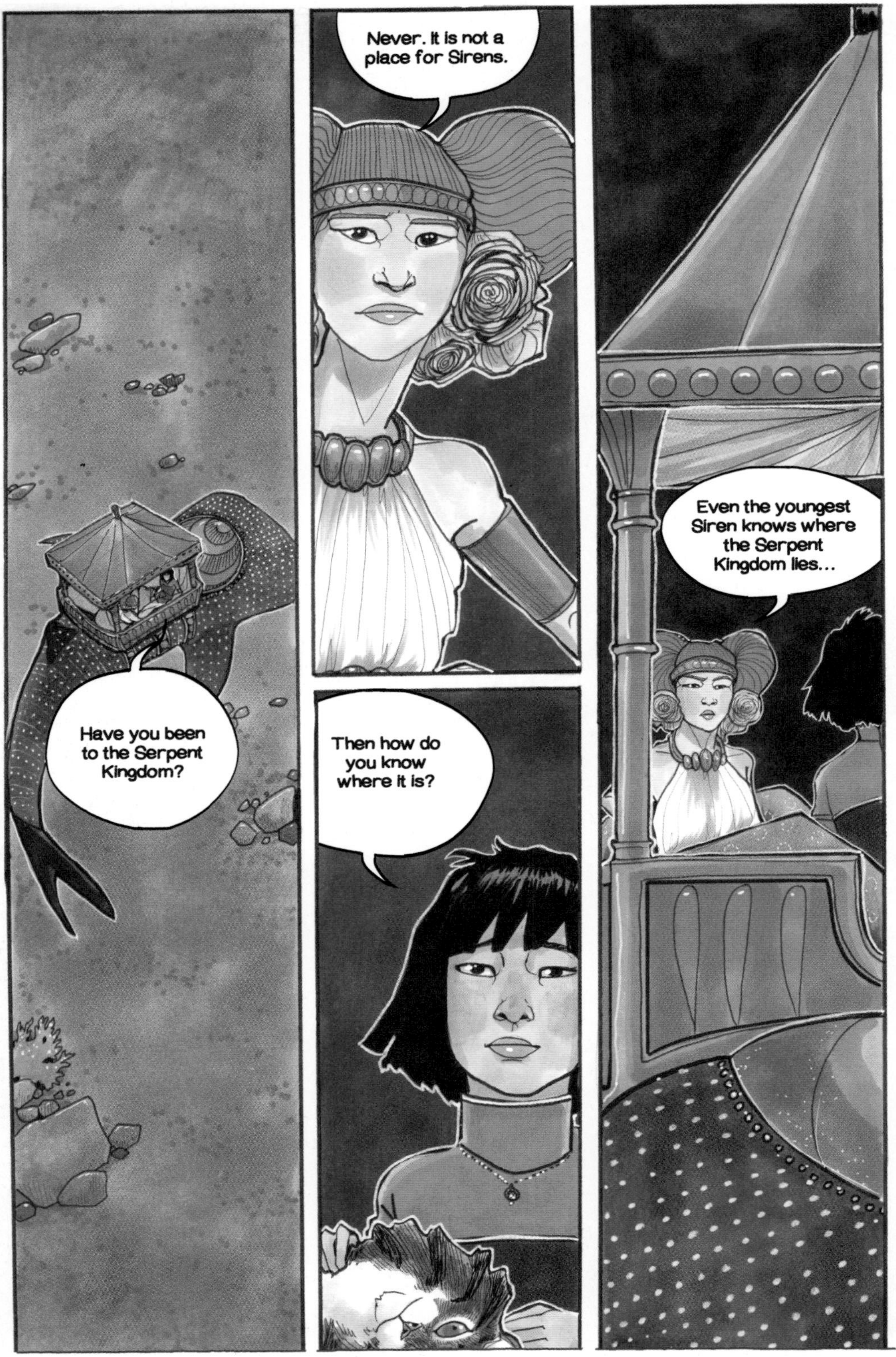
Have you been to the Serpent Kingdom?
Never. It is not a place for Sirens.
Then how do you know where it is?
Even the youngest Siren knows where the Serpent Kingdom lies...

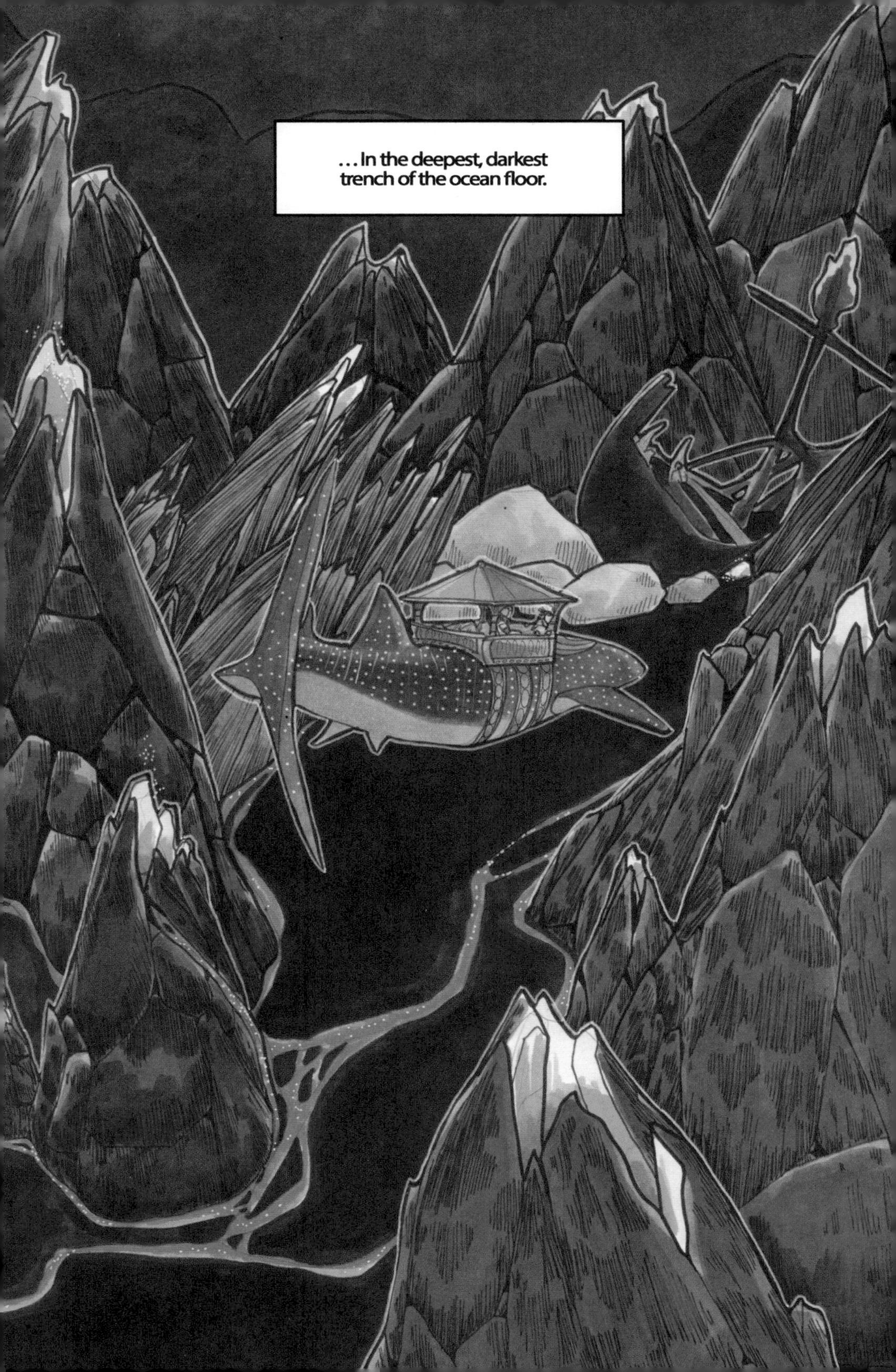
. . . In the deepest, darkest
trench of the ocean floor.

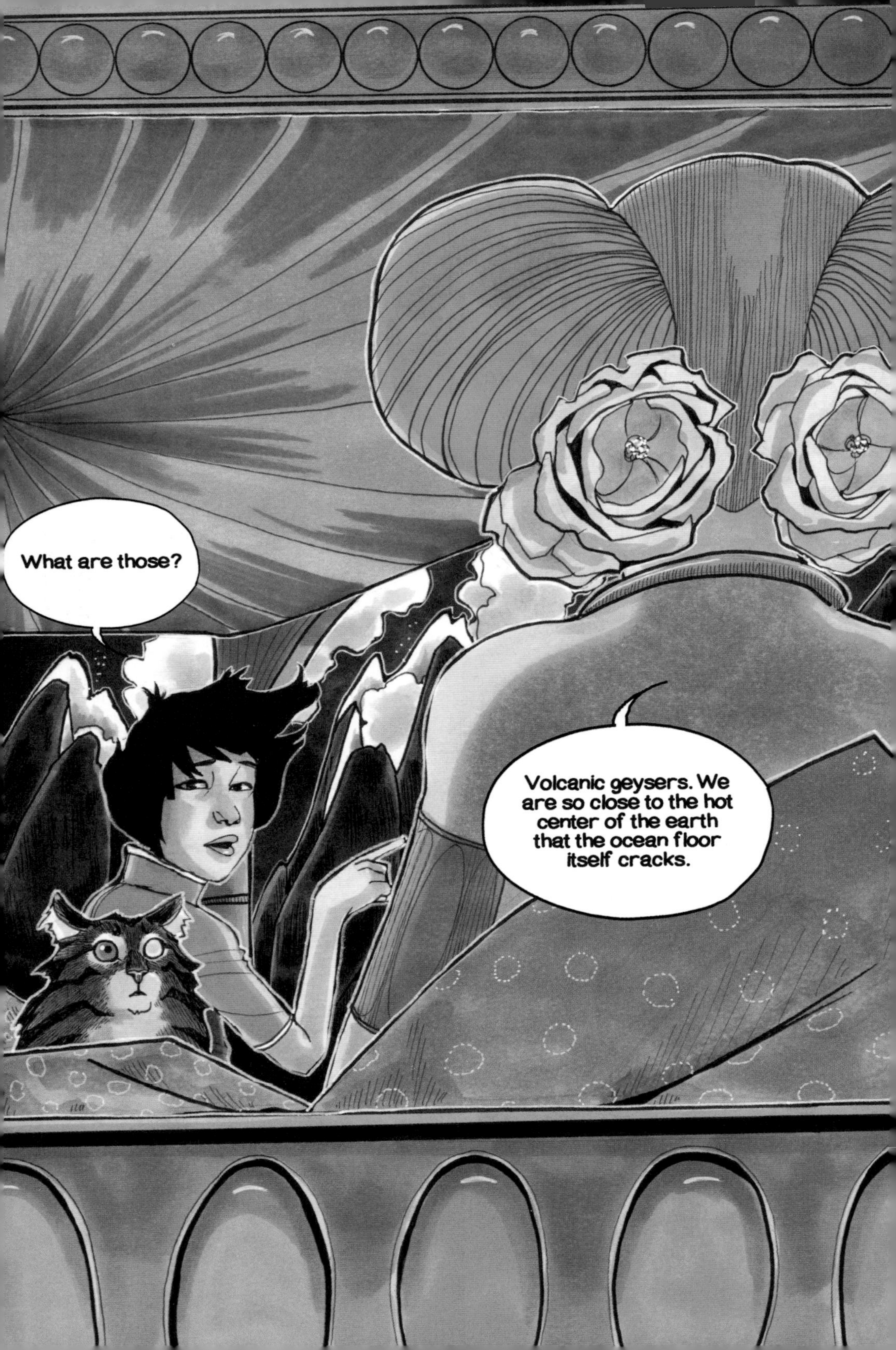
What are those?
Volcanic geysers. We are so close to the hot center of the earth that the ocean floor itself cracks.

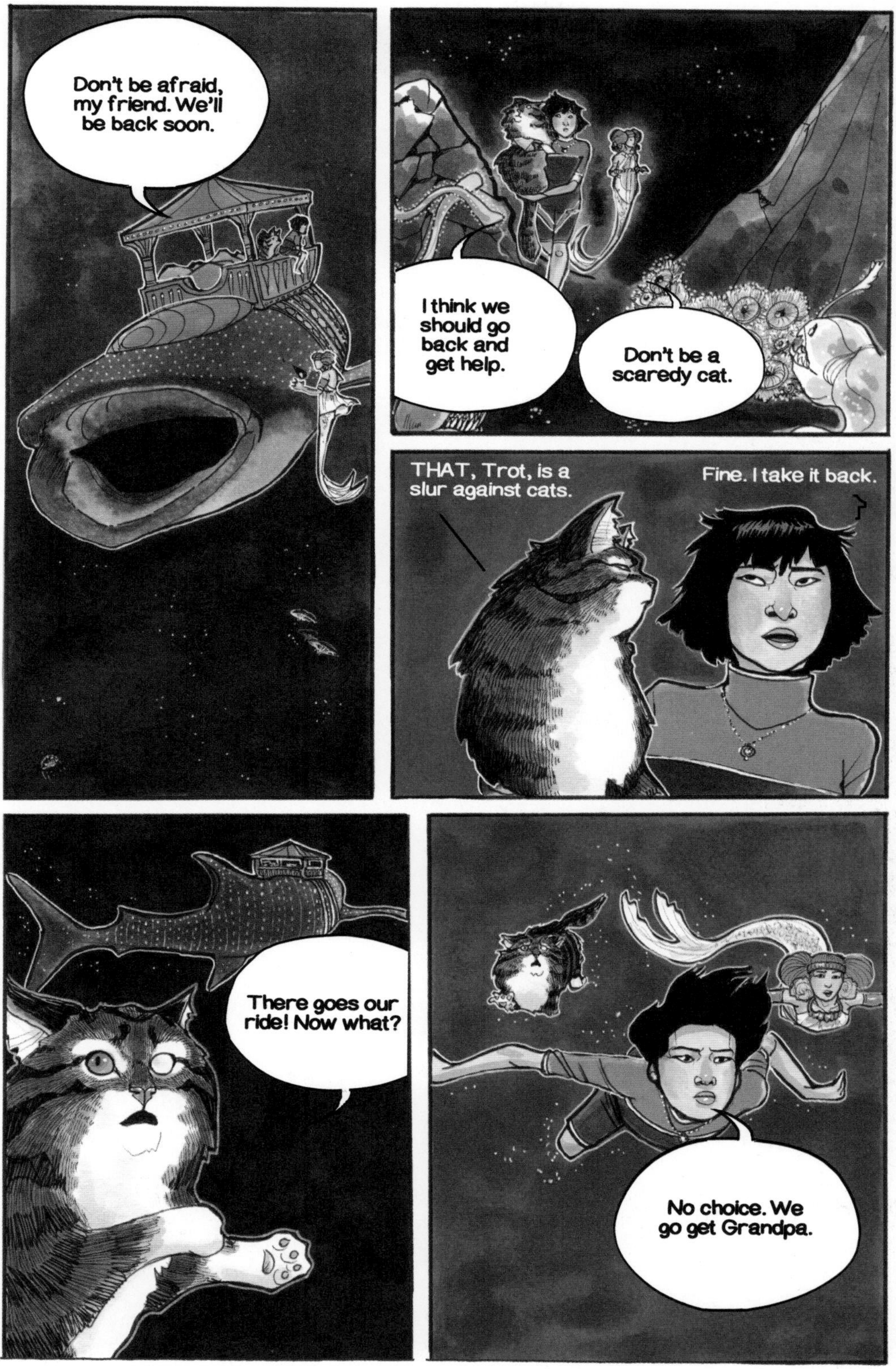
Don't be afraid, my friend. We'll be back soon.
I think we should go back and get help.
Don't be a scaredy cat.
THAT, Trot, is a slur against cats.
Fine. I take it back.
There goes our ride! Now what?
No choice. We go get Grandpa.

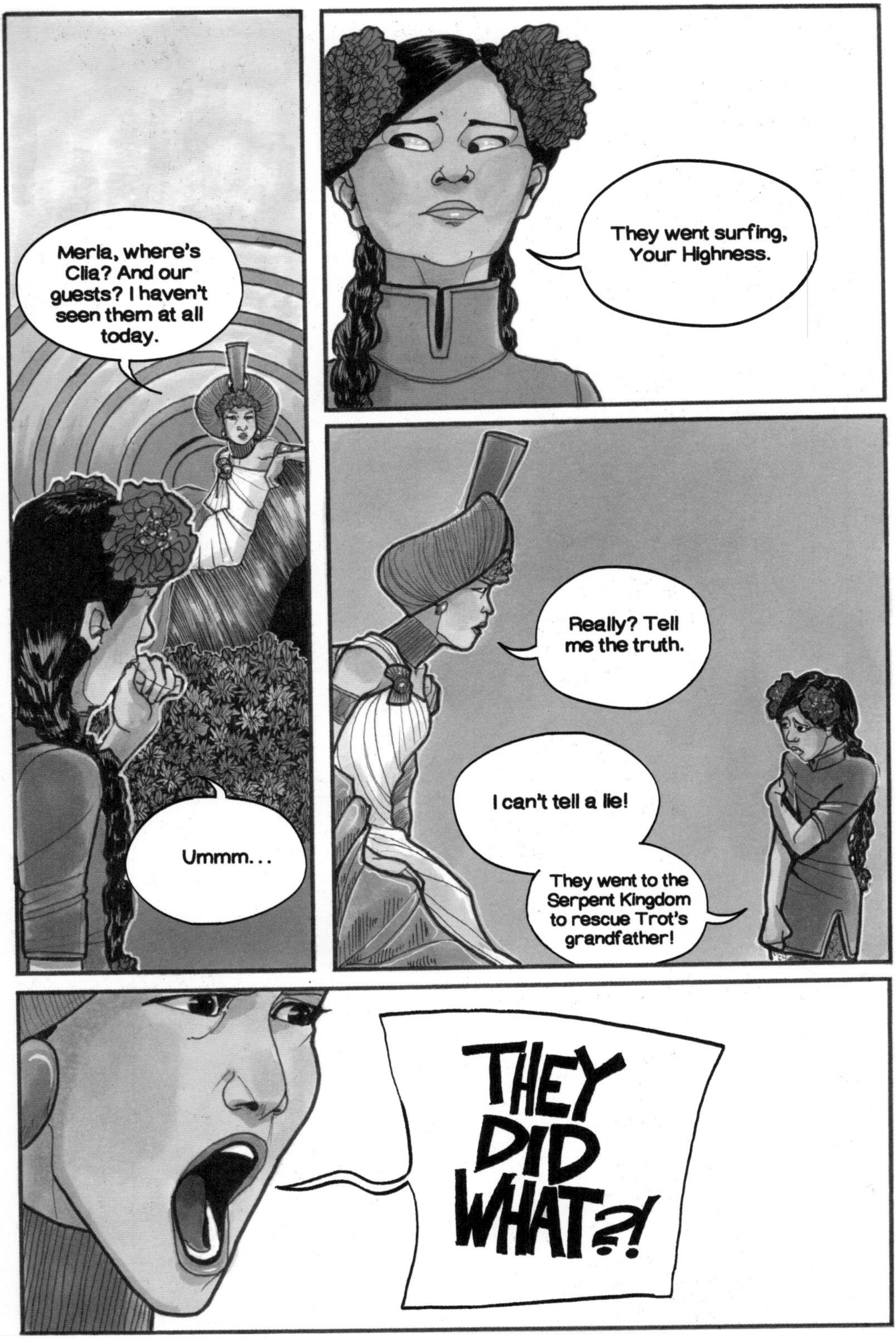
Merla, where's Clia? And our guests? I haven't seen them at all today.
Ummm...
They went surfing, Your Highness.
Really? Tell me the truth.
I can't tell a lie!
They went to the Serpent Kingdom to rescue Trot's grandfather!
THEY DID WHAT?!

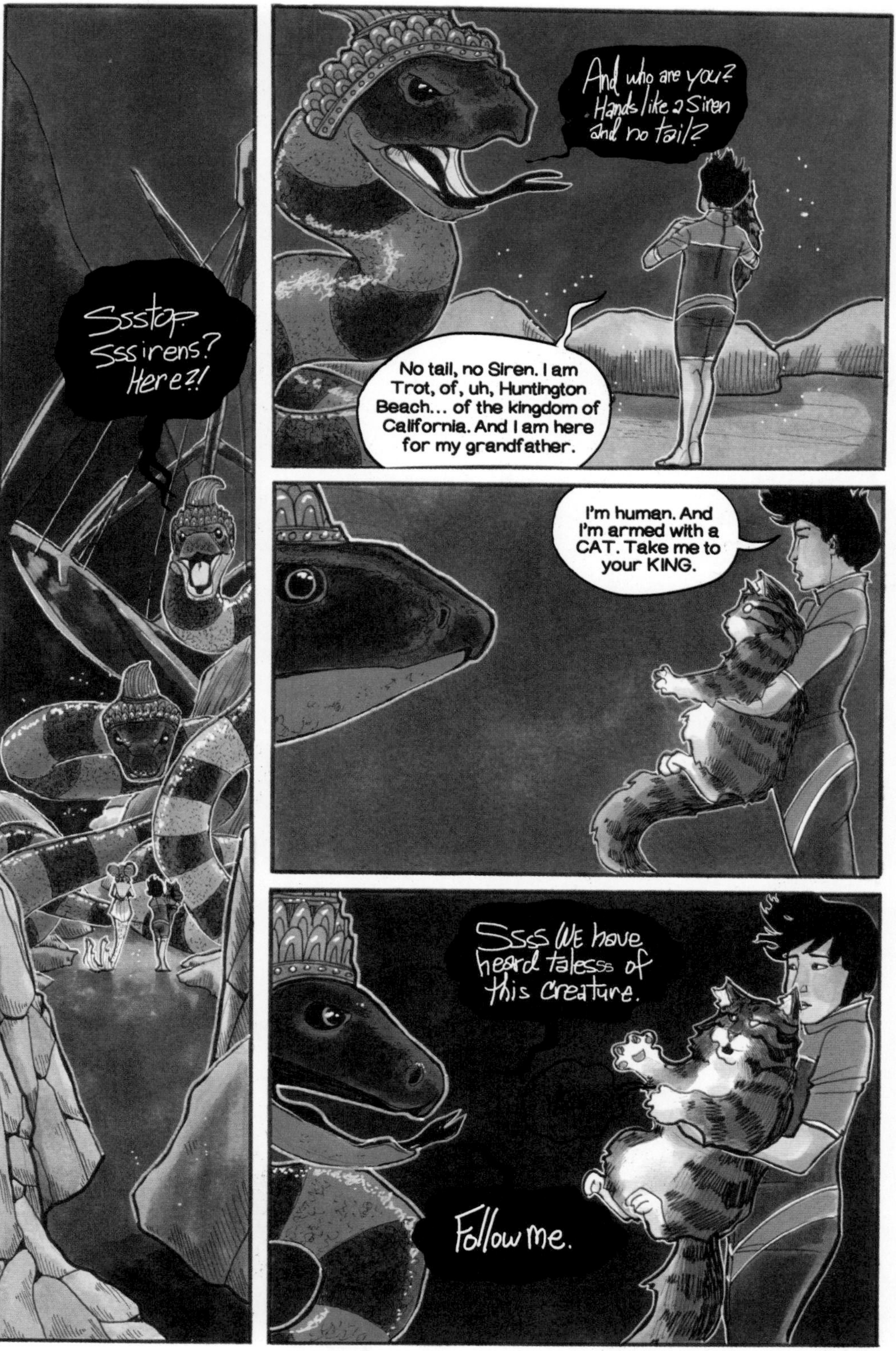
Ssstop. Sssirens? Here?!
And who are you? Hands like a Siren and no tail?
No tail, no Siren. I am Trot, of, uh, Huntington Beach... of the kingdom of California. And I am here for my grandfather.
I'm human. And I'm armed with a CAT. Take me to your KING.
Ssss We have heard talesss of this creature.
Follow me.

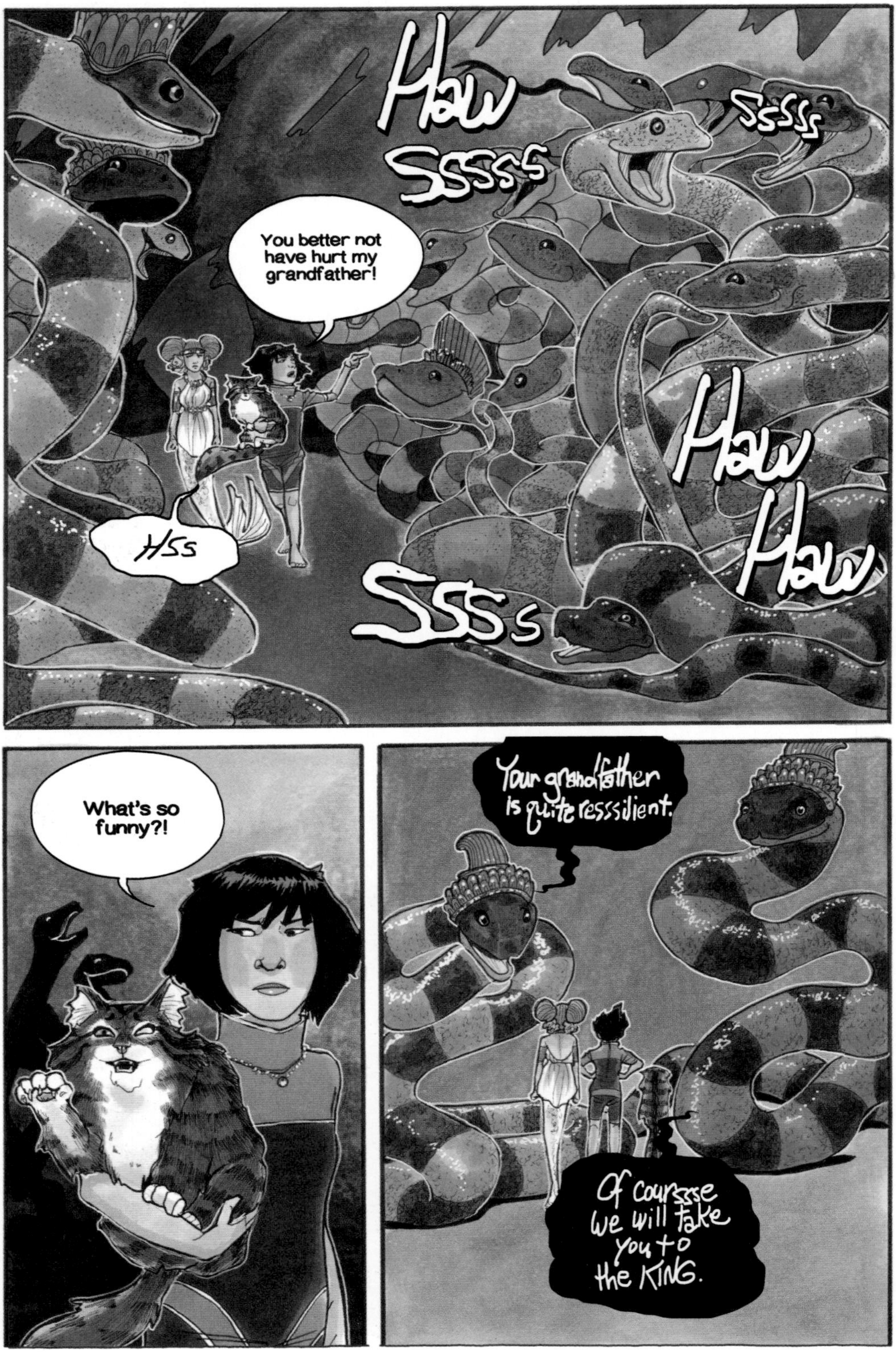
Haw
Sssss
Sssss
You better not have hurt my grandfather!
Haw
Haw
Haw
Hss
Ssss
What's so funny?!
Your grandfather is quite resssilient.
Of coursse we will take you to the KING.

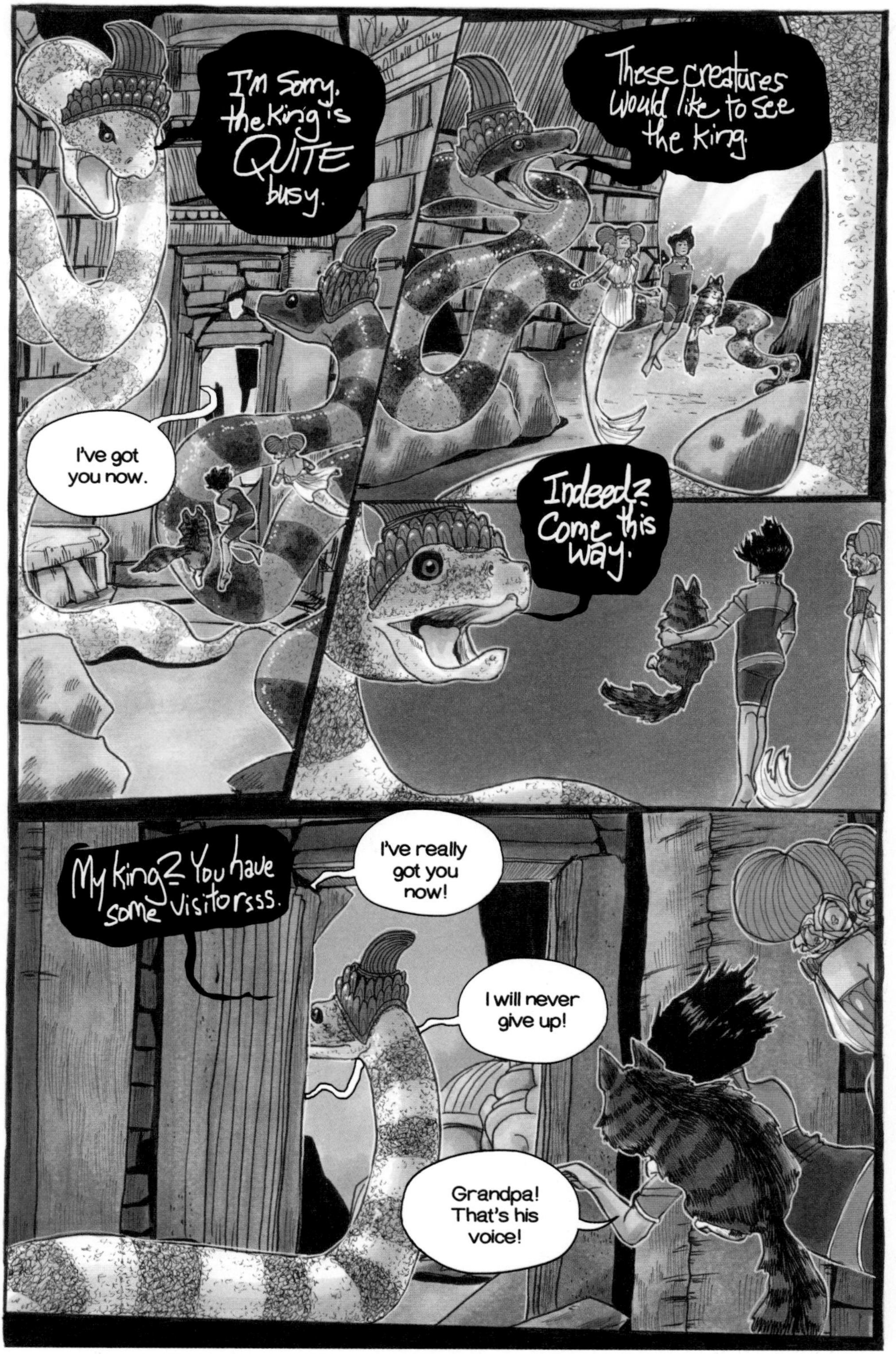
I'm Sorry, the king is QUITE busy.
I've got you now.
These creatures would like to see the king.
Indeed? Come this way.
My king? You have some visitorsss.
I've really got you now!
I will never give up!
Grandpa! That's his voice!

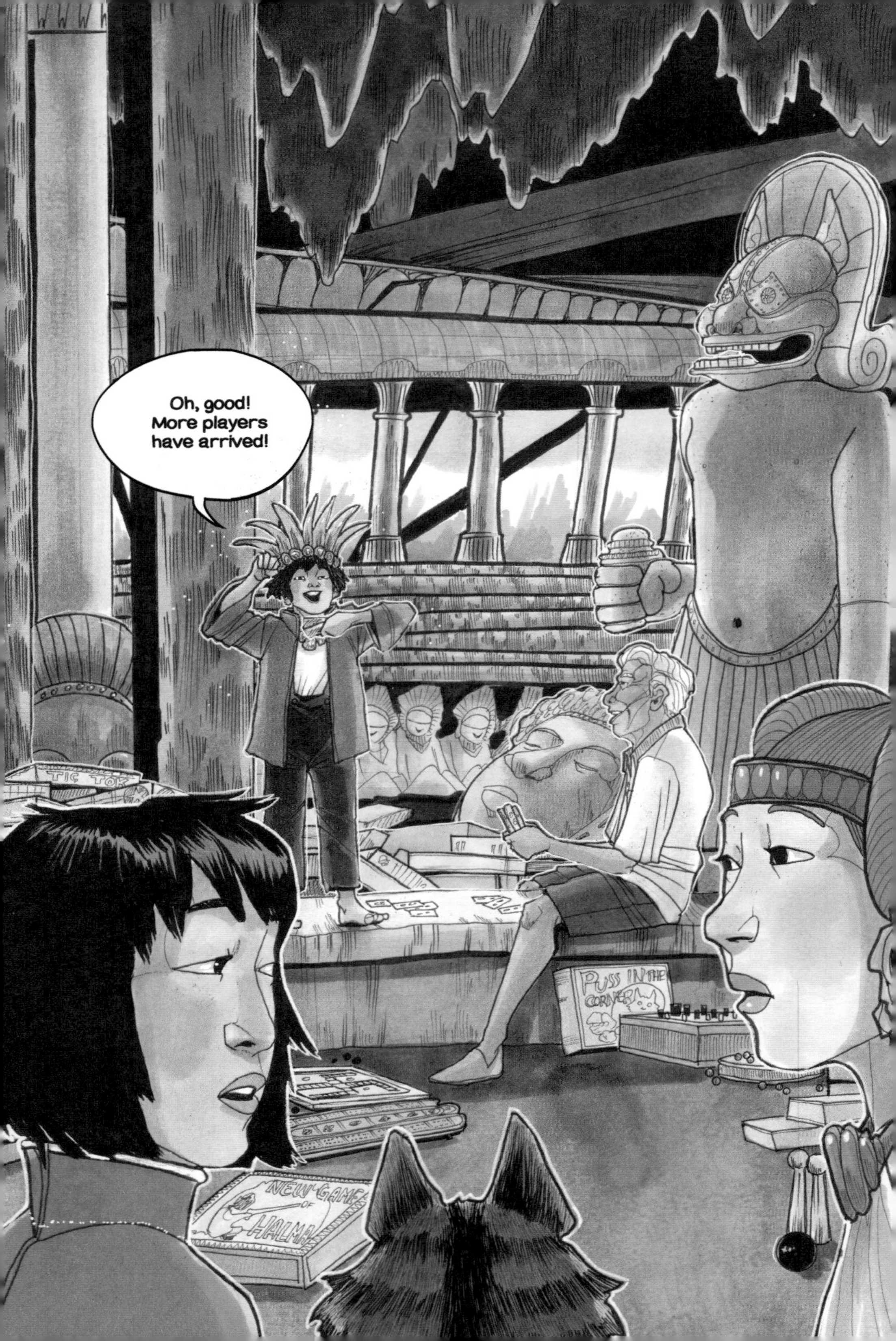
Oh, good! More players have arrived!
TIC TOK
PUSS IN THE CORNER
NEW GAME OF HALMA

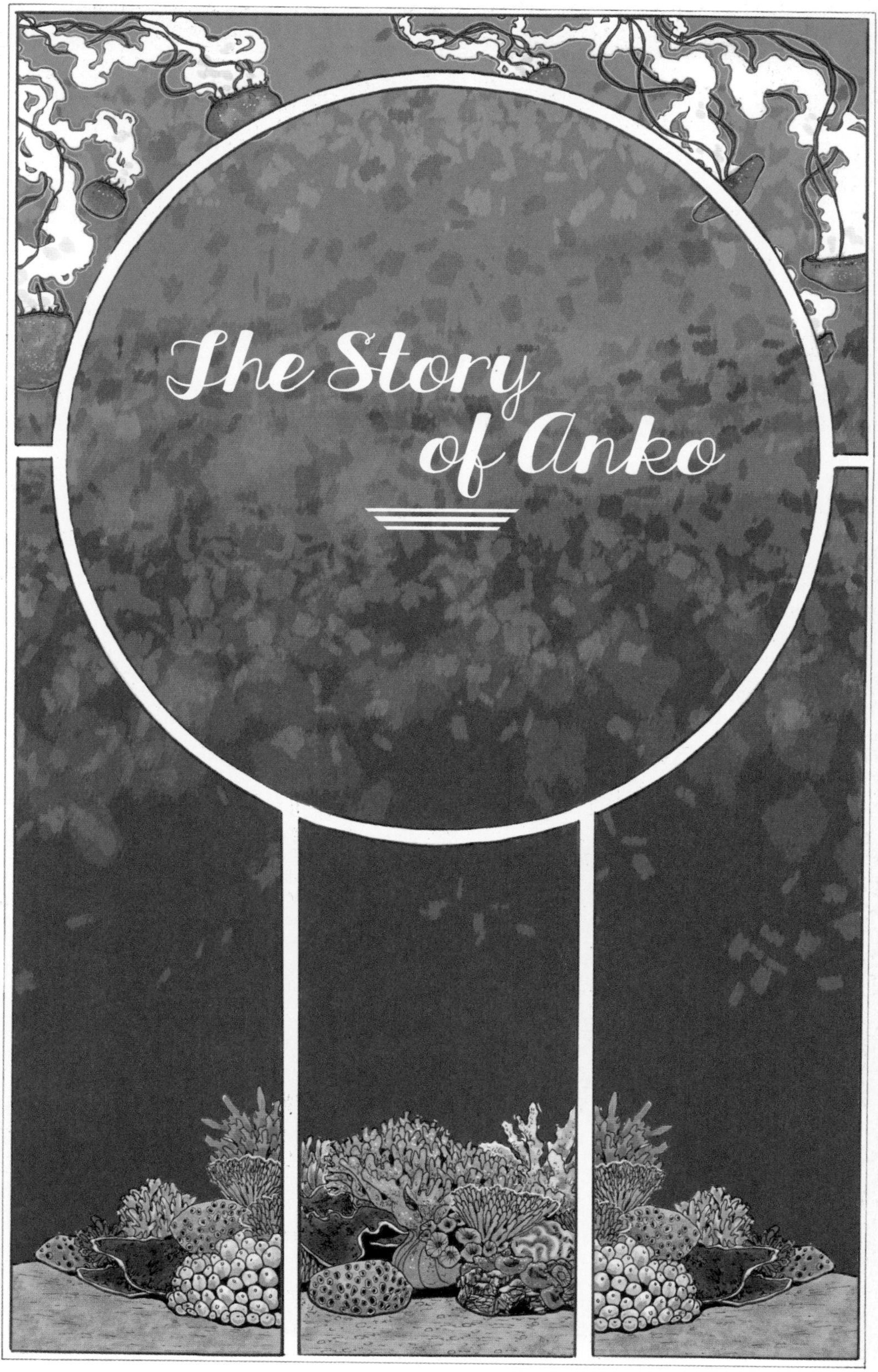
The Story
of Anko

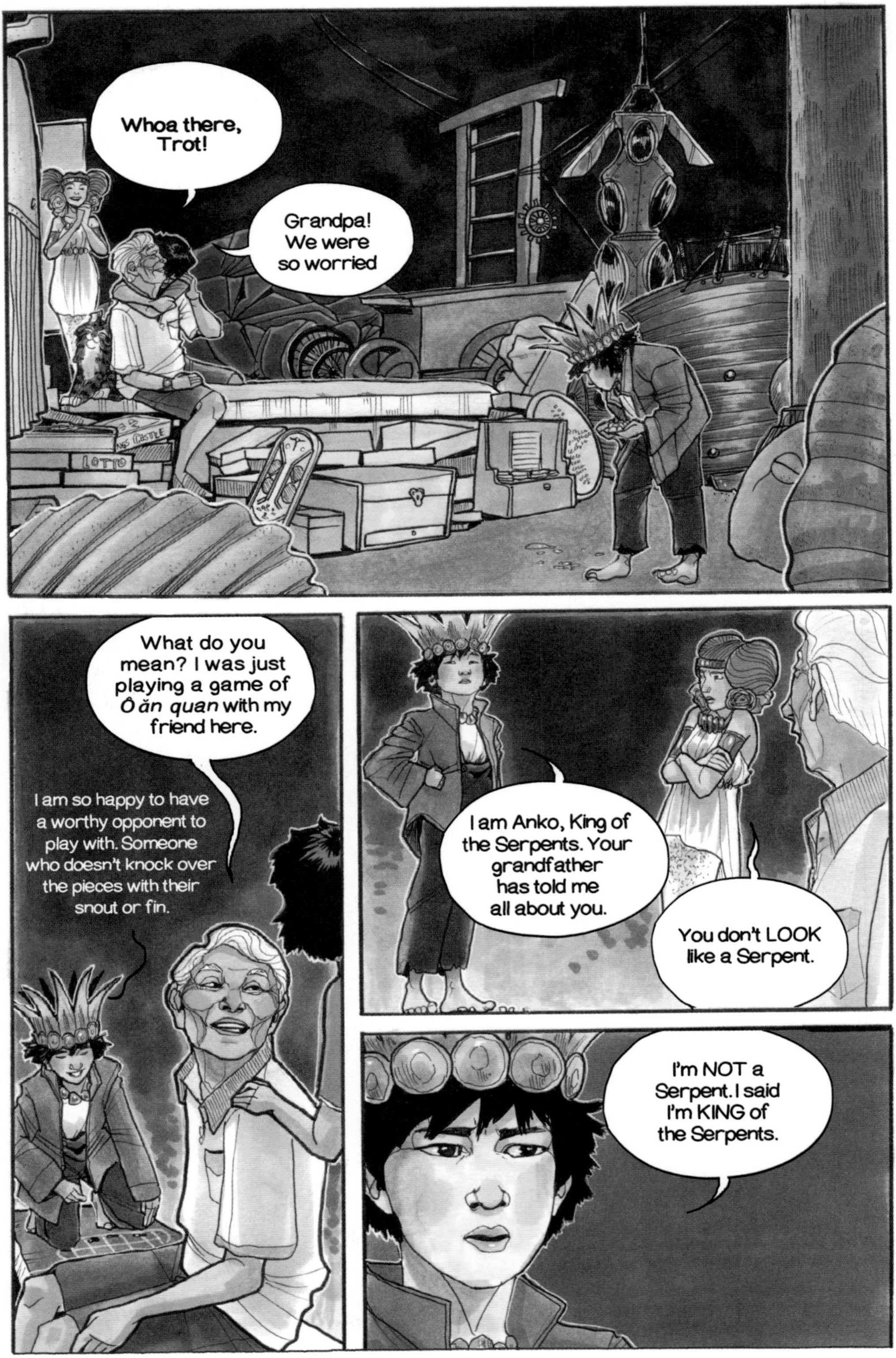
Whoa there, Trot!
Grandpa! We were so worried
LOTTO
What do you mean? I was just playing a game of *Ô ăn quan* with my friend here.
I am so happy to have a worthy opponent to play with. Someone who doesn't knock over the pieces with their snout or fin.
I am Anko, King of the Serpents. Your grandfather has told me all about you.
You don't LOOK like a Serpent.
I'm NOT a Serpent. I said I'm KING of the Serpents.

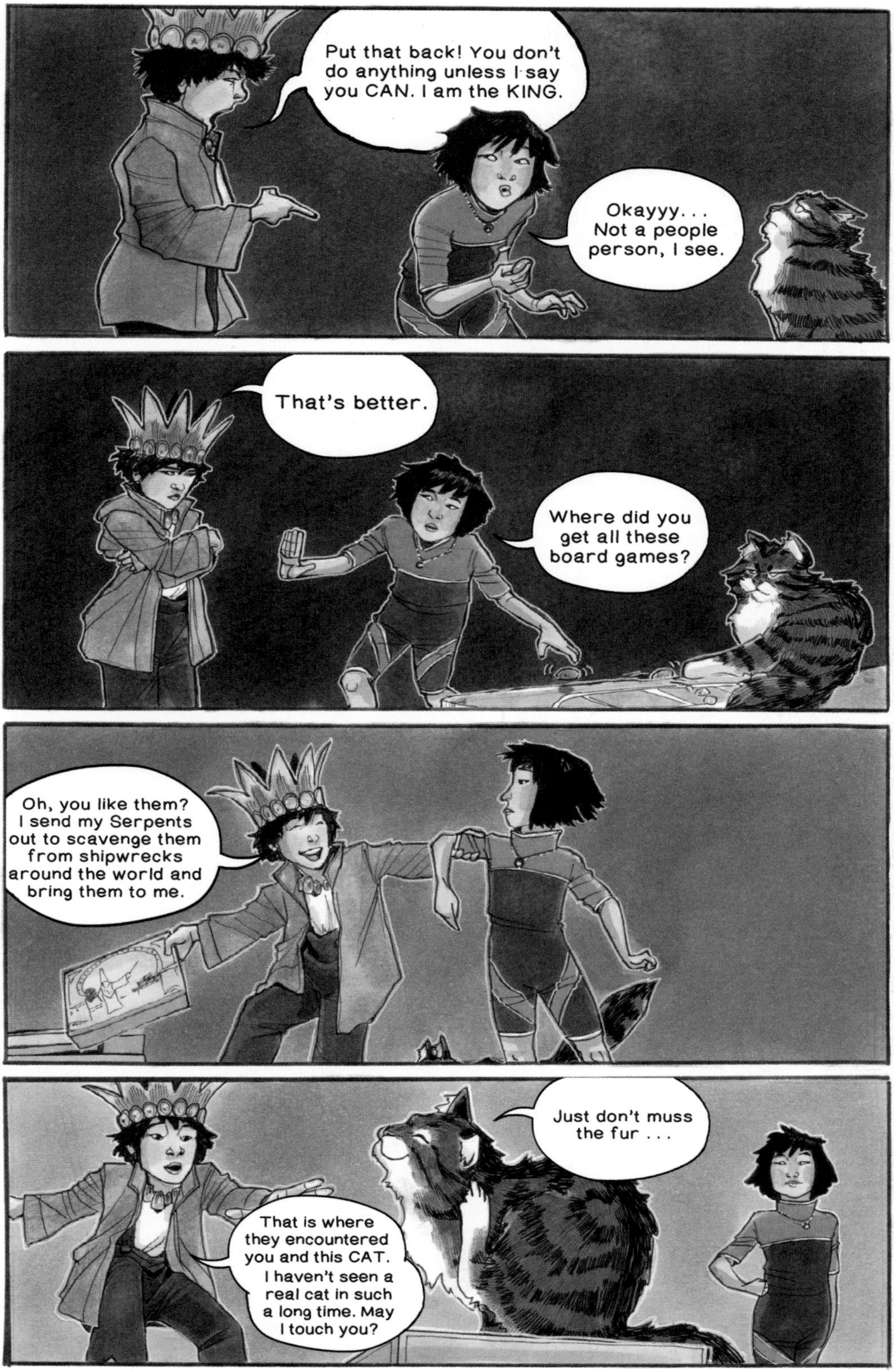
Put that back! You don't do anything unless I say you CAN. I am the KING.
Okayyy... Not a people person, I see.
That's better.
Where did you get all these board games?
Oh, you like them? I send my Serpents out to scavenge them from shipwrecks around the world and bring them to me.
That is where they encountered you and this CAT. I haven't seen a real cat in such a long time. May I touch you?
Just don't muss the fur . . .

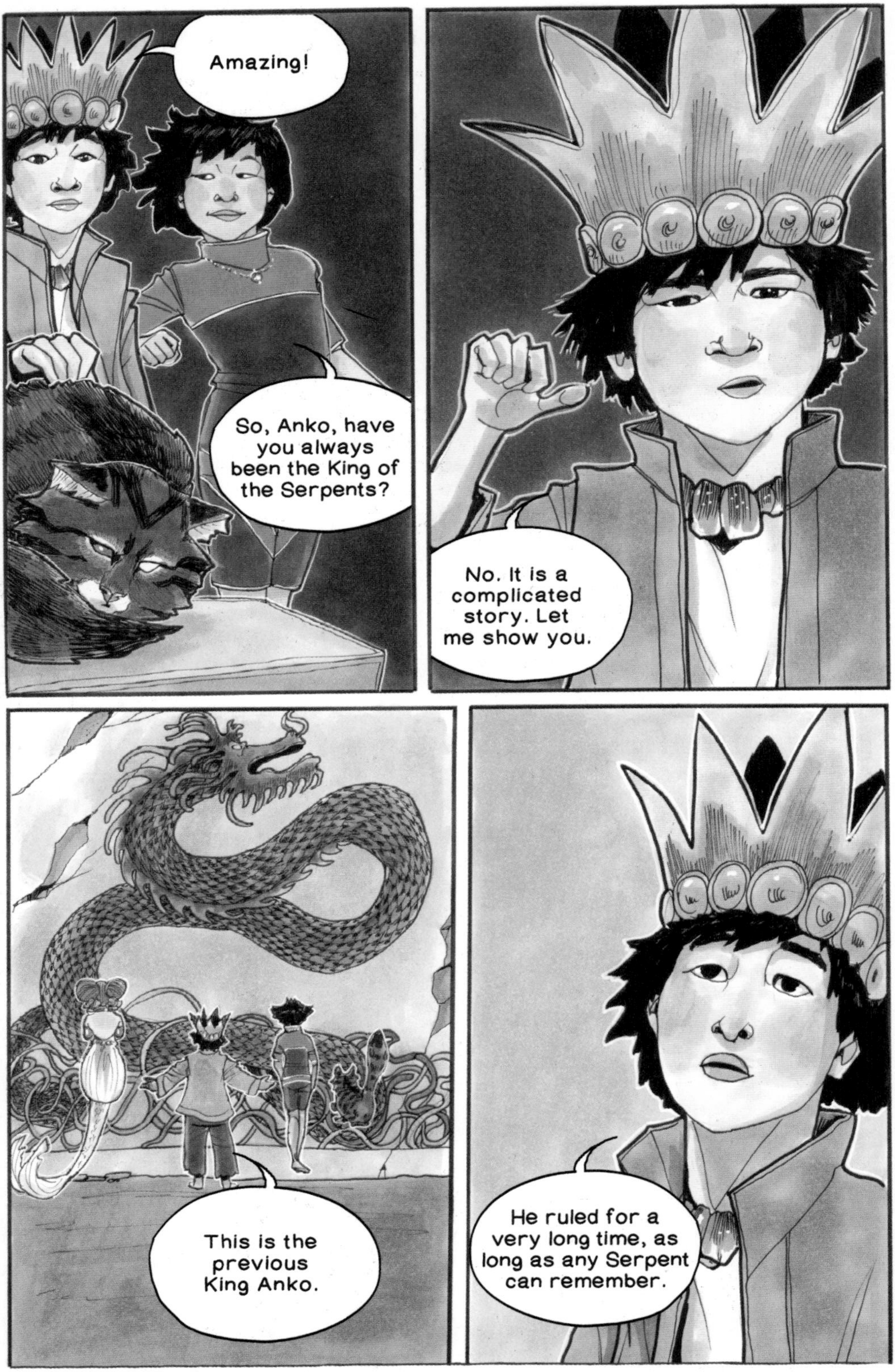
Amazing!
So, Anko, have you always been the King of the Serpents?
No. It is a complicated story. Let me show you.
This is the previous King Anko.
He ruled for a very long time, as long as any Serpent can remember.

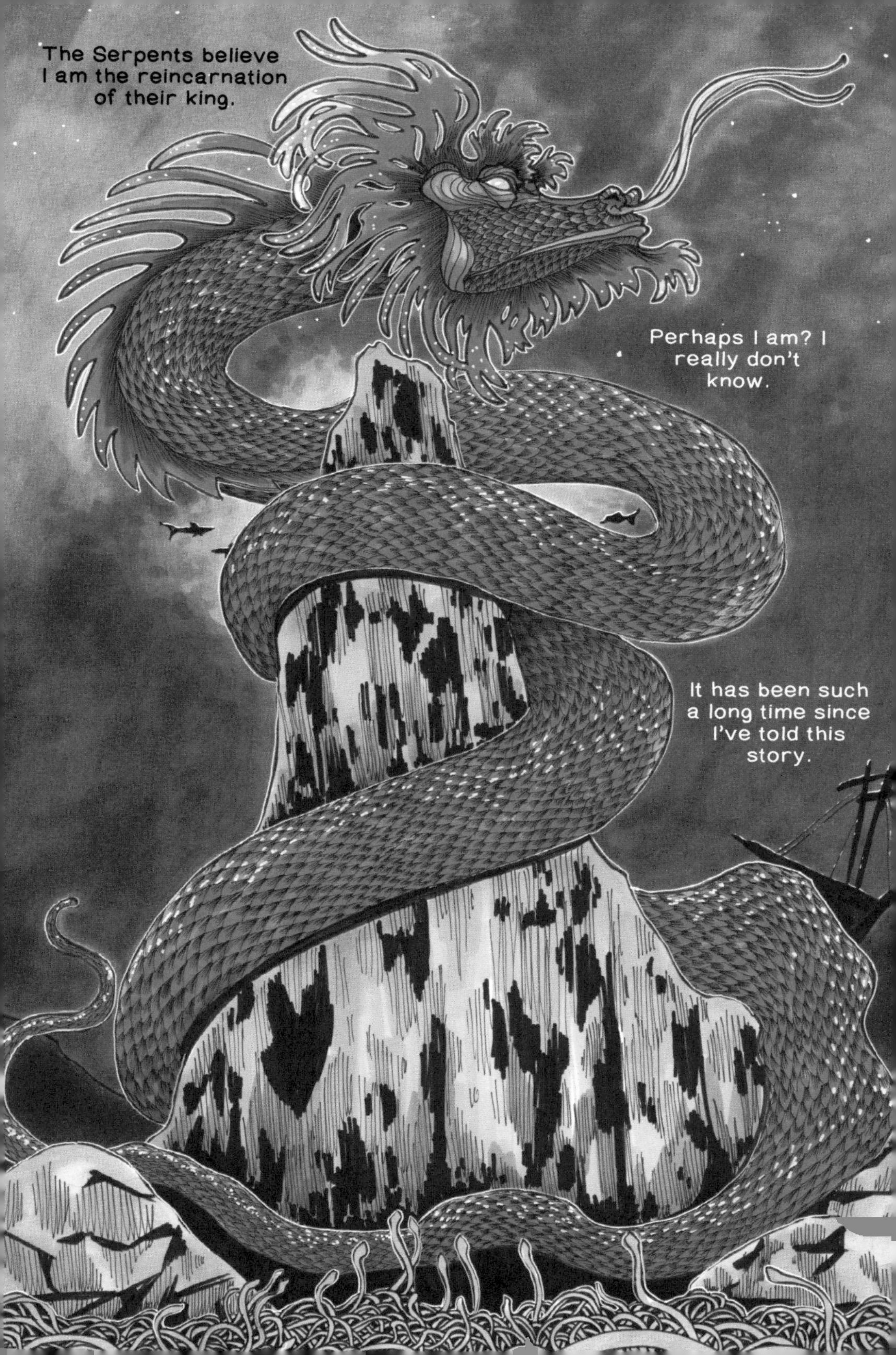
The Serpents believe I am the reincarnation of their king.
Perhaps I am? I really don't know.
It has been such a long time since I've told this story.

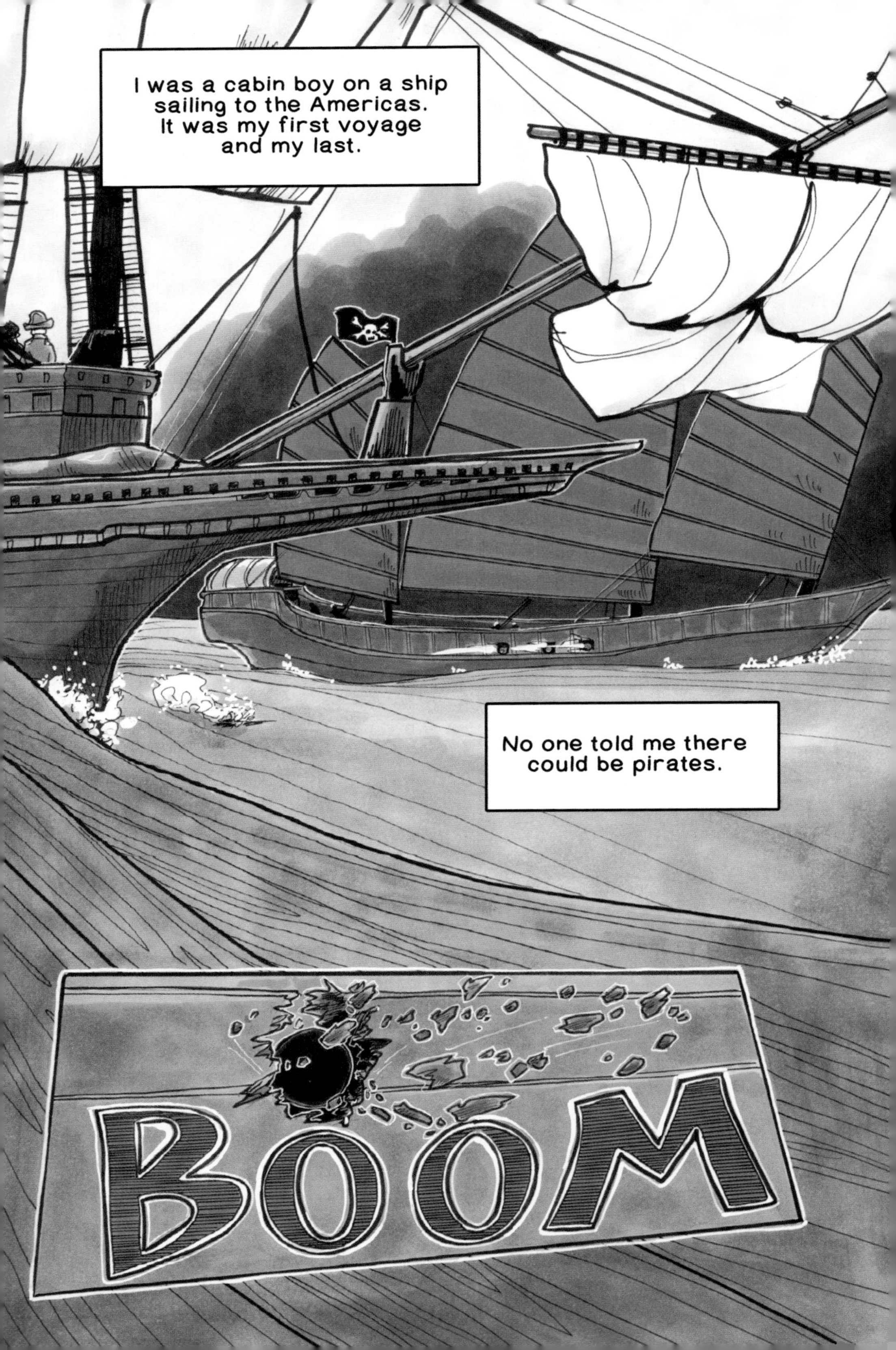
I was a cabin boy on a ship sailing to the Americas. It was my first voyage and my last.
No one told me there could be pirates.
BOOM

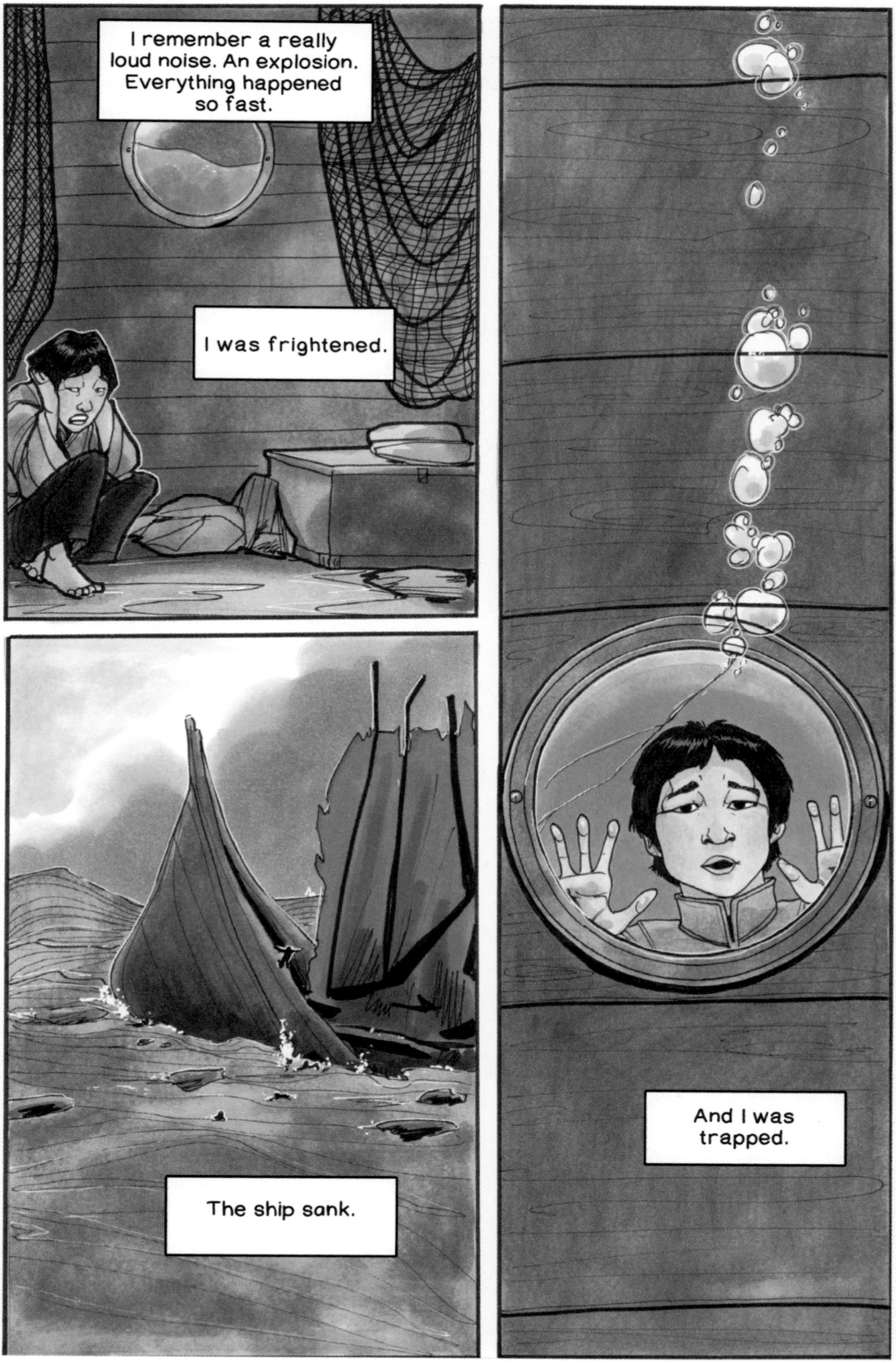
I remember a really loud noise. An explosion. Everything happened so fast.
I was frightened.
The ship sank.
And I was trapped.

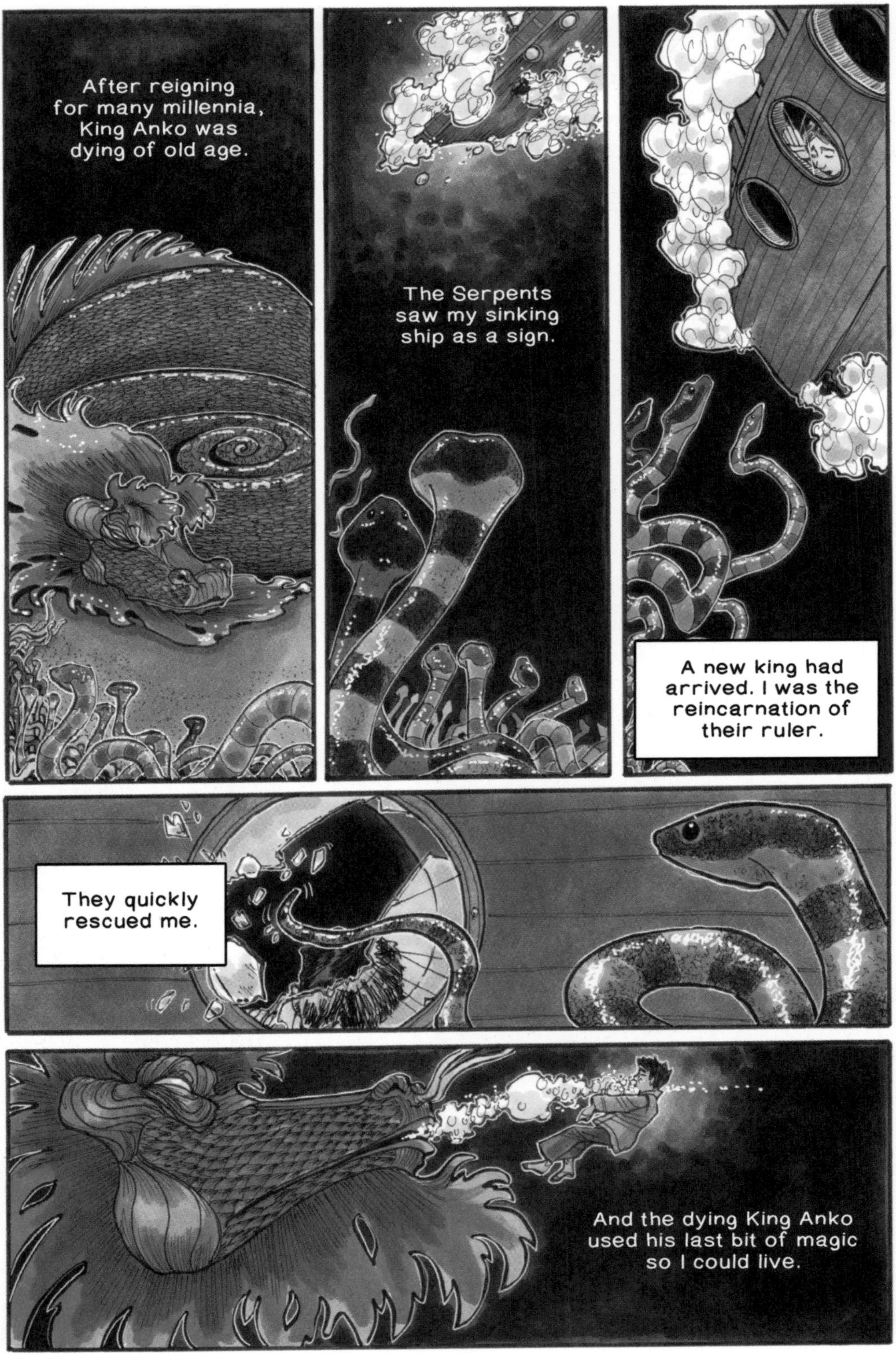
After reigning for many millennia, King Anko was dying of old age.
The Serpents saw my sinking ship as a sign.
A new king had arrived. I was the reincarnation of their ruler.
They quickly rescued me.
And the dying King Anko used his last bit of magic so I could live.

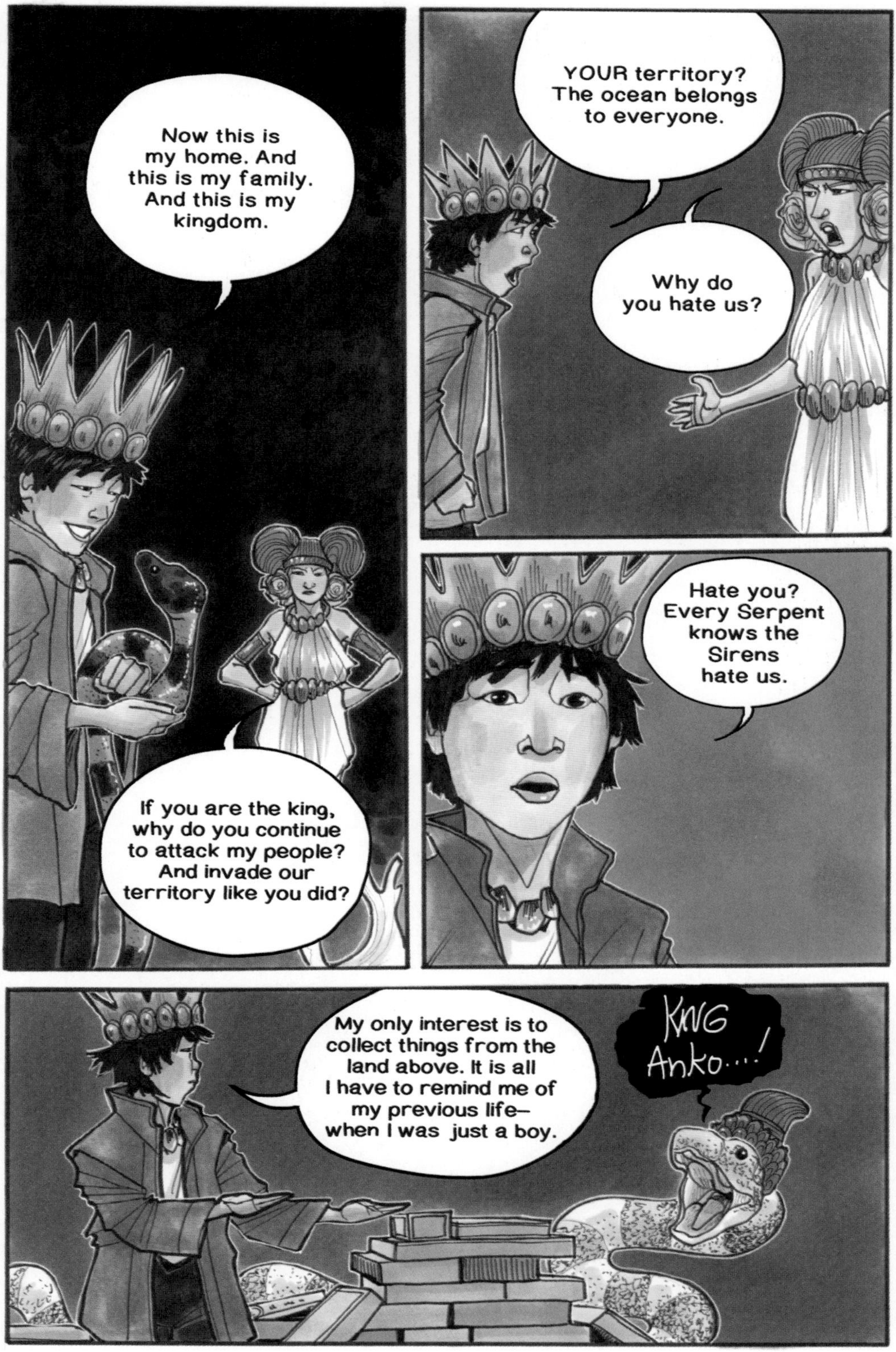
Now this is my home. And this is my family. And this is my kingdom.
If you are the king, why do you continue to attack my people? And invade our territory like you did?
YOUR territory? The ocean belongs to everyone.
Why do you hate us?
Hate you? Every Serpent knows the Sirens hate us.
My only interest is to collect things from the land above. It is all I have to remind me of my previous life— when I was just a boy.
KING Anko...!

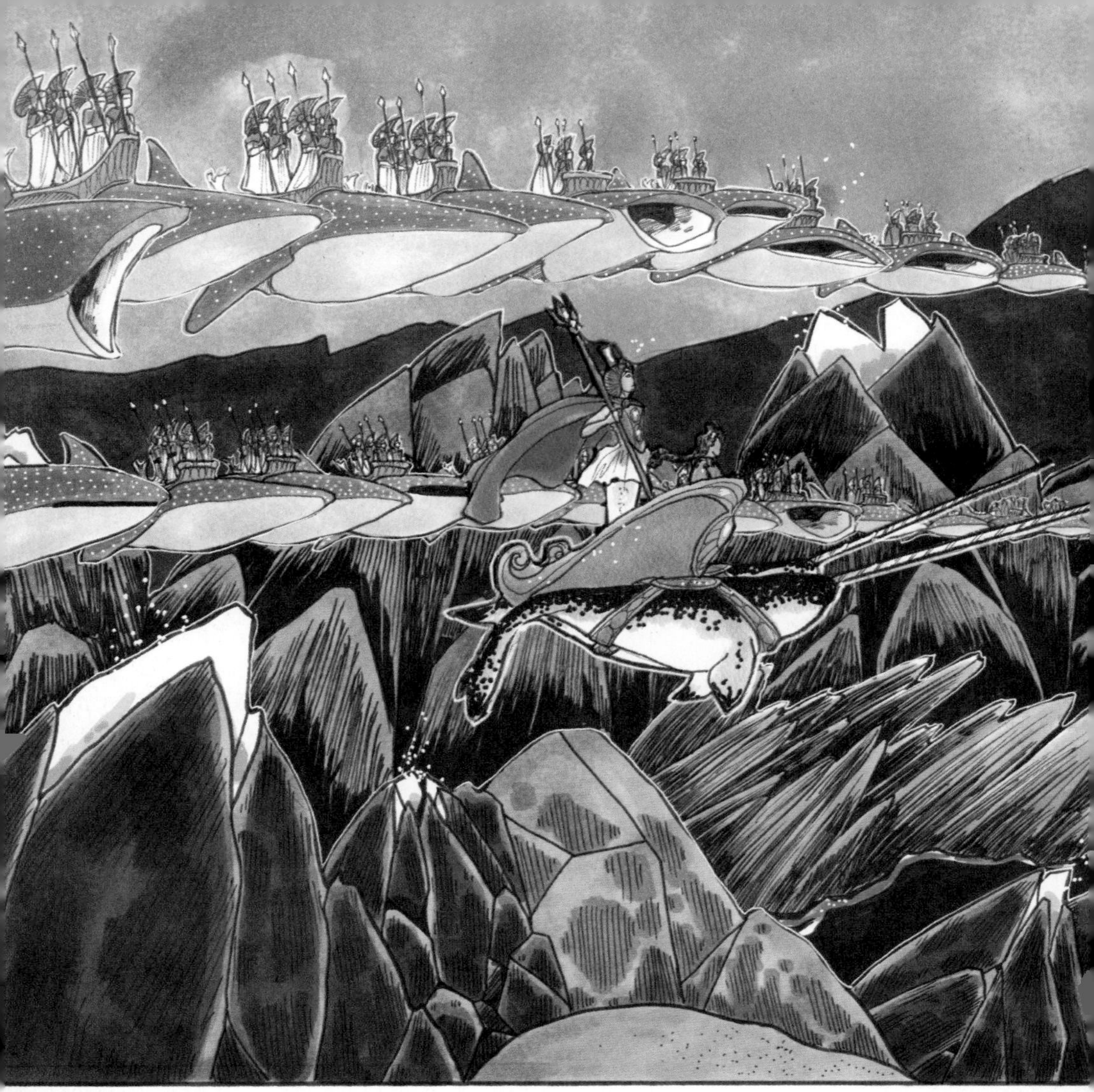

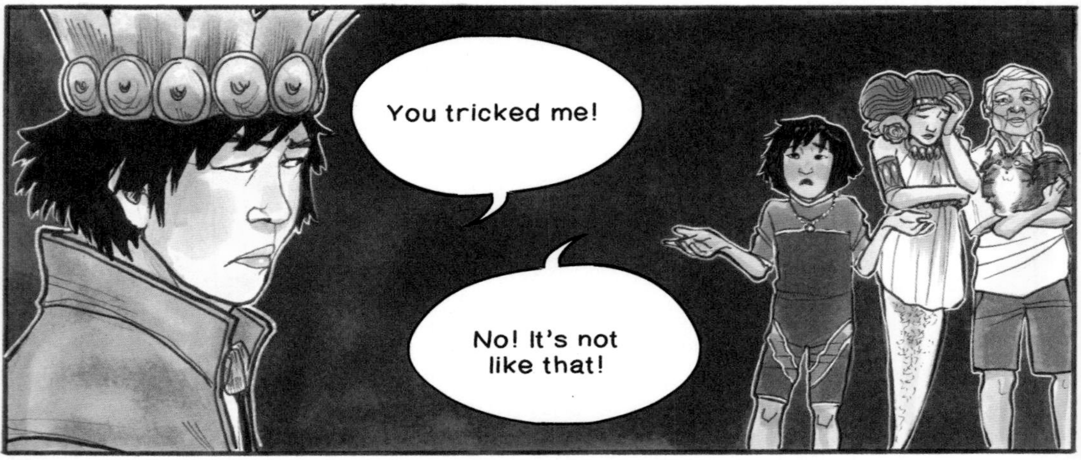
You tricked me!
No! It's not like that!

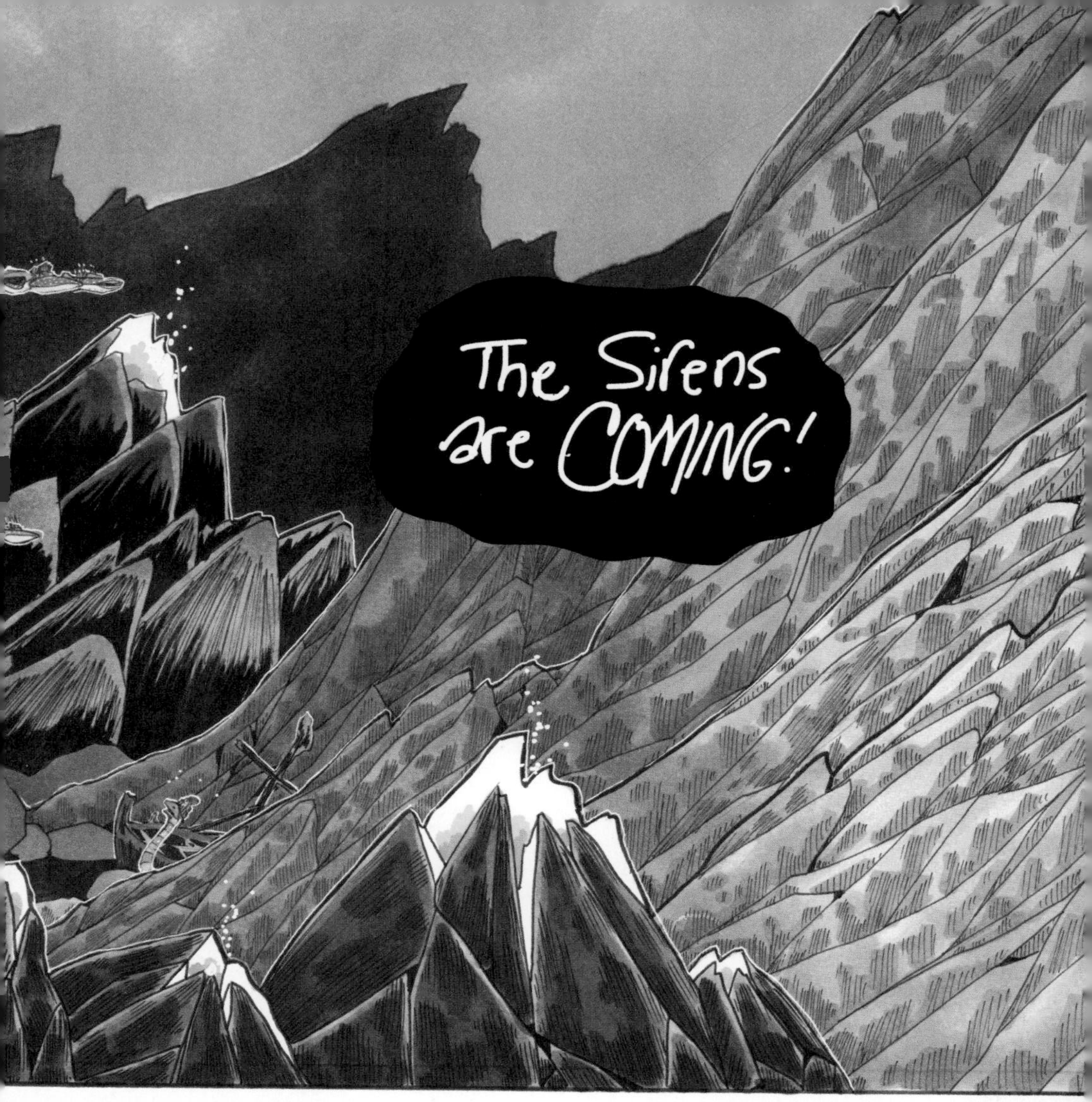
The Sirens are COMING!

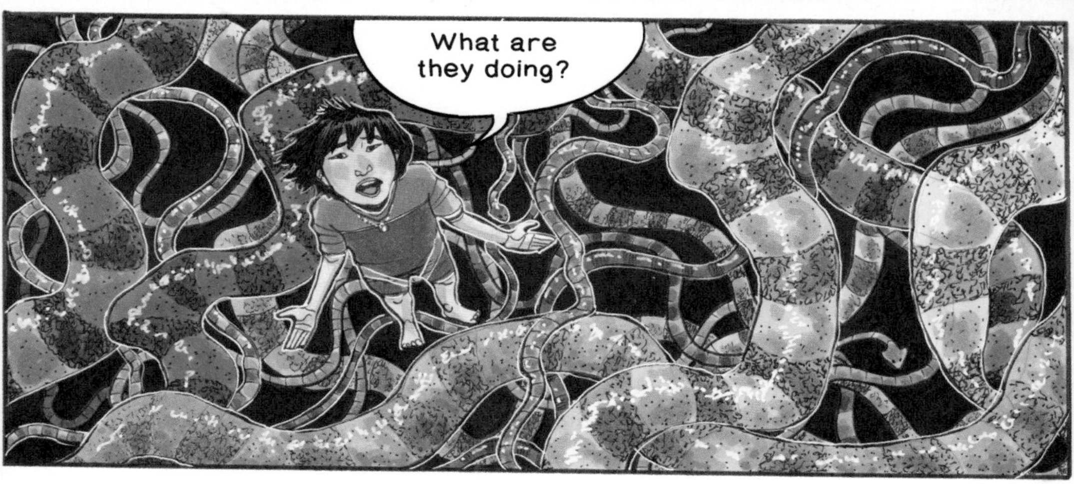
What are they doing?

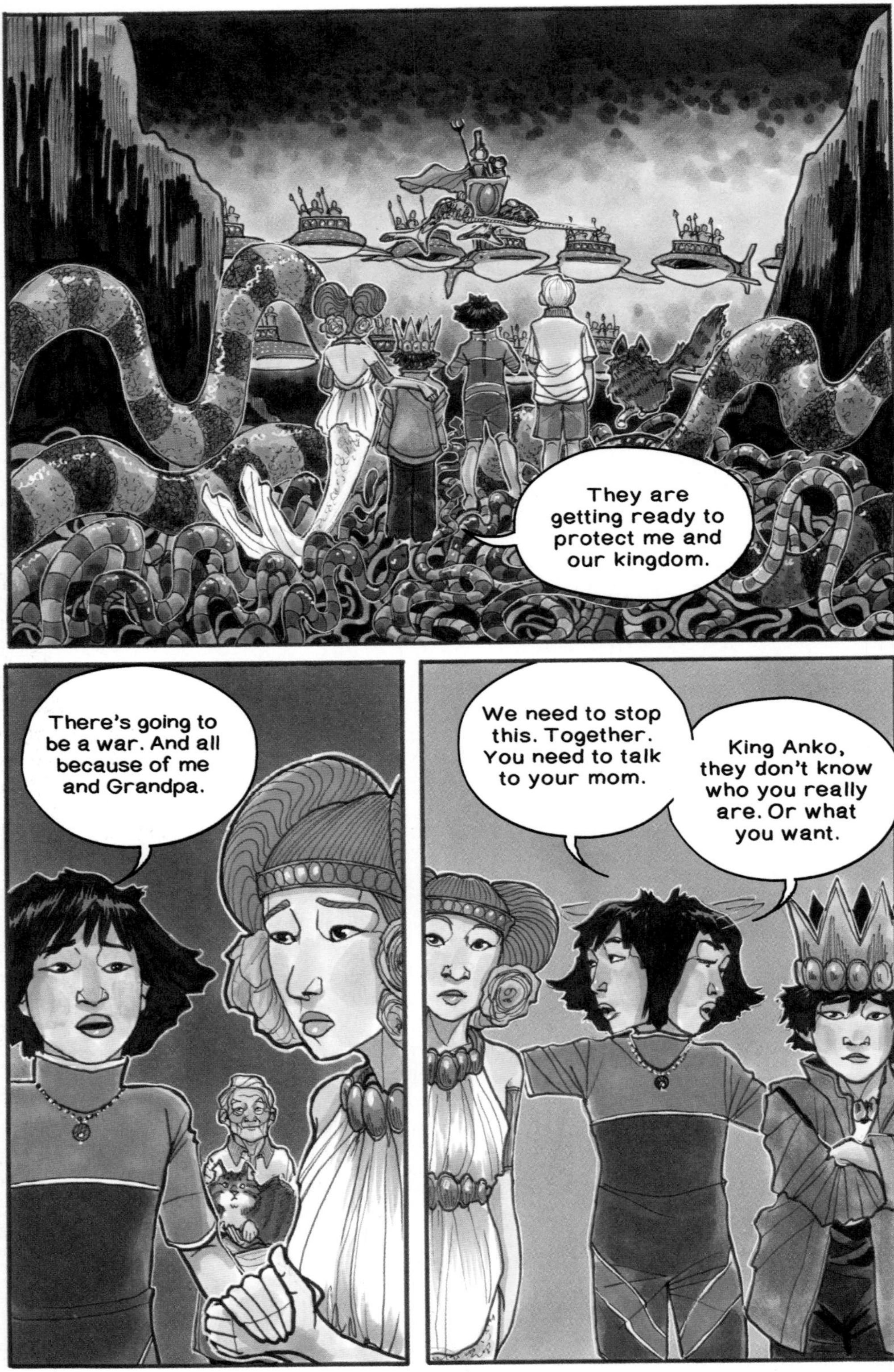
They are getting ready to protect me and our kingdom.
There's going to be a war. And all because of me and Grandpa.
We need to stop this. Together. You need to talk to your mom.
King Anko, they don't know who you really are. Or what you want.

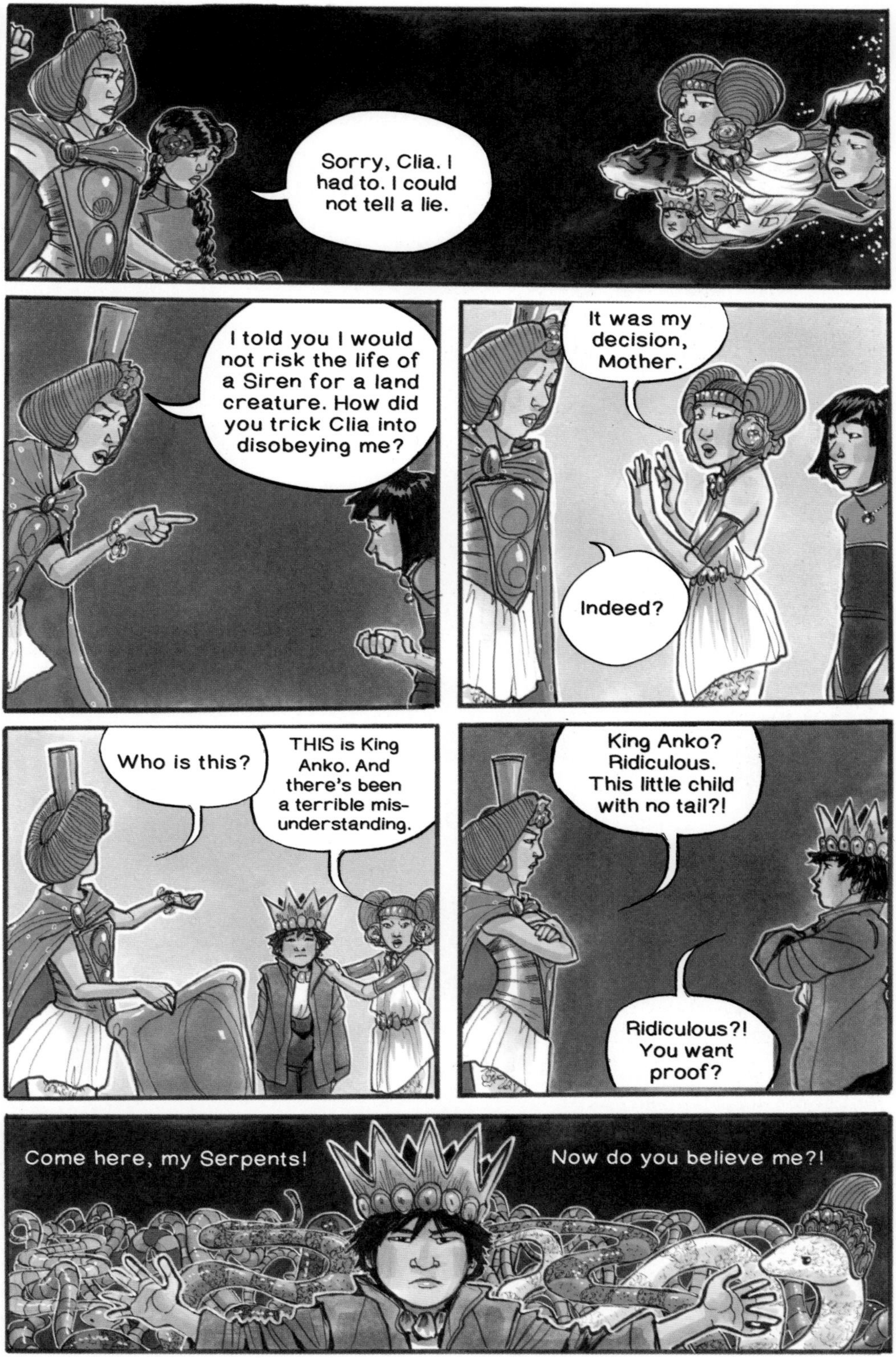

Sorry, Clia. I had to. I could not tell a lie.
I told you I would not risk the life of a Siren for a land creature. How did you trick Clia into disobeying me?
It was my decision, Mother.
Indeed?
Who is this?
THIS is King Anko. And there's been a terrible mis-understanding.
King Anko? Ridiculous. This little child with no tail?!
Ridiculous?! You want proof?
Come here, my Serpents!
Now do you believe me?!

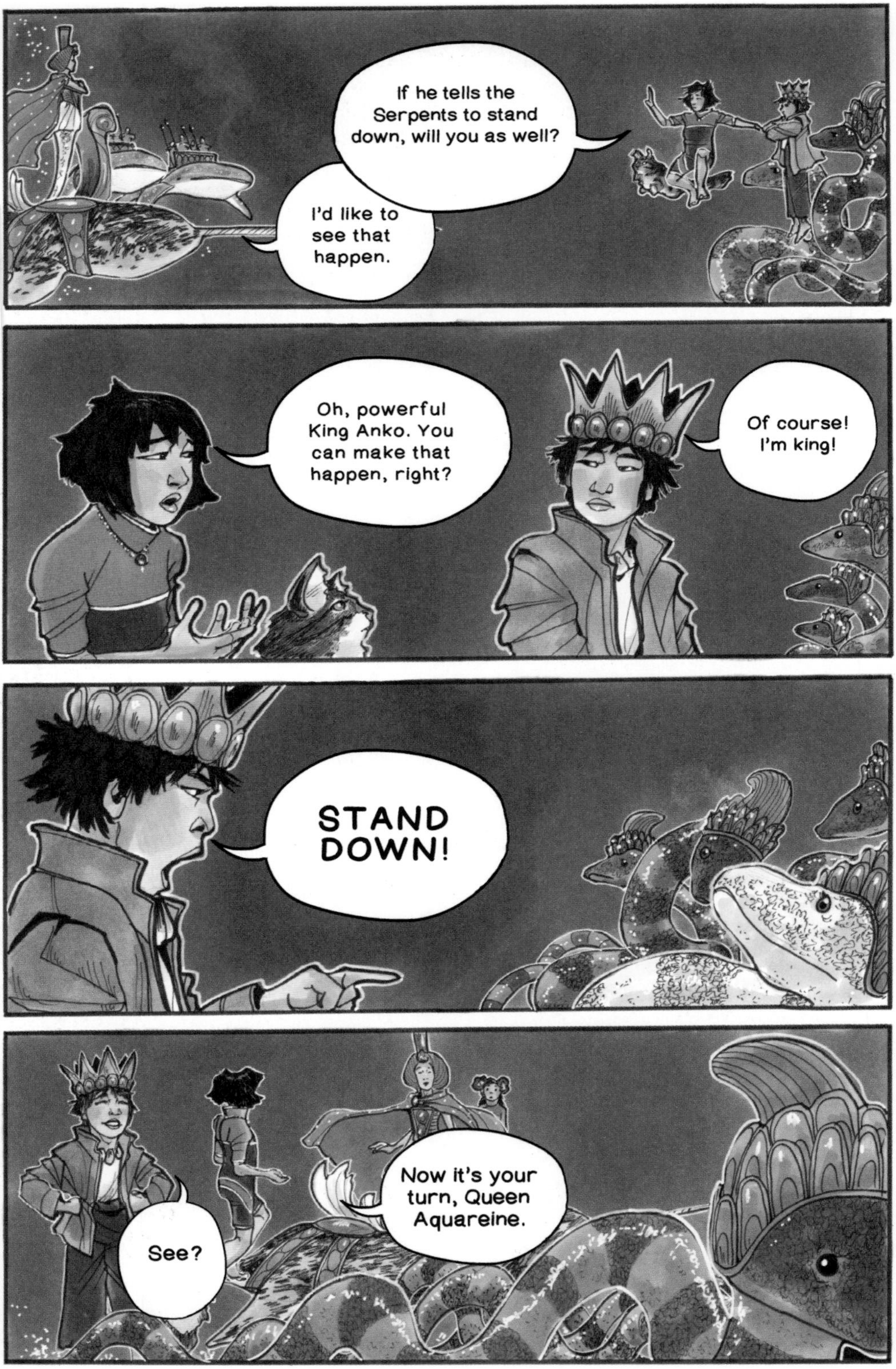
If he tells the Serpents to stand down, will you as well?
I'd like to see that happen.
Oh, powerful King Anko. You can make that happen, right?
Of course! I'm king!
STAND DOWN!
See?
Now it's your turn, Queen Aquareine.

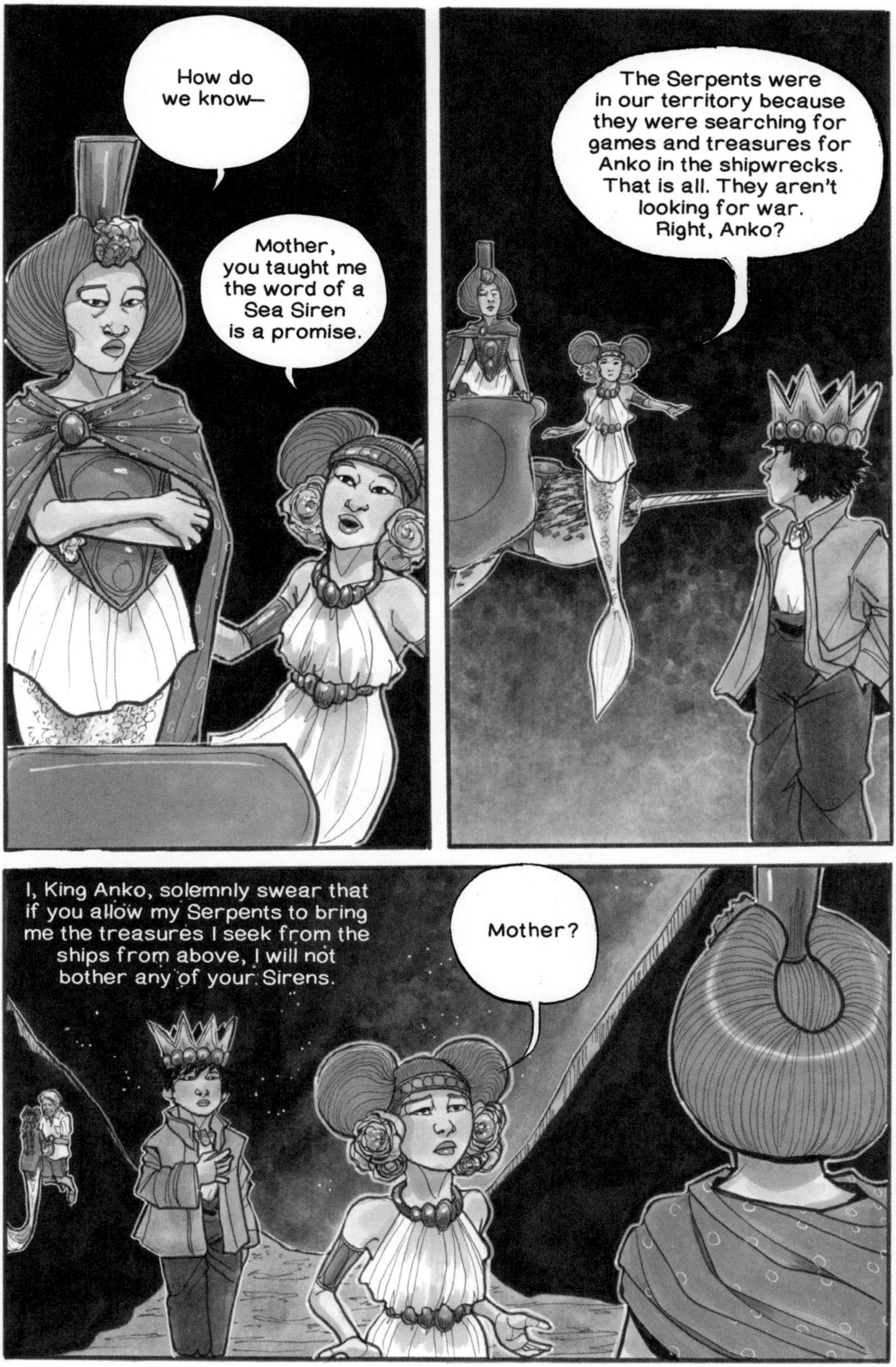

How do we know—
Mother, you taught me the word of a Sea Siren is a promise.
The Serpents were in our territory because they were searching for games and treasures for Anko in the shipwrecks. That is all. They aren't looking for war. Right, Anko?
I, King Anko, solemnly swear that if you allow my Serpents to bring me the treasures I seek from the ships from above, I will not bother any of your Sirens.
Mother?

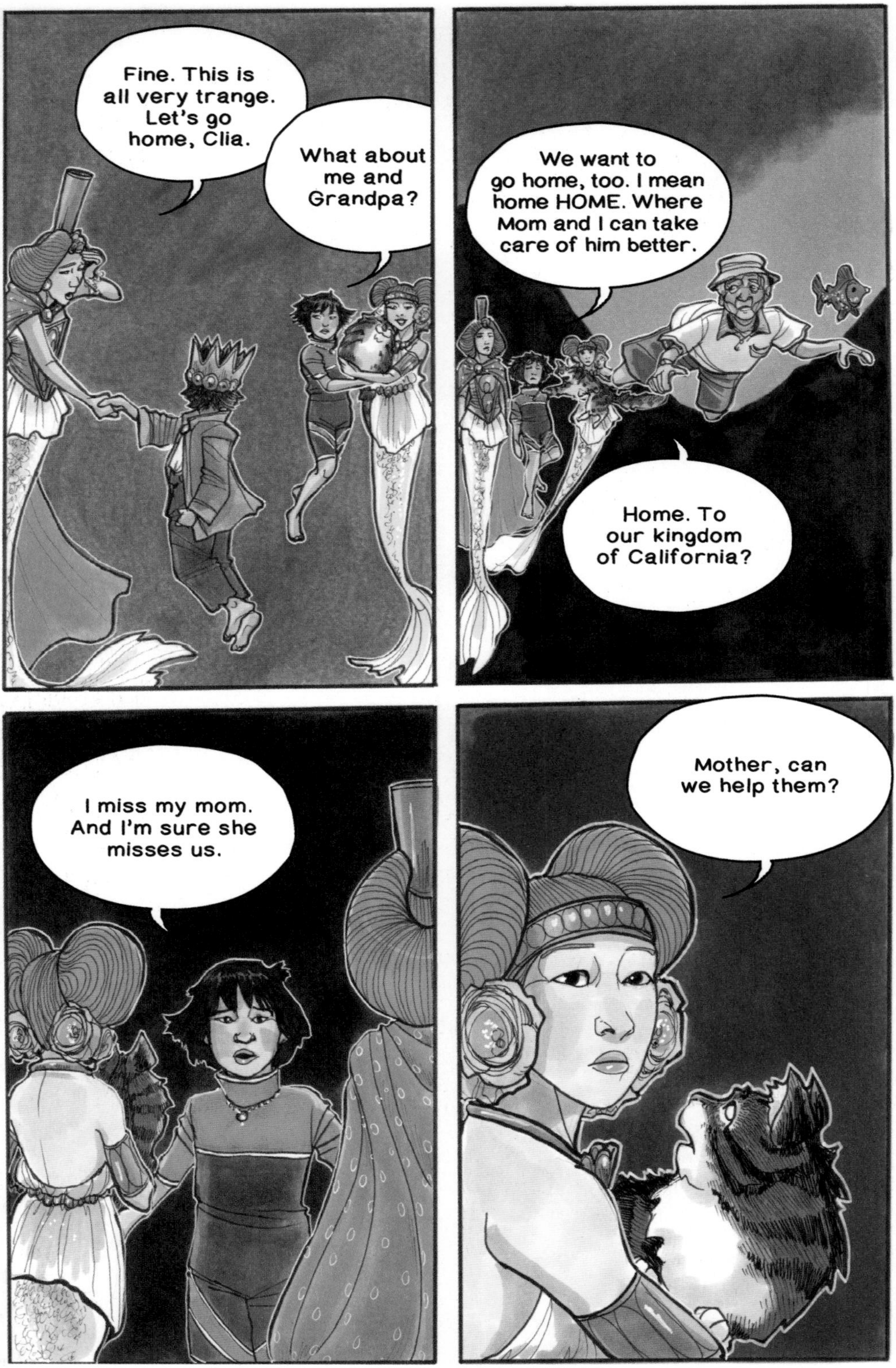
Fine. This is all very trange. Let's go home, Clia.
What about me and Grandpa?
We want to go home, too. I mean home HOME. Where Mom and I can take care of him better.
Home. To our kingdom of California?
I miss my mom. And I'm sure she misses us.
Mother, can we help them?

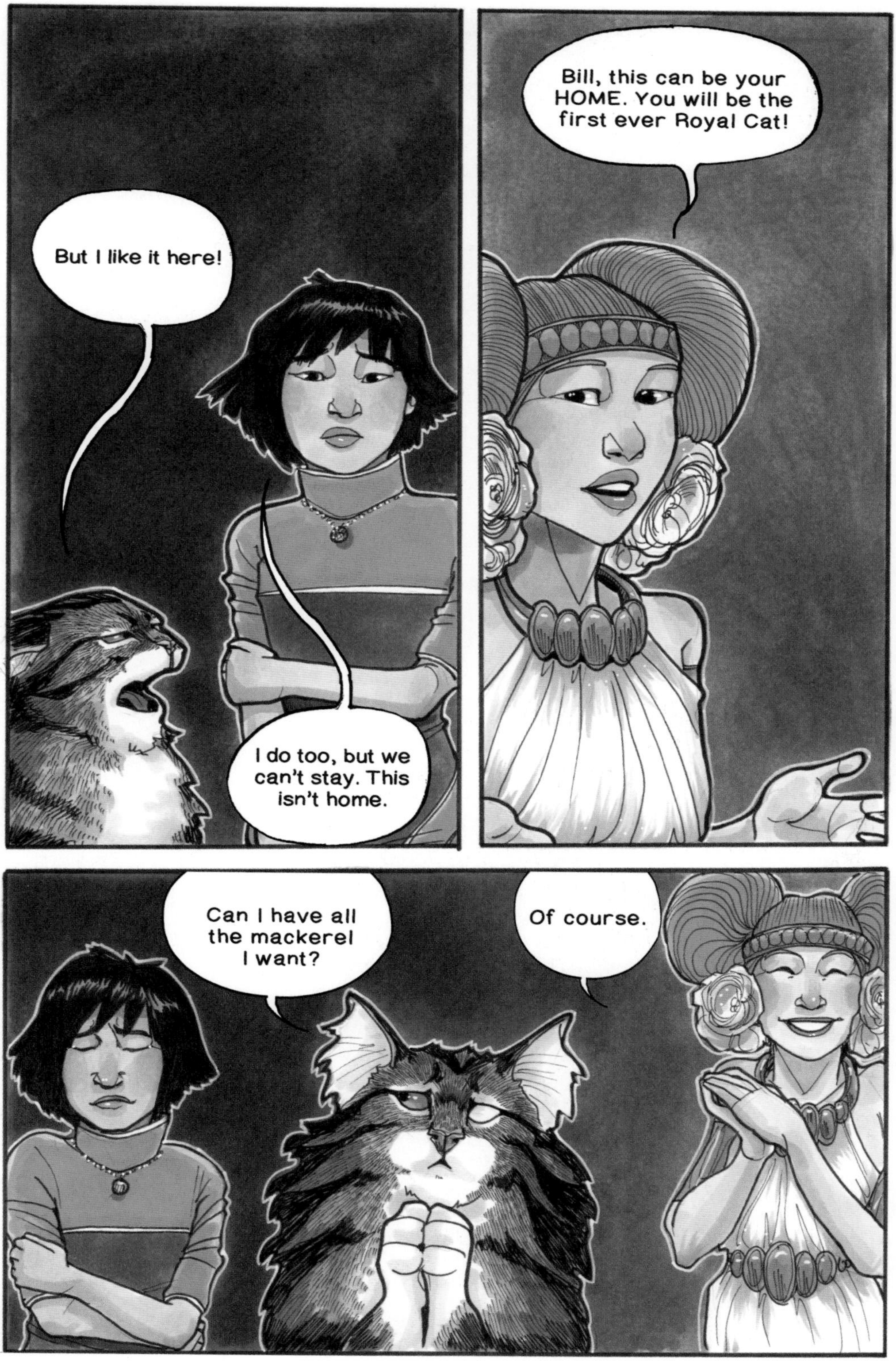
But I like it here!
I do too, but we can't stay. This isn't home.
Bill, this can be your HOME. You will be the first ever Royal Cat!
Can I have all the mackerel I want?
Of course.

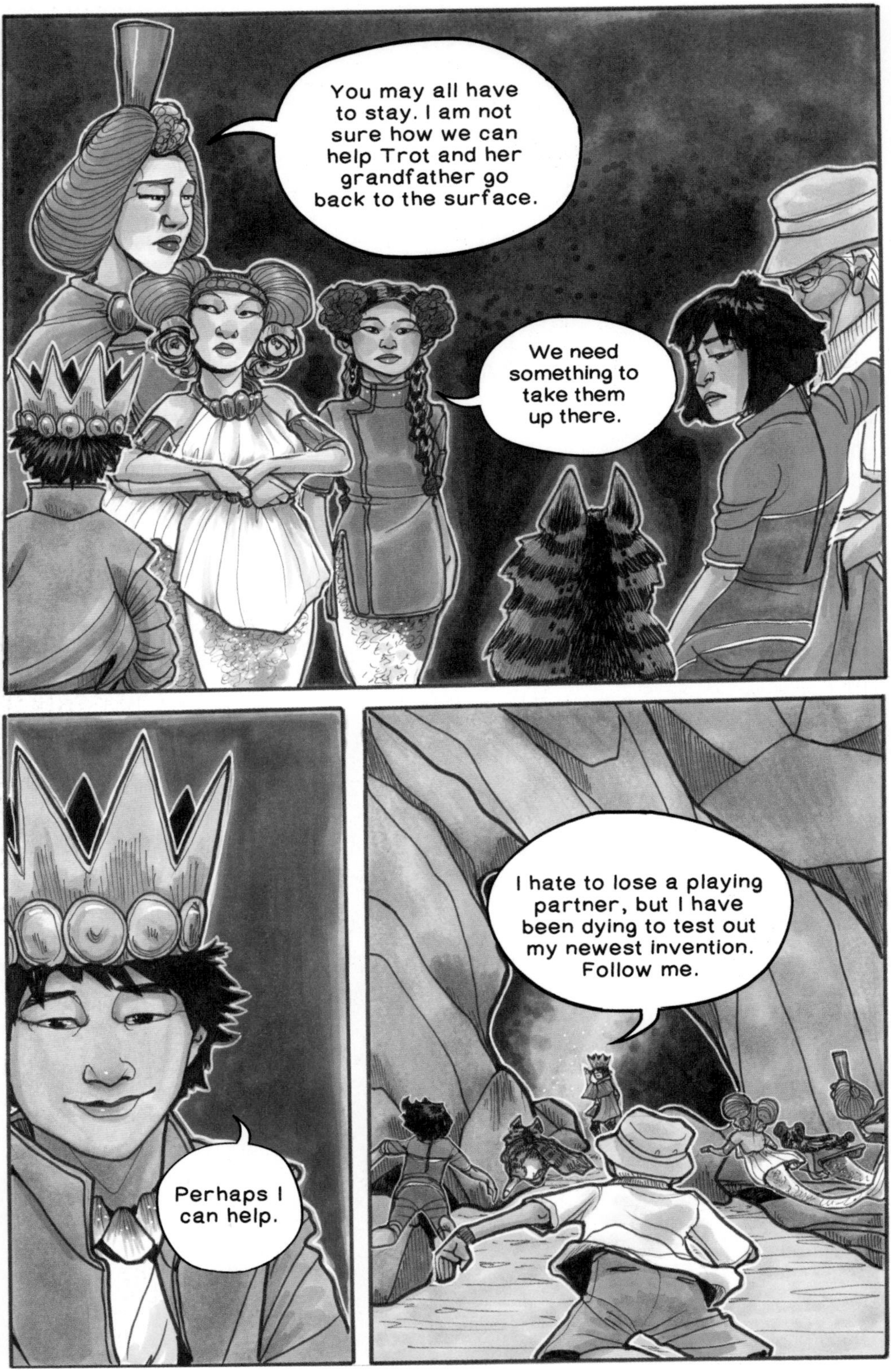

You may all have to stay. I am not sure how we can help Trot and her grandfather go back to the surface.
We need something to take them up there.
Perhaps I can help.
I hate to lose a playing partner, but I have been dying to test out my newest invention. Follow me.

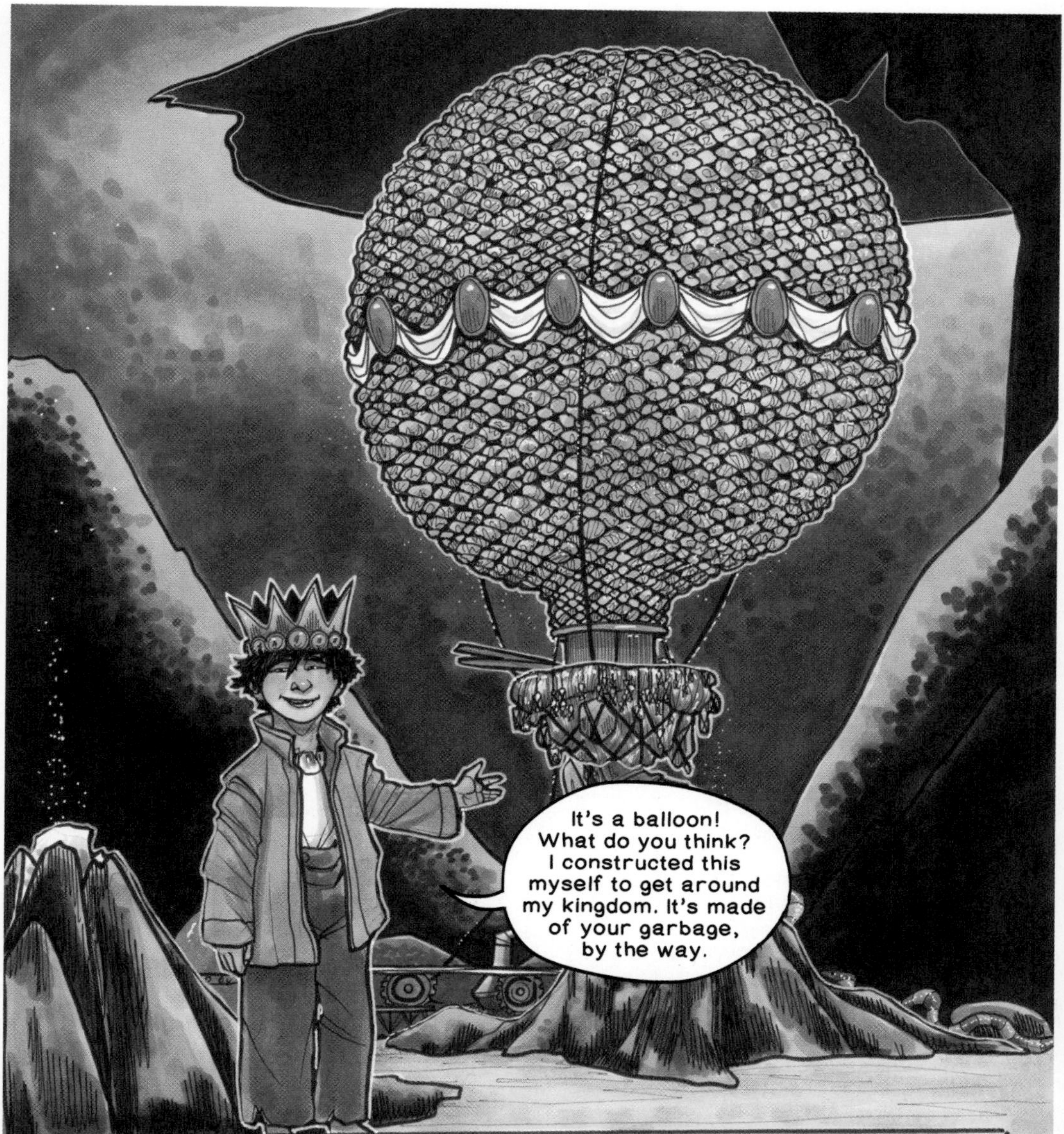
It's a balloon! What do you think? I constructed this myself to get around my kingdom. It's made of your garbage, by the way.

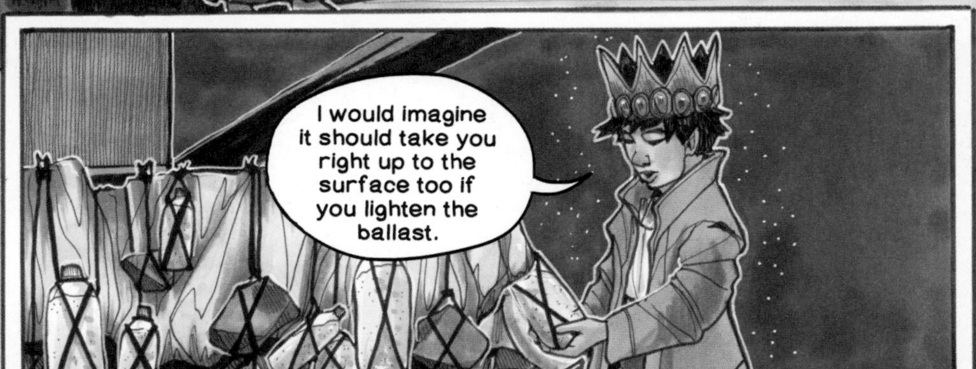
I would imagine it should take you right up to the surface too if you lighten the ballast.

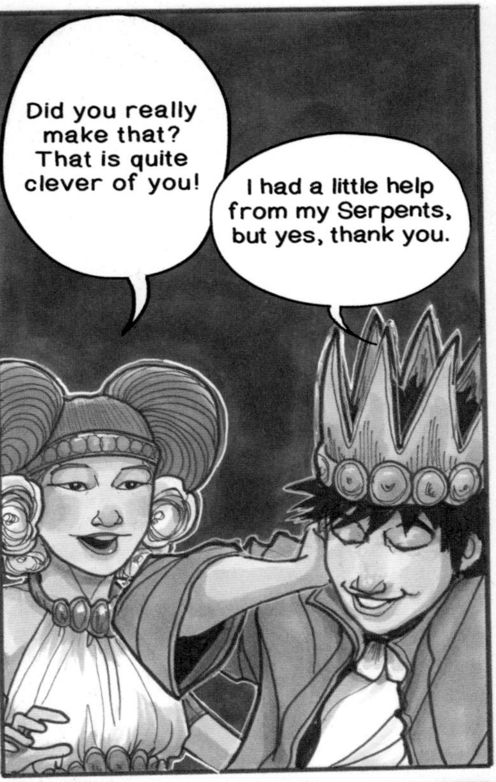
Did you really make that? That is quite clever of you!
I had a little help from my Serpents, but yes, thank you.

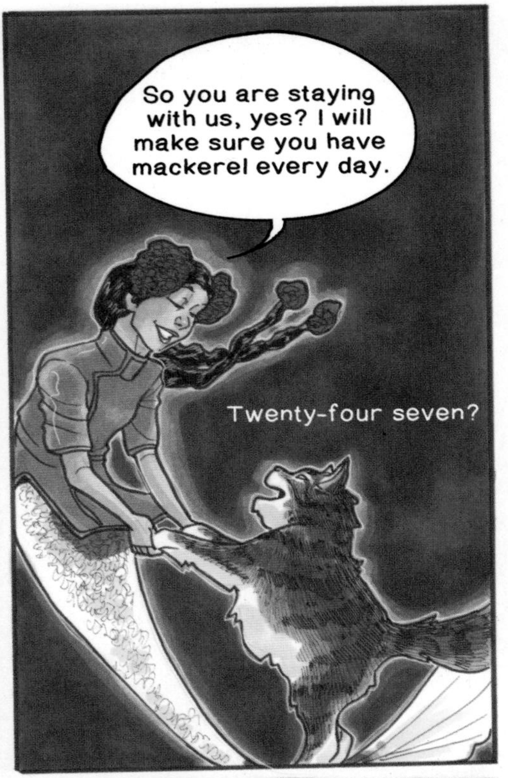
So you are staying with us, yes? I will make sure you have mackerel every day.
Twenty-four seven?

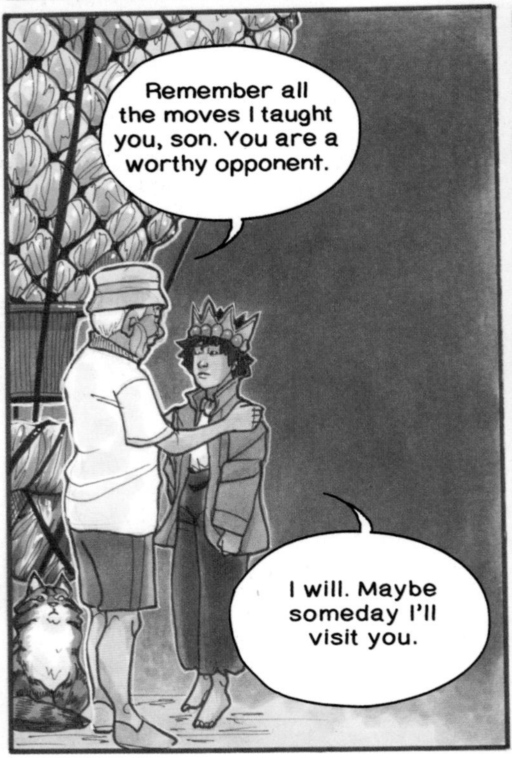
Remember all the moves I taught you, son. You are a worthy opponent.
I will. Maybe someday I'll visit you.

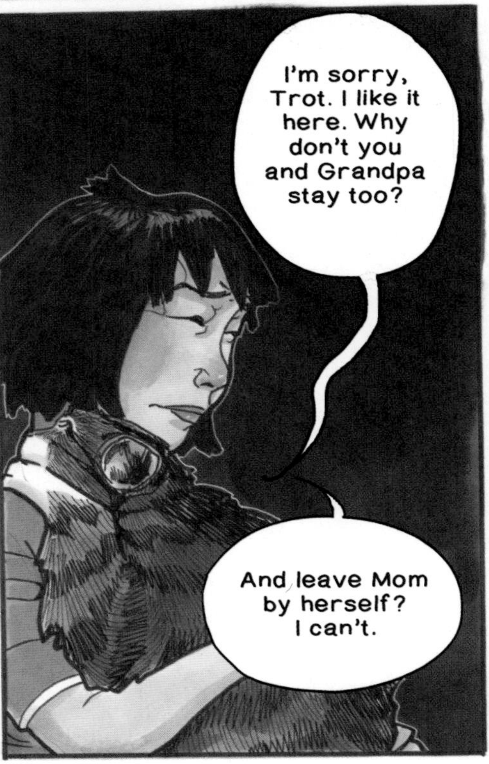
I'm sorry, Trot. I like it here. Why don't you and Grandpa stay too?
And leave Mom by herself? I can't.

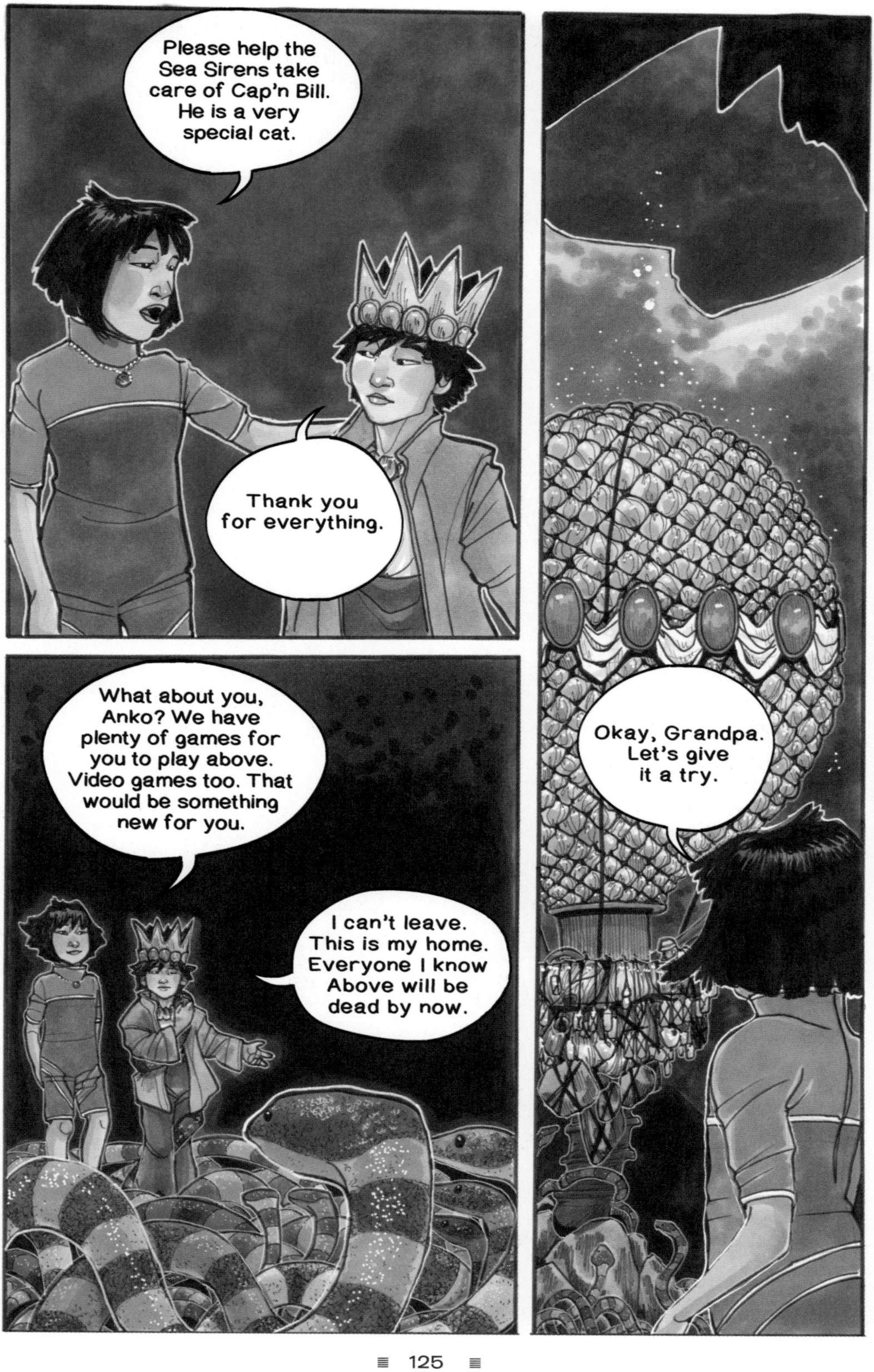
Please help the Sea Sirens take care of Cap'n Bill. He is a very special cat.
Thank you for everything.
What about you, Anko? We have plenty of games for you to play above. Video games too. That would be something new for you.
I can't leave. This is my home. Everyone I know Above will be dead by now.
Okay, Grandpa. Let's give it a try.

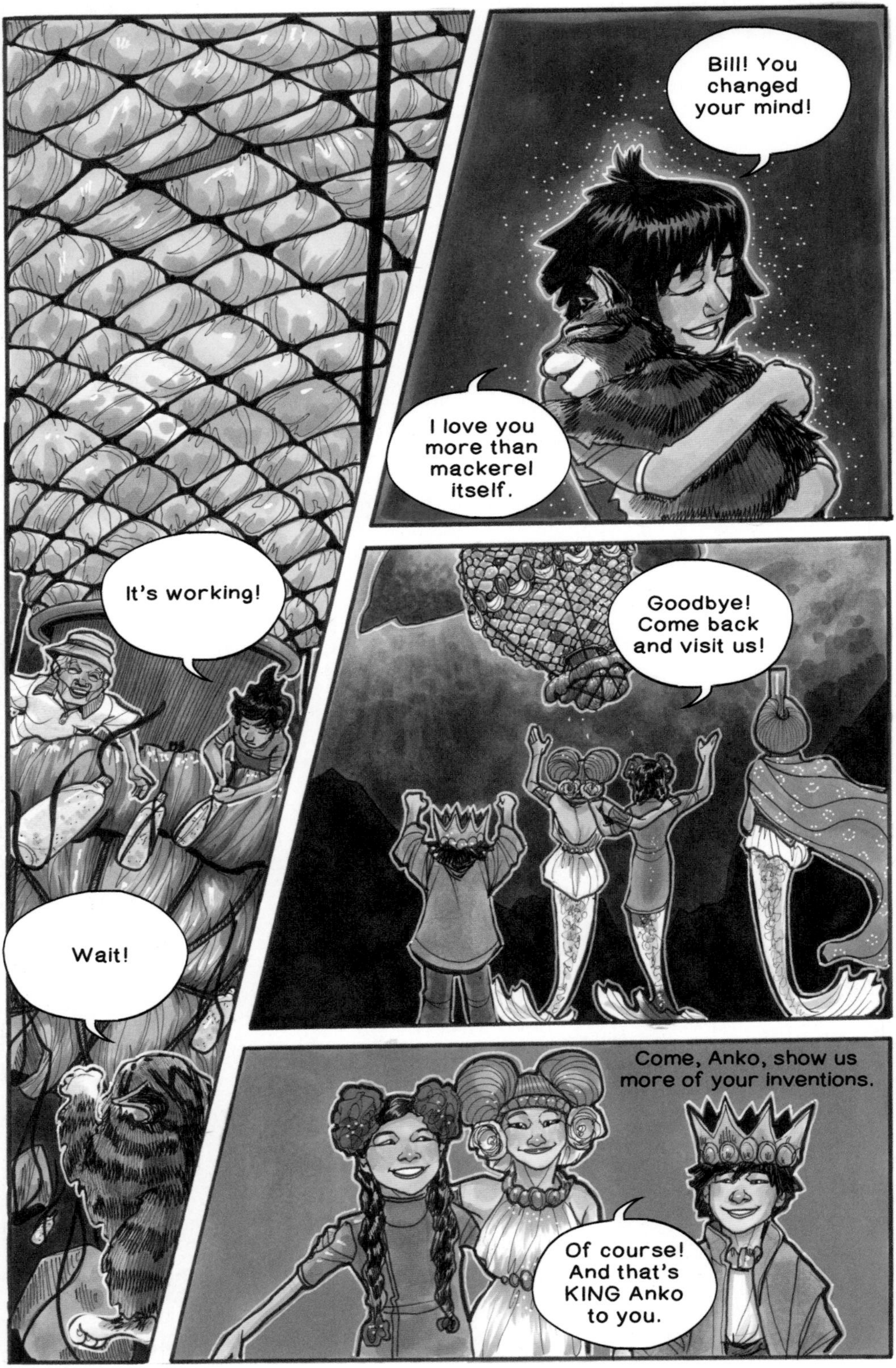
Bill! You changed your mind!
I love you more than mackerel itself.
It's working!
Wait!
Goodbye! Come back and visit us!
Come, Anko, show us more of your inventions.
Of course! And that's KING Anko to you.

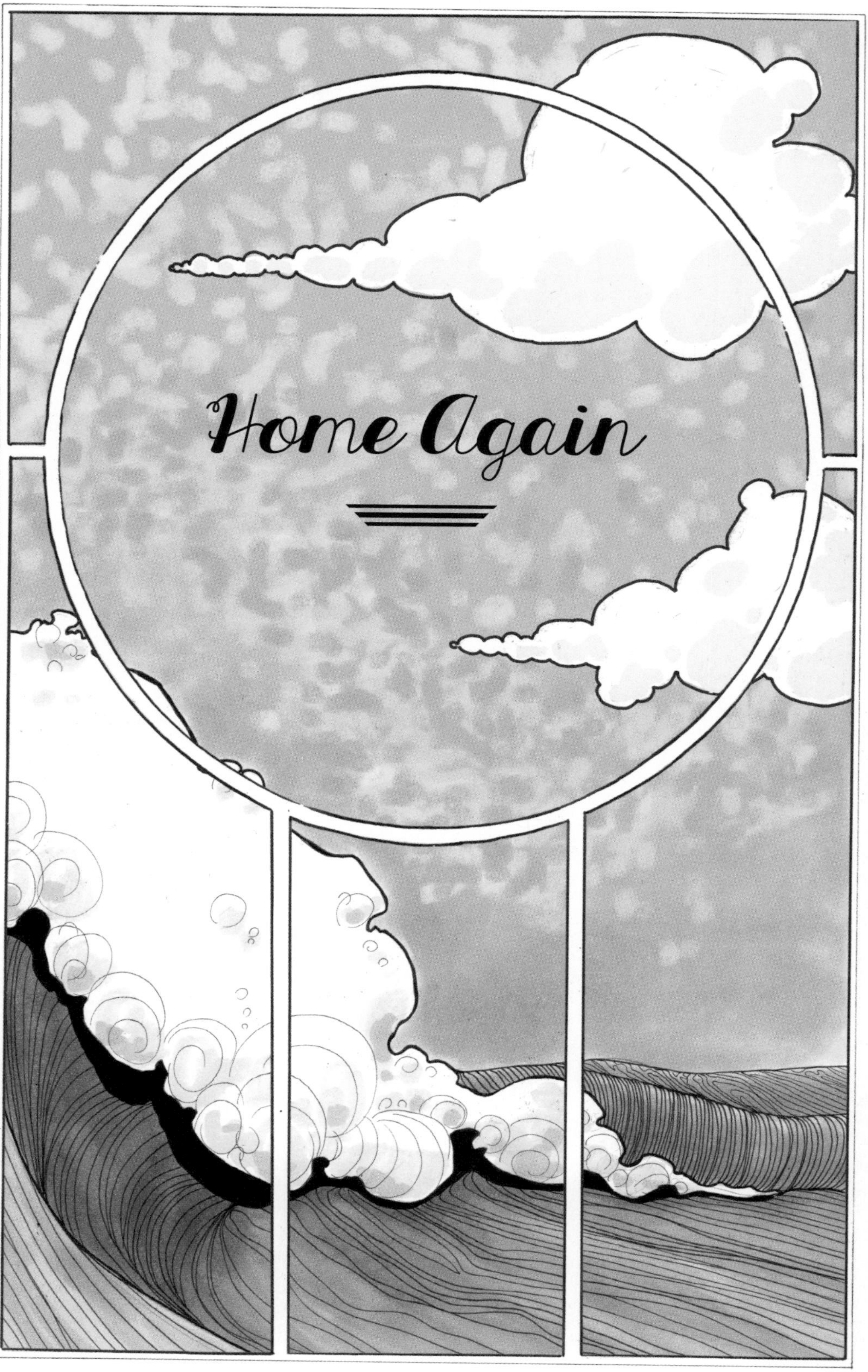
Home Again

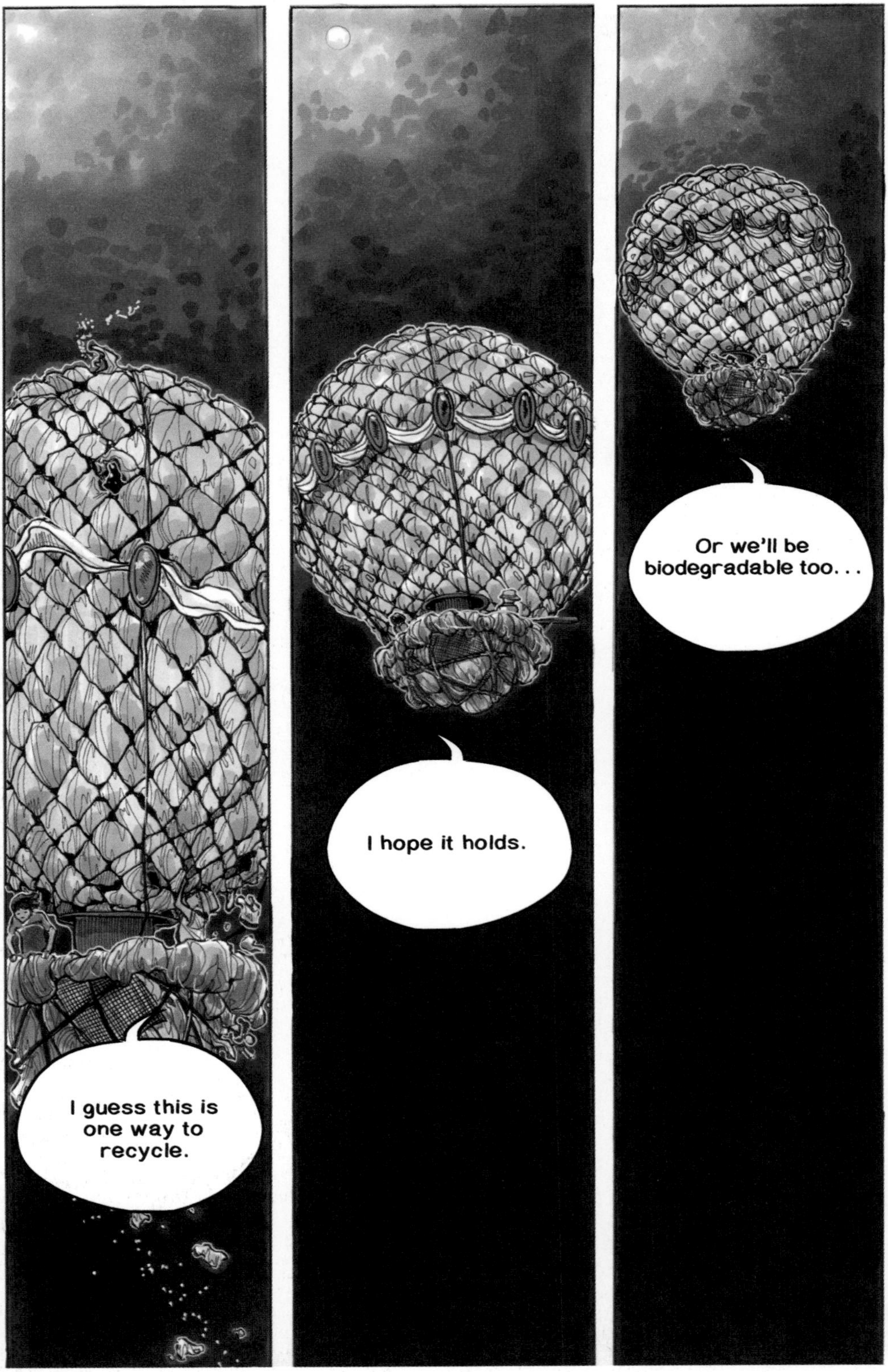
I guess this is one way to recycle.
I hope it holds.
Or we'll be biodegradable too. . .

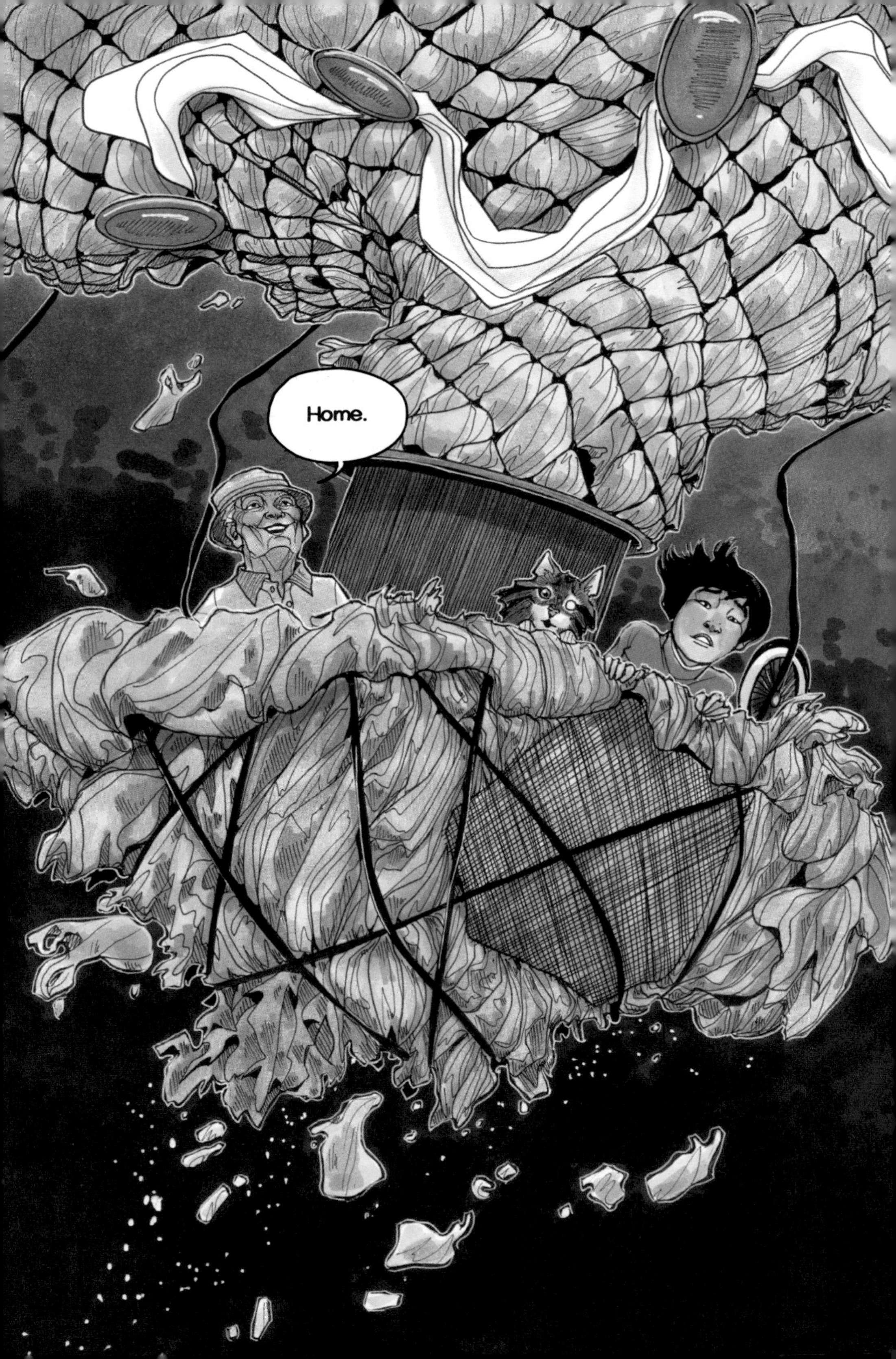
Home.

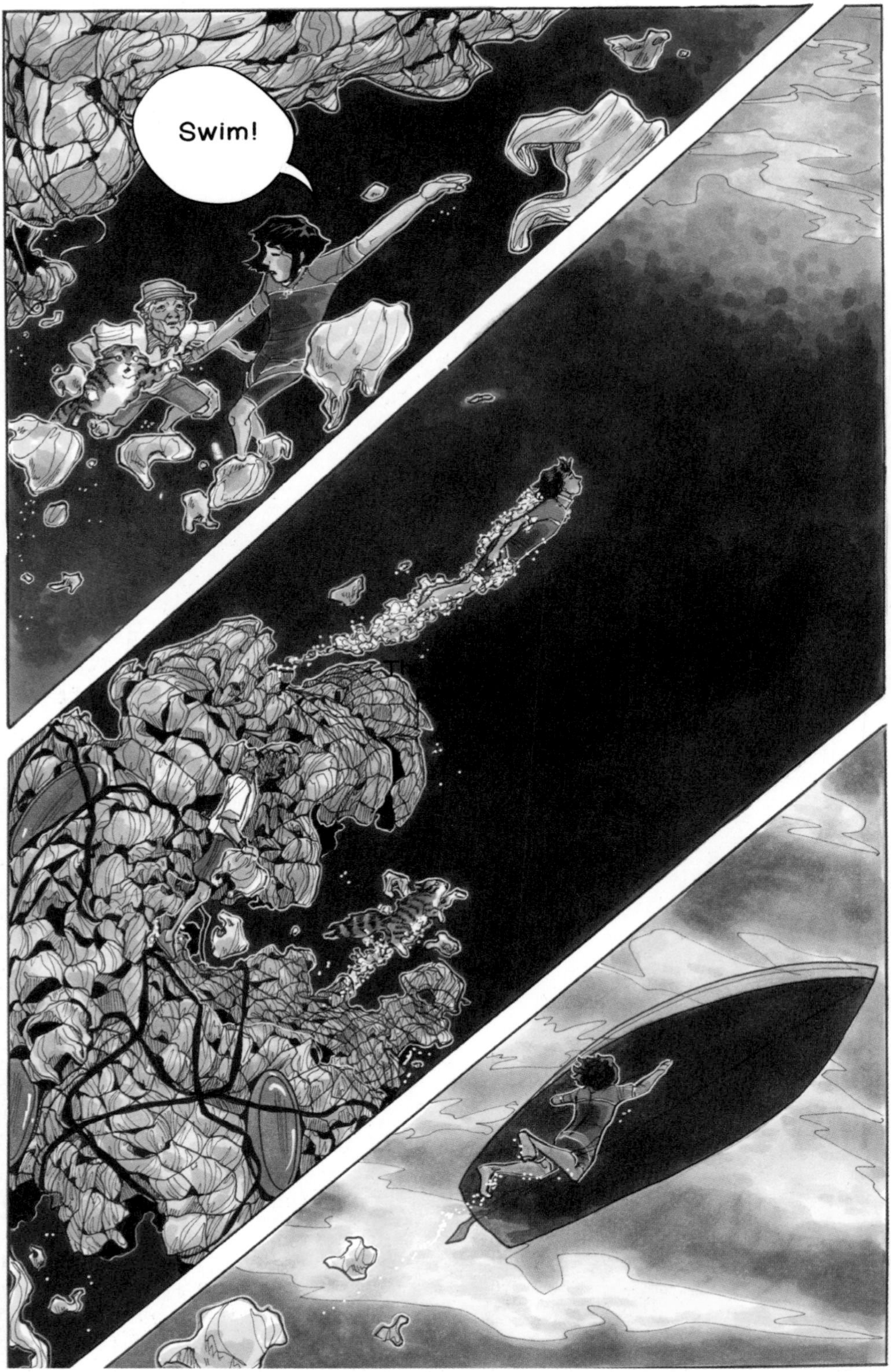
Swim!

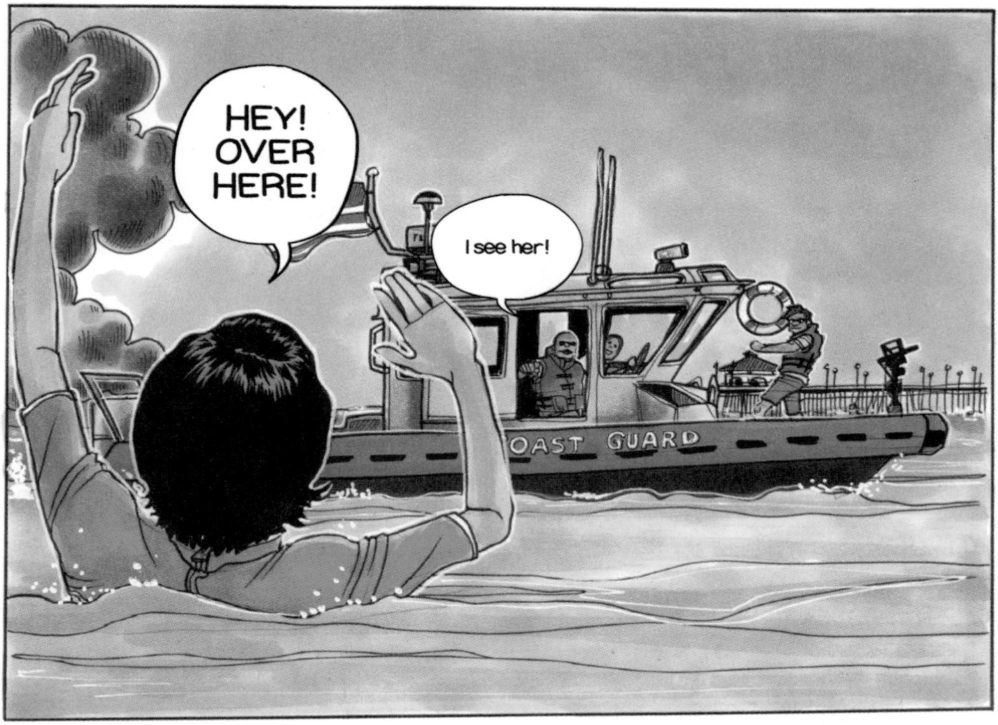
HEY! OVER HERE!
I see her!
COAST GUARD

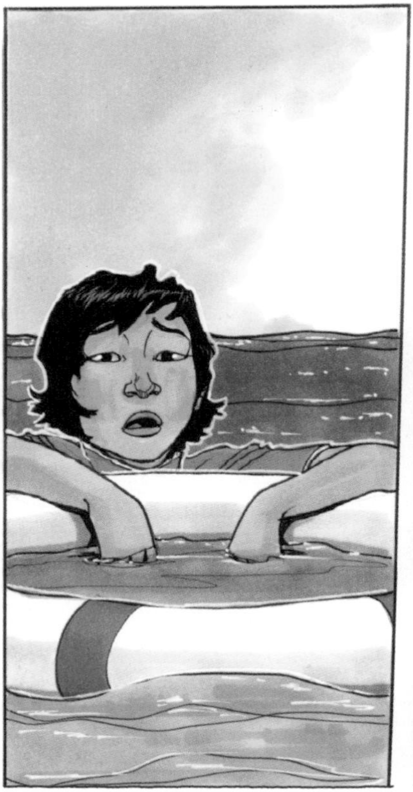

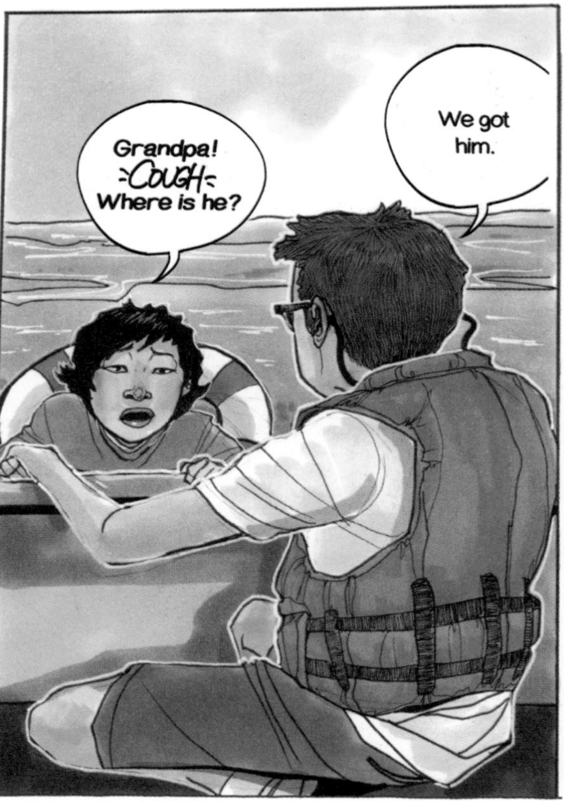
Grandpa! COUGH Where is he?
We got him.

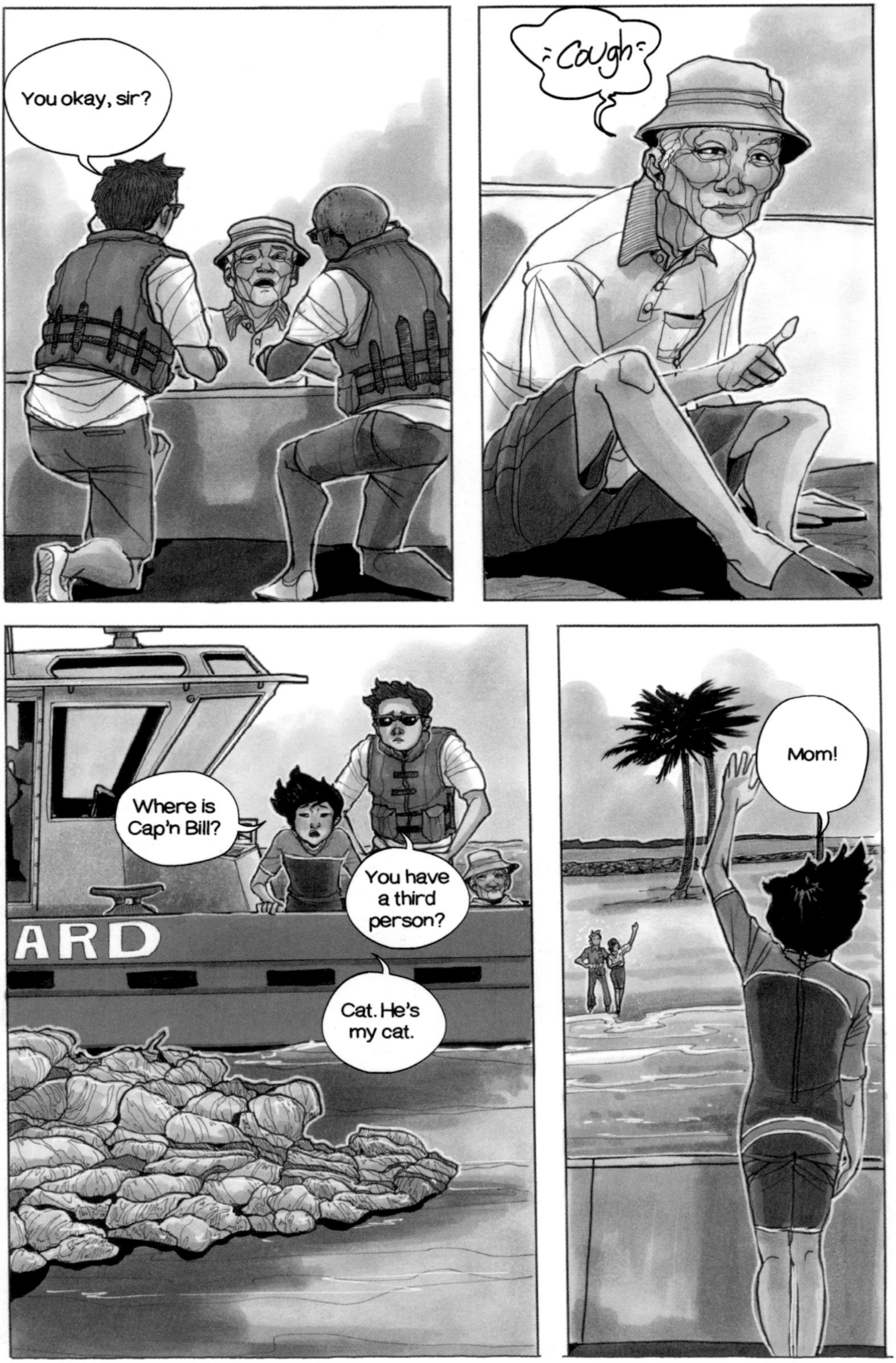
You okay, sir?
Cough
Where is Cap'n Bill?
You have a third person?
Cat. He's my cat.
ARD
Mom!

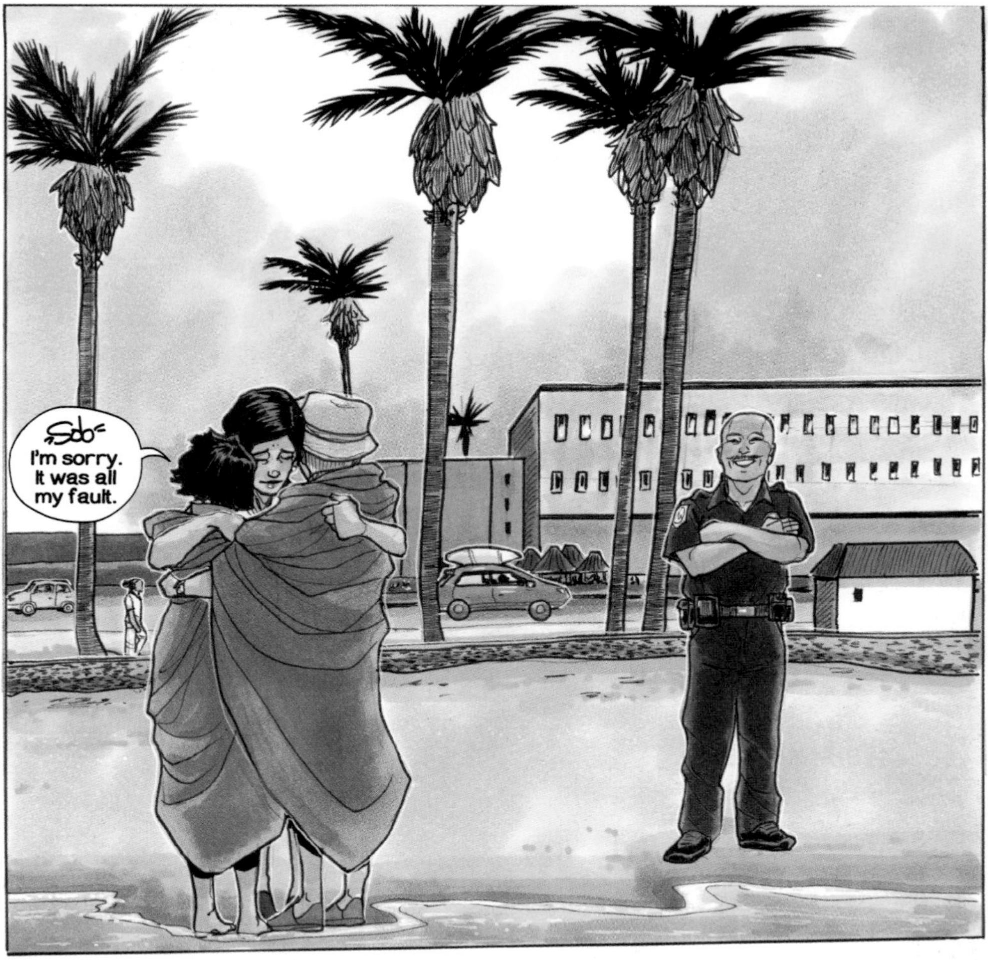
Sob
I'm sorry. It was all my fault.

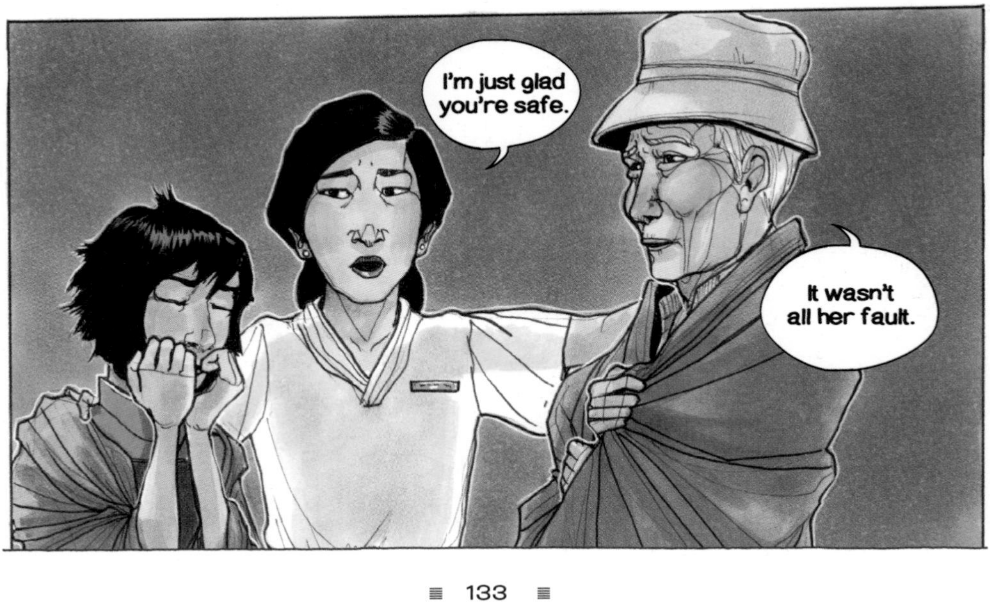
I'm just glad you're safe.
It wasn't all her fault.

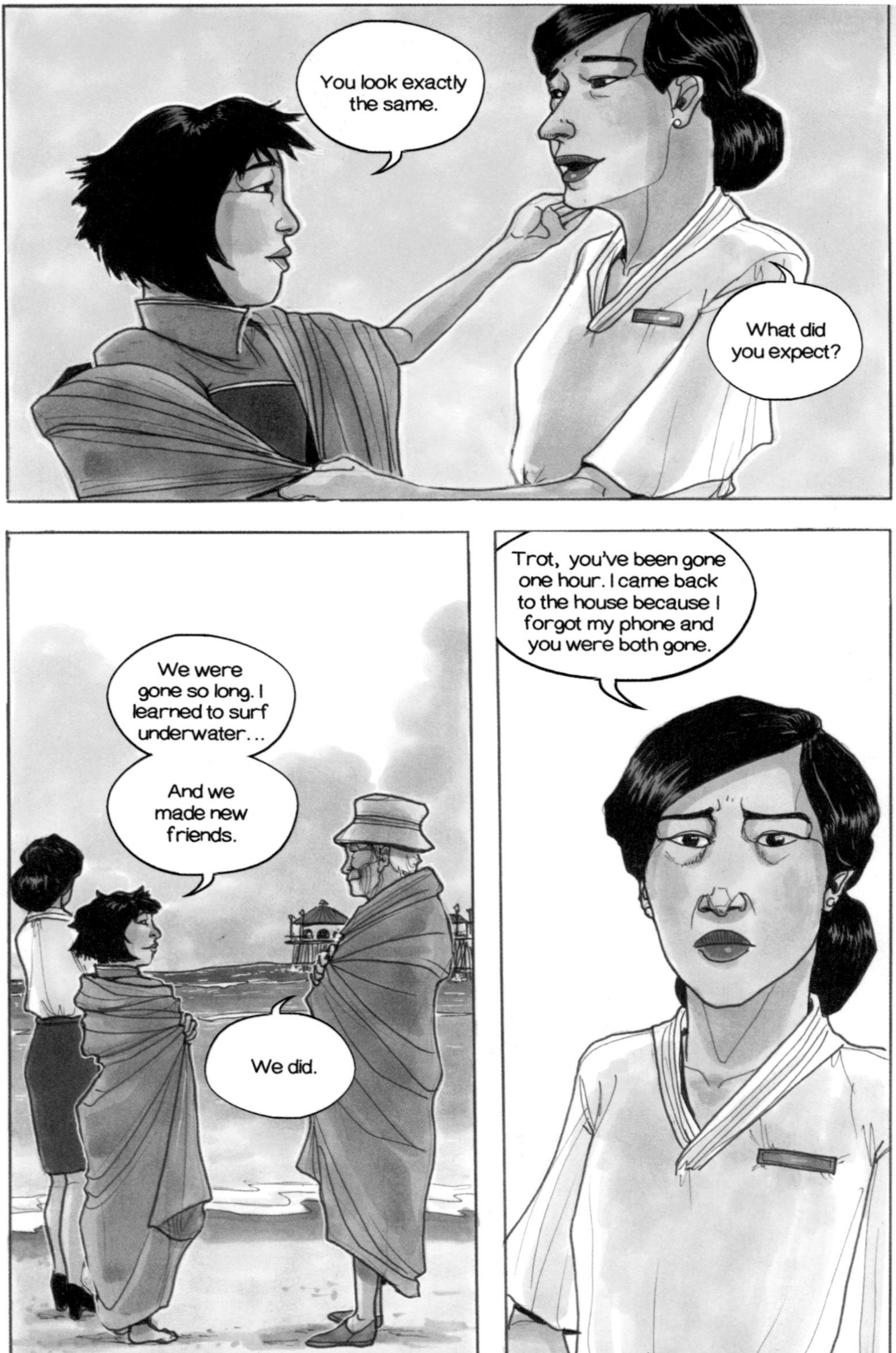
You look exactly the same.
What did you expect?
We were gone so long. I learned to surf underwater...
And we made new friends.
We did.
Trot, you've been gone one hour. I came back to the house because I forgot my phone and you were both gone.

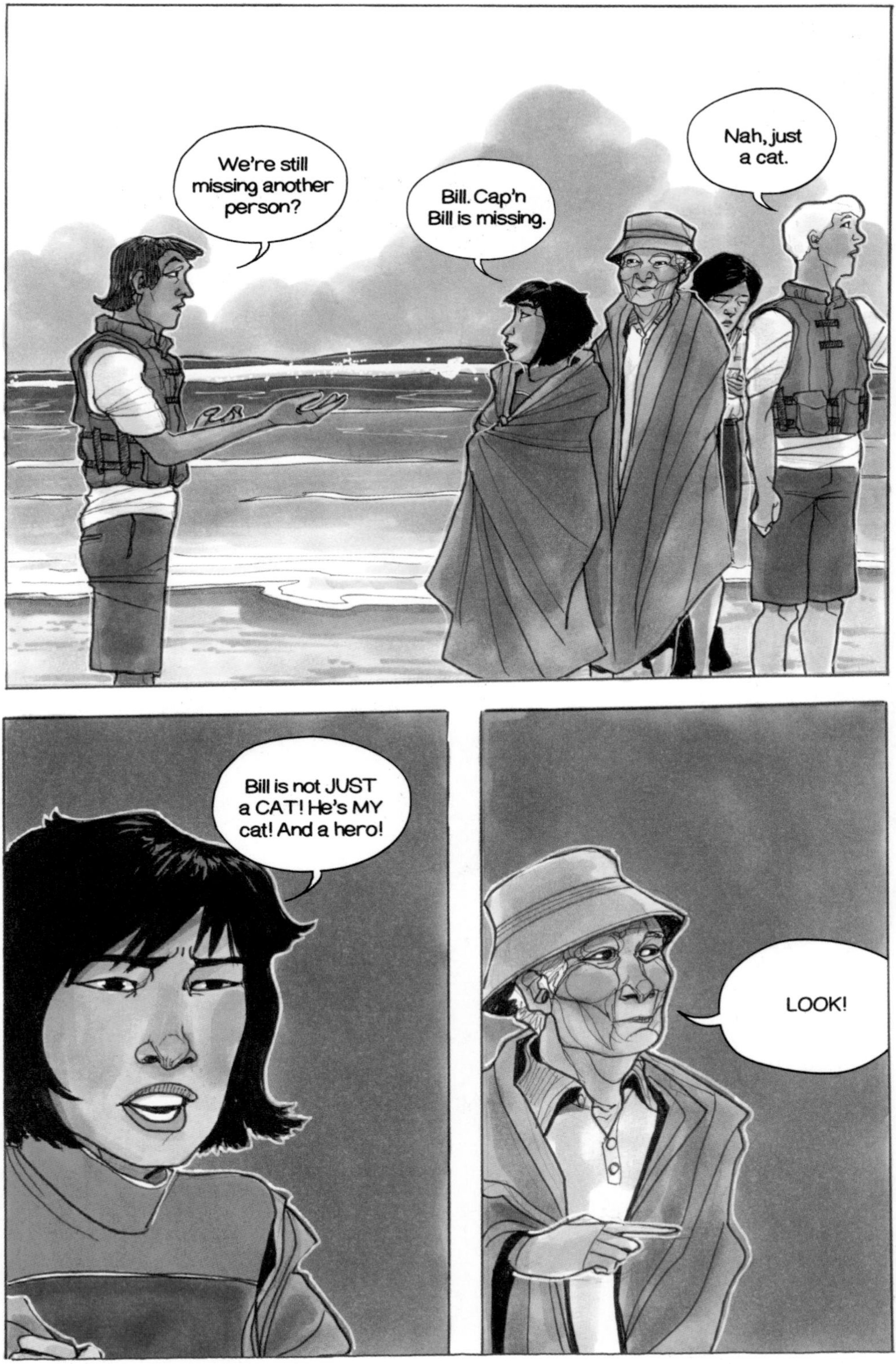
We're still missing another person?
Bill. Cap'n Bill is missing.
Nah, just a cat.
Bill is not JUST a CAT! He's MY cat! And a hero!
LOOK!

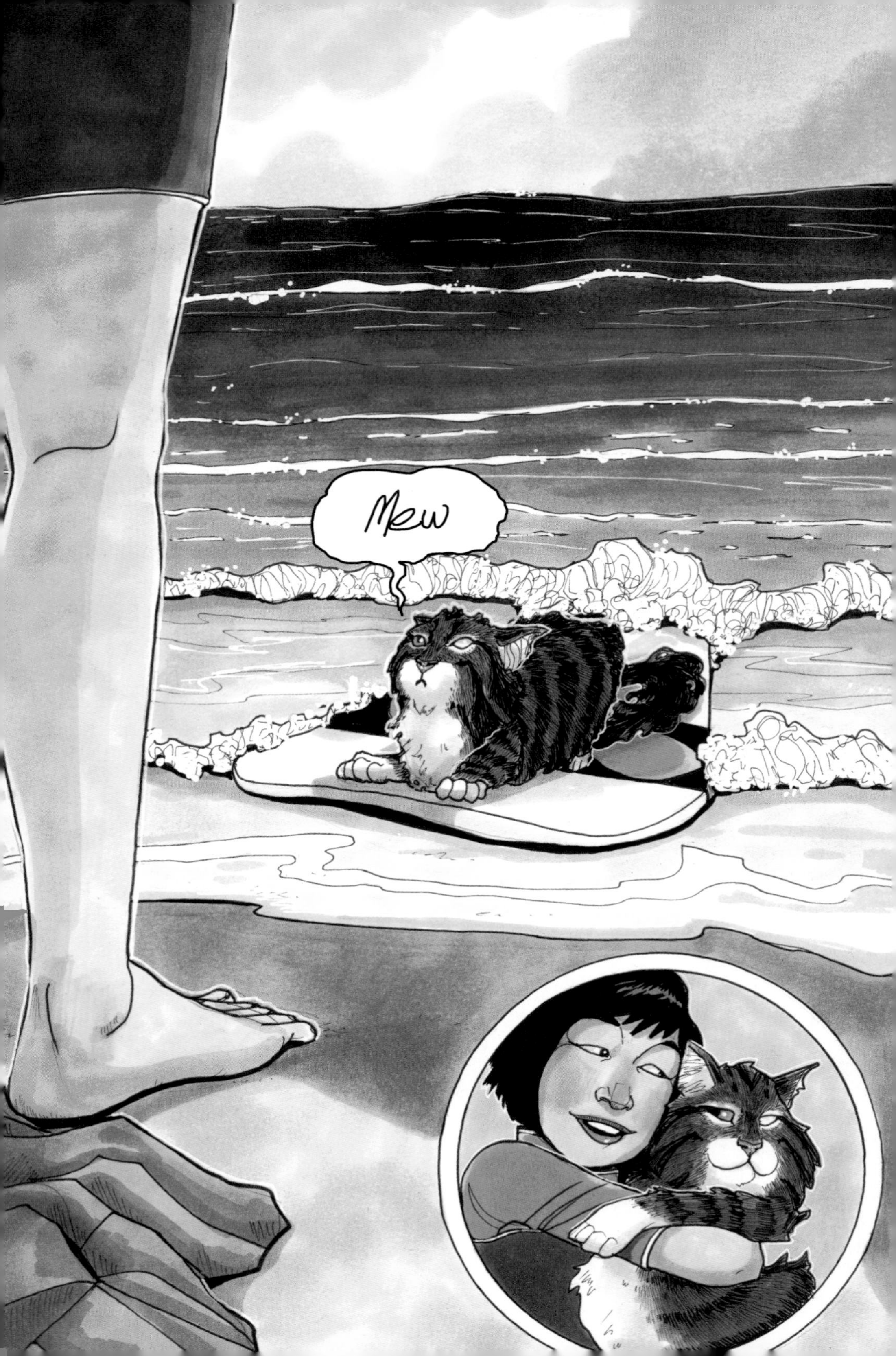
Mew

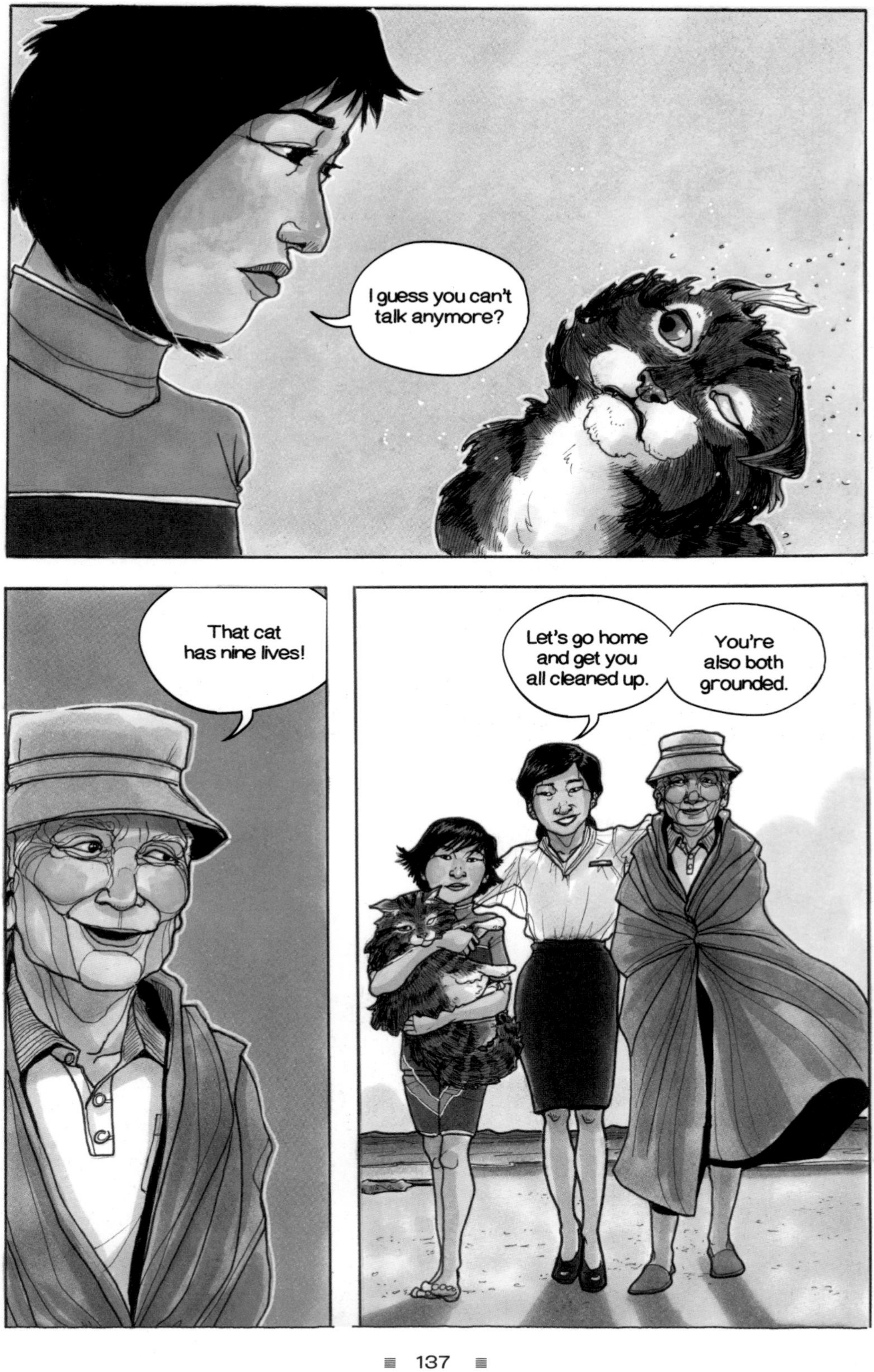
I guess you can't talk anymore?
That cat has nine lives!
Let's go home and get you all cleaned up.
You're also both grounded.

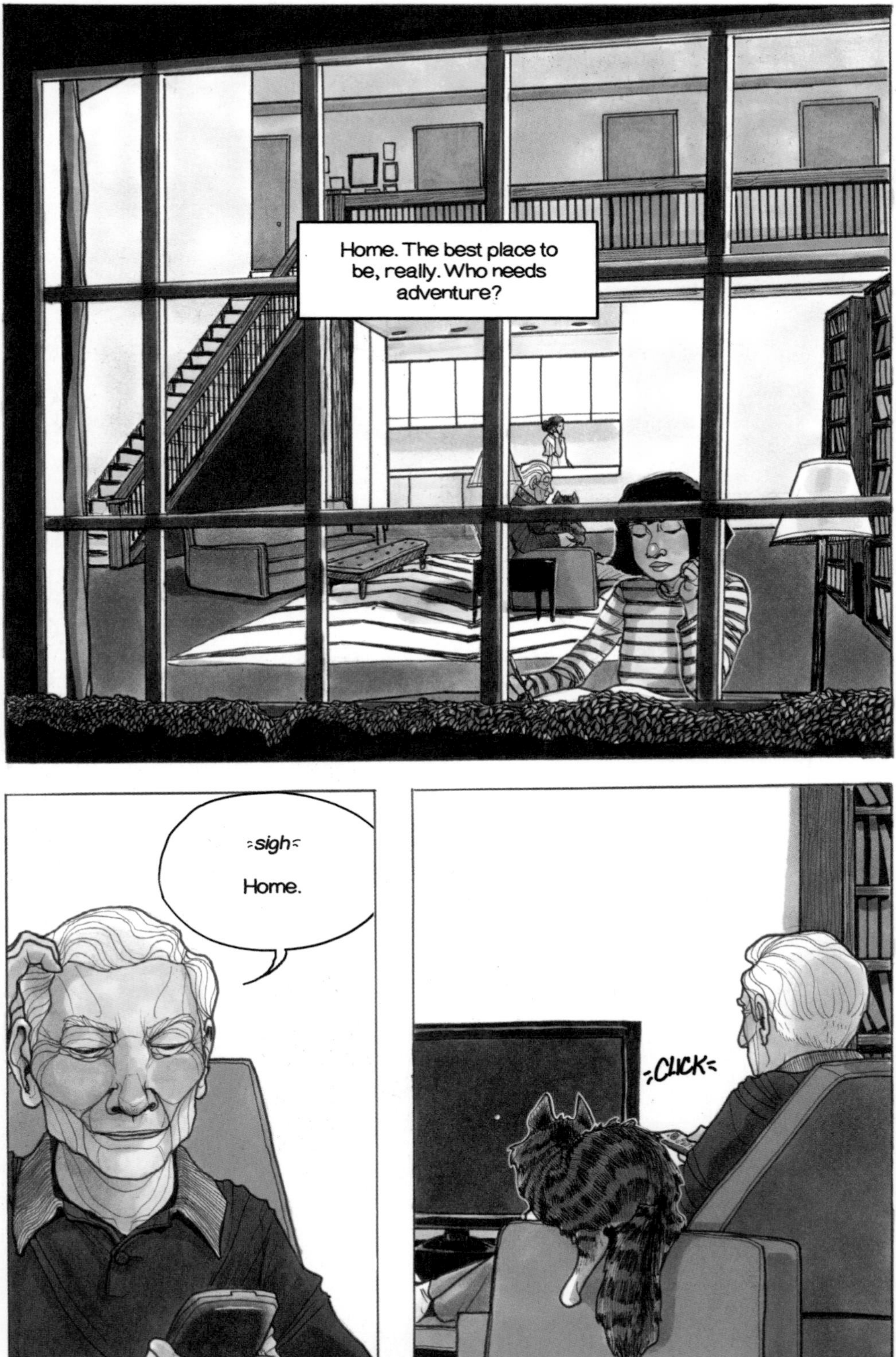
Home. The best place to be, really. Who needs adventure?
sigh
Home.
CLICK

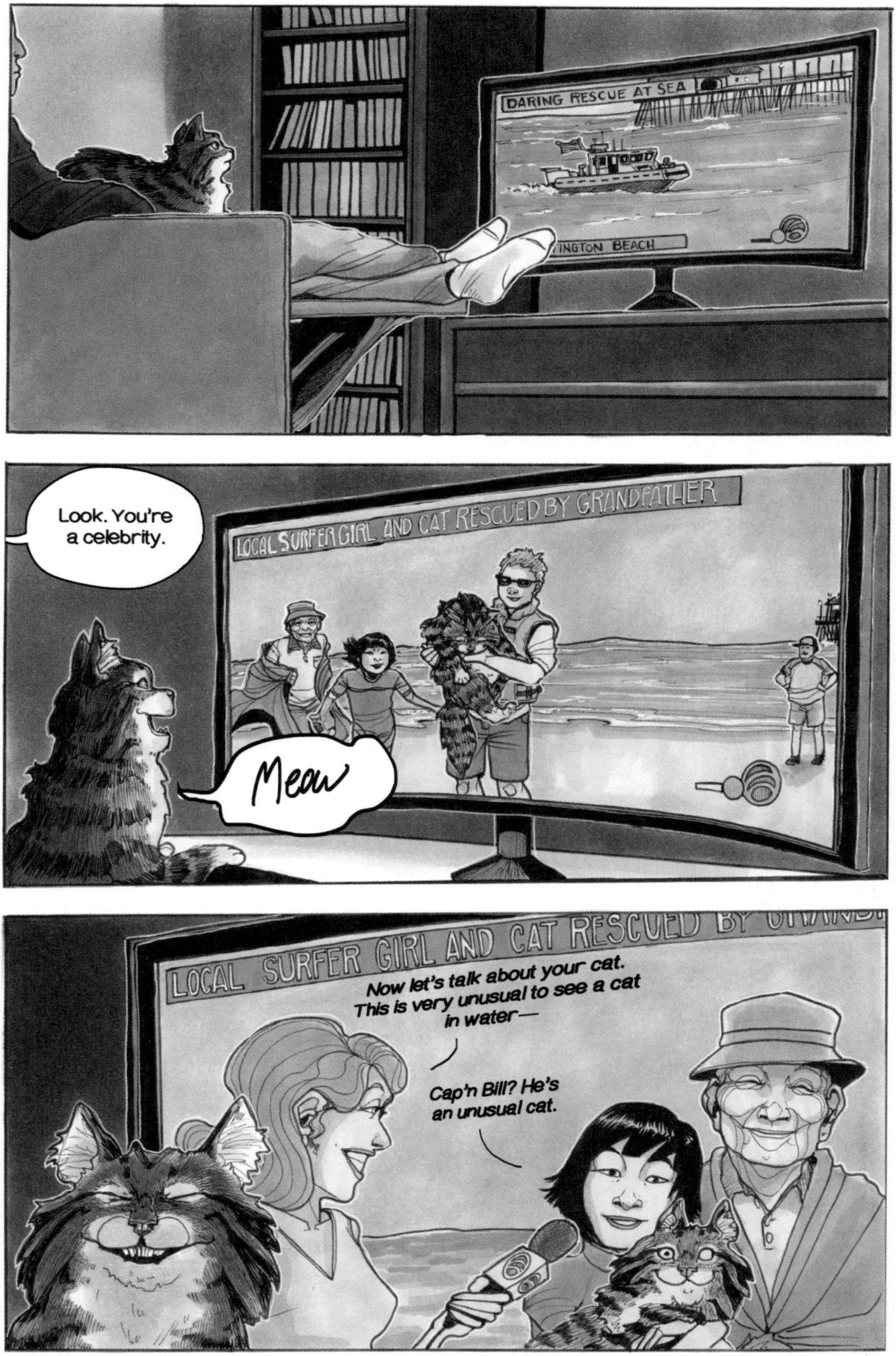
DARING RESCUE AT SEA
INGTON BEACH
LOCAL SURFER GIRL AND CAT RESCUED BY GRANDFATHER
Look. You're a celebrity.
Meow
LOCAL SURFER GIRL AND CAT RESCUED BY
Now let's talk about your cat. This is very unusual to see a cat in water—
Cap'n Bill? He's an unusual cat.

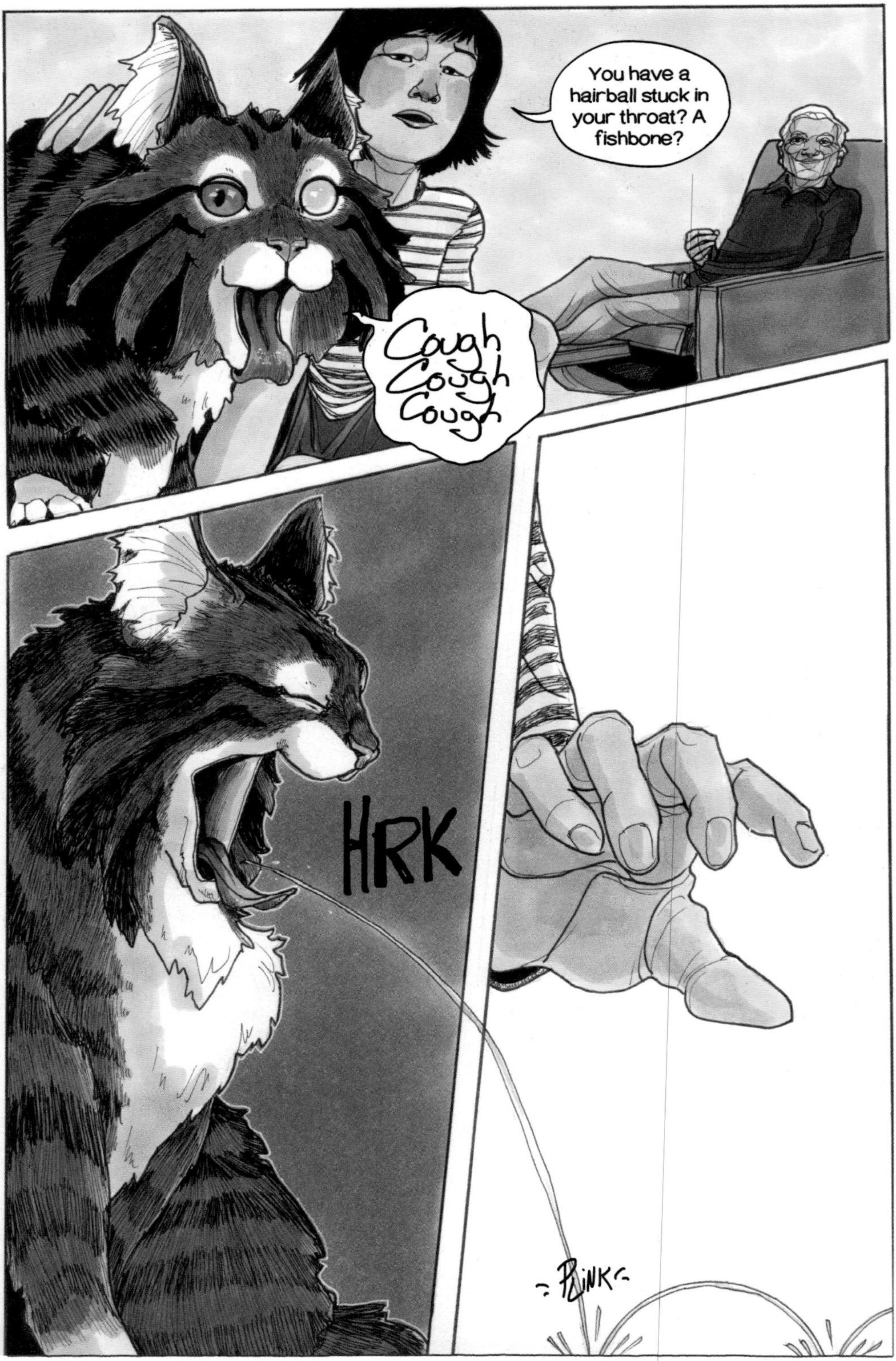
You have a hairball stuck in your throat? A fishbone?
Cough Cough Cough
HRK
PLINK

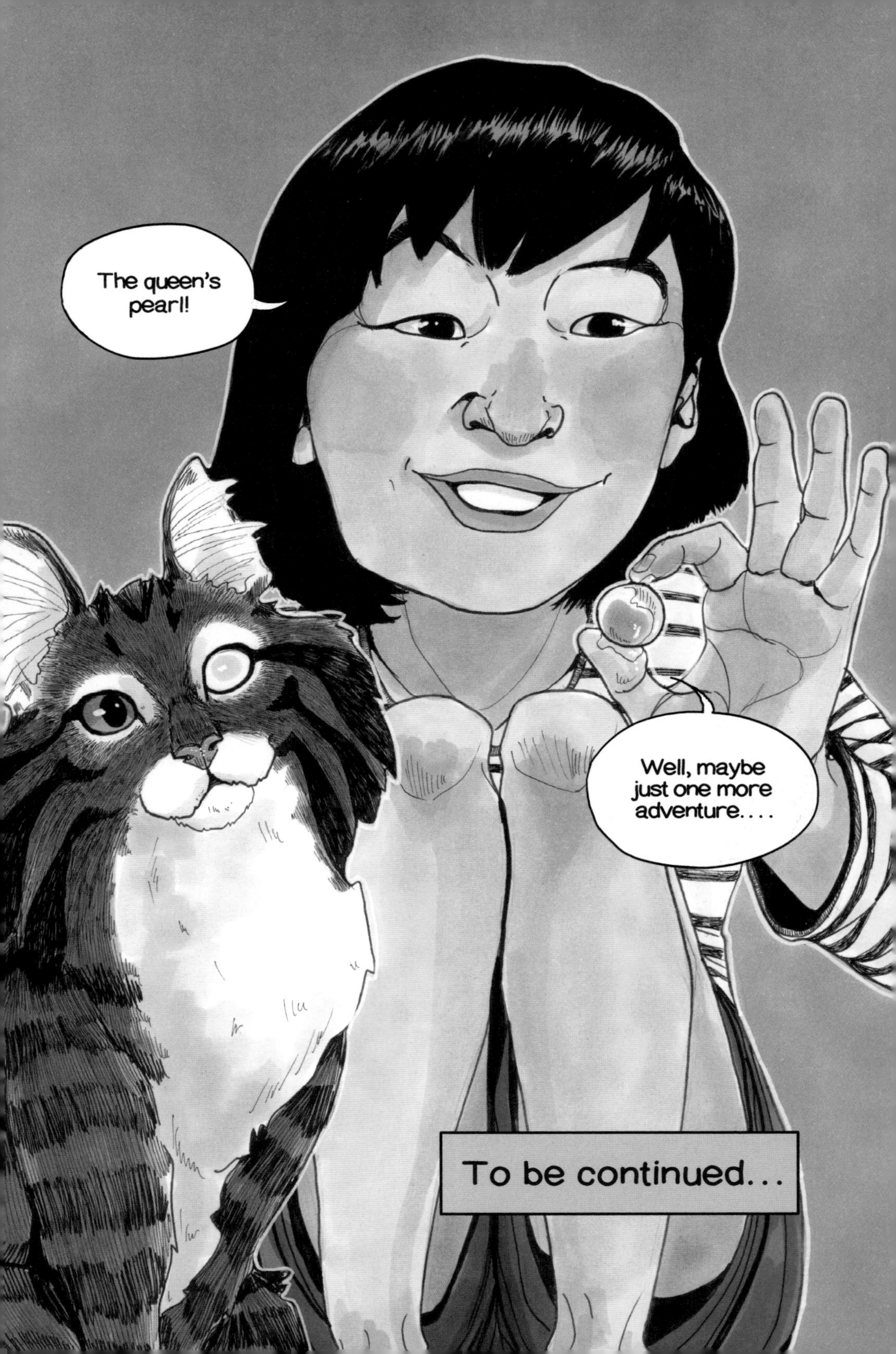
The queen's pearl!
Well, maybe just one more adventure. . . .
To be continued. . .

☙ About the Artist ☙

JANET K. LEE moved from Palo Alto, California, to Nashville, Tennessee, when she was eight years old and has been there ever since. Living so far away from an ocean, she never learned to surf like Trot, but she did have a kitten, Genie, as her first pet, rode a skateboard almost everywhere, and loved to draw. So she created her own newspaper, which featured her first comic strips, and passed that out to friends at school.

Fast forward to adulthood when Janet won an Eisner Award for her first graphic novel, *Return of the Dapper Men*. Now she illustrates comics full-time in a studio surrounded by four cats, one of which bears an uncanny resemblance to Cap'n Bill.

❧ About the Writer ❧

At age eleven, **AMY CHU** wrote her first book. It was about a princess and a magic poodle and went on to win the Best Book Prize in Mrs. Millard's sixth grade class.

Amy is now a professional comic book writer, creating stories for popular Marvel and DC characters such as Wonder Woman, Ant-Man, Deadpool, and Poison Ivy, as well as Green Hornet, Red Sonja, and The Princess of Mars.

Amy was born in Boston, Massachusetts, and has lived in New York, California, Iowa, Oklahoma, and Hong Kong. She now lives in Princeton, New Jersey, with her family and her extensive LEGO collection.

About the Story

SEA SIRENS was inspired by a few things new and old: fond childhood memories of being at the beach; real life stories of cats who like to surf; *The Dragon Prince* and *Why the Sea Is Full of Salt*, two collections of folktales and fairy tales from Vietnam; and a long-forgotten novel published in 1911.

That novel was *The Sea Fairies* by L. Frank Baum, the creator of the famous Wizard of Oz books. Baum wrote two underwater fantasy novels about a California girl nicknamed Trot and her adventures with mermaids and other creatures of the deep.

P.S. No serpents were harmed in the making of this book.

Acknowledgments

Shout out to Jimmy Gownley for his magical letters, Ngoc Cammuso for vetting the Vietnamese dialogue, Peter Nguyen and his family, Stephen Pruett, and all the women of the Comic Book Women support group. Last but not least, thanks to the wonderful team at Viking Children's Books. You guys really do make dreams come to life.